PRESUMED
DEAD

MARTIN KNOX

PRESUMED DEAD
Copyright © MARTIN KNOX 2018

A catalogue record for this book is available from the National Library of Australia

ISBN: 978-0-6481607-7-9

DEDICATION

For Dianne

REVIEWS OF THE AUTHOR'S PREVIOUS NOVELS:

LOVE STRADDLE
Reviewer: Donna Munro, Warm Witty Words

'University life in the 60s is a lot about free love, but with Selwyn being an Engineering major, his reasoning turns to facts and figures. Even in love Selwyn doesn't think like most blokes.

'He has Barbara who seems to care about him and then there's Vicki. Seemingly Vicki is his true love but he always seems to be chasing that dream but never getting there. So, to save himself from heartache he uses his intellect instead of his emotions. He thinks about graphs and strategies and comes to the conclusion that he will think of each young lady as a commodity, much like putting a straddle on a share. So comes the innocuous title 'Love $traddle', note the dollar sign.

'(Selwyn) is a character that is highly intelligent, at the pinnacle of his profession and still bumbles along with his emotional life. It doesn't help that he over-compensates by indulging in too much sex, food, work and alcohol during different stages of his life, or that he can't quiet articulate his feelings properly.

'Author Martin Knox has captured this era and developed characters with believable angst in a real world - that is not just black and white. This is an intelligent novel that makes you think long after you read the last page.'

Reviewer: Vera A. Pereskokova, Luxury Reading

'Readers who are interested in reading a more calculated approach to a love story may enjoy *Love Straddle*, as may those who enjoy an antihero who doesn't always win.'

THE GRASS IS ALWAYS BROWNER

Glossary of Acronyms

CBD   City Business District
ACC   Alexandra City Council
ATV   Alexandra Television
CCC   Crime and Corruption Commission(er)
CS1   Crime Scene 1: City Square car parking garage
CS2   Crime Scene 2: Roadway, Anston Street, Northgrove
CS3   Crime Scene 3: Disused pharmaceutical factory at
      Commercial Road
CS4   Crime Scene 4: Vehicle used to transport victim from CS3 to
      CS5 & CS6
CS5   Crime Scene 5: Hypothetical victim release site
CS6   Crime Scene 6: Construction site where victim rescued
CS7   Crime Scene 7: Hypothetical site where perpetrator received
      payment
CS8   Crime Scene 8: Hypothetical site where mastermind obtained
      funds
CSI   Crime Scene Investigator
DA   Development Application
DCI   Detective Chief Inspector
DI   Detective Inspector
DM   Deputy Mayor
HQ   Headquarters
IB   Immigration Building
IBAG IB Action Group
LM   Lord Mayor
MC   Multicultural Centre
NLP   National Liberal Party
PC   Police Commissioner
PDA   Preliminary Development Application
SLP   Southland Labour Party
UMTS University Materials Testing Services

Contents

PART 1

CONCRETE

CHAPTER 1

In the dim light of dawn, the concreters plodded in funereal procession across the construction site towards boxes in the ground that would mould the pillars of a road overpass. Ready Mix trucks waited in a line to move their bowel contents into a pipeline for pumping across to Norman in his crane. He swung the spout from box to box, playing the knobs like piano keys.

The gouts plopped down into the darkness, over tufts of steel rods. Brian and Bob came close behind with vibrating pokers, jiggling the ooze into cavities.

'Something under!' yelled Bob, pointing to where he had felt a push against his poker. They buried all sorts of things: cans, tools and garments. Perhaps this was an animal or a large bird?

When he jumped in and tried to lift it, he sank up to his waist in the quagmire.

'Help!' he called.

Brian jumped in too and Norman swung his crane over. They hooked their arms over the spout and were lifted up. Holding on to the thing, they dragged it out from under the surface onto the ground. They were amazed to discover it was a woman, in a blouse and skirt, with bound wrists and ankles, a gag in her mouth.

'Alive,' shouted Bob. 'Quick.'

How skinny she was as she lay on her back with arm bones protruding. They removed the gag, pulled off the blindfold and undid the bindings. Norm started pumping her chest. She coughed, gasped, groaned and rubbed her eyes. They rolled her on to her side and hosed away the grit and slurry. Her skin was smooth and grey, her hair lank and matted. She shivered and lapsed into unconsciousness.

Paramedics arrived with a stretcher.

'Almost dead she is,' Norman cautioned as they lifted her on.

They carried her to a waiting ambulance. It rushed away with her, siren wailing.

'Another hour and it would take a jackhammer to get her out,' said Bob. 'What evil bastard did this?'

Police cordoned off the site, keeping the crowd back with crime-scene tape.

A reporter said, 'It could be that city councillor who went missing over a month ago.'

Norman replied with vehemence, 'It's premeditated fucking murder. Whoever did it should be locked away forever.'

'What if she lives?'

'Attempted murder — no two ways about it. Our Jane — after she has done so much good! What a thing to do! He must be a psychopath. Throw away the key.'

The reporter set up his camera on a tripod and stood in front talking to it.

'I am at a construction site where a woman has been rescued from under wet concrete. She was barely alive and has been rushed to hospital. It would be a terrible way to die. If the concrete had set, her body would have decayed to gas and liquid and leaked away slowly, leaving only an empty mould with a brown stain, like they found at Pompeii where a person was buried alive in volcanic ash. She would never have been found.

'The police are investigating how she was buried alive, a horrific crime. We will find out from the hospital if she will survive.

'The victim could be a councillor who disappeared five weeks ago on her way to a meeting in City Hall, but her identity has not been confirmed. There is no evidence that this cruel attack was politically motivated.'

The picture switched to a uniformed police officer, who said, 'We have located a place where we believe she was held captive before she was brought here. We are following leads to find the abductors. If you have any information would you phone this number: 3386 1190.'

The reporter said, 'We are awaiting developments. This is Grant Summers for ATV.'

PART 2

JANE

CHAPTER 2

I met Jane Kenwood two years before she was found buried in concrete, when I went on an excursion to the beach in a coach with other National Liberal Party (NLP) councillors and their families. Alexandra was the capital city of Roberta Province in the former British colonial independency of Southland. It was a city with two million inhabitants descended from European, Indian, African, Asian and Indigenous forebears. It was governed by a Council having 24 elected members.

As couples descended from the bus, I noticed that one in each pair would direct where they went. It was like an outing of blind people each with a seeing-eye dog. When I had been in a couple, I had wanted to be neither the leader nor the follower but equally balanced. My marriage had ended in divorce when I had wanted to have children and my wife didn't. We had wanted to go in different directions. We didn't make it as a pair.

'Are these couples balanced?' I wondered.

I was enjoying life as a single again. I was well known, physically okay and my job as a city councillor was prestigious. I met plenty of attractive women. For four years I had partnered a series of females and when one intruded into my space I moved on to another. They said I didn't have feelings. I did have feelings but they were not the ones they wanted. I was better off on my own, I thought, unless I met someone exceptional.

There were only a handful of singles on the bus. I was pleased to see Jane Kenwood getting off, joking and laughing with her friends. She was the sassy councillor who kept us on the edge of our seats with her invective and wit in Council meetings. I had heard she was single but because she was a doll I assumed she would have a partner. Today she was on her own.

I had been at uni with Jane but I hadn't talked to her because she always had people with her and I had been too shy. She was a law student and prominent in campus politics. I was studying Science and into sport. I had been interested in politics too but in students' union elections I was limited to handing out leaflets. I was not a talker, being shy and terse.

Debating was Jane's forte. Like Marilyn Monroe, she was in her element before an audience. She had a coy naïveté that was captivating, belying her kickass attitude and razor-sharp intelligence. Now she enlivened our weekly Council meetings, putting the Government dullards on their mettle.

As I waded through the foam to catch another wave, she looked across at me and gave me a wry smile, sharing in my obvious enjoyment. She turned away to dive through a wave. My legs pranced towards her underwater, while above the surface my torso was immobile like a duck's.

When I was close enough I shouted through the din, 'Hello, Jane.'

Her voice tinkled in the roar. 'Hi, Phillip. How are you doing?'

'Is there enough water for you?' I said, as we stood chest deep, side by side, bobbing up and down. Her auburn hair was plastered on her head. She was pretty.

'No. I like bigger waves.'

'This beach is too high for that,' I said.

She gave me a puzzled look.

'You mean there isn't enough water?'

'That's right. The biggest waves will be at high tide.'

'You surf?'

'Not much now. I was into it once.'

'What happened?'

'I don't have enough time now.'

'Me too but I body surf sometimes,' she said.

'I thought making waves was more your style.'

She smiled. 'Ha-ha. How do you like our Council meetings?'

'They seem to be staged,' I said, 'except for your err ... polemics.'

'Thank you,' she said. 'The meetings *are* staged. The Government puts on a demonstration of its authority.'

'By virtue of its superior reasoning?'

'No, its bovine will,' Jane said.

'I would say porcine. Once their snout has an opening, they push and push and there is no stopping them.'

'Yes,' she said, laughing. 'That is exactly what they do.'

'Pigs are difficult to stop. A pig farmer holds a sheet of galvanised iron to drive them along. The Opposition has to have a solid barrier.'

'The meeting rules are full of holes.'

'Until you block them,' I said.

Jane's self-appointed role seemed to me to persuade our indolent Government to obey our rules of meeting procedure.

'Oh look, let's catch this one.'

We rode in on a large wave and waded out again.

'Do you ever get out of your depth?' I asked, smiling.

She cupped her hand to her shell-like ear, but the next wave smashed into us.

'DO YOU EVER GET OUT OF YOUR DEPTH?' I yelled, but she did not respond. I felt foolish and shrugged in defeat.

She came towards me and peered up into my face, smiling, waiting for me to say it again. I reached out and held her gently by the arms, in front of me. She quivered like a bird, living quickly. Holding each other at arm's length in the foam, we chatted and laughed.

Her warm smile uncovered perfectly white teeth. Her right eye calculated my details while her left ran a cool appraisal. Her nose, almost straight, had a slight downward curve but I saw neither disdain nor narcissism.

'I could get out of my depth with you,' I said. I had not met anyone like her before. I had heard it was better when meeting girls to pretend to be underwhelmed, so they would think you didn't like them, causing them to want your approval and open up to you. I would conceal that I was in awe of her.

She cocked an eyebrow.

'You will have to swim.'

'I refuse to crawl.'

'Let's not get in too deep.'

We grinned at each other, having fun.

She was trusting; her body arched to meet mine, her hands holding my hips, keeping me close – but not too close. I could hardly believe

11

that someone so beautiful would flirt with me like this, with our colleagues watching from the beach.

She steadied herself in the soft sand. I was a head taller and bent down to kiss her for the first time, slowly and gently, her soft mouth searching my lips. We heard yells and whistles and broke apart, diving under the next breaker, swimming alongside each other, sharing a wave, laughing.

'Do you want to stay shallow?' I asked as I braced against the backflow, holding her to stop her being washed away. Water tore at our legs.

'We won't know until we've tested the water,' she quipped.

'Do you think there could be any sharks?' I asked, keeping the patter going.

'What do you think of Hubbard?' she said. Martha was Lord Mayor (LM) of the two million people who lived in Alexandra City. We could see her holding court on the beach.

'She is totally up herself,' said Jane.

'Half a million citizens voted for her.'

'For the NLP,' Jane corrected.

We were both members of the NLP.

'I don't like the way she matronises us.'

Pouting and with a long upper lip, Jane imitated the LM, 'I'm not sitting in the cheap seats ...'

We laughed together.

'Perhaps she is the only one who knows what is really going on,' I said.

'Privilege is a bad look as far as I'm concerned,' said Jane. 'The Government should be transparent.'

I was going to say *'me too'*, but I caught myself in time. It was my first encounter with open dissent in the NLP ranks. Jane seemed conflicted by a renegade tendency. She had spoken a heresy as casually as commenting on the weather and it resonated with something inside me that I hadn't realised was there — something rebellious. Jane fascinated me. I wanted to be on her side.

We waded side by side against the current, chatted and then sat on the beach until we boarded the coach. We rode back, sitting together in companionable silence. I was talked out.

CHAPTER 3

Jane and I got together often. We dated, went to movies, restaurants and parties. She was an extrovert who liked to be with people, whereas I was a nerdy introvert who waited for social occasions to end so I could be alone. Although we were socially different we were both intuitive thinkers. We pooled our information and reanalysed it, concocting new realities. Our ideas often kindled and burned together for hours. A difference was that her thinking diverged and tended to float away on gusts of enthusiasm, whereas mine became smothered by practicalities. We kept each other going. I imagined us becoming councillor buddies, with skills that complemented each other. I could create plans to achieve Jane's inventions and she could persuade people to adopt them, mitigating the social deficiencies that held me back.

What I lacked in empathy and sophistication, I could make up for in smarts and affection. Maybe I wasn't a great lover but I could become so with her.

She was a thrilling catch. Because she was only loosely hooked I wondered how I could play her in and land her. Would she find out that I was something of a Lothario and assume I wanted to add her scalp to my belt? Or would she see me like a naked mole-rat scurrying blindly from its burrow, looking for a mate for life? It was an issue to be addressed early, for I ached for sex with her.

I have never been able to gauge with accuracy a partner's desire for sexual intercourse. Sex was easier to do than talk about. I figured a boots-and-all approach could work as well as hanging back, waiting for an invitation. But I would not try to jump on Jane from out of the blue. 'Shall we do it?' had to be built up to.

Romancing Jane didn't get me as far as I wanted.

'Nice try,' she would say with a mischievous wink, as if I was an opposing player.

'Are you getting over someone?' I asked her.

13

'I think so,' she said. 'I am finding myself as fast as I can. Thank you for your patience.'

I was rapt. This exotic individual was unlike anyone I had ever known. Always questioning, often preoccupied with work, she seemed not to realise the effect she was having on me. Whenever she was near me, in a meeting or in a crowd, my attention was riveted on her, wanting to see what she would do next. I was jealous of her interactions with other men. I wanted her intensely and it distracted me from everything else.

*

Starting a relationship with the woman who later would be found in concrete lifted me up to a higher level of caring than with anyone before.

People gathered around Jane like planets around a sun. Her gravitational field, like the kernel of a new galaxy, attracted nebulous lives to draw close, coalesce, fuse and shine like stars. I was in a box seat to watch her causes unfold and marvelled as all sorts of people put themselves out to take her side.

Jane was idolised for her sassiness in the debating chamber and she was the bane of the lackadaisical government. Her motives for her trenchant opposition puzzled me.

'Why are you so troublesome in meetings?' I asked her.

'I want true democracy,' she said. 'Councillors should be concerned with residents' wants. The NLP sells off public parks, gets political donations from developers and they build apartment blocks. The people who live in those apartments need a public park for recreation — but there is no land left. Councillors are boofheads who fail to ensure the public good. They suppose it is enough to encourage market capitalism. They concern themselves with wooing private developers. That is wrong. They were elected to administer public assets for the public good of the greatest number, through efficiency, humanity and conservation of the environment, to name but a few of many relevant philosophies of government. I try to stop this misbehaviour and get them to behave responsibly.'

'I like what you're doing, so don't get me wrong,' I said, 'but are you saying most councillors are on the take?'

'There are few who give like you. Councillors obey the party bosses who may be honest when they are first elected but succumb to self-interest.'

'Adam Smith regarded self-interest as the origin of public good.'

'Their self-interest is opposed to the wider public good.'

'Vigilance can stop it. We cleaned up some of it two years ago,' I said, referring to my famous discovery of systematic theft from Council's property rates accounts by senior officers.

'I remember,' Jane said. 'Your evidence put some of them behind bars. It was brilliant. But there's plenty of corruption still going on.'

'Henry Kissinger said, 'Corrupt politicians make the other 10% look bad.''

'Ha-ha. We independents are the other 10%. Our names don't go up in lights because we don't prostitute ourselves to get donations. To make up for our lack of advertising hype, we have to serve voters well.'

'Are you a do-gooder?' I asked.

'No. I believe in taking care of myself first; and trying to help others afterwards.'

'Have you taken care of yourself?' I asked.

'Yes,' she said. 'I have everything I want. How about you, Phillip?'

'I have enough. My material needs are simple.'

'We can try and help others.'

CHAPTER 4

We had been dating for about a month when I booked a table at a classy Italian restaurant with a dance floor and a DJ.

'Will I pick you up?' I asked.

'No, thank you. We can meet outside.'

Jane usually preferred to be independent. She arrived on time, her slender body poured into a little black dress, with heels that trimmed her legs.

'Awesome dress,' I said.

'Thank you. You look becoming yourself.'

She adjusted my collar.

Over dinner I tried to get her to talk about herself.

'Tell me your big picture. How do you see yourself?'

'You go first.'

'I am enjoying being a city councillor,' I said. 'I'm not sure if I'm made of the right stuff to rise in the NLP. Development of the city is not my Holy Grail. I'm more into civil rights.'

'There are other NLP councillors opposed to mindless growth too,' said Jane. 'You could join the liberal faction.'

'They don't value rational thinking as I do. They manipulate people, which I am not good at. I lack emotions, empathy and social skills. At school and uni they called me Spock and ridiculed me because I was unable to interpret vague instructions. Now it is the other extreme: the Party demands my blind obedience. I feel unfulfilled.'

'You seem to want more influence,' she said. 'What do you do best?'

'I observe and I analyse. I lock on to something and I don't let go. When I was given a Rubik's Cube, I kept at it for 12 hours straight until my fingers bled.'

'I see,' she said, eying me thoughtfully. 'Maybe the NLP find you a bit too intense. You don't seem to have found your niche yet.'

16

I shrugged. 'No.'

'What you need is a new technology to concentrate on and analyse. How about Political Science?'

'Political Science? Hmm,' I said. 'Is politics a technology?'

'It is a tool they use to get their own way when it is not rational. You could become a political powerbroker.'

'Politics is too trivial and fickle for me.'

'Then make it into something worthwhile. You could lead the NLP in a cultural revolution like Mao's.'

'I could send the intellectuals out into the country to do real work — on the land.'

'To discover the wants of real people.'

'To learn that politics is shit,' I said.

'Not everyone is capable of reasoning and compromising.'

'I agree, that is the problem,' I said. 'Now tell me about you. What is your big picture?'

'Until I was in third year I wanted to be the best,' she said.

'What at?'

'Everything. I had to be under the spotlight and the applause had to be for me. I worked hard, competed strongly and came top.'

'It sounds like you had narcissistic personality disorder.'

'I did until I was brought down. My professor sent me to a provincial business school for a week of role playing. There were about 200 of us, all research students. We played a game called Society for three days. We put in $50 each and everyone signed on as a worker, manager, owner, entrepreneur, politician, journalist, policeperson, or stayed unemployed.'

'What did you do?'

'I signed on as a politician and they elected me Prime Minister. The first national project was a competition between the companies to construct a model town with matchsticks. Entrepreneurs rushed through the town, buying up boxes of matches. Managements paid extortionate prices for them. Then construction began but vandals smashed the matchstick towns. The police wanted a pay rise to catch them and my government paid up.

'I led the Government well enough until I made a wrong move and was reviled in the press, with character attacks and outrageous lies.

17

After a no-confidence vote they dumped me and chose another PM. I had nothing to do except write my memoirs. I was devastated. It was a salutary lesson for me. I learned that the higher you rise, the harder you fall.

'After three days and three national projects they stopped the game. Then a group dynamics expert observer summed up the game. The job that had made most money was the police. They had extracted huge regular pay, they had taken bribes from the villains and they were paid protection money by the companies.'

'What if the Government and companies had not given in to them?'

'I think the crooks would not have been paid off by the police.'

'It was a dismal outcome.'

'I think it showed that effects can be opposite to the purpose intended. But that's enough of what I think. What do *you* think of me?'

'Ha-ha. I'm wondering how ambitious you are. Would you run for Lord Mayor?'

'Yes, but only because I am ambitious for my ideas.'

'That is a noble purpose. Why?'

'It is not noblesse oblige. It comes from inside me,' Jane said with a shrug. 'It's the way I am.'

'Do you like the Lord Mayor's ideas?'

'Hubbard is a dictator,' she said. 'She doesn't have any interest in what my constituents want. The NLP's agenda addresses the Party's needs, not the people's.'

We changed to speculating about the individuals at the nearest tables.

'What do you think his big picture is?' she asked, referring to a middle-aged man in a blazer sitting alone.

'He looks like a sea captain,' I replied.

'Why do you say that?'

'He is scanning the horizon.'

'He could be a castaway.'

'No. Castaways don't eat in restaurants.'

We speculated about several other diners. People fascinated her and she could see the good in everyone.

We danced half the night away with the solo steps of salsas and sambas as foreplay to holding each other in bouncy milongas and merengues. Then we danced fluid tangos with our bodies pressed tightly together.

'Where did you learn to dance?' she asked.

'Argentina. You?'

'Brazil.'

'I can do any dance when I can copy someone else's steps,' I said.

'So if the lights went off you wouldn't be able to dance?'

'No.'

'Then I would have to find someone else to dance with.'

'I wouldn't like that.'

'You should bring a flashlight with you so you could watch their feet in a blackout.'

'Not cool,' I said. 'You will just have to put up with my shuffling.'

Being so drawn to someone was unfamiliar territory.

The music was too loud for talking and we danced without speaking.

'I like being with you,' she said, in a lull in the music.

'Me too.'

'You aren't as cold as you seem.'

I knew from the wicked glint in her eyes that she was teasing me.

'Have you stopped giving backhanders?' I said in riposte.

'Sorry. I meant it as a compliment.'

'Thank you,' I said. 'You are less disagreeable than you seem.'

She eyed me with respect, grinning.

'Do you need people to agree with you?' she asked.

'I like having my own way,' I replied. 'Is that a problem for you?'

There was laughter at the corners of her eyes.

'You won't have your own way with me,' she said. 'My personal space is huge and has no rights of way.'

I realised, uneasily, that she was calling the shots in this conversation.

'Perhaps we could find some common ground?' I suggested.

'If we had some overlap,' she said.

'Overlap?'

'Like between two Venn diagrams.'

19

I liked it that she could talk dirty with maths.

'Something common?' I said.

'We can get as common as you like!'

'Your place or mine?'

'Phillip!'

She batted me on the upper arm.

'Sex is off, love,' she said pertly, like a café waitress. It reminded me of how a mare kicks at the stallion when she isn't ready, to keep him away.

'Too bad,' I said. 'How about overlapping with a coffee at your place?'

'I prefer lapping tea.'

'Fine. I'll follow you.'

We went outside to the car park and her sulphur yellow Porsche.

'Very nice,' I said. 'It sets a certain tone.'

'It's the best colour for safety,' she said apologetically.

'A yellow Volvo would be safer.'

'Ha-ha.'

'A bigger car would be safer; a Cadillac is the Rolls Royce of cars.'

'Ha-ha again. I like your jokes.'

They aren't jokes. I'm serious.'

'No matter. You're funny.'

I followed her, hardly able to keep up in my Toyota wagon. In the back were signboards, a projector screen, folding tables, chairs and a public address system: the paraphernalia of a local politician. Her driving was lead-footed but law-abiding. The route she took was circuitous.

'I wanted to check something — an idea.'

'What idea?'

'I am proposing a new public transport hub.'

Jane's mind was always trying for new ideas, whereas mine was always looking for patterns in data. Our minds churned like washing machines.

'Communicating with you is like yelling in a laundry,' I said.

'To have a conversation with you, I have to drag you out of your cave,' said Jane.

She would interrupt my train of thought by climbing onto my lap or wrapping her arms around my head or tongue kissing me. Jane made demands but I wasn't complaining.

CHAPTER 5

Jane's house was a 1930s two-storey red-brick rectangular prism with an octagonal gazebo at one front corner and at the other a cylindrical tower with an observatory. Along one side was a row of large circular portholes with nautical scenes in stained glass.

'My grandfather sailed,' said Jane.

A sweeping driveway skirted a Japanese garden: a lagoon with an arched bridge, spreading orange maples, an ornate gazebo, sculpted azaleas, boulders and a Buddha statue.

'A neighbour helps me with the garden,' she said.

Inside was art deco with high ceilings, vertical lines and angular patterns. Arched doorways held semicircular lunettes with ornate mouldings of cupids, angels and cherubs. Large rectangular windows had vertical white shutters. The floor of the living area was gleaming herringbone parquetry in red hardwoods. A wide staircase wound upwards.

On the walls were paintings in modern styles and spotlighted in alcoves were installations of glass, ceramic and metal arts. Antique chairs and tables displayed ornamental art pieces, some in radical designs. Her home displayed timeless elegance.

'My sister and I inherited this place from Grandma. She collected over a lifetime — there isn't a piece I don't like. I'm trying to buy out my sister — she lives in the UK.'

We sat in a love seat, sipping wine, and discussed a Kirchner 1911 oil painting of a husband standing lighting his pipe beside his part-naked wife.

'It's an experiment in Expressionism,' she said.

'It seems to satirise Gainsborough's Mr and Mrs Andrews,' I suggested.

'I know that one, but I don't like it. Mr Andrews looks anal retentive.'

'So does this poser,' I said. 'He should be happy. His lady is voluptuous.'

'Perhaps she has a lover and he is jealous,' said Jane.

'She seems saintly. Perhaps he feels inadequate and is passively aggressive. I feel like that about you sometimes.'

'Do you?' she scoffed. 'A saint I ain't.'

'You perform miracles in getting the council to behave responsibly.'

'Does that make you feel inadequate?'

'Maybe — it could be jealousy. I too want them to behave better but they take no notice of me.'

'That's because you are a control freak.'

'Am I?' I said lamely.

'Yes. You are like a sheepdog. You are always trying to round people up and drive them through small openings.'

'Do I really do that?'

'You do — but driving people never works. If you give them half a chance, they bugger off.'

'How do you get people to do what you want?'

'Take the lead. Go in front and they flock after you.'

*

I had been lured into politics by the novelty of trying out in a people job. When I was doing forensic science, people experiences were few and far between. The Council corruption case had whetted my appetite for public notoriety, government and politics. I was fascinated and when I was offered the opportunity to run for council, I had leapt at it. It would be an adventure.

As it turned out, my people skills were not up to the job. I wasn't any good at sassing out what residents wanted. Nor did I make them feel better by listening to their concerns by the hour before realising that what they usually wanted was my attention. I wasted my time getting a duck pond in the local park but residents seldom went there. When I opposed creating a flying area for drones, residents got up a petition. Council approved setting one up and to my surprise it was popular.

I did have some successes. People sought my advice on preventing and solving crimes. I was effective in helping residents deal with bureaucracies, interpreting laws and regulations. My work as a councillor seemed stuck with endless cycles of planning.

I could never be a dyed-in-the-wool NLP member. I wasn't a joiner of groups. I didn't set out to merge my interests with others. I had to learn to disguise my dislike for people and to pretend affection. From Jane I learned to remember names, ask them about their interests and chewed the fat with them. I chatted with Party people whenever I could and pretended to be a regular NLP wallah. Jane helped me in the job and I began to feel I was succeeding.

When I first met Jane, her ex-boyfriend, Manfred, was staying at her place. They had lived together for two years. She had finished with him six months before and he had gone away but he had come back. My jealousy was ugly.

'Why did you finish with him?' I asked Jane.

'We were incompatible.'

'Tell me about him.'

She had met Manfred at a Samba school in Rio de Janeiro. She was there with a girlfriend for Carnival. He was with his sailing crew, celebrating their win in the annual Cape Town to Rio yacht race. He had been womanless at sea for five weeks. They partied all night.

Manfred had won Olympic gold and was a legend in sailing circles. He was wealthy, having a large income from his father's property empire. He took Jane sailing but she became seasick and wouldn't go again. She paired up with him for the rest of her holiday. Leaving his crew to sail his yacht to the UK, he came back to Alexandra with her.

At first, Manfred joined in with Jane's full social life. They went out almost every evening to functions or private parties, mostly in government circles. He had no interest in government and preferred to spend his time at Alexandra Yacht Club. He went away frequently, to skipper or crew in races. In-between he lived with Jane in her luxurious house.

'Each time he returned, we had to start over,' she said. 'It was like he was in the Navy.'

'I'll bet it didn't bother him,' I said.

24

Manfred was an adventurer and risk-taker. He put together a consortium to challenge for the America's Cup.

'At first his public profile gave me kudos,' she said, 'but some of my constituents saw me as a wealthy playboy's girlfriend dabbling in Town Hall politics. Manfred's profligacy conflicted with my humanitarian goals.'

Jane had given Manfred an ultimatum. 'Choose between sailing and me.'

He was running too hard to change his sails. He continued on and she finished with him. Although six months had passed, he still had his gear at Jane's place.

'Why don't you make him take his stuff away?' I asked.

'I want to stay friends with him,' she said.

'I don't like him hanging around.'

When our paths crossed we bared our teeth and growled.

I was spending my spare time at Jane's place but I returned to my apartment to sleep alone. Jane was seldom cautious except with me.

*

In the Council, Jane was on a collision course with the NLP. She opposed the Government's hegemony, secrecy and corruption. Her antipathy was reaching new heights. After months of rocking the NLP boat, matters came to a head when she voted with the Opposition.

'O'Connell called me a scab today,' she told me.

He was the Deputy Mayor.

'What did you do?'

'I stuck my tongue out at him. I told him I could vote for whoever I liked, whenever I liked.'

'Good for you.'

The NLP majority was slender.

Later that week they expelled Jane from the Party. For the final year of her four-year term, Jane was on her own.

For the Council election, Jane mobilised a hard-working team of supporters and mounted a campaign of door knocking and public appearances. Although the NLP and SLP tried to discredit her, Blake Ward people recognised her worth and re-elected her.

I was returned for Byron Ward when my corruption-busting halo again attracted votes. Grateful residents had voted me in as their councillor when, as a forensic scientist with the police, I had exposed a ring of corrupt City Council officials.

CHAPTER 6

I was running late for the Council meeting. A button had come off my shirt and changing it had delayed me. As I drove, an item on the nine o'clock news caught my attention.

'The Government is inviting proposals for casinos to be built in Roberta's major cities.

'Today Bentley Leach, Premier of Roberta, announced that companies who submitted winning tenders would get licences to build casinos. 'New casinos will attract gamblers from China, India and other countries, as well as Robertans. They will boost tourism and employment.'

'Geoff Nash of the Salvation Army made this comment.

"Casinos ruin people's lives. Victims end up on welfare, in mortuaries, hospitals, mental institutions and prison. Tourists deserve better. Roberta has other better attractions for tourists to spend their money on.'

'The Premier said, 'Tourism is declining in Roberta due to strong competition from places offering world-class integrated casino and resort accommodation. We need casino resorts.'

'Today Premier Leach is holding further talks with Runyon Casinos. Six new casinos have opened worldwide this year. The Government's strategy is to catch the next wave of demand for gambling by wealthy players. A new casino will take at least six years to construct. Growth of high-roller gambling may depend on continuing prosperity.

'Nash of the Salvation Army said, 'If there is a recession, casinos will rely on machine gaming, which causes addiction to gambling with serious social consequences. Casinos sometimes reward lack of reward. This is called operant conditioning and can cause addiction.'

'Speaking for Runyon Casinos, Andrea Gough denied this. 'We cannot disclose our rewards system, to be fair to all players. Random payout would not generate enough profit and taxes. Our gambling machines do not reinforce player continuity on the same machine. They are not addictive.'

'The Roberta Government wants casino developers to submit proposals immediately.

'This is Sophie Little reporting for Radio Southland.'

This news annoyed me. As usual, the Government was trying to prevent debate. There might not be an opportunity to oppose them. A government was supposed to bring benefits to its people. A casino was about as beneficial as a brothel; some people would get hurt and others would get nasty habits. Gambling hit on the little people. The Government was mesmerised by a mirage of tax loot. It was bad government and by my Party.

I parked in my bay in the garage under City Hall and took the lift up to street level, nodding to well-wishers. I was still a public figure from my corruption-busting days. I hurried across the square and between the Corinthian columns, scattering the pigeons to their roosts above the capitols.

It was 9.54 when I pushed through the glass door into City Hall, crossed the atrium with its polished marble floor and followed the brass handrail to committee room number three. I was four minutes late, just within my tolerance.

Usually, I was first to arrive but Trudy Munster was already there, seated at a mahogany board table large enough for table tennis, in a room hushed by soft green carpet and illuminated by suspended brass lights. She presided over eight empty redwood chairs with plush green upholstery. Erskine from Executive bustled in and dealt out paper around the table. A café bar in the corner scented the air with fresh coffee, adding to the impression that we councillors were appreciated, despite our meagre remuneration.

'Good morning, Phillip,' said Trudy, with a thin smile. She was a stalwart of LM Hubbard's cabinet team and Chairperson of the DA Committee. She oversaw building approvals for the City.

Next to arrive was Grant Fenwick, Deputy Chairperson and Whip. He was a mean and vindictive person known as Attack Dog. Martha Hubbard, the Lord Mayor, kept him on a leash and released him to intimidate erring NLP councillors. He sat down at the head of the table next to Munster.

Next the SLP contingent arrived, Penny Redford and Shelly Burton. Penny was a veteran urban planner.

'Good morning, Spock,' Penny said. 'I liked your reply to that whinger in the Standard.'

I was pleased she had seen my letter but I only nodded. I liked to stay at a distance from colleagues, so they wouldn't expect me to support their causes when I didn't believe in them.

'Monorails are crap,' I replied. 'If buildings were of standard height, as I proposed, aerial railways could go from rooftop to rooftop.'

'Pie in the sky,' said Munster, without looking up from her reading.

She didn't like my ideas and knocked them back regularly.

'I'll give her pie in the sky,' I thought bitterly. *'Her comment shows a lack of imagination.'*

'It would stop one-upmanship.' said Shelly, supporting me. She was a friend of mine and Jane's. 'Do tall buildings have any advantages at all?'

'You can see further,' I said.

Trudy said, 'Efficient use of space; less infrastructure; lower cost of accommodation; more tax revenue.'

'More isolated, lonely and slower to get down in an emergency,' said Shelly.

'Slower climbing up when there is a power cut,' I said. 'People could be trapped or homeless. Rooftop precincts at standard height could connect and give better access.'

'The CBD would look like a biscuit tin,' said Trudy flatly. 'We don't want aerial tubeways like in that movie *Metropolis*. Railways have to be at ground level.'

Because she was the Chairperson her assertion was enough to dismiss my idea. She only allowed development that had NLP approval. Their majority accepted my statistics, logic and science then rejected my ideas. They left me out of discussions on values and relationships, citing senses and feelings that contradicted science as well as my intuition and thinking. Nothing was ever debated thoroughly in this committee. It was unjust that I was so powerless.

Richard Barber, aka Cutter, came in dishevelled, glanced blearily around, sat down tiredly, reclined with his legs thrust out and linked his hands behind his head. He was wearing a white suit he had made himself. He aspired to be an artist. He affected the manner of a dissipated aristocrat. Attractive in a rakish way, he had a bohemian tendency and held cannabis tea parties which were reputed to degenerate into soirées, with everyone going to bed with everyone else. His lifestyle was oriented towards pleasure, sometimes to a self-destructive degree.

At other times he could be a charming companion and conversationalist, delivering fine work as a policymaker, debater and people's representative. Despite his social lapses he was a friend.

'How are you?' I asked him.

'Morning,' Cutter said curtly, rolling his eyes as if it was not at all good.

The others sat around and made small talk, waiting to start. The minute hand on the wall clock crawled around to 10.00 am.

Several officers from the Council's administration came in: an architect, a civil engineer, an environmental engineer and a financial analyst. They were there to provide advice, or out of interest and sat around the outside of the room.

A young woman looked into the room hesitantly.

'Runyon Casinos?' said Trudy, standing up.

'Yes. I'm Andrea Gough.'

'Welcome. Your seat is there,' Trudy pointed to the other end of the table.

Erskine showed her the projector controls and she plugged in a message stick. He took his seat on the other side of Trudy from Fenwick. He would chair the non-partisan part of the meeting.

He looked at his watch. 'Good morning, Councillors. We'll expect Councillor Kenwood when she arrives.'

When Jane was late it was because she meant to be.

First up was a motion to accept Runyon Casinos' preliminary development application (PDA). It was to check the proposal before the developer spent millions and years on preparing a DA that would be rejected. The Committee would look for any major problems that needed to be addressed.

Erskine delivered his standard spiel. 'This meeting will decide whether to recommend to Council to accept Runyon's PDA. Your recommendation will go to the full Council for approval.

'We have with us Andrea Gough who will present Runyon's proposal.'

Andrea, in a pigeon-grey business suit with a pink blouse, stood to one side of the screen, her face a picture of responsible precision. She used the remote to show PowerPoint slides and read out a voiceover. In the first slide she stood with a middle-aged businessman in front of a solid modern building with the name 'Runyon Casinos' carved in marble over the door.

'Here I am at our Singapore office with Don Sindona, our CEO,' she said. 'I am manager of our Alexandra project. My presentation today is to give you a first look at our proposal.'

The door opened and Jane came in two minutes late. She was prim in a knee-length canary yellow shift, with matching shoes and handbag. Andrea paused for her to sit down.

'Sorry I'm late,' she said. 'I was held up. My fingernail broke and my mobile was difficult.' She turned to face Andrea. 'I'm Jane Kenwood.'

She had an unerring ability to self-promote. Most people wanted Jane to be part of their lives after only a brief meeting.

CHAPTER 7

The woman who would be found in concrete gave me a quick smile and slid gracefully into the empty chair. The committee had four councillors from the NLP, two SLP and independent Jane.

'Good morning, Councillor Kenwood. I'm Andrea Gough from Runyon Casinos. I'm showing a presentation of our company's proposal.'

'Please continue.'

'For centuries, gambling has been a favourite pastime for people from all walks of life and it continues to be today,' she said. 'Runyon Casinos is a public company that has operated casinos for 15 years. The sun never sets on our empire. We have built 10, one in each of: Sydney, Melbourne, Perth, Mumbai, New Delhi, Vancouver, Toronto, Montreal, Cape Town and Johannesburg. Starting a casino needs more than a passion for gambling: it requires a significant investment, accurate planning and good business management. We are negotiating for a site in the CBD with your Government.

'High rollers from China and India want privacy, luxury and prestige.'

She showed images of three tall mushroom-shaped buildings towering over the city centre.

'Our vision is a resort that is a landmark. The significance of the mushroom design is that good luck can grow quickly and spread. The mushrooms would be visible all around as far as the city periphery. They would be the nation's tallest buildings, with spectacular views. Bradfield, our architect, has set out to create a resort with the highest standards of provision for customers. The caps contain two gambling floors, six movie theatres, four auditoriums, ten restaurants and a total of 1200 rooms. The stalks are for lifts and business offices. At ground level, the site has a public swimming pool, a health and fitness centre and a public park.

'Construction would create 2000 jobs onsite for six years and 6000 permanent jobs afterwards. Here are some artists' views.'

Ten views of the sumptuous interiors made it evident that the development would be iconic.

'Wealthy customers will want the excitement of playing games with a high limit in an exclusive atmosphere. For them we have the Sky Suite, which is a club where they can gamble for seven days and 24 hours. It is for people who want to have fun with their money.'

'Now, I expect some of you may be concerned about the welfare of our customers and that they make sensible decisions about how much they can afford to lose. Our receptionists interview every client and ascertain their financial situation, what conditions could cause them to want to quit and that they would choose to do so when necessary.'

Andrea showed more images and ended her talk with a photo of the province's Premier, Bentley Leach, shaking hands with Runyon's CEO on the steps of Alexandra's Immigration Building (IB).

I thought, *'Leach seems to be selling the old IB site to them. He hasn't the authority to do that. Even the handshake is a bit rich when Council hasn't approved their PDA.'*

'I hope you approve of this project,' said Andrea, ending her presentation. 'Thank you.'

It was apparent she expected us to decide it without further ado.

'We'll break for five minutes,' said Erskine. 'After that there will be discussion and an opportunity to question Andrea.'

I had a few words with Cutter at the café bar. I had met Richard Barber, my best friend, at university. We had both studied Science and were members of the NLP. He had become a school Physical Education teacher while I had stayed on to do research. We had met regularly for a drink and a natter, or to go on a double date. After several years he became a taxi driver.

'I'm finding out from my rides how this city works,' he said.

He was active in the NLP and was elected for Wordsworth Ward where he lived three years before I joined him on the Council. He was a 'lifer' who protected me, a naïve new inmate, in the prison of Council politics.

'What do you think of the casino?' I asked him.

'Another provincial snow job.'

Jane walked over to us.

'Aren't those mushrooms ghastly? You can tell it isn't kosher by the way it's being rushed through. Until today we have heard nothing about it. They know people won't want it. After today it will be out of our hands— unless We Do Something,' she said, mouthing each word for emphasis.

The 24 councillors were affiliated: 13 NLP, 10 SLP and independent Jane. The NLP juggernaut seemed certain to approve Runyon's proposal. I doubted there was anything I could do to stop it.

CHAPTER 8

'Councillor Munster, the first question is yours,' said Erskine.

'Thank you, Mr Chairperson,' said Munster. 'Andrea, would the mushroom shapes be safe in a cyclone?'

'A strong wind can blow off a cap,' I said with a smirk.

There were smiles. Trudy scowled.

Andrea answered, 'Mathematical models show they are safe even under extreme conditions. Alexandra University will test a physical model in their wind tunnel.'

'Thank you, Andrea,' Erskine said. 'Next question?'

For the next hour, councillors asked about the proposal and Andrea provided details.

'If there are no more questions, thank you, Andrea,' said Erskine. 'Would you wait outside and we'll let you know what we decide.'

Andrea left the room.

'The committee will discuss the PDA and decide by voting whether to recommend it to Council,' Erskine prompted.

Jane spoke quietly and sweetly.

'Mr Chairperson, Councillors, I am concerned about the process we are using here. In my opinion, voting is not the way to decide this application. We need to consider not only this casino but other casinos too — and other alternatives such as a multicultural centre (MC). We should compare PDAs and make a reasoned choice.'

'There aren't any other PDAs,' said Fenwick. 'The Government hasn't sought proposals.'

'A multicultural centre should be considered... other alternatives too.'

'What is a multicultural centre?' asked Munster,

'It is a place where people from all nations can celebrate their unique cultures before public audiences,' Jane said. 'The IB could be restored and an auditorium and theatre built on.'

'But multiculture is a catchword. It doesn't mean anything,' said Munster. 'It glosses over racial differences that cause problems, such as languages.'

'On the contrary, it enables cultures to recognise and respect each other. The Arborville rioting is a heads-up.'

Ethnic gangs had clashed recently in a suburb of Alexandra.

'Is there a MC proposal?'

'Yes. A group has been meeting for a couple of years.'

'Who are they?'

'The IB Action Group (IBAG),' said Jane. 'My contact is their chairperson, Sunita Lovelock. She works at the university.'

'Oh her,' said Trudy Munster disdainfully. 'Hippy activist type — I doubt she'll be able to raise the funds needed.'

'They are too late,' said Fenwick. 'They should have put in a PDA.'

'IBAG's project isn't ready yet. They didn't know we would be considering proposals. The Council should call tenders.'

'No. We have to decide the casino proposal now,' said Fenwick.

As usual, the Government's consultation was token. Fenwick's smile was frozen; his engagement with the issue was shown by his distended right eye and his aggressive talk. His left eye coolly surveyed demeanours around the table. His nose was pulled back, withdrawn from considering the matter by reason.

'Why is it too late?' Jane asked. 'You are not being fair.'

'If Runyon's could make an early-bird proposal, why couldn't your Miss Lovelock?' Fenwick said with contempt, 'instead of trying to worm her way in at the last minute with this MC nonsense?'

'Why has only Runyon's been able to make a proposal?' Jane asked indignantly. You can't tear down the IB willy-nilly. A city needs to cherish its heritage, so people can grow roots, feel secure and take pride in their past. Alexandra should not become a soulless pile of concrete, steel and glass, like the battle planet in Star Wars.'

'Runyon's are prepared to pay most for the site — end of story,' said Munster.

'The IB site is not like a heap of coal the Government can flog off to the highest bidder,' said Jane. 'It is a site of iconic cultural heritage. The people have owned it and used it for 150 years.

Destroying it to make way for a casino is desecration. There is a better public good.'

'Runyon's casino would pay most taxes,' said Munster. 'A MC would pay only a pittance.'

'The aim of government is not to collect as much tax money as possible,' Jane said patiently. 'A MC would bring racial harmony and a more secure civil society. Music can heal rifts between individuals and within communities. It can forge friendships between different ethnic groups.'

'Bravo, Jane,' I thought. I wanted to openly support her but could not because I needed NLP endorsement at the next election.

'Encouraging them to retain their cultures will slow down assimilation,' said Fenwick. 'They have to forget their foreign ways and adopt Robertan culture as quickly as possible.'

Fenwick's words were tantamount to fascist nationalism. I was ashamed to be in the same party.

'People need their cultural heritage preserved and renewed,' said Shelly with indignation. 'People who are in touch with their own culture are more contented.'

'They left their roots behind when they immigrated here,' Munster said. 'The IB no longer processes immigrants and is of little interest to anyone.'

'The IB is an iconic emblem. It symbolises that immigrants are valued highly here,' said Penny. 'It has helped keep their roots alive and growing. It dignifies their cultural heritage and contributes to their sense of belonging.'

Shelly and Penny were doing what I wanted to do: confront these NLP extremists.

'High rollers need privacy and one-stop access to tourist destinations for their families but if the resort is in the CBD they will hardly get that,' I said. 'On the other hand, a MC does need a central location and the IB site is ideal.'

'People who work in the CBD will be able to go to the casino after work,' Fenwick said.

'As usual, Councillor Fenwick is blind to the humanitarian aspects,' said Jane quietly. 'Workers will lose their shirts, become poor, create unrest and crime will flourish.'

'You can't save people from themselves,' said Fenwick.

'We can save them from bad developments,' Jane said, 'by opposing this PDA.'

Jane had caused Fenwick chagrin in the past and it made him circumspect in confronting her now.

'I don't see that there is anything to be gained by more debate,' he said. 'The argument is simply that we represent different people. Our supporters want growth and jobs; yours want handouts. We have a majority. You lose.'

The way Fenwick was trying to steamroller us irritated me and put me on Jane's side.

'Many people either don't want to gamble or can't afford to,' she said. 'What people really want is for the IB site to be used for the most benefit to the community.'

'Runyon's resort will be of the most benefit,' said Munster. 'They would pay most for the site and pay most taxes.'

'But those are only capitalist economic benefits. Only a few of our constituents are capitalists. Benefits by other economic theories such as Marx's socialism, the greatest good of the greatest number, resources efficiency, humanism and conservation cannot be ignored.'

'How could we consider other alternatives at this late date?'

'We should not abandon reason and recommend Runyon's proposal just to kowtow to the Premier. We should survey city residents to find out what they want done with the IB site – a casino, a MC or something else.' Jane sat back.

Shelly, Penny and I clapped. 'Yay!'

Munster and Fenwick looked at me anxiously. It was the first time I had come out against the NLP. My dissent threatened the NLP majority.

'Hmm. If we did a survey, people would want a casino,' said Munster. 'People want Alexandra to become a world city. The hideous old IB is holding us back.'

'To test that hypothesis we need a survey,' I said.

'There isn't time,' said Fenwick. 'We should decide now with a vote.'

My vote was critical. I could vote with either the Government or the Opposition. I would have to decide between loyalty to Jane or to the NLP during this meeting. Would siding with Jane be worthwhile if we lost? Should I follow my heart and go all the way with JK?

CHAPTER 9

'Now Councillor Munster will take over the chair for a political item,' said Erskine.

The committee did political business with a partisan chair.

'Thank you, Erskine,' Munster said. 'Before we get carried away with philosophy, we need to discuss the Premier's visit this afternoon.'

'It isn't on the agenda,' said Jane. 'He can't just barge in on us.'

'I didn't find out until yesterday. He is coming to inform Council about the casino. Then we will vote on the PDA.'

The committee could only recommend: approval had to be by the full Council.

'We should recommend it,' Fenwick said. He was a staunch NLP cabinet member.

'I disagree,' I said, declaring my opposition. 'A casino will condition customers to keep playing and putting up more than they can afford to lose.'

Fenwick shook his head angrily.

'Runyon's have denied that,' said Munster.

'It is a lie,' said Jane. 'There are many well-authenticated reports that casinos operant condition. When a player is losing, the machine is programmed to payout seed money to lure them to continue. It creates a gambling addiction. That is how they get return business.'

'Not all addiction is acquired,' I said. 'Some have a compulsion.'

'Casinos nurture it,' said Jane. 'Can we ask the Premier how the losers are likely to be affected?'

'Certainly not,' said Fenwick shaking his head. 'The Premier needs our support.'

'Gambling transfers money from the impatient poor to the patient wealthy,' said Jane. 'That is not my idea of a public amenity — although it might be yours.'

'I personally would not go to a casino,' Munster said, 'but the taxes it would collect would do a lot of good.'

'Believing one thing and doing another is called hypocrisy. A person who abjures gambling should act to stop a casino being built.'

'How quaint and Christian of you to do to others as you would be done by,' said Fenwick. 'But it won't wash here. If we had to follow precepts of universal good, we wouldn't be able to do anything.'

'Our personal views don't count here,' said Munster. 'What matters is having a future for the city. When the Premier wants a tourist renaissance led by a casino, our job is to lump it.'

'Bollocks,' said Jane, her glossy auburn ponytail bobbing. 'The last thing residents of this city need is a casino in the CBD, even if it is the Premier's pet project.'

She glared at Trudy.

'The city centre is dying,' Fenwick said. 'What are you going to do about it, Jane?'

I knew Jane had a manifesto of futuristic ideas in astonishing detail. Now she didn't hesitate.

'Firstly we need a MC to make everyone feel welcome in the city centre. Then we need an underground railway to bring them in.'

I had heard this before.

'Would a MC boost the CBD as much as a casino?' Fenwick asked, stubbornly trying to narrow the consideration of possibilities down to commerce.

'Yes, absolutely,' said Jane. 'A MC would transform the city centre after hours from empty office buildings into a vibrant people-oriented community. Is anyone interested in joining me in a brainstorming session after this meeting to nut out the alternatives?'

'I will,' I said, making my disaffection for the NLP plain.

'Me too,' said Shelly.

'Not me,' said Fenwick. 'I've heard enough shit for one day.'

'Fenwick, you are a disgrace to the office of city councillor,' Jane said.

'I am not obliged to listen to hare-brained schemes,' he said.

'We will revert to recommending approval of Runyon's PDA,' said Munster. 'Erskine, would you resume the chair?'

The executive chaired non-policy matters.

41

'This will be interesting,' said Jane. 'I wonder if the Government will have the numbers.'

They all looked at me.

CHAPTER 10

'Okay,' said Erskine. 'Does someone have a motion?'

Grant Fenwick applied the committee mantra to the casino proposal.

'I move that we recommend Runyon's PDA.'

'Seconded,' said Trudy Munster.

The NLP were in automatic, having their own way as usual.

'Those in favour, raise an arm,' said Erskine.

Trudy, Grant and Cutter.

'Doctor Keane?' said Trudy.

My name is Phillip Keane. They say: 'Keane by name, keen by nature. I have a doctorate in Forensic Science. When they address me as 'Doctor' it is usually to remind me that I am overqualified for practical matters and I should do what they want.

'Is this a conscience vote?' I asked.

'Yes, Doctor, it is,' said Erskine.

'In theory,' said Trudy, 'but it has never happened.'

Council's committees were nominally non-partisan to ensure they would get a majority. The Government stacked the numbers and appointed the Chair.

'Those in favour, raise an arm,' Erskine repeated.

My arm stayed down.

'Excuse me, Mr Chairperson,' said Fenwick. 'Would you hold on while I speak with Doctor Phillip outside?'

'Two minutes,' said Erskine.

'Phillip?' said Fenwick, pointing to the door with his lips.

I followed him out. When we were alone he said, 'You have to vote with us, Phillip. I know you don't want a casino — none of us do — but we have to support it.'

'Why?'

'Our Party leaders want it.'

'But I haven't had a say.'

43

'None of us have. What's your problem?'

Grant Fenwick was aggressive. He left the Army at age 40 and went into a job as despatch manager for a supermarket chain. A Party man, the NLP nominated him for a safe seat. Cold, officious and without friends, he was influential in candidate selection. He used this in his position as Whip, demanding compliance from NLP councillors. He didn't get the nickname 'Attack Dog' for nothing.

'I don't have a problem. I want a say.'

'Why? Whether we have a multicultural gizmo or a casino doesn't matter at all. Whether people gamble or get cultured doesn't make any difference, as long as they keep working, earning and spending.'

He was serious and I was appalled.

'I think it does matter,' I said, confronting him.

'You can raise it in caucus. Topple the leadership. Run for leader yourself. In the meantime, we have to vote for the casino.'

'What if I refuse?'

Fenwick took a step closer. 'You will vote with us, right?'

I shrugged with my face. 'Maybe not. It's a conscience vote.'

He looked as if he was about to rip out my throat. 'If you don't, you are dead. You won't ever get Party endorsement again. If you run as an independent, you won't win. Don't let Jane fool you — she only got in by the skin of her teeth. She will be out next time. If you want to stay in politics, you have to vote with us.'

'Go fuck yourself, Fenwick,' I said, taking deep breaths for control, keeping my fists by my sides. I despised violence even more than I despised him.

'Don't tangle with me, Keane,' he snarled, 'or you'll regret it.' He thrust his face up close to mine, glared, bared his teeth, spun on his heel and stomped back into the meeting. It was political death to go against the NLP. The best I could hope for was to follow Jane on to the crossbench.

I knew Jane would approve of me confronting Fenwick.

*

My commitment to Jane had been steadily growing, while Jane had continued to go on dates with friends, both female and male.

44

When she explained her other dates were platonic, I was not totally reassured and decided to bring the whole deal of exclusivity out into the open.

'Jane, you can be the only woman in my life,' I said, 'if you want.'

'Until when?' she replied.

'Permanently,' I said, trying to hide the regret I felt in denying the dictates of my promiscuous Bonobo ancestry. Bonobos are regarded by biologists as humans' closest ancestors, by the large size of their genitalia. They copulate promiscuously with evangelical zeal.

I had stopped seeing my previous girlfriend, Sandy. We had been together on and off for six months. We had only ever been temporary, both of us waiting for the real thing to come along. Now it had and I was apprehensive.

'My equipment is too big for fidelity,' I thought despondently. *'If my ancestors were gibbons, my tool bag would be better equipped to mate for life, as they do.'*

'Monogamy is not a death sentence,' Jane said. She was good at reading me.

'If you want, you can have an exclusive deal,' I said, pretending to be casual. I was standing on the edge of a cliff. It was possible to climb down and continue philandering, but there would be no way back to Jane.

'Several men are going to be unhappy about this,' she said, 'but I'll reciprocate.'

'What do you mean?'

'You know I like to flirt.'

'I didn't know.'

'Well, I'll keep my flirting for you alone from now on. Okay?'

I couldn't tell if she was serious.

'I'm sorry if I cramp your style.'

She burst out laughing and threw her arms around my neck and we kissed.

'Got you going, didn't I? It's a deal,' she said. 'I don't want anyone else.

Faced with the need for irrevocable commitment, I finished with Sandy.

'The real thing has come along.'

'I'm happy for you,' Sandy said. 'Goodbye.'

It was one small step for me and a giant leap for womankind. Jane and I had an exclusive deal. It was a milestone.

*

I decided there and then to desert the NLP. I would not have the likes of Fenwick riding herd on me. No longer would I have to toady to the ruthless near-psychopath to get endorsed by the Party. My ambition was to serve friends and the community where I lived. They would appreciate my work and that was enough for me. I would vote on my conscience and the NLP could go hang.

I would no longer get member benefits. The briefings, policy guidelines, position papers, advertising, pork barrelling and leader visits to my electorate at election time would cease. Without them, I would become an independent like Jane, doing my own research at weekends, deciding every issue myself and campaigning alone.

If I did what a majority of my constituents wanted, I would oppose the casino. I could be gallant in support of Jane.

I went back inside.

Erskine said, 'Those in favour of recommending Runyon's PDA raise an arm.'

As before, there were three. Munster and Fenwick looked at me daggers. Cutter was examining his fingernails. The lower lid of my right eye gave a twitch as it did sometimes under stress.

'Phillip?' Fenwick prompted.

'Sorry, guys,' I said. 'My residents do not want a casino.'

'What's that got to do with it?' said Fenwick angrily. 'You just wait.'

'Grant, you are an embarrassment,' said Jane. 'Bullying people is bad behaviour.'

'Three Fors,' said Erskine. 'How many Againsts?'

Jane, Shelly, Penny and me.

'Four. The motion is defeated.'

'Nice one, Phillip,' said Jane jubilantly.

I gave her a high-five and sat back. We had rejected Runyon's PDA. Everyone looked at me and I supposed they wondered why I

46

had jumped ship now, whether I had quit the NLP for good, whether there would be an election and what their chances were of being elected.

Our lives could be changed forever.

CHAPTER 11

Munster looked at her watch, as though she wanted to end the meeting.

She said to Jane, 'Turning down that PDA is a travesty.'

'No it isn't. Recommending Runyon's without calling tenders would be a travesty.'

'It would take too much time,' Munster said. 'Runyon's want an answer now or they will go somewhere else.'

'Too bad,' said Jane. 'A survey will find out if it is a casino that people want, or something else would be better.'

'It has to be a quick survey,' said Trudy. 'Let's check if Runyon's can wait.'

We went out and found Andrea.

'Andrea, we are thinking of calling tenders. We would also do a survey of what residents want and decide in a month's time. How would Runyon's be with that?'

'Not happy at all,' said Andrea. 'The Premier didn't say anything about delaying, calling of tenders or doing a survey.'

'That's our Bentley,' Jane said. 'He forgets that it is the Council that has to approve a development.'

'A month is not long,' said Munster, placating.

Andrea pouted but was silent, then gave a shrug, resigned.

We went back in.

'Okay, let's do it,' said Munster.

'Erskine, Councillor Kenwood has a recommendation for Council.'

'Do you have some words?' asked Erskine.

Jane spoke carefully as Erskine wrote. 'The DA Committee is to seek proposals for development of the Immigration Museum site, by 10th June, with assessment subject to a survey of residents' gambling and other preferences.'

He read it to everyone.

'That puts it back five weeks,' he said. 'Seconder? Okay, seconded by Shelly Burton. All those in favour?'

Jane, Shelly, Penny and me.

'Four Fors,' said Erskine. 'Against?'

Munster, Fenwick and Cutter.

'Three. The motion is carried.'

'Yes,' said Jane with an air punch.

Munster was disoriented by the loss of Government control and seemed to be sleepwalking. She brought Andrea in and told her of the recommendation.

'It's disappointing,' Andrea said. 'We worked hard on that PDA.'

'Thank you for coming, Andrea,' said Munster. 'I'm sure your proposal will get Council's approval in a month's time.'

'We thought you would approve it today.'

'Why not gamble on having better luck next time?' I said with a grin.

She glared at me and left.

'We'll meet in the Councillors' Lounge at midday to discuss alternatives,' said Jane to everyone.

Munster looked at me as though I smelled bad.

'Scabbing against the party that elected you is pretty low,' she said. 'You are committing political suicide. A deserter loses their next election.'

'I didn't lose when I crossed,' Jane said.

'That was a fluke. It'll never happen again,' said Munster, shaking her head. 'Phillip is making a big mistake.'

'Are you kidding?' said Jane. 'He is going in to bat for his constituents instead of skulking in the NLP pavilion.'

I liked Jane sticking up for me.

'I won't be able to overlook this, Phillip,' said Fenwick, scowling.

'Bugger off, you pathetic bully,' I said.

'Now, now,' said Munster. 'It's all good fun. What would we do without adversarial politics?'

'Get a proper job, I suppose,' Shelly smirked. Soon she would be stepping back from the fray to have a baby.

'We can't all have babies,' Munster said.

She was single and dedicated to her job. Her remark sounded less like envy and more like a personal catechism.

'Make love, not war,' said Cutter. 'This committee needs to lighten up.'

'Is there any other business?' Erskine said. 'No? Your recommendation will go forward to Council.'

He ended the meeting.

*

The seven of us went down in the lift together. I stood with the Opposition: Jane, Shelly and Penny, chatting and laughing. On the other side were Fenwick and Munster, with Cutter standing gloomily silent. He would be smarting from having towed his party's line and opposed Jane and me, his friends. He was hunched up as if he wanted to disappear. The NLP group was like a ticking bomb. Trudy Munster's head was down, wearing a frown. She whispered into Fenwick's ear and he nodded, with his hands clenched and his eyes unseeing, as if he might explode.

CHAPTER 12

Jane and I crossed City Square to have lunch together. My breakout from the Party straitjacket gave me a wonderful feeling of freedom. Jane walked with her head up and shoulders back, happy after our triumph, taking in faces with a smile and a nod. Shoppers in our path sensed her leadership and parted to let us through.

We bumped into Julie Dawson, Leader of the Opposition.

'In the DA Committee just now, we rolled them. We got the casino put back a month.'

'The Premier is coming this afternoon,' said Dawson. 'I expect he wants approval for the casino. Your delay will piss him off no end.'

'Good,' said Jane. 'He shouldn't try to sideline us.'

Julie Dawson was elected leader of the SLP after successfully opposing several tall residential tower blocks.

'We are meeting at midday to talk about alternatives to a casino,' said Jane. 'Can you come?'

'I'm at a Party meeting, sorry. See you later.'

'I'm famished,' Jane said to me. 'Let's eat.'

'What do you think Julie was doing with that spade?' I asked.

'What spade?'

'It was wrapped up.'

'For gardening, I suppose. What else?'

'Perhaps she is going to uncover or hide something,' Jane said.

'What?'

'No idea. Let's get a gyro.'

We went into a Greek restaurant. Over coffee I wound down from the tense meeting. Relaxing was my latest priority.

They brought us pita breads stuffed with succulent meat shaved off a vertical spit. It was a great taste, a welcome respite. I wanted to detach from politics and sat quietly beside Jane in my cycle of Buddhist reincarnation. The corners of my boulder-like psyche were being worn down by the elements, a chip here and a chip there, as I eroded and returned to nature.

We ate pieces of Turkish baklava, rich and sweet. The world had seemed tough but now it mellowed. We drank more coffee before heading back. Then I remembered I had deserted my sponsoring political party. If I did not return to the party fold, I would be out in the cold. My halcyon days as a NLP backbencher would be over. It was like finding myself without pants.

As we walked, I noticed Jane did not give way to oncoming pedestrians until they yielded, sometimes at the very last minute. Jane's sense of territory was self-centred but I didn't say anything. That was the way she was made. Her brinkmanship was unconscious: a camel doesn't know itself by its hump. Jane got her kicks from pushing back boundaries but she didn't realise she was doing it.

'How long did it take you to make up your mind to leave the NLP?' I asked her.

'A few weeks,' she said. 'Why — did you quit the NLP on the spur of the moment?'

'It was the last straw when Fenwick threatened me.'

'What do you think of the casino proposal?'

'Not much. Those mushroom things would turn the city into a tinsel town like Vegas.'

'What do you think of Vegas?' she asked.

'I don't like it,' I said. 'It is spiritually vacuous.'

I was trying to impress Jane that I was more than an unfeeling science nerd.

'Really?' said Jane. 'You are such a purist. I don't like Vegas because gambling is boring.'

'Then you are okay with people going to casinos?'

'Absolutely not. It can ensnare them. We need to protect vulnerable people from being exploited. A casino should be at a remote location, certainly not in the CBD.'

'I'm with you all the way,' I said with a friendly smile.

As we strolled back across the square, I was thinking that life was alright. I felt fortunate to be in a relationship with such a talented and lovely woman, doing a job that had a personal challenge and making a difference to so many lives. It couldn't get much better than this.

We paused beside a busker playing on an amplified classical guitar. Jane smiled as she listened. She caught my glance.

'What?' she said.

'Is this the life you want?' I asked, litmus testing her commitment to what we did. She contemplated my question with a small frown. We both put a small note in his instrument case and strolled on.

'I suppose I'm happy enough,' she said, 'but I want society to be more civil and I want government to be better than it is now. I feel dishonest and deceitful taking part in meetings which are set pieces, with outcomes decided by loyalties rather than by reasoning.'

'Reasoning by logic is from Ancient Greece and is as exotic in Alexandra as the gyro we had for lunch,' I said. 'Getting any more reasoning may not be possible.'

Jane stopped and faced me.

'I am trying to get more reasoning, today and every day. The politicking has to stop. Isn't that what you want too?'

I felt prickling at the nape of my neck as the hairs stood on end. This woman's determination and selflessness were awesome. Reasoning was important to me too. She was already making an outstanding contribution to our city's government. I admired her goals. Fate had brought us together.

Around her I could dare to be myself.

CHAPTER 13

Back in City Hall, I sat with Jane and Cutter in deep armchairs, talking as we waited for the others to arrive. The Councillors' Lounge was a sumptuous room, with a high embossed ceiling, gilded cornice mouldings and a crystal glass chandelier. In other parts of the room, councillors stood in knots.

Several NLP councillors were looking across, probably talking about us. I was an absconder and they could be wondering why I was keeping company with Jane and Cutter. Bona fide party members didn't hang out with independents.

Jane was using her phone.

I said to Cutter, 'Can we block Runyon's proposal this afternoon?'

'What? Betray our Party?'

'Why not?'

'The NLP is a cult,' Cutter said. 'The leader is assumed to have divine power. There could be divine retribution.'

'I'm not worried.'

'Will you cross?'

'If I have to,' I said.

Cutter did not rise to the bait.

Shelly arrived.

'Penny sends her apologies, she said. 'She wanted to come but had to go to another meeting.'

'Let's get started,' said Jane. 'We are here because they want to knock down the old IB to build a casino and we need to put in a PDA for an alternative.'

'I thought the IB was heritage-protected,' said Cutter.

'That won't stop them,' I said. 'They will de-heritage it.'

'How?'

They will get their architect to say it's a pile of shit.'

54

'It is a pile of shit,' said Cutter. 'It was built from crappy materials thrown together to accommodate penniless immigrants cheaply. It would cost a heap to restore.'

He was right. Cutter knew a little bit about a lot of things. He was with Jane at her primary and secondary schools and joined the Council in the same election. As far as I knew there was never anything between them although he had always fancied her. They were colleagues and friends. He was sitting close to Jane and his sly advances irritated me.

'Can we get the Government to pay for restoring it?' I asked.

'Would it help their re-election?' Cutter asked sceptically.

Restoring the IB would not be a vote winner.

'If we can adapt it to provide something voters want, the Government could support us,' said Jane. 'How about an immigration museum? Other provinces have them.'

'The word 'immigration' has negative connotations,' Cutter said. 'How about a beer hall?'

'An ethnic art gallery,' said Shelly.

'A multicultural centre'' said Jane. 'A MC.'

'What do you mean 'multicultural'?' I asked.

'Tolerance; diversity; assimilation; ghettos; racism; land rights; reconciliation. Take your pick,' said Cutter. He always helped us to focus, in his sardonic way.

'Multicultural' means that many cultures would be valued there,' she said. 'It respects identity and rejects the melting pot concept. Assimilation is shit. Alexandrans are segregating and forming ghettos. It is a powerful word and a MC is a place where many cultures co-exist, communicate and negotiate.'

'Fenwick wants immigrants to forget their pasts,' Cutter said. 'He wants them to adopt Roberta culture immediately.'

'Does Roberta have a culture?' I asked.

'Yes. Fenwick's idea of culture is voting for the NLP.'

'Or for the SLP. Southland has a bipartisan monoculture,' Jane said. 'To preserve their cultures, immigrants have to go underground.'

'They don't want to go underground,' said Shelly. 'People want to be free to show off their diversity. A MC would focus on ethnicity and unite the community against racism.'

'A MC would prevent racial conflict,' I said.

'I like it,' Cutter said. 'The old IB would showcase respect for ethnicity?'

'Why not?' said Jane. 'It is a heritage setting where re-enactments, exhibits and entertainments will be more authentic, a vibrant hub with cultural depth.'

'Well that's decided. A MC it is.'

It was time to go to the next meeting. Jane's MC idea was now a serious alternative.

CHAPTER 14

Councillors entered the chamber for the weekly Council meeting as I stood chatting with the woman who would be found in concrete. Jane was at her desk on the Chairperson's right, with the SLP benches beside her and the NLP's opposite. My place was on the NLP backbench — but if the Party expelled me, I would be able to sit next to Jane.

Penny came in and paused beside us.

'The Premier is coming today, isn't he?'

'Yes — to tell us his casino fantasy,' said Jane.

'Maybe it's not a fantasy,' said Penny. 'He may have done a deal with Runyon's already.'

'What about due process? I asked.

'This Government's 'do' process is to do what it wants,' said Jane.

Bells started ringing and councillors flooded in.

Dominating the wall on one side of the debating chamber was a full length portrait of the Queen of England. On the other, there was the city's coat of arms. At front centre, facing the semicircle of desks, was the Chairperson's throne, draped with the flags of Southland, Roberta and Alexandra. To her right was a dais for visiting speakers and to the left were desks where the CEO and Recorder sat.

I had first seen this room six months previously, when I was sworn in after the by-election. A NLP councillor had been my guide.

'In this quadrant on the Chairperson's left are the 11 NLP members, on front and backbenches,' he said. 'On their left is the Opposition quadrant with the 10 SLP members and the crossbench with Jane Kenwood. In-between are the LM and Deputy in their box. Counting those two and the Chairperson there are 14 NLP against 10 SLP plus Jane. We usually have it all our own way.'

Councillors sat at their desks, talking quietly to each other.

The Chairperson entered and sat sedately on her throne, chatting with CEO, Ainsley Montague, who turned around to talk with her.

'See you afterwards,' I said to Jane.

My desk was like a pew in a church. The maroon upholstery was reflected as a soft ruby glow from the glossy teak partitions. There was a faint smell of furniture polish. There were networked computer screens at each desk. I brought up the sequence of speakers on my monitor. The Premier would be first.

The Chairperson opened the meeting with prayers, brisk but respectful. Councillors intoned 'Amen' and sat down.

The Chairperson used her mic. 'Premier Bentley Leach is coming this afternoon to tell us about a proposal for a casino.'

We waited. The more important the person, the longer they kept us waiting. Councillors sometimes dozed off. On her throne, the Chairperson continued to confer with the CEO.

'Ah, here's the Premier now.'

A tall man in a dark-blue suit swaggered in from the back of the chamber up to the guest speaker's dais. The Right Honourable Bentley Leach was the top politician in Roberta. Two minders flanked him, large men in grey suits and inconspicuous. I hadn't seen him at City Hall before. Many councillors knew him from five years ago when he had been LM.

'There may be a few minutes for questions after the Premier has finished his talk,' said Chairperson.

'How wonderful!' Jane remarked loud enough for SLP councillors near her to hear and smile. Jane had told me of her contempt for Premier Leach, from a clash where he had behaved badly. She openly rejected his autocratic style.

'Hello, Jane.' The Premier's amplified voice was calm.

'Mr Premier,' Jane nodded.

'So they haven't got rid of you yet?'

'We're trying,' said Fenwick from the Government frontbench.

There were a few laughs. Jane did not respond.

The Premier began his presentation.

'LM, Madam Chairperson, Councillors, thank you for inviting me here today. I have come to inform you about a casino proposed for our city. If you would switch your monitors to desktop and click on the casino icon, you can see what it will look like.'

The Premier waited while we watched our screens. It was a video with the slides we had seen that morning and Andrea's voiceover. When the councillors had finished watching he continued.

'As you have seen, the proposal is for breathtaking new buildings all in glass. Below will be gardens, trees and parkland for public use. It will be the most exotic building in the nation and will mark the centre of a modern vibrant city.

'The casino will be top notch, an attraction of global significance. Fortunes are being made in China, India and the USA. Wealthy people will come here to gamble.'

The Premier spoke with hubris, as if it was his own project.

'We are distant from those nations and can offer surroundings where their gamblers won't be pestered. I do not have a crystal ball, but I believe Alexandra can gain a reputation like Las Vegas.

'Taxes will be collected from gambling, alcohol, accommodation and entertainment. All three levels of government will get a share.'

'Thank you, Madam Chairperson. I now have a few minutes for questions.'

'Thank you, Mr Premier,' said the Chairperson. 'It is a phenomenal vision. You have given us much to think about.'

I hoped I would not have to vote against the NLP. My desertion in the committee could be overlooked as a temporary aberration but going against them in Council would be seen as treachery.

CHAPTER 15

'LM, your question?' said the Chairperson.

'Mr Premier,' said Martha Hubbard, 'thank you for informing us about this exciting opportunity. My question is, why does Alexandra need a casino?'

'Thank you for your question, LM,' said the Premier. 'A casino is needed here now more than ever. Gambling has been a part of everyday life for a very long time. People need hope. Faith in religion has declined and people are reverting to chance, luck and fortune. A casino can foster a vision of what wealth can buy, motivating gambling and also honest toil. A casino is a people's version of the securities market. Those who can afford only a few brief plays have a right to have access to games that could make them rich and follow their dreams.'

'Point of order, Madam Chairperson.' Jane was bending over her mic. 'The Premier has not answer…'

'Councillor Kenwood, your point of order is not accepted,' interrupted the Chairperson. 'This is not a debate. Would you sit down.'

'Madam Chairperson,' said the Premier, 'with your permission, I will hear what Councillor Kenwood has to say.'

'Councillor Kenwood?'

'Madam Chairperson, the Premier has not answered the LM's question which concerned what are the advantages of locating a casino here in the CBD *rather than somewhere else.*'

'Point of order,' said Trudy Munster. 'Councillor Kenwood is elaborating the LM's question.'

'Objection sustained. Councillor Kenwood's point of order is rejected. The next question is from Councillor Dawson.'

I felt indignant. The Chairperson had enabled Leach to evade an important question.

'Mr Premier,' said the Opposition Leader, 'what social effects will a casino have on people who live in the CBD?'

'Councillor Dawson, thank you for your question,' said the Premier. 'There will be little social effect on those people because few of them will use the casino. For the 6000 people who will be employed, the social effects will be very beneficial.'

'Hear, hear,' resounded from the Government side.

The Premier sat down.

Trudy Munster was next with a question: about city growth. The Premier answered by trumpeting about how the Government was nurturing development.

'Councillor Kenwood, your question.'

Jane leaned forward a little, with a hand resting on the partition in front of her desk, looking at the Premier. She brought her mouth close to the mic.

'Mr Premier, thank you for telling us about Runyon's casino resort proposal. Was the winning tender Runyon's?'

'Thank you for your question, Councillor Kenwood. Tendering was not necessary. The Government gets proposals all the time. Runyon's proposal was outstanding. We were elected to govern, not to hold wasteful competitions. Our priority is to pay down the debt we inherited caused by the previous SLP Government's mismanagement.'

'Mr Premier, my question is: 'Did you invite tenders for entertainment projects that would conserve this heritage building?' Jane's voice was restrained and reasonable. 'Did you consider an auditorium, or a theatre, or a cultural precinct, or a Disney World, or a history theme park, or my preference, a MC? Did you invite alternatives?'

'We concluded that a casino would be best,' said Leach.

'By what process was that?'

'Cabinet discussed it.'

'Cabinet's proceedings are not available to councillors. How can we assess and approve a proposal it if the Government has not called tenders nor disclosed the alternatives it considered nor revealed its evaluation process?'

'We have passed the tendering stage,' said the Premier. 'Runyon Casinos would win.'

'Madam Chairperson,' said Jane, 'there are other types of entertainment that could bring more benefit to the people of this city than a casino. The Premier wants the Council to rubber stamp this development without calling tenders or debating alternatives. It's a disgrace.'

'Hear, hear,' said the Opposition.

'Councillor Kenwood, be seated.'

'Promises of taxes aren't everything,' she said and sat down.

'Madam Chairperson,' said Leach, 'it would be a rare day when Councillor Kenwood did not try to stop us doing what the people elected us to do. It must be that over at her Blake Ward they don't understand the realities of government. Perhaps they think that money grows on trees. We must have funds to maintain our schools, our buses and our roads. None of the alternatives Councillor Kenwood has mentioned could hold a candle to a casino for raising money.'

'Point of order,' said Jane, standing up. She spoke quietly but clearly. 'The Premier has not answered my question. Has the Provincial Government considered alternatives for this site?'

'Overruled. This is not a debate. Councillor Kenwood be seated.'

'It is a fair question,' Shelly Burton called out. 'What alternatives have been considered?'

'No calling out,' said the Chairperson.

I couldn't watch this David and Goliath contest any longer without slinging a stone. My reflex was to oppose demagogues, self-appointed alarmists and fear-mongers who had displaced objective analysis with populist lies and half-truths. The Government's neglect of the tendering protocol shamed their leaders' offices.

'Point of order,' I said.

Heads swivelled.

'The Premier has not answered the question: 'What alternatives have been discussed?''

'Overruled. This ...'

'Madam Chairperson,' said the Premier, flustered by the unexpected barrage. 'We could, I suppose, delay for a short time for people to realise that the alternatives are inferior. If someone has a proposal and sends it in pronto, say by one month's time, it will be looked at. It will have to contribute a lot of taxes to be taken seriously. Now I have to return to Parliament for a meeting.'

'Jane has won a window of opportunity for a MC,' I thought. *'She has thrown a spanner into the NLP works — and into mine too.'*

Jane flashed me a victory grin.

The Chairperson spoke. 'Thank you, Mr Premier, for coming and informing us of this important proposal.'

Flanked by his minders, the Premier stalked out of the chamber.

'We will adjourn for afternoon tea,' said the Chairperson.

*

I sat with Jane, drinking tea.

'Thank you for siding with me.' she said. 'Tongues will be wagging.'

'There will be hell to pay,' I thought. *'I have crossed the Rubicon. I have rebutted and contradicted the Premier.'*

My audacity had surprised me. I had wanted to impress Jane with my independence.

'I will like myself a heap better on the crossbench,' I said to Jane as we drank our tea. 'I have been wasting my time on the backbench.'

I had drawn close to her and I wanted to know if there was a method to her madness — or was she just ornery, a maverick, magnificent but unknowable?

'Tell me, Jane,' I said, 'am I right in thinking you want voters to have more say in how they are governed? Isn't it enough to make a cross on a ballot paper once every four years?'

'Of course not. We should have a real democracy with government out in the open, with consultation and plebiscites, with argument and reasoning in public.'

'Do you want to have more say yourself?'

'It's not quite that simple,' she said haughtily.

'I would never call your approach simple,' I said. 'After all, you tied the Premier up in knots.'

She laughed.

'The Premier is a bit loopy to start with,' she said, 'like all NLP members. All they care about is getting re-elected.'

'I too care about getting re-elected but I won't know where to start as an independent.'

'Begin with voters; you will have to be their guardian angel.'

'How did you get your people to trust you?'

'I spent time with them,' she said. 'I found out about them.'

'I'm not that interested in mine.'

'Well, you should be. It will grow on you. You get on well with people.'

'I'm not an extrovert like you.'

'They like you and will vote for you.'

'Thank you for your encouragement.'

We finished our tea and returned to the Council chamber.

CHAPTER 16

Councillors talked quietly at their desks as they waited. Coloured light filtered in from a side window with Queen Alexandra depicted in stained glass. Tiered brass chandeliers diffused light from candle bulbs through white frosted lamp glasses.

The Chairperson resumed her throne and the chamber hushed expectantly.

'LM, you have an announcement?'

'Yes, Madam Chairperson,' LM Martha Hubbard spoke from her box on my left, between NLP members and the Opposition. 'Councillors, I want to inform you of the new city plan we are releasing today. It will transform Alexandra into a global city. The casino resort is one of many developments that will provide prosperity for all.'

Before her election to the Council a decade ago, the LM had been a lawyer. Now in middle age, she was personable, well organised, expansive and charismatic. She held her lapels like a demagogue and ranted about the failures of the SLP previously and how much the Council had provided under her leadership. She was an outspoken advocate of market economy and laissez faire government.

She was renowned for saying: *'People who want a higher standard of living should get better-paying jobs.'*

She was reported to have said: *'Helping the disadvantaged is a matter of ensuring they are able to participate in economic markets, for jobs, money, transport, goods, services and whatever. Those who choose not to participate have only themselves to blame.'*

Another of her sayings was: *'What the inhabitants of Alexandra think of me is less important than what I think of them.'*

These attitudes had polarised her rating in the community. While voters on the right applauded her, she was unpopular with the left.

As the LM's rant continued, Opposition catcalls and muttering became louder until she was yelling to be heard. Eventually she finished and sat down.

The Chairperson said, 'Now we come to the LM's Question Time. We have 45 minutes. Questions must be asked in under two minutes and answered in less than five. Trudy Munster, you are first cab off the rank.'

'Thank you, Madam Chairperson,' Munster said. 'LM, can Council oppose the casino proposed by the Premier?'

'Councillor Munster, thank you for the question. This is like asking a child whether it can disown its parents. If you think we are able to decide what we can do, then think again. The Provincial Government holds our purse strings. We can't go our own way. The Premier clearly told us what he wanted this morning: a casino. I know he will not be thwarted. The Provincial Government could cut off our money.'

Jane called, 'Rubbish. They wouldn't dare. We should ...'

The Chairperson raised her voice, drowning Jane's words.

'Councillor Kenwood, do not call out.'

The LM continued, 'Madam Chairperson, the Opposition foolishly blocked Runyon's PDA in committee this morning but we are going to approve it this afternoon. Not only are we not going to stand against the Premier, we are going to give him our full support.'

'Hear, hear,' said the NLP members and they drummed on their desks with their fists, drowning out the Opposition's booing.

'Point of information.'

'Yes, Councillor Dawson.'

'Madame Chair, the LM is subordinating our city plan to the Provincial Government's proposed casino.'

'She is bending over backwards to kiss the Premier's ass,' said Jane.

Laughter.

'Point of order,' said Julie Dawson. 'Councillor Kenwood is misleading the chamber. The LM could not possibly bend over backwards and kiss someone's ass at the same time.'

Guffaws. I suspected that Jane had planned this repartee with Julie beforehand.

'Sustained,' said the Chairperson. 'Councillor Kenwood, would you back flip, I mean retract that image.'

'I retract. But it is pretty low behaviour.'

Chuckles.

'It is what we have come to expect from this Government,' said Jane. 'We have the results of a survey which shows that a majority of Alexandrans do not want a larger city, nor high-density living, nor congestion, nor escalating demands on roads, parks and parking spaces. This Government is allowing developers to exploit infrastructure belonging to communities, lowering qualities of their lifestyles. Do we really need this casino?'

'Madam Chairperson,' said the LM. 'Councillor Kenwood's survey probably asked people if they wanted more people here and of course they said no. It is the NIMBY syndrome, Not In My Back Yard, which omits to have a prosperous community. If they had asked people if they wanted more opportunities they would have said yes and that is exactly what this Government will provide.'

The NLP members drummed again.

'We can't rely on people to tell us what they want,' said the LM. 'Henry Ford said that if he had asked people what they wanted they would have said faster horses. We need to think outside the box. We really do need this casino resort. Without it our city could sink into oblivion.'

She sat down to applause.

The Chairperson said, 'A question from the Leader of the Opposition.'

Julie Dawson said, 'LM, did you see an article in the Standard a few days ago that referred to a crime syndicate run by Runyon Casinos? Does the article show ...'

'You have asked your question, Councillor Dawson,' interrupted the Chairperson. 'Would you be seated, LM.'

The Chairperson's bias against the Opposition was blatant.

'Yes, I did see the article,' said Hubbard. 'The incident was in Johannesburg. Unlike Councillor Dawson, I am not sitting in the cheap seats. I know what happened there. The police have investigated and assured me it could not happen here. Thank you for your question.'

Hubbard sat down.

I thought, *'The casino proposal could go through without important questions being answered. Will Jane be able to stop it?'*

CHAPTER 17

'Councillor Fenwick, your question?' said the Chairperson.

'Madam Chairperson, my question is...

'Point of order,' Dawson interrupted. 'Madam Chairperson, the LM has not answered my question which was 'Does the article show ...?'

'... The LM has answered it,' interjected the Chairperson.

'But ...'

'Councillor Dawson, be seated. You may not like the answer, but it is an answer.'

'She wasn't able to complete her question,' said Shelly.

'Councillor, do not call out.'

I was feeling exasperated. There was too much bickering. The Chairperson bulldozed onwards.

'Your question, Councillor Fenwick?'

'Point of order, Madam Chairperson.'

'Yes, Councillor Kenwood?'

'Madam Chairperson, I draw to your attention that the rules of procedure require questions to go from side-to-side. The next question should be coming from this side of the chamber, not from Councillor Fenwick, because the previous question was Councillor Munster's.'

'Not sustained. Councillor Dawson forfeited her side with her newspaper article question. Now it is the other side's turn. Councillor Fenwick, would you ask your question?'

Jane was confronting the brute force of the Government's majority. I wanted the pantomime of the LM's Question Time to be over.

'LM,' said Fenwick, 'my question is this: Why does the population of the CBD have to increase?'

It was a cue for Hubbard to put up a straw man.

'The Opposition do not have a vision of Alexandra growing into a global city,' she said. 'They oppose development. Their idea of planning is to grandstand what we are doing and pick holes in it. The CBD has to increase in population, because it is like the trunk of a young tree growing to maturity. The larger our city grows, the longer it will live. We will build an architectural wonderland, with hanging gardens, waterfalls and walkways connecting high overhead. It will be an exciting place to live, work and visit. The casino with its mushroom towers will attract people from far and wide.'

She sat down.

'Thank you, LM. The next question is from Councillor Redford.'

'Madam Chairperson,' said Penny, 'if you had allowed Councillor Dawson to complete her question she would have asked: 'Could Runyon Casinos operate a crime syndicate here as they have in Johannesburg?''

'Councillor Redford,' said the Chairperson, 'the LM has already answered that question in saying that the police have assured her not.'

'What assurances .. ?'

'Details of police methods cannot be made available here. The question has been answered.' Jane was scheduled to ask a question for the Opposition after the next NLP speaker. I was counting on her to put a dint in the shiny casino proposal.

'Councillor Barber, your question.'

They had given a question to Cutter to ask, possibly to secure his loyalty after they saw him fraternising with me and Jane.

'Madam Chairperson,' said Cutter, 'my question is to the LM. What is your vision for the development of tourism in the CBD?'

The question cued the LM to spruik her Government's tourism plans. I slouched back in my seat, not wanting to hear more of her self-promotion.

'Point of order,' said Jane.

'Councillor Kenwood.'

'Madam Chairperson, while the LM has been speaking, Councillor Munster has been in discussion with Councillor Fenwick. I draw your attention to this behaviour because you said at the last meeting it was a disorder and not allowed.'

'Councillor Kenwood, I am perfectly aware of what is going on in this chamber and able to manage it without your intervention. Thank you, LM.'

'You should apply the rules —' said Jane.

'Councillor Kenwood, as Chairperson I have discretion as to what constitutes disorder in this place. Those communications were not acts of disorder whereas yours was. This is a formal warning. If you persist, you will face the consequences — you may be excluded from the chamber for up to eight days. LM, please continue.'

The Chairperson had warned Jane in earlier meetings. She was a notorious miscreant, having been sent out several times.

'I have finished, Madam Chairperson,' said the LM.

'Councillor Kenwood, your question.'

'LM, will the Council compare the proposed casino with alternative uses for the site?'

It was an incisive question and difficult for the LM to dismiss.

'Councillor Kenwood,' said the LM, 'the site proposed is an old building on the heritage list, formerly used for immigration. Because it is unsafe it has been disused for many years. It would be very expensive to restore it for public use. I realise that some people get concerned about knocking down old buildings but in this case they will be outnumbered by those who approve.'

The LM sat down.

'Point of order,' said Jane. 'LM, would you answer my question. Will the Council compare alternatives?'

Jane's opposition was respected by party members on both sides. She spoke for their consciences.

'Yes... the normal process will apply,' said the LM. 'As the Premier indicated earlier, proposals must be received very soon.'

'Thank you,' said Jane with a smile. She had got what she wanted: an opening for a MC to be considered.

The Chairperson said, 'Thank you, LM. There will now be a break for tea.'

In the tearoom, I took my mug and sat with Jane.

'I liked your questioning,' I said. 'We have our foot in the door.'

'Thank you, Phillip. Do you think they'll buy a MC?'

71

'Yes, it is possible,' I said. 'We have muscled our way into contention. We still have some way to go but a majority is possible.'

'They will try to push the casino through today,' said Jane. 'If we can get a week's delay, enthusiasm for a casino will wane and they will be more receptive to a MC.'

'I agree. If we can get a better-considered response it will work in our favour.'

After tea, before the Council could debate our committee's recommendation of a month's postponement, Jane spoke up.

'Madam Chairperson, I move that we delay for a week our debate until we know if there are other development alternatives such as a MC, that would make a month's postponement necessary.'

No-one contested her motion and it was carried unanimously. Jane, a lone independent, was fighting above her weight and winning.

*

When the meeting ended, I went over to Jane's desk.

'Will you be long?'

'I've had enough for today,' she said. 'What are you doing now?'

'I have to go to the government bookstore,' I said. 'I want to get a copy of the provincial budget.'

'Will it be open?'

'Yes. They close late on Tuesdays.'

'Would you get something for me?'

'Of course. What?'

'A copy of the Heritage Conservation Regulations. The IB is heritage listed. That must count for something. It's $28… here…'

She fumbled in her bag.

'I'll get it from you later,' I said.

I felt privileged to be able to do Jane a favour.

CHAPTER 18

The next day, Cutter and I went with Jane to meet her friend, Sunita.

'She's a bit eccentric,' said Jane, 'and she doesn't like men.'

Jane relished diversity so I expected Sunita would be out on the tail of the bell curve. We found her in a cloud of incense smoke, playing Mah Jong in a Greek restaurant. She had medium-length blonde hair tied in bunches, wearing a tight flowery chemise, a sarong, sandals and every inch a hippy.

'Hey, Sunita!' Jane said. 'What's hanging?'

'Jane! Great to see you.' She got up and Jane introduced us. 'I'll be finished my game in a mo, dig?'

We ordered coffee and a hummus dip. Sunita joined us.

'We need your help, Sunita,' said Jane. 'We want to save the IB. That's your gig isn't it?'

'Fuck, yes.'

'What's your expertise, Sunita?'

'History — Colonial Roberta, especially Alexandra City. I'm a lecturer. We have been trying to save the IB for years. What are y'all — history freaks or sumpin?'

'We want the IB for a MC,' said Jane.

Sunita thought for a moment.

'What kind of multiculture?'

'Megasize entertainment,' I said.

'In the IB?' she asked like it wasn't a good idea.

'In a couple of new theatres at the back,' I said.

'Far out. Who is going to be in on it?'

'Hopefully the Council.'

'Fat chance! Missus Hubbard into multiculture? The Bitch? Get real, man. The Bitch does not want multi nor does she want culture. She won't be in it unless it gets votes, gets donations or gets taxes. We have been trying to set up an immigration museum in the IB since forever. We got 7000 signatures on a petition, but the fucking Council didn't do a thing.'

'Who did you give it to?' I asked.

So far she had ignored me.

'Leach's lot. You know, the Man,' she said as if I might not be aware that the Provincial Government's rule was authoritarian.

'The Man wouldn't want to restore the IB,' Jane said. 'Could you submit it again, this time to Council?'

'What's the difference?'

'The three of us are on the Development Committee, so it will get a hearing,' Jane said.

Jane explained the casino proposal to her and that we were opposing it.

'A MC is like an immigration museum, right? Can we use the signatures we have already collected?'

Jane laughed, 'Close enough. I'll table it.'

'The Bitch won't be able to ignore a petition from you, huh?' said Sunita.

'They won't be able to ignore our PDA for a MC. Can you come to a meeting with us tomorrow?' Jane asked. 'How about 11 am at Marco's?'

'Okay. See you there.'

Sunita was as distinct as Jane was — as reactionary as she was idealistic.

*

We went off to our ward offices. In the evening I had dinner with Jane at her place. Although Jane and I were partners, our intercourse had so far been verbal, not for want of my trying. Then something happened.

'Are you going to be tied up after lunch tomorrow?' Jane asked the following day.

'No, why?'

'Would you do me a big favour. Tomorrow would you pick me up from outside the Indian Club in Worthington Heights? I'm going to a Kipling's Day lunch. It will be difficult to get a taxi and I can't be late getting back to work.'

'I'll be pleased to. At what time would you like me to be there?'

'At 1.30 pm outside the main entrance,' she said.

*

I was there precisely on time but she was not there. The Indian Club faced on to a busy one-way street with no stopping either side. I circled around the block twice and when Jane wasn't there I was annoyed. I pulled up outside in a bus lane with my motor running. When a bus came and blew its horn I drove up onto the footpath. Pedestrians gave me dirty looks as they stepped around my car. If a policeman happened by I would get a ticket for sure. I waited anxiously.

I called her mobile but it was switched off. When at last she came out, she got in with a smile, as if parking on the footpath was normal.

'What happened to you?' I asked with my nerves shredded.

'Are you mad at me?' Her voice climbed in surprise.

'A little,' I said tersely.

'Sorry. I ran into Sue Dent and we talked for a few minutes. Was that wicked of me?'

'No.' I shook my head grimly. *'Not wicked,'* I thought, *'but bad.'*

I'm really sorry,' she said.

'It's fine,' I said. 'Jane, I'm not going to play Nureyev to your Fonteyn.'

'I don't want you to,' she said huffily.

As I drove to City Hall I said to her, 'Jane, I want to explain something. Giving you a lift today was what the Japanese call an 'amae'. It was to create in you an obligation to make our relationship kinder. My indulgence is supposed to strengthen our bonding. But it could have come between us.'

'No, it did work!' she said, kissing me with fervour. 'Thank you, Phillip! I appreciate you fetching me very much. I do want to be kinder to you. Can you climb down from your high horse? I can't reach you up there.'

Her affection and respect brought a quantum leap in intimacy although I still feared the consummation of our love, simply because it was so long-awaited. I had never waited so long before. My intuition was it wouldn't be long. Could it possibly be as good as I was anticipating? I felt potent but feared ultimate rejection as it neared. Drowning in commitment, I clung to the independence that remained to me.

CHAPTER 19

Next morning, Cutter and I were at Marco's waiting for Jane and Sunita to arrive.

'Hey, Cutter, I noticed you were in a swoon about the casino yesterday,' I said. 'I thought you would have shown more interest in the public good.'

We were often blunt with each other. It prevented misunderstandings.

'Fuck you. Spock,' he said mildly. 'It must be lonely for you sitting on the fence.'

'At least I'm doing what I want.'

'If you want to get Jane, you'll have to get down from there.'

She had quit the NLP more than a year ago. She never said it directly but I knew she wanted me to leave too.

'Maybe. It seems to me like you have sour grapes, Cutter.'

I had had relatively more success with Jane.

'I have something real,' he said disdainfully.

Our conversation lapsed into a comfortable silence, as we watched people near us drinking coffee.

*

Jane and Sunita joined us. We talked about where to get the money to prepare a PDA.

'Could we put on a concert?' asked Jane. 'A huge multicultural one.'

'I know of some artistes who would donate their performances,' said Sunita.

We discussed it as we ate and fixed to hold it on a Saturday night, several weeks ahead. Multiculture was a hot issue because there was racial tension in Arborville, a rundown city suburb with few social amenities where people from more than 70 countries lived. There was youth unemployment, poverty, gangs and violence. Tribal rivalries had spilled over. There was little respect for the police. Fighting had erupted in the streets and escalated until troops brought it under control.

The venue we wanted was the basketball stadium. It had seats for 8000. Performers would fill the playing area, with the orchestra in front and the choir on raised platforms behind. We would ask Andrew Kervelas, who had directed the Commonwealth Games opening and closing ceremonies, to be music director. He would conduct a 100-piece orchestra, a 2000-voice massed choir, an opera company, ballet and dance troupes and half a dozen rock bands. The performances would be televised and broadcast enter nationally. Ticket sales would create a fund for the MC project.

'Do you want your concert bent or straight?' Sunita asked Jane.

'What's the difference?' asked Jane.

'Bare asses and sex stuff,' said Sunita. 'I can get all kinds of transvestite troupes, queer acts, skin shows and risqué comedians. Or we can have a family show with musicians, recitals, drama and some modest burlesque.'

'I think we need to have an authentic multicultural flavour,' said Jane leaving it to Sunita. 'Bent culture is derivative. Ethnic acts would be better.'

'I will need assistance with direction, production and effects; they will be amateurs,' said Sunita.

'How many people do you need?' asked Jane.

'To begin with, a person to liaise with the groups and an event coordinator.'

'How about an enthusiastic local girl with common sense?' said Jane. 'Barbie works for me in my ward office. She's only 18 but she knows how to make things happen.'

'She sounds perfect.'

'I'll get her to phone you.'

Jane discussed with me and Sunita how to assemble the concert programme.

'The performers will have to make fast entrances and exits,' Sunita said.

'Could we have three stages, one setting up, one performing and the other taking down?' I said.

'Awesome. It will be a huge construction task.'

'We can get plenty of help,' I said. 'The difficulty is to get people to think big enough. They cannot imagine a concert this big.'

'If we show it to them a bit at a time, they'll be curious and get interested,' Jane said.

'How will you do that?'

'The same way that I have led walkers up a mountain,' Jane said. 'After the fitness freaks had set off self-guided, I persuaded those who did not want to climb to come with me for a stroll around the corner to where there was a great view for taking photos. When we got there I took them to even better views higher up, stage after stage of non-threatening climbs. I never told them they were going to the top. When we reached the summit they were surprised and delighted.'

'You decomposed the task and repackaged it.'

'Exactly. Our mountain is high. We aren't fitness freaks and we won't get up in one session. Could we get together at the Arts Centre with the choir, dance, theatre and music people?' said Jane. 'Sunita, how about calling a meeting on Saturday?'

'What would be the purpose?'

'To plan.'

'Isn't Saturday rather close?' I said.

'We don't have forever. Runyon's have already submitted their PDA,' Jane said. 'We need the concert money to pay professionals who will work on ours.'

'If we tell them to come at 6 pm,' I said, 'they can go off afterwards for their leg-overs or whatever.'

'You are such a romantic,' said Sunita.

*

On Sunday afternoon Jane, Sunita, Barbie and I went to the City Arts Centre, where a melange of 60 exotic characters was gathered, like the bar scene in Star Wars.

'Good afternoon, everyone,' said Jane. 'My name is Jane Kenwood. I'm councillor for Blake Ward. This is my ward assistant,

79

Barbie. Phillip here is on the City Council too. We are members of a group who want a MC. Most of you know Sunita — she is our concert director. She has a wealth of experience in directing and producing this type of event.'

Sunita, in skinny black jeans, faced the seated group.

'We asked you here because you are Alexandra's leaders in putting on cultural entertainments. We are seeking your help to put on a huge concert in Arborville basketball arena, to raise money for a MC. It will be multicultural because almost everyone in Roberta has an ancestor or relative originally from a different culture. I see some of you have come in your national costumes as we asked.'

'Is this an audition?' asked an African with face paint dressed up as a warrior.

'What do you do?'

He performed some fancy break-dancing. Sunita had probably set this up.

'That was great,' she said. 'We need more dancers for a group act. Could you find some other people in your community to dance with you?'

'Maybe.

'How about you others?' Sunita scanned the audience. 'Which of you could prepare an item?'

Arms went up.

'Now, let's organise into groups. Your task is to get together and work out an item you can put on. It can be music, song, dance, drama, comedy or just about anything that an audience will like. Be ready to tell us when we come around.'

For an hour there was a hubbub of discussion. Jane, Sunita, Barbie and I circulated, giving encouragement.

Jane scheduled the items into a concert programme. Then she called everyone together.

'If you haven't nominated yet, there's still time. The concert is in three weeks and you need to finish planning, hold rehearsals and get you friends to buy tickets. Keep in touch with Sunita who is putting it all together with Barbie helping. Let's meet again next Sunday to have a run-through of your acts. Leave your contacts with Sunita. Thank you everyone for coming.'

After they had gone, Jane and I were alone for the first time since the meeting started.

'Thank God that's over,' I said. 'Facilitating groups is not my idea of fun.'

'That's because you are a control freak,' said Jane. 'I like working with groups. Today we accomplished a lot. People are preparing for the concert!'

*

We all got together again at the weekend in the basketball arena and the groups started rehearsing. Sunita had asked the City Opera Company, Repertory Theatre Company and Ballet if they would put on items. They sent groups to perform tasters and Sunita accepted them gladly. Our concert programme filled up. There would be almost 3000 individuals performing. We printed tickets and started selling.

CHAPTER 20

With preparation for the concert underway, we met to design a MC. We wanted to show Council a plan for a self-sustaining enterprise. Cutter, Sunita, Jane and I met at a sushi bar to discuss how it could operate.

'Foreign touring companies could put on ethnic musicals and stage shows,' I suggested.

'Immigrants would come for family reunions, commemorations and celebrations — they would spend up big,' Cutter said.

'Ethnic foods, à la carte dining, a German beer hall, a theatre restaurant, bars, singing and dancing,' added Jane.

'Bastille Day, American Independence, Halloween, Hogmanay.'

'Places and events for expatriate singles to meet,' said Cutter.

'Foreign film festivals,' I continued. 'An Eisteddfod. Talent shows.'

'Local theatre groups presenting ethnic works.'

'Local ethnic groups showcasing their culture.'

Jane said, 'There's plenty.'

'We have to plan a season of high-quality productions,' I added.

'I know someone who can help us,' said Jane. 'Martha Van Tromp used to be CEO of the Performing Arts Complex — a sort of impresario. She has brought performers from overseas and made a profit. I'll try and arrange a meeting with her.'

'That would be terrific.'

'We also need to find local leaders and get them to work up ethnic acts,' Jane said. 'Our concert has set the ball rolling. Remember the mountain. We can climb it bit by bit. We need writers, choreographers, actors, directors, producers, stage managers, light and sound technicians.'

'For how many theatres?' asked Sunita.

'Phillip, can you work out the best number?'

'No. It's not deterministic.'

'What does that mean?'
'There is no simple answer.'
'How about we have one auditorium and one theatre,' said Jane. 'Any advances on that?'
No-one said anything.
'Well, that was easy.'
'Awesome,' I said.

*

Jane leapt high buildings but her committee of IBAG people was sluggish. She held weekly MC meetings with all and sundry. Sometimes there were 40 people present. Jane planned from the bottom-up whereas my planning was top-down.

'We are not making enough progress during meetings,' I said to Jane. 'People are blathering on and on as if they are social occasions. People have to suppress their anecdotes and emotional arguments. They need to make decisions based on reason.'

'Not everyone objectifies like you and me,' Jane said. 'Their selfish interest stands higher than reason and logic. They don't want to take risks. By attending our meetings, some of them are going against their bosses' interests and they could find themselves out the door.'

'We need to get more done,' I said. 'Meetings always get bogged down. They only agree on lowest common denominators. It is not enough. Those meetings are toxic. Bottom-up planning is not getting us anywhere. They use my plans as a whipping post to disdain central planning. I will not go to any more meetings. I will study feasibility and prepare a PDA. I'll show you my plans and you can use them or not, as you see fit.'

'If that is your dummy spit, okay. Your problem is that you live in the future; you expect people to want change.'

'Isn't that what people come to meetings for?'

'No. They want most things to stay the same. They don't like you dominating them and insisting on having your own way. You are bombastic and arrogant. You cannot decide everything yourself.'

'They should consider my plans,' I said.

'Why?'

'If we leave it to them, they will probably come up with something we don't like.'

Jane's voice hardened.

'What if they don't like your plans?'

'I would alter them. But they would not change theirs. We would be stuck with them. It's best not to involve them in the first place.'

'You have a top-down bias,' she said with distaste.

'Correct. We are at the top and it is us who will do the implementing. We should have right of veto.'

'Rubbish. Everyone will help implement our plan. Unless the people at the bottom want it, your plan will be a waste of time. Our planning has to be bottom-up.'

'Can we trust them?' I put on a sceptical face.

'Them? You mean us. It will be *our* plan, everybody's. It has to go to the group to be discussed, instead of you trying to ram it down our throats.'

'When a group tried to design a horse, they got a camel,' I said.

Jane displayed patience. 'What is your plan, Phillip?'

'It's not ready yet. I don't have the details worked out.'

'We don't need details yet. We need to mobilise people. They can work out the details for themselves.' Her phone rang. 'Excuse me.'

While she took the call, I thought about what to do. My way wasn't working. I had to change.

'Okay,' I said to Jane. 'We'll do it your way.'

*

Her people were quite different from the planners I had come across. When I was with the police, planning was always top-down. In the following weeks, I stopped going to the meetings. Jane had my plans and they helped her to concentrate. We worked together hand in glove.

Later I showed Jane my sketches for a MC atrium and grand central stairways that led up to the two theatres.

'That's fantastic, Phillip,' she said. 'How did you think of that?'

'I saw it in a theatre in Vienna, on a smaller scale.'

'It's sumptuous.'

'I'm glad you like it.'

I loved Jane's enthusiasm. It was a moment worth all the drudgery and negativity. I luxuriated in her approval and set my sights on seeing crowds thronging in on opening night.

CHAPTER 21

Jane and I usually spent our weekends together. One Saturday evening we were preparing our evening meal in the kitchen at Jane's place. It was baked fish with potato chips, broad beans and capsicums. While Jane shelled the beans, seeded and sliced the capsicums for the microwave, I poured glasses of wine and kept an eye on the oven.

Jane was at the kitchen bench when I reached around her with both arms and cupped her breasts. I tried to sing to a hesitant tango rhythm like Magaldi in the musical *Evita*, in a strong sentimental baritone.

On this night
On this night
On this night of a thousand stars
Let me take you to heaven's door
On that magical day when you first came my way — mi amor.

I spun her around and kissed her passionately.
'That's not allowed,' she said.
'Why not?'
'The fish will burn.'
'Since when do you play it safe?'
'That's not fair! Always.'
'Never, you brinkster! I know you better than you know yourself.'
'That's what you think. Typical of a control freak.'
She tried to turn away but I held her back.
'I know what's best for you.'
We kissed. Then she broke away.
'The fish is burning,' she said.
'We have bigger fish to fry,' I said, as I took the fish out of the oven.
'Like what?'

'Like… nothing,' I said. 'Just testing.'

'Perhaps we should talk more.'

'You never agree with anything I say.'

'We would eventually,' she said, 'but you always get physical.'

'You are too cute by half.'

I slid my hands down to hold her butt.

'It's too early to go to bed,' she said.

'We should eat first.'

'No. I mean, we aren't ready to have sex yet.'

'I am.'

'But you hardly know me.'

She wasn't wrong. Most of our private time had gone into the MC project. While I knew Jane-the-councillor quite well, it was frightening that I hardly knew the rest of her at all. I didn't know whether she was interested in nature, history, literature, travel, sport, family, friends or children. I wanted to know. I didn't want any surprises, as had happened with Connie.

I had met Connie at university while I was doing a PhD in Forensic Science and she was doing one in International Relations. We both liked reading, movies, theatre and music. Our friendship grew and I moved in with her. We studied together. After two years we were awarded our doctorates. I started work with the police and Connie joined the Immigration Department. We got married and bought a house together.

I wanted to have kids.

'I do not want a child,' Connie said.

I was surprised. 'Maybe you will one day?'

'Never.'

'But that's why we got married!'

'Not me. I never agreed to have children.'

It had been implied and I felt cheated. I thought she might change her mind. Connie had a separate social life with her Immigration Department colleagues and consulate people. They partied loud and long, with much dancing, alcohol, marijuana and cocaine. Connie came home to rest up for her next social.

I was not gregarious and disliked parties. I was investigating corruption in the City Council. I worked long hours, received anonymous threats and was often stressed. I seldom saw Connie. I suspected her of infidelity but had no evidence.

Habitually suspicious, I saw enough to accuse her of cheating. She denied it and stayed out for days without explanation. We began sleeping apart.

I was interested in local government and joined the NLP. Connie was not interested in our local community. She announced she was going to a Foreign Office position overseas. Our jobs would be in different places and compromise was impossible.

'You can come with me if you like,' she said.

I wanted to separate. She took her things and was gone. I sold the house, added up our worth, divided it by two and sent her share to her. We had been together for five years. I was sad and regretted marrying her without really knowing her.

I would not make the same mistake with Jane. Before we became too involved, I needed to find out everything about her. I needed to be sure of her with confidence and know she had told me everything and honestly.

Jane seemed to be sizing me up too. Understanding another person was like opening up someone's cupboard crammed with their things and finding out which items were precious and needed careful handling.

'Sunita said she saw you with a girl the other night,' Jane said, in the measured tone I knew was serious dissatisfaction. 'Who was she?'

'A mate from uni who was in town. I told you about that.'

'It sounded like a guy,' she said. 'I won't accept you seeing girls.'

Jane had assumed it was a guy, but I wasn't about to quibble.

'She was here for a few days from London.'

'Why did you meet her behind my back?'

'I didn't want you to worry.'

'You made me look foolish.'

'You should trust me.'

'You should have told me.'

'I'm sorry. In future I will.'

After that my Bonobo-inspired fantasy of a sexually open relationship faded but my residual interest in other females, although conjectural, continued unabated.

CHAPTER 22

At the next Council Meeting, Fenwick accosted me as I went for tea.

'Err, Phillip,' he said, 'how do you like being on the Council?'

I knew he was not interested in my job satisfaction.

'I can't keep everyone happy.'

'Quite so. You have to keep your eye on getting re-elected though.'

I was down to speak for the Opposition in the debate and he was trying to whip me back into line, threatening my job.

'I am working hard in my ward.'

'That's not important.'

He was Chairman of the NLP candidate selection committee. His cynicism and hubris affronted me.

'That's your opinion,' I said.

'You have to get endorsed.'

'If I stay with the NLP.'

'Why wouldn't you?'

'I want to represent my constituents, not the NLP.'

'They voted for the NLP, not for you.'

'That's not true. They voted for me to represent them. The NLP doesn't let me do that.'

'You came in after we had discussed and agreed our policies. You have to follow them even if your personal ideas are different.'

'Why can't my ward have policies its people want?'

He tossed his head impatiently. 'That wouldn't work at all. There has to be parity between wards. Suppose bicycle lanes changed width at every ward boundary. It would be dangerous. The public need a uniform approach.'

'I don't agree. Where bicycle lanes can be wider, they should be. The lowest common denominator is the worst of all possible worlds. To get parity, provision is spread so thinly it is not worth having.

'Parity is hardly ever desirable. Liberals are supposed to bring freedom to every individual. Under the uniformity you espouse, the city's accommodation is mostly samey drab boxes. People need to be able to share – open spaces, places, things, chores, children and chatter, with their neighbours and with their community.'

Fenwick stared at me in dismay.

'Phillip, I have heard enough. There has to be a compromise between individuality and community. The Government provides parks, buses and much else. People can express their individuality in their religion, in their careers and in choosing products to consume. Consumption has to be organised. Demand is boosted by having many small separate living units. Group living would consume less and it is therefore less desirable. The wheel of community has already been invented and it works okay.'

'If you cross the floor, you could force an election and some of your colleagues would lose their seats. Believe what you like, say what you like, but think of your colleagues and vote NLP. If you don't you are finished.'

'Fuck you, arsehole,' I said to restore my sense of self. His contempt for people, his party's protection racket and his bully-boy behaviour were intolerable.

*

When we went back in, I sat with Jane on the crossbench, feeling less alone than with the NLP robots.

Next would be a debate of our Opposition motion to delay for a month a decision on Runyon's PDA. The Affirmative speakers were me first, then Jane. The Negative team was Munster and O'Connell, their two most able speakers.

'Nervous?' Jane asked me.

'A little.'

'I would be too if I was up first.'

'It's easier than seconding,' I said. Jane would have to rebut the points put by Munster, then develop and summarise the Affirmative case.

'They will play dirty,' said Jane. 'The Government has never lost since it was elected. They will try to stop us.'

90

'I'll try not to let you down.'

She turned to me and squeezed my arm. 'I know you will,' she said with a smile.

Jane had warmed up to me slowly. I was a divorcee and she may have thought at first I could be flawed or damaged. We worked together and she could lose face and be stuck with a child that would make it difficult to get another mate. She would not want to make a commitment until she was sure of me. Her reluctance to get into the sack with me was par for the course.

The Chairperson rapped her gavel.

'Councillor Munster, will you report your committee's proceedings.'

Munster stood up. 'At the meeting of the DA Committee a week ago, a motion that Runyon Casinos' PDA be accepted was narrowly defeated. An Opposition majority recommended that alternative PDA proposals be sought by 10th June, with a survey of residents' gambling and other preferences. Ratification was delayed for a week until today.'

'Thank you, Councillor Munster,' the Chairperson said. 'Is there a proposer for a motion to accept the committee's recommendation? Thank you, Councillor Dawson. Seconder? Councillor Burton. We will now debate the motion. Proposer for the affirmative is Councillor Keane.'

I was on.

CHAPTER 23

I stood up and adjusted my mic. Every face in the place was turned towards me. The NLP members' faces showed their dislike. My desertion threatened their incumbency. The voting line up was 11 NLP, 10 SLP, plus Jane and me. Cutter had not appeared yet. The NLP would be counting on him to make it 12-all and then our motion would not succeed.

This debate probably wouldn't change anyone's mind but you never could tell. My job was to come out fighting, put our Affirmative case, anticipate the Negative case and damage it.

It was the first time I had spoken in a full Council debate. I was wearing my lucky navy mohair suit to bolster my confidence. I had a card with a list of points to mention. It was good to have Jane beside me on the crossbench.

'Go for it,' said Jane, looking up at me.

'LM, Madam Chairperson, Councillors,' I said. 'The committee's recommendation is to delay, invite and survey. These steps are necessary for proper consideration of the casino proposal.

'Your support for this recommendation is important to the people of Alexandra. Our province's Government is about to sell a site owned by the people for a controversial activity: gambling. The City Council has all responsibility for the outcome but so far alternatives have not been considered. This motion is to allow due consideration to occur.

'High rollers do not need the casino to be in the CBD. A resort filled with foreign gamblers and their families would be out of place in our city's commercial and business centre.'

I paused and then spoke harshly.

'Gambling is addictive and causes poverty, illness and violence. Many of our residents regard a casino as immoral and offensive. It is supposed that it would be a bonanza for our city but, in fact, the cost of rectifying the social and psychological damage may exceed the taxes collected.'

I softened to a persuasive tone.

'If the Government is allowed to fast-track this project, it will neglect to consider an alternative that we think would be better. A MC is a better alternative. It would be accessed by more locals and by more visitors than a casino. It would deliver high-quality cultural and educational experiences. It would take advantage of the heritage value of the site instead of destroying it. It would bring racial harmony that we badly need.'

'Point of order.'

It was Grant Fenwick.

'Yes, Councillor.'

'Councillor Keane's talk about a MC is digression.'

'Upheld. Councillor, confine your remarks to the matters considered in the committee report.'

'Point of order.'

'Yes, Councillor Kenwood.'

'Point of order, Madam Chairperson,' said Jane. 'Under Rule 3.6 Councillor Keane is allowed to speak on matters within the responsibilities of the committee and that's what he is doing.'

It was strengthening to have Jane speaking out eloquently on my side.

'Overruled,' said the Chairperson. 'Under Rule 5.17, I can rule out of order any aspects not relating to the debate and direct they be raised during general business. Councillor Keane may not speak now about some other development, such as this... MC. Now continue.'

'Madam Chairperson,' I said, 'I am merely establishing that there is at least one alternative to a casino.'

'Point of order,' said Fenwick. 'The councillor is failing to comply with your direction.'

'Accepted. Councillor Keane, I am warning you, if you fail to comply with my direction and commit a further act of disorder, you may be suspended for up to eight days.'

If I was sent out I would be unable to vote. I must be careful not to do anything that could be construed as disorder.

'Madam Chairperson, I urge NLP members to show their loyalty to residents by voting for this motion. It is momentous for the future of Alexandra City. This prominent site should be thrown open to all-comers to make proposals. A month is not a lot to ask when there could be such important benefits.

'If you vote against this motion, you are voting for Runyon's application to be approved without the merits of the project being considered. Councillors, if you refuse to accept your legal obligations you have under the Local Government Act, what hope is there that the casino managers will operate within the law? Gamblers could lose more than their shirts. The people of Alexandra could lose an important part of their heritage and be stuck with a sleazy future. I urge you to vote for this motion. Thank you.'

I sat down. There was little chance that any councillor would break ranks from the mindless herd. The 11 NLP members present were under orders. Their allegiance would flow in like the tide, whatever storms blew up on the surface. The most I could hope for was that all 10 SLP members would vote for the motion. Jane's and my votes would then result in a majority of one.

'Thank you, Dr Keane. Now, for the Negative,' said the Chairperson. 'Councillor Munster.'

'Thank you, Madam Chairperson,' said Trudy. 'We on this side are opposed to delaying Runyon's proposal. Adding these frills to the Council's process is a waste of time. We have been elected, all of us, to serve the City as a whole. Runyon's proposal is very attractive and the sooner we approve it the better. The Opposition pretends to want development but really it is opposed to it. This recommendation is nothing more than a delaying tactic.'

'Point of order,' said Jane. 'Councillor Munster is imputing the Affirmative side's motives.'

'Sustained. Councillor Munster, you will retract.'

'I retract. Madam Chairperson, I reiterate that if the recommendation succeeds it will disadvantage our city's people. It is imperative that we in the Government engage with Runyon's project before they lose patience and go elsewhere. The approval they are seeking now is preliminary. If there is a problem, they will have to fix it before they get our final approval.'

Munster wittered on about Government leadership and deploring the actions of the Opposition.

'Point of order, Madam Chairperson,' said Jane.

'Point of order against you, Councillor Munster.'

'Madam Chairperson,' said Jane, 'it's very obvious that Councillor Munster is filibustering. She is not addressing the motion. She is asserting that Runyon's application should not have to follow the usual process of calling tenders, without telling us why not. This is ludicrous, Madam Chairperson.'

'Yes, thank you, Councillor Kenwood. I agree it is ludicrous, but if that's how Councillor Munster wants to waste the chamber's time, she has the right to do it. Keep going, Councillor Munster.'

'Thank you very much, Madam Chairperson,' said Munster. 'I appreciate this opportunity to speak to this motion here today. So thank you very much for that.'

'Get on with it,' said Jane loudly.

While Munster continued speaking, Jane sauntered across the chamber to Munster's desk, leaned on the partition and gazed at her raptly as if she was a rare zoo animal. The Opposition councillors chuckled at Jane's display of contempt for this so-called debate.

'Councillor Kenwood, resume your seat,' said the Chairperson, exasperated.

Jane strolled back to her desk.

A few minutes later the Chairperson said, 'Councillor Munster, your 10 minutes are up.'

'Madam Chairperson,' said Munster, 'I hope that councillors will vote against this motion so that our government can continue to bring in changes that the community wants and stop Councillors Kenwood and Keane from wasting our time with this ridiculous motion.'

Trudy Munster sat down.

'Councillor Kenwood,' said the Chairperson. 'Your turn.'

'Keep your cool,' I said to Jane quietly, as the woman who would be found in concrete got to her feet.

CHAPTER 24

Jane surveyed the chamber. Attention turned to her and she smiled confidently.

'Madam Chairperson, LM, Councillors, I rise as seconder affirming the recommendation to put back consideration of Runyon's PDA for a month so that alternatives can be considered.

'My colleague, Dr Keane, has objected to the content of Runyon's proposal. Now I will object to the process the Government is using. They want to impose this monstrosity on the unsuspecting people of Alexandra. They are trying to rush it through. Last week, the Premier wanted the Council to kowtow to the Provincial Government, which is secretly and improperly negotiating with Runyon's. Now the LM is cajoling us not to consider other alternatives and approve the casino without the usual assessment being done.

'The proper processes are not being followed and we cannot allow it. The Government has to evaluate all the alternatives. The people of Alexandra expect us to apply reason and consider the moral aspect and public welfare effects. They do not expect us to prostrate ourselves before the NLP's hunger for funds.

'Council is the planning authority but its consideration of this matter has so far been cursory. It is being led to ingratiate itself with the Provincial Government.'

'Point of order.'

'Yes, Councillor?'

'The speaker is imputing councillors' motives,' said Trudy Munster.

'Upheld. Councillor Kenwood, you will retract that.'

'I retract. Councillors are not being motivated by the Premier's demand.'

Jane had highlighted with irony the fact that many councillors resented the way the Premier was subordinating them. Jane's mud would stick. Her head had an affable backward tilt, her worldly right eye gleaming, with a smile crinkling her nose and with dimples in her cheeks. Her voice tinkled with laughter.

'The Council has not investigated alternatives to a casino, as it is obliged to do in the public interest,' she said. 'Councillors, stand up for your constituents' rights by voting for this motion.'

'Point of order.'

'Yes, Councillor O'Connell.'

The DM's words were garbled. He had a reputation for drinking before meetings.

'Point of information: the casino is being properly considered by the Government and the full situation cannot be revealed, now or ever. Negotiations are confidential. Delay will not clarify the situation.'

'Madam Chairperson,' said Jane, 'I am shocked by the DM's hypocrisy. His job is responsible to the community but he doesn't want the community to know what he and the Government are doing. That is not good enough. What is so hard about this negotiation that we cannot be told what alternatives are being considered?'

'Point of order, Madam Chairperson?' said the DM, his diction indistinct. 'Claim to be misrepresented.'

'Sustained,' said the Chairperson. 'The DM gave a reason — that negotiations were confidential. I will obtain information about what is allowed to be commercial-in-confidence for our meeting next week. Councillor Kenwood, continue.'

'Madam Chairperson,' said Jane, the DM used the word 'confidential'. He is using confidentiality as a smokescreen to hide what the Government is doing. The public should be informed what is going on and be able to express their views.'

'Point of order.'

'Yes, Councillor Keane.'

'Madam Chairperson, your information about what is commercial-in-confidence will not be obtained in time for today's motion. To be duly cautious, councillors should vote for a delay. If the information favours the casino they can vote to approve it in a month's time.'

'Councillor Keane, that information was already available to councillors. Do not interject with inessential information again. Councillor Kenwood continue.'

'The DM is sitting in this Council chamber,' Jane said, her arms wide, 'a place where elected councillors bring forward ideas and views from the community for consideration. But the DM's model of how Council works does not allow questioning or any opposition. The Government is hiding what it has been doing. We know from experience that this Government does not take a blind bit of notice of anyone else. The DM needs to get up to speed on what democracy is all about and how debate in this place is supposed to work.'

'Point of information.'

'Yes, Councillor Fenwick.'

'Madam Chairperson,' said Fenwick, 'is Councillor Kenwood aware that in the real world no-one is able to find out everyone else's business? Commercial organisations guard their money-making ideas. They demand confidentiality.'

'Point of information, Madam Chairperson,' said Jane.

'Yes, Councillor Kenwood.'

'Just to help you out, Madam Chairperson, 'commercial-in-confidence' means…'

'No,' the Chairperson interrupted, 'I do not need helping out. I realise, Councillor Kenwood, that you think you know it all, but I freely admit I do not.'

'Madam Chairperson, point of information,' said Jane. 'There are rules that apply to commercial-in-confidence and I refer you to the City of Alexandra Act particularly—'

Jane had worked for a developer and knew the topic of confidentiality and the Act better than anyone in the chamber.

'I do not need your assistance —' said the Chairperson.

'Well, you said you didn't know.'

'Councillor Kenwood, continue on with your speech.'

'Am I not allowed to make a point of information?'

'Councillor Kenwood, in future, make sure it is a proper point of order.'

Danger loomed. Jane was already on a warning for interjecting. The Chairperson was NLP and if she sent Jane out, we would lose our majority and the motion would be defeated.

'Point of order,' said Attack Dog. 'Councillor Kenwood is misleading the chamber by building a straw man around the legality of one option or the other. Madam Chairperson —'

'Point of order,' I said.

'Yes, Councillor Keane.'

I was going to Jane's support. I would ridicule the hateful Fenwick.

'Councillor Fenwick is misleading the Chamber,' I said. 'There is no straw man. What Councillor Kenwood was doing was addressing Councillor Fenwick's false dilemma: that there is a choice to be made between no public disclosure, or total public disclosure. He is implying that it is not possible to have a position in-between. What utter rubbish! The Government can disclose details of what it is doing without revealing commercial secrets. It could disclose it now, but it will not do so because what it has been doing is improper. The straw man Councillor Fenwick speaks of is himself, as he has stuffed it up and is grasping at straws.'

There was applause from the SLP and jeers from the Government benches.

I continued, 'The deceit of Councillor Fenwick's fallacy compounds the Government's lack of transparency. The NLP are verballing Councillor Kenwood because she has stood up to them and shown that what they are doing is improper —'

'Order. Councillor Keane, be seated.'

I sat down amid an uproar of boos and cheers. I had achieved what I wanted when I stood up, which was to oppose Fenwick's insidious attack on transparency, the central tenet of Jane's canon.

'Councillor Keane, you have not made your point. Councillor Fenwick's behaviour is normal rhetoric and has not been disorderly. Councillor Kenwood you have two minutes left.'

'Madam Chairperson,' said Jane, continuing, 'Government confidentiality is not justified when information is withheld for political advantage. Transparency is essential, for accountability and for people to adjust to the new situation.'

'Point of Order,' said Fenwick. 'Transparency is a word, not a practical government process. Government is less able to interact the way it needs to when people are looking over its shoulder. The information Councillor Kenwood is demanding is part of a commercial negotiation and has to be kept confidential. I urge you to choose good government by throwing out this motion.'

'Point of information,' said the LM. 'The site is owned by the Provincial Government. Before Runyon's will buy it they will require that the Council approves their DA. Delaying the preliminary approval is pointless.'

'That is hypocrisy,' Jane scoffed, 'because if you win this motion you will go on to approve the PDA, making the DA virtually unstoppable. The Provincial Government is being sneaky and trying to present us with a fait accompli. They will say we should have objected earlier, which is hypocrisy because they are trying to stop us objecting right now.'

'Councillor Kenwood, your time has expired.'

'Councillors, I urge you to remember that you represent residents who want transparency and reason,' said Jane. Her smile was inscrutable, with her soulful left eye round and smiling, and her mouth pouting thoughtfully under the superior arch of her nose.

She sat down.

Cutter had still not arrived and there was only O'Connell left to speak. There were 11 NLP and 10 SLP plus Jane and me. We could be in front 12:11 at this stage but it could easily go the other way.

CHAPTER 25

The Chairperson said, 'Councillor O'Connell.'

The DM stood up unsteadily in the Mayor's box. He was the last of the four speakers. Like me and the other male councillors he was in shirtsleeves and tie with suit pants. He leaned on the partition, speaking into the mic.

'Madam Chairperson, I rise to second for the Negative.'

At this point Cutter walked in with his hair mussed up, his shirt tail out, his tie loose, looking as though he had been in a fight or a debilitating tryst.

He dropped onto the Government's backbench and put his head in his hands. Councillors craned to look at him. Cutter's presence was a catastrophe for us. He had taken away our majority. Government and Opposition now had 12 members each and our motion would not carry.

O'Connell saw him arrive and was heartened.

'A casino has wide support,' he said resolutely. 'We oppose this motion to delay and consider other alternatives. We will unite to approve Runyon's proposal.'

'Point of order,' said Jane. 'Councillor O'Connell is misleading Council. If you defeat our motion Runyon's PDA still has to be approved.'

'Whatever. You are splitting hairs. This Council will approve it. The casino is a fantastic opportunity. Absolutely terrific.'

O'Connell swayed slightly on his feet and paused to sip from a glass that I suspected contained more than water. His voice was slurred.

Cutter said in a hallowed tone: 'Let him who is without gin be the first to get stoned.' He was audible to councillors but the Chairperson did not hear.

Laughter.

'I rebut the assertion of Councillor Keane that residents are morally opposed to gambling,' said O'Connell. 'It is a common pursuit and it is increasing in popularity.'

'Point of order, Madam Chairperson,' said Jane. 'Is the increase in gambling greater online than in casinos?'

O'Connell pondered.

'Councillor, do you elect to answer or refuse the question?' said the Chairperson.

'My answer is that I do not know, Madam Chairperson,' said O'Connell smugly. 'Runyon's would know and they are betting the demand for a casino in Alexandra will be sufficient.'

He sipped again, toad-like — squat, with a rotund face and bulging eyes.

'Point of order, the councillor is refusing to answer my question,' said Jane.

'Councillor Kenwood, indeed he has,' said the Chairperson. 'You may not like the answer but it is allowed under our rules. Councillor O'Connell, continue.'

'Thank you, Madam Chairperson,' he said croakily. 'I rebut ... rebut ...'

'Ribbit, ribbit,' said Cutter.

Guffaws from the Opposition benches and a chorus of 'Ribbit, ribbit, ribbit, ribbit.'

'Order, order,' the Chairperson banged her gavel.

'Point of order.'

'Yes, Councillor Kenwood.'

'Councillor O'Connell has not answered my question.'

Jane was irrepressible. No matter what distortion of the rules they used to try and silence her, she demanded answers.

'Councillor Kenwood, I have made my decision,' said the Chairperson. 'It was not a refusal. He answered that he didn't know. If people would accept more often that they don't know, we would all be better off.' She glared at Jane.

Jane turned to the LM. 'Councillor Hubbard, you don't know why the Premier is promoting this private investment, do you?'

'Good question,' said Shelly.

Jeers from the Government benches.

Her question could suggest that Leach was corrupt. I hoped that Jane would have evidence of some impropriety if the LM challenged her aspersion.

The LM squirmed in her seat. Councillors knew that Jane's animosity towards the Government ran deep. Even so, it was reckless to verbal the Premier like this.

Hubbard said, 'Indeed, I do know. It will benefit all Robertans.'

'Pig's arse,' scoffed Jane.

'Councillor Kenwood, do not call out,' said the Chairperson. 'Councillor O'Connell, would you continue for the negative.'

'Not content with making unsubstantiated allegations and badmouthing the Government's initiative, Councillor Kenwood has put up flimsy proposals of her own that no-one wants.' His voice was loud and resonant. The metallic timbre excited him and his bombastic monologue continued. 'She has rolled her Trojan horse, a MC, up to the city gates and is now trying to persuade us to come out and bring it inside. But what will we find? It is an empty idea. The MC is merely a vehicle to carry her peculiar notions about tendering, consultation and transparency. They can't make it in their own right and she is trying to get them in by trickery.'

'Hear, hear,' was called from the Government benches.

O'Connell drank from his glass again.

'Councillor Kenwood is stuck in a rut,' he said wetly. 'Her wheels are spinning but she's going nowhere. Einstein said that doing the same thing over and over and expecting a different result is insane. She must therefore be mad. She keeps yapping about tendering, consultation and transparency as if they are the only possible way to run a city, when good governments have often restricted them in the public interest.'

'Point of order,' said Jane.

'Yes, Councillor Kenwood.'

'Information: Councillor O'Connell is not speaking to the motion. He has given no reasons for rushing ahead with a casino instead of waiting while alternatives are considered.'

'Councillor Kenwood, they have denied that delay will produce a different result. I do not uphold your point of order. I am formally warning you that if this is repeated you may be banned from the chamber for eight days. Councillor O'Connell, continue.'

I wanted Jane to stop her assault. She had warnings on two different calls and with the vote tied, we were in a perilous position. If she was sent out our motion would fail.

O'Connell continued, 'All I can say to Councillor Kenwood is that we have explained to you the necessity for confidential negotiations; that formal tenders are not always desirable; that Runyon's need our approval now; and your MC proposal is too late. If you still don't know what's going on — well, resign. Do everyone a favour and stop coming in here and trying to use your ignorance to disrupt proceedings. Either that, or get your SLP colleagues to slowly explain to you how government of this city works and maybe at the end of that you might get it — '

'Point of order,' said Jane.

Her face was flushed and her jaw was clenched. I was furious too. It was a derisory and unfounded personal attack. Even though O'Connell's game was obvious, my angst was almost uncontrollable. I hoped Jane would not take the bait. I projected a thought to her: *'Keep your cool, girl!'*

'Claim to be misrepresented — ' Jane said.

'Not upheld. Councillor Kenwood, I am warning you, you may be excluded from this chamber if you continue to interject.'

'Point of order.'

'Councillor Kenwood,' said the Chairperson.

'Madam Chairperson, what is the rule of procedure that led you to warn me just now?'

The Chairperson said, 'It is the Chief Legal Counsel's ruling. The Chair may determine when a person is making too many points of order that are not upheld.'

I could see the Chairperson was itching to use her power to eject Jane, as she had done several times before during my time on the Council. The NLP wanted to shut Jane down.

'But you are holding down my points of order unfairly.'

'Jane, don't argue!' I said in my head. Jane's brinkmanship was an aspect of her behaviour that at times seemed self-destructive. She thrived on confrontation and danced along the very edge of the stage,

104

where she was in danger of falling off into the orchestra pit. It was arrant bravado. That was her nature – it fascinated and delighted me. She played by rules to their limits. There was nothing I could do but watch her, as like a matador she flicked the cape of procedural rules and enraged the wounded government bull to make a fatal error.

'You are entitled to your opinion, Councillor Kenwood, but not to state it during a debate. Be seated.'

Soon the debate would finish and the voting would be 12 votes each. Our motion would most likely fail.

CHAPTER 26

'Councillor O'Connell continue,' said the Chairperson.

'If Mike Harris had won Blake, he would have provided residents with what they wanted.'

It was untrue. Since soundly beating Harris in the election, Jane had been assiduous in serving her constituents. She was an outstandingly effective councillor. O'Connell was pressing Jane's buttons, taunting her, trying to goad her into committing a misconduct so they could expel her. I hoped she would not be lured into his trap. We needed her vote to win.

O'Connell said, 'Blake residents have been suffering while Councillor Kenwood pursues her pipe dreams. She is too busy Twittering to find out what they want.'

The reality was that Jane's use of social media set a high standard no other councillor had matched. She had achieved much for her residents – a public park, a community building and sports centre. She had led a campaign to stop the sale of public parkland for private development, earning the ire of the Government.

'Point of order.'

'Yes, Councillor Dawson.'

The Leader of the Opposition was coming to Jane's defence.

'Councillor O'Connell is not addressing the motion. Events in Blake Ward are not relevant.'

'Sustained. Councillor O'Connell, would you address the motion. You are almost out of time.'

'Councillor Kenwood should attend to the needs of Blake Ward,' said O'Connell, squat and hateful. 'She has been trying to whip up a moral crusade against a casino. When will she stop using her residents for her own political purposes? When will she start actually representing their needs instead of trying to get projects she wants that no-one else wants? How hard is it? The rest of us do it, so why doesn't she? Obviously, for Councillor Kenwood it is too hard.'

O'Connell was winding her up. Jane, of all the city's councillors, was closest to her ward residents.

'Too, too hard, Madam Chairperson,' he continued. 'How absolutely childish that Councillor Kenwood sits in this chamber and wastes our precious time, when she doesn't do her job and she doesn't talk to her locals. She doesn't actually utilise the system as it currently exists. Coming in here and trying to derail the casino with this hare-brained MC is an absolute joke.'

O'Connell's rhetoric applied the philosophy of 'opposition' called 'deconstruction', formulated by Derrida. He was trying to destroy Jane's credibility as a representative. His 'evidence' was completely false. 'Post-truth' prevarication had become common in Council meetings. I had had enough of this nonsense. We were tied at 12-all and would lose the motion unless we could pull something out of the hat. We had to fight the NLP. I would back up Jane and try to stop O'Connell's rampage.

'Point of order,' I said.

'Councillor Keane.'

'The councillor has digressed.'

'Sustained. Councillor O'Connell, address the motion.'

'I am, Madam Chairperson. I am showing that Councillor Kenwood's alternative is uncompetitive. Doctor Keane must know that casino gambling is not harmful and has many benefits.'

Jane spoke, 'Point of order, Madam Chairperson. The councillor is not providing any information relevant to dismissing alternatives to a casino. He has used weasel words to evade acknowledging that casinos cause addiction to gambling and crime. He is claiming that gambling 'has many benefits' but the evidence is that the benefits are less than the costs.'

'Rubbish,' said O'Connell.

'Councillor O'Connell,' said Jane, 'I will send you a reference to where this evaluation has been published. Councillor Keane has told you correctly that a casino would be of no benefit *overall*. That is our proposition and if Councillor O'Connell is unable to refute it then it is wrong to oppose this motion. His words do not address people's concerns and are irrelevant. '

'Councillor Kenwood,' the Chairperson interrupted her. 'His words do provide information of a sort.'

O'Connell was a skilled infighter. His pummelling had softened up Jane and now he moved in for the knockout.

'I do refute it,' he said, smirking. 'My information is objective.'

'It is lies,' said Jane.

'Councillor Kenwood! You will not interject ... As I was saying, if statements have to address points fully and accurately, most of us would rarely speak.'

'Good — o,' said Jane, clapping.

The Opposition councillors laughed and stamped their feet, chanting, 'Good — o, Good — o.'

The Chairperson punished the wood block with her gavel.

'Order. Order. Order. Councillor Kenwood, I warned you earlier that if you made a further point of order that was not upheld, you would have to leave the chamber. I do not uphold your point of order. Would you now leave us.'

There was a moment of shocked silence followed by applause from the Government side.

'Yah — boo — hiss,' said the Opposition.

Jane was on her feet, at the mic. 'I have a right to have my question about gambling online answered. When a speaker's words are not relevant to the motion, I have a right to point it out.'

'Would you leave now.'

'I am not leaving.'

She sat down, folding her arms resolutely. People in the gallery applauded loudly with calls of 'Good on you, Jane'.

Jane's ego sometimes verged on hubris. She could be over-zealous, over-confident, ego-centric and even self-aggrandising. Stopping short of recklessness, her brinkmanship was full on. I found this trait absolutely endearing. I would always be on her side, despite her crazy behaviour, unconditionally. I hoped I would be able to protect her from adverse consequences.

'Councillor Kenwood, you have every right to adhere to the rules of this chamber. But week in and week out, you misbehave very deliberately—'

'Hah,' she said, jeering. 'I obey the rules. I do not deceive people with weasel words. My statements can be tested. I do not misbehave ... We all know who misbehaves, don't we? The Government. They hide what they are doing, they refuse to answer questions, they break the rules and you allow them to get away with it.'

'I warned you. Now leave the chamber at—'

'— under what rule of procedure did you warn me?'

'I gave you the Chief Legal Counsel's ruling ...'

'No, I didn't ask for 'a ruling'. I asked what was the rule I broke?' said Jane shrilly.

From where I sat next to her, on her left, I could see the set of her jaw, her lips pulled back in a confident smile, her nose engaged, her mouth projecting assertively, her wide and vigilant right eye measuring the situation. She was formidable.

The Chairperson was unable to answer. Whereas Jane had objected to O'Connell's irrelevancies, the Chairperson had condoned them. I had never seen them so at each other before. Cheryl Purser had been running Council meetings for the past two years. Jane had been disputing chair calls for even longer and her knowledge of the rules was at least equal to hers. The Chairperson was a popular councillor who tempered her loyalty to the NLP with enough fairness for her subtle biases to be overlooked. But today it was more than a ritual confrontation as Jane was determined to be heard and the Chairperson was equally determined that she should not.

'Councillor Kenwood, leave the chamber.'

'What rule was it? Nowhere did I refuse to accept the rules. Look on the record.'

The Chairperson could not respond because her warning would not stand scrutiny. She had allowed O'Connell's calumny and irrelevancies to provoke Jane.

'Councillor O'Connell, your time has expired,' said the Chairperson. 'The debate has ended.'

The LM spoke. 'I propose that the meeting adjourn for a period of five minutes to allow Councillor Kenwood to leave the chamber.'

'Seconded,'

'Meeting adjourned.'

The councillors filed out of the chamber.

109

Jane did not budge. The Chairperson directed two Council officers to escort her out but Jane continued to harangue her.

'I want to know what rule I broke.'

'You should have accepted my points of order.'

A Council official beckoned to Jane. 'Come with me, Councillor, please,' he said.

Jane ignored him. 'I demand that the question of what rule I broke is placed on notice.'

Chief Executive Officer, Ainsley Montague, used his telephone and a few minutes later two police officers in uniform sauntered in with holstered guns. Montague pointed out Jane to them.

'What's the problem?' said a policewoman to Jane.

'A political party game: it's called pass the question.'

'That's funny,' she said grimly.

'Not really. It's a fucking farce.'

'I am ordering you to come with us now.'

Jane's stride was jaunty as she left the chamber, with the policewoman following her. I was proud of her. I felt bad that I had not spoken up more on her side but I was on a warning and could have been sent out too.

I followed Jane outside. She was talking ruefully with the Opposition. Cutter was there too.

'The Chair was totally unfair,' said Shelly.

'O'Connell pressed my self-eject button,' said Jane. 'I'm sorry for letting you down. Being out here is a bummer.'

'It was a set-up,' said Cutter.

'Hello, Cutter,' she said, turning to his dishevelled self. 'It looks like you overstayed your welcome somewhere.'

'I had to leave in a hurry.' He was bashful.

Jane turned away — a put-down. Cutter was NLP.

'It looks like we are going to lose 11 to 12,' I said.

'Dammit. We were so close,' Jane said. 'I shouldn't have let Jock antagonise me.'

I was standing on her left and could see her left eye was wide and bright. She was self-actualising healthily. Her right eye smiled confidently. She knew what she was doing. Her nose had the slightest upward curve of inner satisfaction and she spoke with the calmness of a cleric.

'I have to leave the building. I'll see you later, Phillip. I'll keep my fingers crossed for the voting.'

She walked briskly towards the exit.

CHAPTER 27

I went back in. As I passed O'Connell I said to him: 'You are a turd. Rot in hell.'

His behaviour in the debate had been despicable. I didn't hear his reply.

'We will resume the debate,' said the Chairperson.

'Without Jane,' I thought, *'we are doomed.'*

'Councillor O'Connell has seconded for the negative,' said the Chairperson. 'We will proceed to a vote. The motion is that alternative proposals be sought, for a development on the site of the IB, to be received by one month from today, with assessment subject to a survey of residents' gambling and other preferences. All those in favour say Aye.'

A chorus of Aye.

'Those against.'

Another chorus of Naye.

'Division. Proposer?'

'Yes,' said Julie Dawson.

'Seconded,' said Shelly.

'Ring the bells.'

Distant tinkling summonsed councillors.

As I stood to vote I knew the best we could hope for was 11 for and 12 against. I had ruined my career in politics in vain. But I would not accept defeat until the casino had opened for business. Today's confrontation had been a battle but the war would go on.

I walked up and stood on the Chairperson's right. Standing with the Opposition was a new experience for me. There was a pin-drop silence as I was stared at by 22 pairs of councillor eyes, plus those of officials in the chamber, as well as reporters and strangers crowding the gallery.

The Government would have a majority of one and our motion would fail.

The Chairperson said, 'The count pl ...'

We heard gleeful laughter from the public gallery above and looked up. They were watching Cutter, who was standing back, counting the sides. Then he walked across and stood beside me. The gallery erupted with whoops and clapping. The Chairperson stared in disbelief. The faces of the NLP showed fear — we had the numbers to force an election and could oust them.

'The count, please,' the Chairperson asked the CEO.

'For: 12. Against: 11.'

'The motion is carried.'

My arms shot up in victory. I wanted to hug Cutter but I gave him a high-five.

Cutter's crossover had been decisive. The Government had never been defeated before. I savoured my new pivotal influence in the Council.

The NLP were subdued as they returned to their desks. The SLP councillors broke into excited chatter. The Labour councillors came over and shook Cutter's and my hand.

'Good move, you two,' Julie Dawson said. 'We are going to have a motion of no-confidence.'

'Order,' said the Chairperson. 'We will adjourn for tea.'

I was pleased we had halted the Government's reign. Now that it was hung, the votes of we independents would be decisive. It was not a position I relished but I had no qualms. If councillors had properly represented their constituents, rather than obeying party dictates, the Council would not be hung.

The tearoom was a hubbub of voices. People were speculating about an election.

Jane was not answering her mobile — she was probably driving home.

Cutter was standing by himself and I went over. I wondered if he had crossed for Jane, reacting to her cold shoulder earlier. I was not jealous; most men wanted Jane and I was used to them trying to latch on to her. Part of my friendship with him was that we both had shares in Jane.

'That was perfect,' I said to Cutter. 'Shut the gate.'

We were rebels together.

'I hope they don't gang up on us.'

'They will at the next election,' I said.

'It's a year away.'

'It's a new ball game right now.'

We both faced consequences from the NLP. My desertion was cataclysmic for my political ambitions. Yet it felt good to have stood up for a cause I believed in: councillor independence, Jane-style.

'What will you do?' Cutter said.

'They will try to bribe us. We could get cabinet seats.'

'Do you want to form a party and go into coalition?'

I shook my head.

'I couldn't bear to work with them. I can achieve more for my constituents by playing it fast and loose.'

Cutter would make a better independent than me. He was an extrovert, able to tune into people with warmth and feeling. His most endearing trait was spontaneity, unlike my calculating approach. It puzzled me that people overlooked his erratic, self-indulgent and lascivious lifestyle and preferred him to me. My reliable Spartan ways were dull by comparison. Yet today I felt vindicated and proud of my Council work. I might be able to make it as an independent — but it would take all the courage and energy I could muster.

After tea we went back in.

'Any other business?' said the Chairperson.

Julie Dawson, the Labour leader, stood up. 'I move that this chamber has no confidence in the Government.'

'Seconded by Councillor Redford.'

During the recess, Cutter had asked me, 'Do you want an election?'

'No,' I had said. 'I don't think a SLP government would be any better than the NLP.'

He didn't say how he was going to vote and I didn't ask. Cutter kept his cards close always. When we divided, Cutter and I were the last to walk up. We stood with our former colleagues in the NLP.

The count was 13: 10 and no-confidence was lost. The SLP had been counting on us and were stunned. The NLP heaved a sigh of relief and shook our hands.

114

'Just in time,' Trudy Munster said. 'We'll forgive and forget, you know.'

I had heard that miscreants can only return to the NLP by doing some dirty deed, such as making a scurrilous personal attack on an Opposition member, which I would never do. There was no way back.

As we walked to our benches, Dawson came over, furious.

'What's wrong with you? Don't you have any guts?'

'Sorry, Julie, my constituents wouldn't want an election just now,' I said.

'Nor mine,' said Cutter. 'Too bad.'

'You'll regret this,' Dawson said, wading away like a rice farmer in a paddy. She made heavy going of opposing the Government and was less effective than light-footed Jane.

'You can't make an omelette without breaking eggs,' I told Cutter. 'The parties have been beating up the same bipartisan recipe for development of this city for far too long. There is a new ingredient — independent representation. Today it controlled outcomes.'

'It feels right,' he said. 'The people have taken back control from the party hacks.'

When the meeting finished, I went home, exhausted. It didn't seem possible that the Council could continue to be so tense.

CHAPTER 28

That evening, I ate with Jane at her place. I told her how we had won.

'Fantastic,' she said 'Thank God Cutter crossed! What made him do it?'

'He didn't like what the NLP did to you.'

'He's a good friend.'

'How do you feel about being ejected?'

'I am determined to stop the development game being played by cheats.'

'What will you do?'

'I'm going to stop the political parties running the Council.'

It seemed impossible but I could see she was serious. Her tangle with the Government was no storm in a teacup. Although I admired her resolve, I had misgivings.

'It seems like holding back the tide,' I said. 'Could you be biting off more than you can chew?'

It was more polite than telling her she was crazy.

Jane looked at me confidently.

'I'm sure I can do it. Will you help me?'

'I will as much as I can. I believe what you are doing is right.'

'I know you do,' Jane said. 'Thanks, Phillip. And how is it going with you? Was your week eventful too?'

'Too eventful. I won't forget the nastiness of NLP members when I crossed — such meanness of spirit.'

'That's the kind of people they are. All they care about is being re-elected. You have overturned their apple cart.'

'What should I do next?'

'Carry on as an independent.'

'What can I achieve?'

'You can keep the Government honest.'

'By objecting when they break the rules?'

'That's right,' Jane said. 'Otherwise they will think they can do what they want.'

'Will making them follow the rules make any difference?'

'Yes, of course. Otherwise it is tyranny.'

'Why are you the only one confronting the Government?' I asked.

'There isn't genuine opposition. The SLP and NLP rub together like two cheeks of the same arse, hiding the dirty business.'

I laughed.

'Do you believe your testing of the rules and consequences in Council meetings will change anything?'

'Yes. If we don't keep to the rules they will be ignored. The party bosses will decide everything in collusion.'

'Your stand today was magnificent,' I said. 'I think you are so brave.'

'You too. Going against the NLP took real guts. Now you can do what you want.'

We hugged each other. We had become close and comfortable together, able to share concerns. If the worst came to the worst and I had a bad accident or was paralysed, she might consume her life caring for me. I wouldn't want that. She should do whatever she thought was fair. Trusting Jane wasn't like following a straight line or even a branching algorithm. It was a feeling of oneness with her that was growing steadily within me.

As we lay together I wanted her urgently.

'We'll do it soon,' she said.

*

The next day, the NLP offered Jane, Cutter and me cabinet seats. Not to be outdone, the SLP would give us cabinet seats too, if we would vote with them in a no-confidence motion. But we knew in an election we could lose our seats and we turned down both offers.

'I represent my constituents, not a party,' said Jane.

'I will let my conscience be my guide,' I said.

'I want to avoid those party creeps,' said Cutter.

The NLP banned Cutter and me from caucus meetings and started proceedings to expel us. We no longer got party briefing papers or the

117

Government agenda. We could make up our own minds. When you stepped off the party's gravy train, politics was hard work.

There wasn't much glory by yourself. My work as an independent seemed disconnected and ineffective. One thing I was accomplishing was getting the MC proposal worked out in detail. It was a worthy cause, one I believed in — but it was taking all of my spare time.

CHAPTER 29

On Friday evening Cutter, Sunita and I went with the woman who would be found in concrete to Alexandra's finest restaurant, the Moulin Rouge. We sat quaffing red and talked about the week.

'Tonight is for celebrating a memorable event,' said Jane. 'We rolled the NLP!'

'Let's have a toast,' said Cutter. 'Fuck the NLP!'

We stood up and raised our drinks. 'Fuck the NLP!' we said in unison, clinking glasses. 'Long may they fester!'

Tony Hart arrived. He was a friend from my ward committee, a libertarian who worked for a conservation group. Tony's political activism had a surreal quality. He had no commitment to any party or ideology and regarded the Council as a conspiracy.

'Council politics are a problem,' he said. 'Political parties usurp collective wisdom. Councillors should be able to vote freely.'

'I agree,' said Cutter. 'You should be on the Council.'

'Nah. All that bullshit would drive me crazy,' Tony said.

He took a call.

'No, Rupert,' he said. 'Phillip and the others are here too. We are talking about politics. We're going somewhere to eat. Don't worry. See you later.'

He looked at us, rolled his eyes and put his phone in his bag. Rupert was Tony's lover and checked up on him regularly. Tony flaunted his relationship with pride.

Society had threats to his homosexuality that could have contributed to his feeling like an alien amidst potentially dangerous beings. He feared politicians especially. His dealings with Jane and I had gradually gained his trust. He was curious about politics like a botanist exploring a new ecosystem rich with unfamiliar species.

'Can we watch TV?' Jane asked. 'I did an interview with City Matters about the Council meeting. I was spitting blood. Maybe I went too far.'

There was a TV above the bar. We sipped our drinks and watched.

'Good evening, viewers. Welcome to City Matters, your civic current affairs programme. I am Graham Wallis.

'The police were called earlier this week to City Hall and escorted Councillor Jane Kenwood out from a Council meeting. She was banned for eight days. She left the NLP three years ago. Without her the Government has a narrow majority unless more councillors change sides. Already this has happened and the NLP has suffered its first defeat. We invited the LM to comment but she declined. I have independent Councillor Jane Kenwood with me here in the studio. Good afternoon, Jane and welcome.'

'Thank you, Graham. It's good to be here.'

'Why did you leave the Council meeting, Jane?'

'The police made me. Since I left the NLP, three years ago, I have been targeted and sent out half a dozen times even though I have always followed the rules.'

'Why have they targeted you?'

'I complained about Council meetings. The Government won't answer questions or engage in debate, which they must do if we are to have true democracy under the Westminster system.'

'What was the issue today?'

'The Premier has been secretly selling off the IB as a site for a casino without calling for tenders.'

'What happened?'

'They wouldn't tell us about the Government's negotiations with the casino company.'

'What happened?'

'I was sent out.'

'Are they allowed to keep them secret?'

'No. The Government has to inform councillors what they are doing but they claimed the deal has to be kept confidential.'

'Does it have to be confidential?'

'No. They can disclose what they are trying to do without revealing commercial secrets.'

'What happened this afternoon?' Wallis asked.

'I complained that the DM was not addressing the topic being debated. The Chair sent me out.'

'Why?'

'I don't know. I hadn't broken any rules. You would have to ask the Chairperson.'

'By sending you out, did the Government get a majority?'

'Yes, it set them up to win, but another councillor crossed and they lost.'

'Is the Council now hung?'

'Yes, three councillors have quit the NLP and the Government cannot count on getting a majority.'

'How bad is what they have been doing?'

'They have not been administering public assets in the best interests of the community. Selling a heritage site without considering alternatives or calling tenders is bad government.'

'Will your opposition achieve anything?'

'It will if they become more answerable.'

'That's all we have time for today, Jane. The Government could be in a spot of bother here. Thank you for coming in.'

'Thank you for having me on your show, Graham.'

'That was Jane Kenwood. Is she a people's hero or a renegade? We at City Matters will be keeping an eye on events at City Hall in the coming weeks.'

'Here's to Jane,' said Cutter when the programme ended.

'To Jane,' we echoed.

'Also to Cutter for saving the day,' I said.

'I did what came naturally,' he said. 'Voters in Wordsworth want the casino decision considered properly. I have a clear conscience ... and an unclear career.'

'Leaving the NLP is the best thing you have ever done,' said Jane. 'You will be a great independent — honest and fair.'

'You won't have to be loyal to a party now, Cutter,' said Sunita. 'You only have to think of yourself — it's what you do best.'

Cutter smiled, unprovoked.

'I wish I was as public spirited as you, Sunita,' he said with a straight face. 'I would be as humble and sweet as you are.'

Sunita glared at him. We took our drinks through into the dining room and ordered our food.

121

'You were terrific, Jane,' Tony said. 'You demonstrated that the Government is immoral and self-serving.'

'They will realise that their bullying tactics won't work,' I said.

'Cutter, Phillip and I hold the balance of power,' said Jane.

Our situation at the brink of anarchy held her enthralled, but for me it was a nightmare. I liked to have my next moves planned, like a chess player, with the way ahead decided. There were too many possibilities. I was unlikely to win the next election as an independent and I didn't have any other plan. Perhaps I could have a leading role in developing a MC.

'We have a month to prepare and put in a PDA,' Jane said.

'You should get a fair hearing now,' said Tony.

'We need to dispel any idea that a MC is whimsy,' Jane said. 'Our PDA has to establish our credibility on four fronts: demand; heritage; feasibility; and finance.'

'Is that 'demand' the interest out there now, or what we get them to want?' I asked.

'We need ethnic leaders to support our bid and have their people buy our tickets.'

'They can foster local productions,' said Sunita.

'We can tee up money and designs for theatres,' said Jane. 'We are going to extend the IB, aren't we, Phillip?'

It was one of those rare moments when the spotlight was on my plans.

'We will need to restore the IB and construct a new building behind it,' I said. 'We need professionals to draw up plans.'

'Can you find us an architect?'

'I'm not sure. It could be difficult to find one prepared to take on the Government for that site, when it is their favourite project. But I'll contact architects experienced in adapting heritage sites.'

CHAPTER 30

It was a friendly and relaxing dinner. We paid for ourselves and I drove Jane home afterwards.

'Tonight I feel more secure than I have for years,' she said as we arrived at her place. 'After I went independent, I was on my own and it was tough. Having you and the others with me now, I feel I can relax a little.'

'It was a good night,' I said.

'Are you going into town tomorrow?'

'Only to the government bookstore.'

'Would you get something for me?'

'Of course. What?'

'A copy of the Heritage Conservation Regulations and a Directory of Multicultural Organisations. Here ...'

She fumbled in her bag. 'My purse is here somewhere ...'

'I'll get it from you later.'

'Thanks,' she said.

She seemed to be testing whether she could rely on me. I was pleased to oblige because although we were independent I did want her to be able to depend on me — not completely, but more than at present.

She got out of my car. I expected to have to wait before we would sleep together. She had told me a few days earlier, 'I want to be sure that you are the one. I made a mistake with Manfred. I want to get to know you first and that takes time.'

I understood why she was slow to trust me but it didn't make it any easier. My urgency was selfish and there was nothing else I could do.

*

On Saturday Jane and I went to a South American festival in Blake. Jane had helped the organisers obtain a permit, apply for a grant from the City Council and rent a stage. There was a programme with local bands, singers and dancers. There were stalls selling food, drinks, handicrafts and manufactures. Others gave out information about causes, careers, courses and community. Jane was guest of honour and she made the opening speech. I sat on the stage beside my distinguished girlfriend and the other dignitaries, sopping up the esteem.

After the speeches and after watching dance school students strut their stuff, we strolled past the stalls.

'Would you like an empanada?' Jane said. 'It's a savoury meat pasty.'

'No thanks,' I said. 'I don't take chances with food.'

'Rubbish. The stall has been inspected.'

'Can I give it a miss? Thanks.'

I seldom try new kitchens, whereas Jane will try anything for a change.

By now it was nightfall; a band started playing salsa and people were dancing in a lighted part of the street.

'Do you want to dance?' I asked Jane.

'Oh yes!' she said, grabbing me and heading there.

For a couple of hours we stepped in time and entwined around each other. It was an effort to keep my hands off her.

Afterwards, she came back to my apartment and we had our long-awaited first sex. It was spontaneous and mutual, with the time for it just right. We trusted each other and our sex was the icing on the cake.

She stayed all night until mid-morning.

I was in a daze. I wanted to do it again and again.

'Let's go to the dance school's party tonight,' I said.

'I'm all danced out,' she said. 'Let's do something else.'

She fed my goldfish.

'They are guileless and flighty,' she said, 'like you.'

We went to a pub with a rock band. We had to shout to be able to converse with friends we ran into there. One wanted me to buy a share in a racehorse. I said I had invested all my mad money in a maple syrup plantation. It could have been true.

Whenever Jane had sated an appetite, she wanted to try something else. Over the next few weeks we made love often but never in the same place twice. We enjoyed outdoor locations, her garden, beaches, a swimming pool, the ocean, a mountain top, various vehicles and boats. Indoors we plied our trade in rooms in public buildings, a lift, a library, an art gallery and a museum. Finding new places kept me busy. It seemed we would never settle into a comfortable routine, as I wanted, but I was not complaining.

CHAPTER 31

'What was Jane like at school?' I asked Cutter.

'She was phenomenal in primary, always under the spotlight,' he said. 'At high school she became sultry, anti-establishment and champion of the underdog. She argued with teachers and led students in revolt.'

When I asked Jane about this she told me, 'When the school used results of academic assessment to separate students for academic, skilled and unskilled careers, I protested that it was unfair. Every student had the right to succeed and if they failed, they should be able to repeat and get remediation. No-one should be stopped from attempting to complete a course or by removing opportunity.'

Cutter said that by the end of Year 11 she had finished all the school's humanities units and went to the university for classes two days each week. But her repudiation of school authority continued.

'Jane's Waterloo was her refusal to wear the school uniform,' said Cutter. 'She is acquainted with trouble and being despised.'

Jane told me of her confrontation with the school's principal.

''Wearing a uniform avoids a fashion parade by well-off students,' he said. 'We want you to experience representing an organisation.''

''I don't want to represent this school.''

''Why not?''

''I don't like it.''

''What don't you like?''

''I am not allowed to be myself.''

''In what way?''

''I want to wear clothes of my choice.''

''I am empowered to decide a school uniform and punish students who don't wear it,' he said.'

''I will refuse. You cannot prevent me attending classes, nor suspend, nor expel me,' I said. 'I know the rules.''

''I can detain you after school.''

"Someone will have to stay with me,' I said. I wouldn't stay with him alone — the creep.'

"I will arrange it.''

"I may not be able to get home afterwards.''

"I will ask your parents to fetch you.''

"If it interferes with my homework, it will not be legal.''

"You will be able to do your homework during the detention.''

Jane would not wear the uniform and attended detention after detention. The principal and a female teacher stayed late to supervise her. Her parents had left it to Jane to work it out with the school. She was able to take a late bus home.

"Your disobedience is inconveniencing us,' the principal said.'

"I will never wear the uniform,' I said. 'You should exempt me.''

"Why should you get special treatment?''

"Because I am different.''

"You are disobedient.' said the principal. 'Everyone has to conform to a group at some time.''

"That is your opinion. I have a right to be myself. I won't wear any uniform. It doesn't have to affect others.''

Jane was vociferous about individual rights, especially freedom of speech, freedom of action within the law and decision making by reason. In arguments with her father and mother she had learned how to win. She would pursue every proposition until an agreement was reached.

'She once argued with her father that dogs were not smarter than cats,' Cutter told me. 'She eventually persuaded him that 'Cats are smarter at being catty'.'

Cutter chuckled as he recalled Jane the student leader.

'The school had a debating team and Jane took to it like a duck to water. She wanted to argue about anything and everything and her parents and teachers indulged her. She didn't care what the topic was, or which side she took.

'The school's board eventually exempted her as a conscientious objector. The principal disqualified her from candidacy for school captain.

'Jane told me the principal said: 'You could go a long way. You may think you can take on the whole system by yourself, but there

127

will be a reaction. Pushing the boundaries like you do could get you into serious trouble.''

'She told him, 'I will not be treated as if who I am and what I want do not matter.''

I said to Jane, 'I can see now how you got to be so stroppy.'

'Be careful,' she said, pretending to menace.

Jane's skills of rhetoric and research outclassed everyone. She was born to debate and was proficient long before she studied law, became a barrister and was elected a city councillor. Her predisposition was not a recipe for domestic bliss. She was prickly and I learned to steer clear of contentious issues. When she got on her high horse she would argue as if the only thing that mattered was winning.

I also had to learn how Jane operated in other arenas. One day I called at her place to take her to a movie.

'We can't leave yet,' she said. 'Manfred is coming to collect his gear at 6.00 pm.'

'About time too,' I thought.

She had finished with him six months ago. Since he came back from the sea, he had stayed with friends.

'We'll be late. Do you have to be here when he comes?'

'Yes. I want to farewell him.'

They had been together for two years.

'Does he know we are going out this evening?'

'Yes. I told him.'

'Is he often late?'

'Yes, always.'

'We could be held up for hours.' I said, trying not to be gruff. It was 6.30 pm and the movie started at 7.00 pm.

'No. His things are packed and ready to go.'

'Well, he could want to talk to you. I don't have to be here. I am going to the movie. Come as soon as you can.'

I went off, leaving her. I had been looking forward to the movie with Jane but I wasn't going to dance attendance on Manfred. It sounded to me like she had wanted me there to prevent a drama with him. I didn't want any part in that.

I wasn't used to watching a movie alone. Jane never arrived. I missed having her tell me relationships that I hadn't picked up on and discussing it afterwards. I felt bad about going without her, but a date was a date. I phoned her later that evening.

'Did he turn up?'

'An hour late. He had trouble borrowing a car.'

'What time did he leave your place?'

'We talked for a couple of hours. How was the movie?'

'It was okay, but I missed you.'

'It serves you right. You could have been more supportive.'

'What, drop everything to wait on your ex-boyfriend?'

'If you cared about me, you would have noticed that I wanted you to be there when he came.'

'I thought I would be in the way. Why did you want me there?'

'So he would realise that we were over.'

I thought it would be best to appear contrite.

'I see. I'm sorry.'

'I'm sorry too. I should have explained.'

Sometimes an apology doesn't recover everything that has been lost. I was nonplussed that Jane was still so unknown to me. She would realise my unconditional support for her was an ideal; I was not perfect.

Manfred must have left the city because I didn't hear of him again.

CHAPTER 32

'The MC has to promote ethnic diversity,' Jane said. 'It will be a place where people go with kin to celebrate their culture or to discover others' cultures.'

I phoned around for an architect to plan the restoration of the IB and design the MC. None of the large firms wanted to oppose the Council.

'Sorry, we don't have anyone for that,' they said.

They feared that they would be punished by exclusion from other Government work, which was their bread and butter. State control in Roberta was not unlike in Stalin's Russia.

'Ask Colin Winkler,' they told us.

He was a renowned city architect, reputed to be wealthy, a renegade champion of aesthetic designs, whose work had been opposing the Government, rebel causes and representing those disgruntled people with enough means to defy the autocrats at the big end of town. He was just what we needed, but would we be able to afford him?

I called him and spoke about our MC proposal.

'You have a good case for saving the old building,' he said. 'We should meet.'

Two days later, Jane and I, wearing business suits, were hoisted steadily up the Winkler Building, a stylish modern skyscraper, in a paternoster lift. Paternosters had lost favour after several accidents in the 1900s, but the one at Winkler's was recent, made safe by computer-control.

When we reached the roof, we walked along a wire rope bridge suspended inside a huge aviary. The cavernous silence was pierced by bird calls. A lake glimmered far below us, its shallows teeming with flamingos. Around us nectar-sipping birds clambered from flower to flower in the tree foliage and hummingbirds the size of bumble bees zipped about. Above us vultures circled on the updraft from an aircon outlet.

A lanky man in a yellow suit met us.

'Flying feels good, doesn't it?' he said. 'Hello, I'm Colin Winkler. I wanted this design to soar.'

He ushered us into a meeting room where we sat at a round table.

'Tell me what you have in mind,' he said.

He listened attentively while Jane and I explained.

'I congratulate you,' he said when we had finished. 'Your MC concept is more attractive than a casino — except to financiers and the Provincial Government — who are the people that count. Entertainment is a riskier investment than gambling. Gamblers are induced by large prizes paid out a bit at a time. Your audiences will have to pay the full amount well in advance without much enticement.'

'Our prizes will be moments of high drama and epiphany,' said Jane. 'Word will get out. People will come.'

'Financiers could be sceptical about your ability to sustain a fresh theatrical repertoire,' Winkler said.

'I know an entertainments manager for a cruise-ships line,' Jane said. 'He could organise a steady supply of quality shows from overseas as well as nurturing a full programme of ethnic productions from local companies. We could poach him for a couple of million a year.'

'It's a good plan. Are you sure Council will give you the IB?'

'It is a site of cultural heritage and if they demolish it, we could take them to court.'

'A court case would cost heaps.'

'Legal costs would be paid by the loser,' I said.

'You can't count on winning against the Government,' he said. 'They would call it in from court and decide against you.'

'Then we must save the IB without going to court — by persuasion.'

'If you prepare a case for saving and leasing it, I can design for restoring and extending it. How much time do we have?'

Jane smiled. 'We have to submit the PDA in three weeks' time. Could you have a concept to show us by the end of next week?'

131

'I am expensive.'

'We would settle your account when we succeed,' said Jane.

'I will need some payment before that.'

'We are getting some donations.'

'I like what you're doing. I might be able to put in some money myself.'

'It is generous of you. Thank you.'

Going down, Jane high-fived me.

*

We had become known as The Three Scaffolds because Jane, Cutter and I kept the Council hanging. We worked separately at our ward offices, counselling residents and helping to solve their problems. We shared ideas but we avoided colluding with our voting. We were independents and proud of it.

'You three are a disgrace,' NLP members told us.

The Government was finding it difficult to hold their act together in the hung Council. Their impotence made a pleasant change from their former hubris.

Julie Dawson, the Opposition leader, was incensed that I wasn't voting with the Opposition.

'Doctor, your duty is to force an election,' she said. "People want a change of government.'

'I don't see it that way,' I said. 'I believe my duty is to get councillors attending to constituents' needs, instead of toeing lines dreamed up by unelected party boffins.'

'Voting on conscience wouldn't work. There would be chaos without the parties. There is no alternative to partisan government. If an election was held tomorrow, Jane might get back in but you and Cutter would be dumped.'

'I don't think so,' I said. 'Political parties are obsolete. People want a councillor who will represent them, not a party clone.'

'There has been party rule for over a century. That won't disappear overnight. Our party does represent them. Be sensible and work with us.'

Just then Martha Hubbard came along and joined in the conversation. Her duopoly with Dawson was evident in their rapport.

'Holding the balance in a hung Council is fine for you but creates uncertainty for the Executive,' the LM said. 'They need a predictable policy environment, which is what our bipartisan government provides.'

'The Executive is fossilised,' Jane said. 'Its job is to serve residents, not build an empire such as the one that assesses DAs.'

The party leaders looked at each other and walked away together. Their collusion was worrying because without real opposition, Council procedures were being breached with impunity.

*

Jane kept the MC alternative simmering by raising it in Council meetings.

'What are the Government's negotiations with Runyon Casinos?' she asked the LM at Question Time. 'Are they still confidential?'

There were groans of 'Give it a rest'.

'It is disgraceful that the Government has to be shamed into doing the job it was elected for,' said Jane.

'Nonsense. Sit down,' they jeered from the Government benches.

'Order,' said the Chairperson.

'The Lord Mayor assured us earlier that Runyon's casino in Alexandra could not be involved in crime,' said Jane. 'I have information from contacts in Toronto and Cape Town that Runyon Casinos have been involved in drug supply, prostitution, protection and extortion, the same as in Johannesburg. It is common knowledge that they use their influence with those governments to stop cases coming to court.'

The NLP members shouted, 'Rubbish. Sit down!'

'Order.'

'Madam Chairperson, the Provincial Government should tell the Council the nature of their dealings with Runyon's, so we can be assured no undue influence is being exerted here.'

Jeers from the NLP benches.

'Order. Councillor Kenwood be seated.'

133

As usual Jane was trading off adulation from those constituents who liked her opposition, with deprecation by those who thought she could serve them better by refraining from antagonising the Government. Her position was controversial, not for the first time.

CHAPTER 33

'We can object in the Planning Court that it is illegal to demolish a heritage-listed building. If we make the legal case, the court could overrule them.'

'We need a solicitor to prepare our case,' Jane said. 'Heritage is a legal specialisation.'

When I phoned around solicitors in the city, no-one wanted to oppose the Government over heritage.

'Miller and Frost might do it,' someone said. 'They are from out of town.'

They were interested and submitted a quote. It was hefty but they had a footnote: 'Our fees will be charged at a reduced hourly rate, acknowledging the significant public value of your proposal.'

I discussed it with Jane. No-one else had quoted and I asked them to start work.

A week later, they emailed me an invoice for prepayment of $6000.

I was surprised. *'Why have they sent it to me?'*

Jane was asleep. I emailed them back, telling them to resubmit it to Multicultural Centre Pty Ltd, the name on our bank account. I copied the email to Jane and thought no more about it. When she read it she was furious.

'We don't have that kind of money,' she yelled. 'I was counting on you to pay.'

'I don't know why you thought I would pay but you were wrong.'

'Your buck-passing will make them think they are not going to get anything from us,' said Jane. 'They won't start the pro-bono work unless we pay it.'

'I never agreed to cover their bills. If we divide it up between us, I'll pay my share.'

'You should have paid it and claimed it back afterwards.'

135

'Would I have got it?'

'What is wrong with you?' She was splendid, her eyes flashing. 'Of course you would — eventually. You should have *told me*, instead of going behind my back.'

'You were asleep.'

'You should have woken me up,' she shrieked.

'You are so cranky — I didn't want a fight.'

'And why do you think I'm cranky?' Her voice had a hard metallic edge.

''Because you have too much to do?'

'Exactly. I carry more than a fair share. You have let me down. You have betrayed my trust. I am very disappointed. I don't know whether I can continue with you. I need time apart ...'

I couldn't believe that she was calling us off.

'When can we talk?'

'Maybe in a couple of weeks. I don't know.'

She stormed out. I was devastated. My life revolved around Jane. She had suddenly shut me out and I was hurting. Sadly, I sent her the feasibility report I had prepared. She could add the architect's assessment and submit the PDA to Council herself. I was out of it.

It was a storm in a teacup and she was cutting me off without trying to reconcile our differences. Her behaviour seemed excessive, a side of her I hadn't seen before. Neither of us was much good at the pedestrian aspects of life. We were better at flying than walking.

On Friday, I went, as usual, to have dinner with Cutter, Tony and Sunita. Jane arrived with Barbie in tow and ignored me as she talked quietly with the others.

'I asked Barbie along,' Jane said, 'because she has been doing such a great job working on the concert acts with Sunita.'

She had told me about Barbie's thinking skills. Jane was helping her in her ambition to become a councillor.

'I'm glad you could come, Barbie,' said Cutter gallantly. 'I'll sit next to you here. Phillip, you can go next to Jane.'

'No thanks,' I said. 'I'll sit at the end. Tony, you can go next to Jane.'

'What is it with you two?' Cutter said.

'Ask Jane.'

'It's a private dispute,' said Jane querulously. 'Phillip has Let Us Down,'

'She imagines she is my mother,' I said. 'She is applying an inappropriate model to my behaviour.'

'What do you mean by that?' said Jane.

It was shaping up to be a row in public. I was angry with how she had cut me off. I turned away to Sunita and changed the subject.

'You and Barbie were great at our meeting with the performers on Sunday,' I said to Sunita, countering Jane's negativity.

'Thank you, Phillip. We have started working with several of the groups.'

'How's it going?'

'Good. We have enough acts to fill the programme.'

'Phillip, why did you say I was inappropriate?' Jane interrupted.

'Well, you seem to have let yourself go completely,' I said.

'Fuck you.'

It was an unfriendly rejoinder from an erstwhile partner. At least she was speaking to me.

'Charming,' I said.

'She hasn't let herself go,' Sunita said. 'You have.'

'She thinks she is mother of our 'family' and my loyalty requires I donate my savings.'

'You are too selfish to be in a family, Phillip,' said Sunita.

It was possibly true and it stung.

'I don't want to be a member of any family that won't let me do what I want with my money.'

'You wouldn't think of sharing your money, Doctor,' said Sunita nastily.

I had thought of it, but having more than others didn't oblige me to pay a larger share.

'You wouldn't think of paying your share,' I said with equal nastiness.

'Stop it,' said Jane. 'We will pay them somehow.'

'How much is it?' said Tony.

'Six thousand.'

'Cripes! What have they done, rebuilt the place?'

137

Jane said: 'They have been researching an objection on heritage grounds.'

'Do we need that?' said Sunita as if we might not.

'I think so,' Jane said.

'Okay, we need it,' said Sunita.

'You think of everything, Jane,' said Tony sardonically. 'You are my ideal woman.'

'I will take that as a compliment,' said Jane, highlighting Tony's homosexuality. 'I am trying to get us to play as a team.'

'Are we a Tour de France team that will coset Jane to success?' asked Tony.

'No,' said Jane. 'We're a team: One for all and all for one.'

'You are the captain,' I said to Jane.

'It sounds as though you could have problems with that.'

'No. It's all good,' I said. 'But you seem to have some strange ideas about what a player can and cannot do.'

Jane looked around. Everyone was watching us.

'Phillip, can we go outside?'

I followed her out into the street, which was deserted.

CHAPTER 34

'What's your problem?' Jane said, folding her arms.

'Why should I have to pay the solicitor?' I asked.

She put her hands on her hips and rounded on me, spitting out the words fast.

'They did what you wanted.'

'What the group wanted.'

'No. You took it upon yourself!'

'For the group,' I said. 'I ordered it on behalf of the group. You are trapping me. You can't use me as a walking wallet. Just because I have some cash doesn't mean I have to be the one who pays.'

She came at me fangs bared, guns blazing.

'You knew very well that we were expecting you to pay.'

Her enmity frightened me.

'I did not know it,' I rebutted. 'You were involved in hiring them. You never said I alone would be paying. I never agreed to pay.'

This aroused in her even more vitriol. Her eyes bored into me, her perfect teeth fashioned the words that her lips sprayed at me.

'Don't try to wriggle out of it. You hired them without asking us, so it is *you* who are liable!'

She was screaming and I figured she might injure her larynx. Her voice would have cut glass. The street was deserted but people were peering out from windows.

I regretted having provoked this altercation. I had not reckoned with Jane's determination to distance herself from me. For her it was technical rather than personal. She was intent on winning the argument. I was wondering if there was a way of losing with dignity.

'I assumed I was acting for the group,' I admitted. 'Someone had to hire them. I thought I was doing it for all of us.'

'You were not,' she said. 'Why do you think the solicitor sent the bill to you instead of to the group?'

'I don't know. It was their mistake.'

'You hadn't told them otherwise.'

Now Jane went on the attack.

'I think you had intended to pay but got cold feet when you saw the size of the bill.'

This was underhand. She wanted nothing less than to win, treating me harshly as if I was an enemy. For her it was zero sum — she had to win.

'That's not true,' I said reasonably. 'I resent you accusing me of deception. I expected the group to pay. Why else would I return the bill to sender with instructions to forward it to our corporate address?'

'Reiterating something you have done doesn't vindicate you,' she said. 'You were wrong to do it.'

No holds were barred.

'Rejecting my premise that I acted for the group doesn't make *you* right,' I replied. 'You are trying to bully me into paying by pretending I acted alone.'

She raised her voice again.

'I did not *pretend*: you most certainly did act alone,' she said, her eyes wide. 'You didn't have even part of an agreement with the group. It is not bullying to tell it the way it is; nor is it a trap: it is a hole you have dug yourself into, mate.'

'I trusted that the group would accept responsibility.'

'Action groups are bottom-up and commitments are made in full view of all group members.'

'Did you warn me? It seems like I accidentally fell over an authority cliff you didn't warn me about. Why should I be held responsible?'

'You behaved like an idiot and now you expect me to rescue you.'

'I don't need to be rescued. I can walk away.'

'We could take you to court.'

'Would you deny under oath that I could have been acting for the group?'

She would lose in court and she knew it.

She thought for a moment. 'This is ridiculous. I can get the group to pay, but it will take time. We can raise the money at our concert.'

'Thank you.'

'Did you really mean it when you accused me of trapping you?'

'I think it happened inadvertently. You were thinking about something else.'

'Then you will retract that I tried to trap you?'

'Yes. I retract — I don't think that you were ever pretending anything. Shit happens.'

'That's cleared up then. We won't be going up that particular shit creek again.'

'Are we friends again?' I asked.

'Why not?' She turned to face me. 'Sorry. I mean yes.' She put her arms around my neck and kissed me. 'You're back.'

'You're a crazy barrister,' I said.

'You're a crazy planner.'

I liked everything about her, from her fiery screeching to her cute little toes.

'This could become love,' I thought.

We went inside. Cutter and Barbie were talking quietly, while Sunita and Tony were telling queer jokes. We sat and listened to them.

*

Jane and I fitted together like two Lego blocks. We had argued but in the end we had reached agreement. The money incident had opened my eyes to Jane the barrister. For her, an argument was an opportunity to strut her stuff. She held nothing back. It was part of her brinkmanship to fight hard — and if need be, dirty. What mattered to her was winning.

She was the anchor in my life and enabled me to steadily accomplish a great deal of work. I was confident that our PDA would win against the casino. I was achieving something worthwhile.

'Selfie!' said Barbie, holding up her camera. 'Get in here you lot.'

We clustered together in zany poses.

CHAPTER 35

We were on our way to Jane's parents' house. I had not yet met them and was feeling apprehensive. I imagined they would think I was too ordinary for Jane.

A gibbous moon hung outside the train window. Its eccentricity reminded me of our unbalanced relationship. Jane had more inertia than me and more tendency to keep on doing what she was already doing. She had greater momentum and to compromise with her I had to give more than her ground. We couldn't meet halfway because she was more set in her ways than I was.

'I love the way you understand what is important to me,' she said. 'I have to visit my parents regularly.'

'I love it that you are prepared to move away from your commitments to allow me to be myself,' I said. I had persuaded her to keep the visit down to one night.

'Why are you looking so glum?' she asked.

'I'm not.'

'Someone is wishing he could be somewhere else.'

'Back off, will you?' I said.

Sometimes I retreated into my shell, becoming grim, cold and silent. We had left Sunita, Barbie, Tony and Cutter to hold a dress rehearsal for the concert. By taking the weekend off, we would not see the acts until the performance and I was concerned that the staging would be lackadaisical and amateurish. I had wanted the orchestra and choir to have an additional rehearsal together.

'I can read you like an open book,' Jane said. 'You are worrying about the concert. There is nothing we can do. So sit back and enjoy yourself.'

Her parents' architect-designed house was perched on a cliff overlooking the ocean. There were rooms on several levels, connected by a winding internal stairway and a lift. Every bedroom had an ensuite, jacuzzi or sauna and there was a large studio flanked by modern statuary. We could be as public or private as we wanted.

We were in time for Saturday lunch — paella made with local shellfish, prepared by their live-in housekeepers, a Spanish couple.

As we ate together the sea below us stretched away to an empty horizon. Jennifer had retired from a public service position in education. Joe, her father was a retired science teacher. Trying for a topic that we could all discuss, I asked, 'How important is a student's home life for their success?'

No-one answered. Maybe my question was too dumb for them.

'What do you think, Phillip?' asked Jennifer.

I didn't want to answer my own question. 'It all depends on the individual. I heard that Jane learned her debating skills at home, so for her it was important.'

'We encouraged her to use her reasoning ability rather than her feminine wiles,' Joseph said.

'She uses both on the Council,' I said. 'The male councillors are as much under her spell as I am. But I know what you mean — she doesn't expect any concessions for her gender.'

We talked about how the Kenwood household had operated when Jane lived at home. Her say was equal with an adult's and she was able to get her own way by logic and rhetoric.

'She was always very creative,' said Jenny. 'She liked performing and presenting ideas in inventive ways. She had leading roles in school plays.'

'She sometimes got into trouble for revving up the characters she played too much,' said Joseph.

'I like to emote audiences,' Jane said.

At university, she did a double degree in law and drama.

'Her work on the Council has gained her a loyal following,' I said.

'Her ability to observe herself is unusually good,' said Jennifer. 'Self-aware people are often self-conscious and shun the limelight, but Jane has out-of-body perception that enables her to be original and comic. She is extroverted, a clown, adventurous, takes risks and is comfortable with being different.'

'She would have been better off staying at the bar,' said Joseph. 'There is more scope for putting on a performance there.'

'I wish she would keep her head down and stay out of trouble,' said Jennifer. 'Getting thrown out of Council meetings is poor form.'

'It was for opposing the Government's illegal behaviour,' I said. 'I am proud of her.'

'Being a city councillor must be rather dull for you compared with forensic work,' Joseph said.

'Council work is about as exciting as an archaeological dig except for the shenanigans of a certain young lady. When she decides to stick it to the Government, it is the liveliest show in town.'

Her mother smiled thinly. 'She used to be a loyal NLP supporter,' she said with regret.

'They say that ex-drinkers are the most ardent wowsers.'

'Jane tells me that you have been expelled from the NLP.'

'Yes, but I still vote with them sometimes.'

Although her parents disapproved of Jane's tactics, they were solidly behind her stand against the parties.

They hadn't known we were coming and had arranged to go out on Saturday evening. When they left us alone, Jane towed me into the kitchen and began undressing me.

'What are you doing?'

'I've always wanted to make love on the kitchen table,' she said, clearing away dishes and condiments.

I was aghast. It seemed so disrespectful. In other people's territory I am cautious.

'Why not?' she said. 'Come on!'

I was worried that the table legs would loosen up and her parents would notice. As it turned out, they didn't mention it. Jane enjoyed the fantasy.

The next evening we went back on the train in a sleeping compartment.

When we kissed, her mouth was changed, less reluctant, more determined, wanting sincerity.

'I want only you and all of you. I am obsessed with you,' I said.

She hugged me closely.

'Don't take it the wrong way,' I said. 'I'm not your submissive.'
'I don't want you to be,' she said.
I knew it was too early to live with her, but I could hope.
'What are we going to do?' I said.
She kissed me passionately.
We stripped off and lay down together. The rhythmical rocking of the train seemed urgent. We made love. Afterwards, I was gasping.
'I don't know.' She traced my nose with her finger.
'Don't know what?'
'What we are going to do,' she said.
'Does it matter?'
'No, not now.'
The train rattled and bounced through a switchyard and we were silent.
She slept then. We had each other equally and that was enough.
I closed my eyes.
In the difficult days after, this time together was my idyll.

CHAPTER 36

Our fundraising concert was held on a Saturday evening in the city's basketball arena with an audience of 8000. There were 15 items of music, dance, drama and comedy. The proceeds paid for the architect and solicitor up to date.

But we needed more money.

'The time to knock on doors is when funding is the only hold-up,' Jane said. 'First we have to get the IB site.'

'They will want our funding secured first.'

'What about public donations?'

'How much do we have so far?'

'About half a mill.'

'It's a start. We need 20.'

'If we can develop a profitable scheme, financiers will beat a path to our door.'

'Our entertainments will have the allure of culture and be popular even if tickets are expensive.'

Jane had a bigger picture. 'Our prices have to undercut the competition. If we keep prices down and entertain a mass market we can get public funding and government-backed loans.'

On the next weekend after the concert, Jane and I went for our first visit with my parents. My mother, Sigrid, had been a psychiatrist and my father, Leon, had been an engineer. He had invented a syringe dispenser for twin-pack epoxy glue. It was so trivial I was embarrassed for him but he didn't seem to mind.

'For years people dreamed of dispensing two-part glues ready to mix and this container lets them do it,' he said.

'Now they're stuck with it,' I said. It was a family joke.

They had retired to a small island off the coast. We left the car on the mainland and took the ferry. They met us and drove us to their beach house beside a deserted sandy shore.

I had never taken a girl home before. Jane and my father got on like a house on fire.

'I've read in the news about you being sent out from Council meetings,' he said.

'I do other things as well,' she said.

'I expect the Government wants to have everything all its own way.'

'They do. They won't let me have a say.'

'You do right to oppose them,' he said. 'We don't want a dictator.'

'Too late. We already have one.'

My mother checked out Jane's psyche with the determination of a garage mechanic inspecting roadworthiness. She tended to be critical and I savoured her approval.

'Jane is pretty and intelligent,' she said. 'So was Connie. I hope you get on better this time.'

A neighbour called around, inviting us to join in a raid on an absent neighbour's trees that dripped with mangoes. All we had to do was let ourselves in through the front gate and pick them.

'Did he invite us to help ourselves?' I asked.

'No, he probably forgot. But he won't be back for several weeks and they would spoil.'

The neighbours were getting together a raiding party.

'Are you two coming?' they asked us.

It seemed like thieving and it was a dilemma for me, but Jane was all for it.

'Birds raid in flocks too,' she said. 'If we went alone, we could get into trouble.'

We went with the crowd and came away with four buckets filled with luscious mangoes.

That evening at dinner Leon said to Jane, 'Phillip tells me you were elected as an independent.'

'That's right.'

'I admire your pluck. It must be difficult competing with political parties.'

She shrugged modestly. 'Thank you. They are horrible. Character assassination is only part of it. Dirty Tricks is their game.'

'Well, it is to your credit that you were elected.'

'Voters were disaffected from the parties,' she said in her self-effacing way.

'Only in your ward,' I said.

'Jane must have something that the others don't,' Sigrid said.

'She performs well for her residents,' I said.

'You make me sound like a trained seal.'

'You put the Government on its mettle,' I said. 'Voters like that. Dad, Mum, you must come to a Council meeting and see Jane in action.'

'We will, son, next time we come into the city,' said Leon.

I was pleased that they liked her. But when we were going to bed, we found my mother had prepared separate rooms for us.

'We sleep together, don't we?' I said to Jane.

'What will your parents think?'

'They will remember I'm 38.'

Her skin was warm and smooth under the duvet as we held and touched. It was 2 am before we went to sleep. Dawn was breaking when we awoke and made love again.

At breakfast my mother poured orange juice and said, 'Did you two have intercourse last night?'

Jane almost choked on her toast. My mother was always very direct.

'Yes, Mother,' I replied, wondering what was coming next.

'Okay, that explains it. I thought the dog might have had fleas again. There was a sort of worrying and whimpering noise. It went on and on.'

'That was Jane,' I said.

'Very funny, Phillip,' Jane said. 'You know it was you. '

'Some places are hard to get to.'

We all laughed.

'I know where I'm sleeping tonight,' said Jane, 'in the hammock on the verandah.'

It was a two-person hammock on a balcony that was private.

'Is bed too boring?' I asked.

'A hammock is more romantic.'

'You don't imagine having sex in it, do you?'

'Why not?'

'Sex in a hammock is a joke.'

'Where's your sense of adventure?'

Jane liked variety in all things. I realised sex with her would never have a predictable occasion, location and position.

'We could be injured,' I said.

'Nothing ventured ...'

'If one of us gets hurt, you will have to explain to my parents.'

'No way. They're your parents.'

We made love in the hammock. It required more effort than usual. For Jane nothing was sacred.

Next day, on the way back, Jane and I leaned on the gunwales of the ferry and watched the water sliding past. It was peaceful.

'The hammock was not impossible, was it?' she said.

'Shall we stop making love in bed and boring you?' I asked cagily.

She thought about it. 'That is a fallacy: post hoc propter hoc,' she said. 'The premise that I am bored in bed is false. I'm not answering.'

We didn't talk for a while.

'I never want to go back to the city,' I said.

'Perhaps one day you won't have to. Could you live at the coast permanently?'

'I could with you,' I said.

'Hmm. We'll see.'

She didn't reject the idea.

CHAPTER 37

Preparing a PDA was a daunting task for anyone. In my shoes you would want to create plans for a safe, sound and spectacular development. You would have had to overcome the design challenge and the Government's opposition. You would have put in all the time and energy you had, but progress would have been slow.

Working frantically, you would have gone without rest until your immune system said 'I am going to stop you doing this'. Then you would have gone under with a cold and a cough, your body painfully sore and immobilised. You would have despaired about missing the deadline. But the others would have taken over and got the PDA ready for you to submit when you recovered.

*

I became unwell and I was very grateful to the others for completing the PDA.

'I feel so ashamed that I let it get to me,' I said to Jane. 'Thank God it's finished.'

'It wasn't your fault, Phillip. It was ridiculous having to fill in all those forms merely for a preliminary application. No-one could have done it better than you. You had done most of the work and all we had to do was put on a contents page and wrap it up.'

On deadline Tuesday, I was at City Hall before the committee meeting. I sat alone at the board table, filling in the final form before I submitted the PDA.

'You bastards,' I muttered when I came to an instruction requiring an authenticated copy of either my driving licence or passport.

'Who are bastards?' asked Grant Fenwick as he walked in. 'How's your MC going?'

I had regularly updated committee members to get them interested in the progress of our PDA.

'Okay,' I said, not wanting him to see my frustration.

I rushed outside to the photocopier and copied both sides of my driving licence. Shelly, who was a Commissioner of Declarations, authenticated the copies.

I stapled them to the back page of the PDA.

'Here you are,' I said, handing the 600-page document to Munster.

I sat back, able to relax at last. We had achieved something important. I felt like a worthwhile person again.

'Hmmph,' Munster said, hiding her surprise that we had met her deadline. She flicked through it. 'It hasn't got funding,' she objected.

My heart sank. Munster was probably under instruction from the NLP to refuse it if the development lacked funding. The committee could reject it.

'It doesn't have to have funding at this stage,' I said, bluffing. 'Until we have the chicken of approval, we won't be able to get a funding egg.'

'Most developers get their funding first.'

'We can't. I can get a letter from a financier saying that they will lend to us conditional upon the PDA being accepted.'

'Why do your lenders need our approval? It's not usual.'

'Because we don't own the site.'

I was bluffing again. Some developments obtained finance before the location was finalised.

'Hmmph,' Munster said again. 'We now have yours and Runyon's PDAs. We will consider them together next week. I'll get copies made for everyone.'

Phew! Munster had accepted it.

We went on to other business.

Munster had wanted to block acceptance of our PDA, but the Premier had set a submission date and because we were on time they couldn't refuse it. They couldn't insist on definite funding of a MC and keep Runyon's proposal alive at the same time. If they could muster a majority they could reject the MC.

It was a tense situation. I sensed another threat and my unease increased.

CHAPTER 38

Barbie and I had arranged to meet the woman who would be found in concrete at a city centre bar. Cutter, Tony and Sunita turned up a few minutes later. We were meeting to celebrate submitting the PDA earlier that week.

We chatted for a while.

'Where shall we eat?' Jane asked, finishing her drink.

'How about an all-you-can-eat joint?' said Cutter.

Cutter was large and always hungry.

'Where light eaters like me will subsidise you,' said Sunita.

'It is not my fault that you are a lightweight, Sunita,' he said.

She made a face at him.

'How about a curry house?' Jane said.

The six of us strolled to the city centre restaurant precinct. It was a fine evening and already dark. Jane walked beside me, holding my arm, swinging along with her catwalk gait on high heels. She exuded celebrity glamour. People's heads turned and they backed up into doorways to get a better view, to gawp at her.

'Hello, Jane!' they called.

She smiled and waved back. She nurtured her public profile to get re-elected and she made sure she was often in the news. I was less well known and was there as her escort and minder, visibly present but inconspicuous.

Sunita was making an effort to keep up, shuffling along with small steps, her body rounded by meditation, chatting with Barbie. Tony skipped along beside them in a long-sleeved white shirt and gingham pants, gesticulating animatedly.

Cutter, large and uncoordinated, ambled along beside me. After years spent taxi-driving, walking was a challenge for him. He was wearing a black-and-white-checked shirt, blue jeans tucked into calf-length brown leather cowboy boots and a black suede jacket.

We reached Singh's Curry House and paused outside.

'Here?' Sunita asked Jane.

She looked at me. They knew I was a fussy eater.

'I prefer Patel's.'

It was further along.

"The menus and prices are the same,' said Sunita.

'Can we have a buffet,' said Cutter, 'or go somewhere with a smorgasbord, or a bistro, or a steakhouse?'

'No,' said Jane. 'Phillip prefers Patel's. We're almost there.'

She continued walking. We followed her to Patel's and went inside.

Each wall had a row of large murals like windows, opening on to an Indian landscape with turbaned nobles riding on elephants in a maharajah's court procession.

We were shown to a table. Light shone weakly from tasselled linen shades.

'Why do you prefer Patel's?' Jane asked me.

'Just a habit.'

'Lack of imagination,' said Sunita.

Her snide remark annoyed me.

'I only change when there is a good reason to,' I said to her. 'You like change because your life is so boring.'

'Fuck you, Phillip.'

Sunita always played serves and rallies with me.

'Do people who go to Patel's ever try Singh's?' Tony asked. 'How weird is Phillip?'

'Very,' said Sunita.

'Probably not,' said Jane. 'Foodies don't swing like voters. Most people do make the same choices over and over again. Like a person who always votes for the same political party.'

'Why not if there isn't any difference?' I said.

'Patel and Singh compete, don't they?'

'Far from it,' said Jane. 'Think duopoly. Messrs Patel and Singh let people think they are in competition, but they're not. They copy each other.'

'Their menus are the same,' Cutter said.

'Perhaps they share a kitchen,' said Tony

'Perhaps they get precooked meals from the same supplier,' said Sunita.

'Perhaps they have the same owner or manager,' I said. 'Why would they risk full-on competition? Duopoly is more profitable.'

'Like the NLP and SLP,' Cutter said, joining in the discussion. 'Their competition is faked.'

'They stage ritual verbal conflict,' Jane said. 'The Government has a majority and always wins while the Opposition always loses.'

'Perhaps the two sides are secretly in coalition,' said Cutter.

'In collusion,' Jane said, 'they are certainly not adversaries like the philosopher Hegel wanted in his dialectical materialism. He wanted informed debate and synthesis of policy improvements.'

'If the parties choose to work together, isn't that their right?' Tony said.

'Not under the Westminster System. They are supposed to be adversaries. Our debates are a sham. The executive has cornered the information, the experts and the simulation models. The pollies wing it by compromising and converging.'

'Why don't they merge? If Patel's merged with Singh's, wouldn't they be able to make more money?' Cutter said.

'Maybe not,' said Jane. 'The parties' marketing is already merged with competition on certain topics only.'

'The NLP and SLP offer the same shit curry,' said Sunita.

'Too bad if you don't like curry,' Cutter said, 'because curry is all there is.'

'A diet of curry,' said Sunita. 'Yuck.'

'Curry' is all that the main political parties have on their agendas. There is endless kicking around of mindless political footballs,' said Jane. 'If they had issues people cared about, parties would have to really compete.'

'They won't risk that because they might lose. They stick to what they know: curry.'

'Curry is bipartisan fare,' said Tony, 'for people without taste.'

'What if an independent restaurant opened with different food?'

'Most people would never hear about it,' said Jane. 'Independents can't afford advertising. Indie reps are the Davids who wrestle against a tag team of twin Goliaths.'

While we talked, the tables near us had filled.

Jane called the waiter over. 'Could we change to that table over there, please?'

She indicated a table on the other side of the room.

As we moved, I asked Jane, 'Why are we changing tables?'

Jane looked around and lowered her voice. 'We could be overheard or bugged,' she said.

'Who would hear us?'

'Almost everybody. Our talk could be in tomorrow's news.'

CHAPTER 39

Jane was on my left, with Cutter on my right. Across the table were Sunita, Tony and Barbie.

'Would you bring a couple of bottles of house wine, a red and a white,' Cutter said to the waiter. 'Also some pappadums.'

'Just tell me one thing,' I said to Jane, 'if political parties have so little to offer, why do people vote for them?'

'People like to connect in a group,' she said. 'In the Bible, Matthew says, *'Unto him that hath it shall be given.'* People sometimes gather around the nucleus of a political party and it snowballs.'

'Perhaps people huddle together in a party like birds fly in a flock, so they won't be isolated, alone and vulnerable to predators.'

'A party can also go on the offensive, like a gang of bullies.'

'When you follow a party, it takes over, not just the issues you want it to, but every issue, even when your view differs widely,' Sunita said. 'Joining a party gives up your individuality.'

Jane sipped from her glass and said, 'Democracy respects individual rights. Parties stop us having true democracy.'

'Before you totally dump on the parties,' said Tony, 'remember that politicians have always grouped into parties. Giving allegiance to a political party is practical. Members have a right to belong to a political party with kindred spirits, so their views can be considered without giving up too much of their time.'

'It has been a right in the past. Voting is an old-fashioned way of deciding matters by 'might is right' but now the law, reasoning and science are better methods of solving problems. People used to have the right to settle their differences by duelling, but now they have legal recourse it is obsolete. Voting for a party is a grab for power and conscience voting is more democratic.'

'Party voting allows the majority viewpoint to rule.'

'Just because a majority gets the votes doesn't make their view right. Why should a party's view decide every issue? The majority is not identical clones with a single world view. Voters want policy alternatives from all the parties to be considered. They need a representative who compares the alternatives, informs his or her constituents and adopts the majority view on each issue.'

'Parties dominate over constituents' interests. It is undemocratic.'

The waiter poured wine around the table.

'Jane's right,' I said, ignoring Tony's point. 'Joining a party gives up your rights.'

'Political parties weren't allowed in parliament until Edmund Burke, in about 1790, changed elected members from delegates who represented voters into free agents. It was euphemistically called 'representative democracy' but it ended a politician's obligation to represent those who had voted for him or her.'

'There isn't much democracy either. We get fewer than half of 15 democratic rights.'

'Why are we so undemocratic?' asked Sunita.

'The public is being hoodwinked by the parties,' I said. 'They have self-seeking agendas and the public good is a much lower priority.'

'But to get re-elected, don't they have to perform?'

'No. Voters are unable to distinguish good performance from bad. Government is not transparent. Elections are absurd.'

'They are better than nothing. At least we don't have a dictator.'

'But we do ... a bipartisan dictatorship.'

*

A couple threaded their way across the restaurant and sat at a table within earshot. They did not seem to be listening to us and I forgot them.

The waiter brought water and menus.

Jane said, 'How about if we each choose a main and a second preference ...'

She paused as an Indian man in a suit came to the table.

157

'Hello, I'm the owner,' he said to Jane. 'Is everything satisfactory?'

'We're fine, thank you, Mr Patel,' she said, 'but what happened to your menu? There used to be duck and fish.'

'Pressure of costs. I have added more of the most popular dishes.'

'If you don't have the dishes we like, we will go somewhere else.'

'Singh's menu is the same as mine,' Patel said, shrugging.

'Why don't you offer some dishes that Singh's don't have?' I asked.

'I don't need to,' he said as if it was none of my business. 'We get enough customers. Enjoy your meal.' He left.

'We won't be able to curry favour with him,' I said.

'Getting fewer choices isn't funny,' Tony said. He was a staunch libertarian.

'What Patel and Singh do is perfectly legal,' said Cutter.

He had a libertarian side too.

'Duopolies are corrupt,' I said. 'The way the NLP and SLP have carved up the Council is disgusting.'

'It is the political parties that have brought our democracy to its bipartisan knees. They have made it into a virtual two-horse race and it's rigged,' I said.

'Oh, you cynical boy,' said Tony condescendingly. His nose was turned to one side, giving his face a piratical and sardonic look. 'Of course it isn't rigged. Were you an unhappy child?'

'Most of the time the parties are like two cyclists duelling at a velodrome. They follow each other around, swapping the lead,' I said. 'They only race the last bit, before the ballot.'

'Party members compete as a team,' said Cutter. 'In the Tour de France, teams pit their combined nous against others'. It is the team's infighting ability that counts more than the ability of any individual member.'

'People want a good team in government, not superstars.'

'They want team players able to work with others of all persuasions, not sectarian zealots.'

'Are there any governments that do not have political parties?' Tony said.

'Yes, in some Swiss cantons they decide matters at public meetings by a count of raised arms. Many Middle Eastern and small Island nations are non-partisan,' said Jane. 'Louisiana's government and Toronto City Council are non-partisan. In Canada and Hong Kong, they have not had party affiliations named on the ballot paper and have voted according to candidates' merits.'

'Is Toronto well governed?' Tony asked.

'I've heard it's a cool place,' said Barbie.

'Ha-ha. What about Louisiana?' he said.

'They don't let problems swamp them down there.'

We laughed and studied the menu in silence.

Presently Jane said, 'Like the political agenda, Patel's menu has been pruned down to essentials, the same as Singh's. The menu comprises lowest common denominators. Each offers only one soup — soup of the day. You can live on it but it tastes like shit.'

'Voters want more,' I said.

'That's a good twist,' said Sunita.

'Let's order our food as democratically as we can,' Jane said. 'We can order one dish each.'

'A problem is,' I said, 'in any group there are people who get more than their fair share.'

'Is that aimed at me?' said Cutter.

'No. You can't help being greedy, Cutter,' I said. 'Your share can be larger.'

'I don't eat much and I don't mind paying equally,' Sunita said.

'Thank you, Sunita,' said Cutter. 'How about a banquet for six?'

'A banquet is too much food for me and too expensive,' said Jane. 'But I don't mind if Cutter has his own banquet and pays the same as us. After all, it's not his fault he is such a big lug.'

'I'm with Jane. Sharing is cool — eating together is a communion,' said Sunita. 'We don't all have to have the same. We can create our own banquet. Cutter can have the leftovers.'

'I am not a dog,' said Cutter.

'You are more like a waste disposal unit,' I said.

'Full of shit,' said Sunita.

'You should order sweet and sour,' Cutter said to Sunita, 'without any sour because you already have it in spades.'

159

She made a face at him.

'Sunita wants to share and I don't,' I said, as if I was the reasonable one.

'You can take yours and eat it by yourself, like a selfish child,' said Sunita.

'At least I won't be foisting my tastes on other people,' I said.

'We want you to keep your strange tastes to yourself, Phillip.'

'Okay, you two,' said Jane. 'Phillip can keep his food separate if he wants to.'

'Thank you.'

'Sharing is cool,' Sunita said. 'Life would be lonely without sharing. We can share and divide up the bill equally.'

'Hang on,' I said. 'Why equally?'

'Why not?'

'There doesn't have to be parity.'

'For convenience.'

'Some people could be inconvenienced by having to pay for others' extravagances. I think we should each pay for our own.'

'Even when others eat some?'

'Yes. People can treat us if they want. The only fair way is to pay for what we order. We can pay separately — it isn't a problem.'

'We could sit at individual tables too, Phillip. You are weird.'

'Thank you for recognising my individuality.'

'We can pool our food and Phillip can pay for his separately,' Jane said.

'I am hungry,' said Tony. 'Why don't we order?'

CHAPTER 40

Jane called the waiter over. She helped him take our orders with her usual verve. We all chose different dishes.

'This is like a conscience vote,' said Jane. 'A party has its members toe a line set by the leadership. Each gets the same, whether they like it or not.'

'They don't have the resilience to stand alone.'

The waiter collected the menus.

'Isn't it fairest to get the same as everyone else?' I asked.

'Parity is seldom fair,' said Jane. 'The parties are obsessed with parity. They demand every ward gets the same, even those that contribute more, don't need whatever it is as much, or want something different. Every ward is a different situation. People should be able to choose how to spend their share of the budget, or to save up for larger items.'

'If councillors were all independents, there would be chaos,' said Tony. 'They wouldn't work together.'

'That is the straw man put up by party people who voters would not select on personal merit ...'

'... and too lazy to form their own opinions.'

'Would independent councillors be able to work together?' asked Tony.

'Yes, if it was their job to,' Jane said.

The waiter brought our food. We ordered more wine and began eating.

'Can we change local government without changing the Constitution?' Cutter asked.

'There is nothing in the Constitution about local government,' replied Jane. 'We don't even need to change the Local Government Act. Political parties aren't mentioned. Councillors are able to vote from their consciences right now.'

161

'The parties would call it anarchy,' said Sunita, 'because their self-serving role would be ended. How about sharing some of the lamb korma, Phillip?'

Sunita knew how to annoy me. The meat chunks had the texture and taste of green cheese. Delicious.

Cutter took me aside from the others.

'Jane is all steamed up about the parties, isn't she?' Cutter said.

'Yes, quite rightly so.'

'Will she be able to change anything?' he asked.

'If she was elected LM she could,' I said. 'She's probably the best-known councillor after Martha Hubbard.'

In Alexandra the LM was elected by a majority of all voters.

'Without money for advertising, Jane wouldn't stand a chance,' Cutter said.

'Perhaps there is some way of bringing her qualifications for the Lord Mayorship into public awareness,' I said.

'People have heard of her as a renegade. She needs a more positive image.'

'She could campaign to improve democracy,' he said.

'Do you think the party leaders regard Jane as a threat?'

'Martha Hubbard probably has nightmares about her,' said Cutter.

'Could Jane go too far?'

'She doesn't have money or authority to do much other than complain,' Cutter said.

'Could she stage a coup?' I asked with a laugh.

Cutter took it seriously.

'She could bring on a vote of no-confidence and cause an election.'

'She could come out openly against the parties,' said Sunita, joining in.

I looked around and saw Jane was talking with Tony and Barbie.

'If she did, it would open up a can of worms,' I said. 'It is not only Alexandra Council that would be wriggling — but politicians in the provincial and federal governments would be too. Her campaign would crash in slow motion into the NLP and SLP establishments, polarising a split between the party faithful and populists, like the split in Russia before the Revolution.'

'What happened?' asked Cutter.

'Lenin's more idealistic Bolsheviks ousted the milder Mensheviks, who wanted a people's democracy similar to Jane's.'

'That's not encouraging.'

'Times have changed. Jane could succeed now,' I said. 'Voters are on a collision course with the establishment.'

'How soon can Jane make it happen?'

I beckoned to Tony to join us.

'Tony, you see it from outside,' I said. 'What do people think about the Council being hung?'

'They think it's a petty squabble between the parties and they want it sorted.'

'Do they know that Jane, Cutter and I are sitting on the fence?'

'They have watched Jane fighting the parties,' said Sunita. 'They think you and Cutter are following her lead. They see you as Jane-clones trying to lever a hung parliament.'

'The parties will find a way of stopping you,' said Sunita. 'They are ruthless.'

'What would they want Hubbard to do about it?'

'NLP voters are concerned that Hubbard is losing control,' he said. 'They like it that she's holding on but they want a return to naked capitalism.'

'She may be getting desperate,' Jane said.

'Do you think she realises we want the demise of the NLP and SLP?' I asked.

'She may suspect it. She has fought her way up the party hierarchy and won't let us sideline her without a fight.'

While we had been talking, Cutter had finished off the food.

'In other words, Doctor, the politicians we have now are incapable of representing us and the sooner we replace them the better,' said Sunita.

'That's it in a nutshell,' I said.

'Why don't you form a political party, so I can work as a volunteer,' Sunita said to Jane.

'Absolutely not,' said Jane. 'An independence party is an oxymoron.'

'But we are all with you in wanting to stop the political parties, aren't we?' said Sunita, looking around. We nodded.

'I hope our talk here has not been recorded by the provincial police,' said Cutter. 'They have locked up people for less.'

'I am not making an incendiary speech here,' said Jane. 'I am not organising an insurrection.'

I looked around the restaurant. Most of the tables were in use. There could be sensors in the wall hangings, in the table equipment, concealed in nearby diners' clothes or focused on us from a distance.

'We will act independently. That's not illegal.'

'In Alexandra, anything that goes on against the Government can be suppressed.' Jane said. 'What worries me is that Roberta has become a totalitarian state. Our lawmakers have become law breakers.'

'What laws?'

'Corruption, collusion and deception.'

'Collusion between political parties is not illegal,' said Tony. 'There is a fine line between the collaboration that philosopher Hegel sought between adversaries to create good policies and the duopoly of bipartisanship.'

The waiter took our plates away.

Jane was beginning to look bleary. Her eyes were pink and unfocused.

'I've had enough wine,' I said. 'Anyone for coffee?'

They brought the bill and we each paid for what we had ordered.

'I hope everyone got what they wanted,' Jane said.

'There was opportunity with the dishes. Parity of place and time may not have suited everyone,' I said, looking at Cutter, 'but it was necessary.'

'Patel's has been okay,' said Cutter. 'Next time, let's go somewhere different.'

I noticed the couple sitting at the next table and preparing to leave. They had looked across several times.

We went outside.

'See you tomorrow at the demo,' said Jane to the others.

Leaving our cars in the parking garage to fetch the next day, Jane and I shared a taxi to her place. There was a crescent moon. If we were patient, a full view would reveal the elegance of Jane's politics.

The dinner had passed a milestone in laying a foundation of independent opposition to Alexandra's political establishment. We wouldn't turn back now.

CHAPTER 41

It was the first time we had gone public with our MC idea. The demonstration started at midday on Saturday. Jane had obtained a licence to hold the demonstration in front of the IB, closing the street to traffic. I had hired a huge digital screen mounted on a flat-bed truck, operated by a digital technician. It was angled across in front of the IB, opposite a grassy park where a crowd gathered. Our publicity at the concert had brought out people in droves. They thronged the park, with children standing on tabletops to see.

At the top of the IB's entrance steps, Jane talked into a mic.

'Welcome, everyone. Thank you for coming. This is a multicultural event. Tell me, what do you think is the culture of Alexandra?'

Silence.

'We are multicultural. Let's hear it from you. What kind of a city is Alexandra?'

'Multicultural,' said a few voices.

'That's right, multicultural. Tell me again as loud as you can, what are we?'

'MULTICULTURAL!'

'Our Multicultural Centre will be built here,' Jane pointed to the IB. 'I'm Jane Kenwood, I am a city councillor. I'll tell you why I want a MC. I like meeting people from other cultures and sharing views with them. I want people to respect me, where I come from and what I do. I want to know about their lifestyles and find out about things we have in common. A MC is where we can meet and find out about people from other cultures.

'Top entertainers from around the world will come here. Alexandra's people come from countries with wonderful cultures and we will bring performers here.'

The screen lit up with 'Multicultural Alexandra' in huge letters.

'We want a MC that respects the cultures of Roberta's past immigrants. We are proud of them.'

Jane read a voiceover as the screen filled with images of immigrants packed into sailing ships, disembarking into long boats and rowing ashore. The newcomers travelled in horse-drawn buggies, wagon trains and steam trains. There were images of early settlers' dwellings and photos of families living under harsh conditions poorly but proudly.

The presentation had been prepared by Sunita's IBAG people and it was stunning. Refracted through the prism of time was a multi-hued community united by the common good.

My father had come as an immigrant and engaged with a culture that remained largely foreign to him.

'An immigrant sacrifices his life for his descendants,' he had said.

'I'm choking up,' I said to Sunita beside me, forgetting our antipathy. 'This runs deep with me.'

'It should do, Doctor,' she said, 'even though you are a scientist.'

We had agreed on something at last.

Jane's voice was in awe of the ancestral images.

'We need to commemorate immigrants who have brought best practices here that are envied worldwide. Southland's soccer team has players from all over the world. We need to remember the deep roots we have in foreign places.'

There were photos of people whose costumes told their countries of origin. An Italian pizza maker; an Irish potato farmer, an African Masai athlete.

'We need to stay connected with our origins for deep confidence in ourselves, to grow our civil society,' Jane said. 'Roberta needs a MC and the logical place for it is here in Alexandra. It was the place where immigrants arrived and spread out to start new lives.

'The MC will make a spiritual connection between Roberta's people and their origins. The MC will have vibrant entertainment, attracting visitors of all ages.'

There were theatre frontages decorated for celebrity shows and colourful restaurants offering Chinese, Indian, French, indigenous and other cuisines.

Finally we saw an artist's impression of Winkler's design for the MC, with the IB extended to become a much larger building, balanced and stylish, its heritage intact. It looked wonderful. There was applause.

'Multiculture in our society is what wind is to sailors: it will take us where we want to go. We do not know exactly where we are going, but the MC is where we will start our journey together,' Jane said. 'Now here is Maria Andrianos, President of the Ethnic Communities Council.'

She spoke with quiet enthusiasm and dignity.

'The MC will be a focal point for families to enjoy shows from their homelands as well as from local ethnic theatre companies,' said Maria. 'They will eat traditional foods and celebrate their descent. People will discover others' cultures and learn to be tolerant. A MC has my full support.'

'Thank you, Maria,' said Jane. 'The bad news is that the Government wants to destroy this building to put a casino here.'

There were boos and cries of 'Shame!'

'Let us protest. Let's sing together loudly, showing that we are opposed to the Government's plan. We want the IB preserved, restored and used for a MC. Hester and Fester Bronsky will lead our singing.'

The sisters were a well-known comedy act who had performed at our concert. They walked on to loud applause, Hester with her violin and Fester with her guitar.

'Good afternoon, multicultural Alexandra, I'm Hester and this is Fester. We all want a MC, don't we, not a casino? WE WILL OVERCOME. Let's yell that out, so loudly they will hear it right across Alexandra, because we want it A LOT.'

'We shall overcome,' sang Hester while Fester chorded. The computer operator had the words up on the screen for everyone to sing. Voices wound around each other and wove into a solid sound that set the pigeons swirling down the streets, bringing people running.

After that we sang 'There is a Season' and the crowd pushed in together, lines of singers putting their arms around each other's shoulders, swaying in waves like wheat before the wind. Hester sawed on her violin soulfully as voices rang out in harmony.

Suddenly, on the other side from us, from behind the screen, a group of young men pushed forward through the crowd, shouting.

'Who are they?' I asked Jane.

'Rent-a-riot,' she said. 'We're in trouble.'

Police in helmets, carrying clubs and riot shields were streaming through the throng from buses pulled up in the distance. They assembled in ranks near us, watching, waiting.

TV cameramen pushed through to the front, while others stayed back and climbed on to walls, surveying the crowd.

When the sisters switched to 'The Times They Are a-Changing' there was a ruckus in the audience and fighting spread outwards. The singing faltered and faded. There were screams and a policeman with a loud hailer announced, 'Attention! For your safety, this event is now cancelled. There is no cause for alarm. Do not push. Stay calm. Leave slowly and go home.'

The fighting had reached the stage, where we had posted a handful of bouncers to keep people back from the performers.

'For your safety, leave calmly and quietly.'

'Follow me,' yelled Jane.

We pushed through the melee and ran to the Bronsky sisters. We dragged them away, jostling to get through. The police threatened us with their clubs.

'Don't you poke me,' screamed Sunita, squaring up to a policeman who had prodded her with his baton. He grabbed her arms. She swore at him while another policeman handcuffed her.

'She hasn't done anything,' I said to the policeman. 'Let her go.'

He grabbed my arm and wrenched it behind my back.

There was uproar in the crowd, with shouts and screams.

'You're arrested,' he yelled in my ear. 'Come quietly now.'

'What have I done?' I cried, trying to break free.

He grabbed my ear, twisted it and dragged me towards a police van with the help of another policeman.

'Inciting,' he said.

I pulled away and he clubbed me behind my knee and I fell. He pressed my face into the tarmac of the road with his boot. The resistance went out of me.

'Do what I say or you will get hurt. Get up.'

Jane, Sunita, Cutter, Hester and Fester and I were surrounded by about eight policemen. They forced us into a paddy wagon and drove us to the city watch house where we were herded into the reception area. It was bedlam.

'Jane Kenwood?' called a senior policeman.

It went quiet.

'Yes. Here!'

'Jane Kenwood, you may be charged with incitement.'

'I did not incite anyone.'

'Your event was supposed to be about 'multicultural unity' but you were singing 'We shall overcome' and 'A time to fight'. That is incitement. Incitement is a felony,' he said. 'Anymore law-breaking and you will all be charged. Now go home.'

We left. Jane and I walked back to the IB to meet a TV interviewer.

'Who set that lot on us?' I asked Jane.

'Someone who doesn't want a MC.'

Whoever it was had stopped our peaceful demonstration. But we would never give up.

CHAPTER 42

We got to the IB at 6 pm for an interview with ATV, a public channel. Andrea Gough of Runyon's was already there, talking with their journalist in front of his camera on a tripod. We waited and he came across to us.

'I'm Miles,' he said. 'Were you caught up in the fighting?'

'Yes. We were holding a peaceful demonstration until thugs moved in,' Jane said. 'We are trying to find out who they were.'

'I can't help you with that. What happened?'

I told him about the fighting and how we were arrested.

'That's awful,' he said. 'Are you okay to do this now? I can put it off until tomorrow if you prefer.'

'Now is okay.'

'I am doing a story for our weekly magazine on Sunday after the evening news,' said Miles. 'I want to put the two proposals out for the community to vote on. I'll do you first and Runyon Casinos afterwards.'

I liked that — we would be first in and best addressed.

Miles stood us at the top of the steps in front of the handsome IB. He had questions written down. Jane and I shared the answering. After about 15 minutes we finished.

'Thank you. That was great. I have too much material so I'll be cutting it,' he said. 'I want to get a balance that is fair.'

'Thank you. Don't worry if Runyon's don't seem as good as us — that's real.'

He smiled. We said goodbye and left him with Andrea.

'How do you think we did?' I asked Jane.

'Competing with Runyon's glitz won't be easy,' she said. 'ATV usually pander to the Government's whims, so we won't get a walkover.'

It was late and we were exhausted. We went to Jane's place, ate, turned in and slept.

171

The next day was Sunday. Jane and I planned our speeches for the Council debate on Tuesday. In the evening the group came to her place to watch the ATV interview. I poured drinks as they lolled on Jane's stylish furniture. The news report began with the title 'Gambling or Multiculture?' followed by a zoom into fighting in front of the IB.

'Good evening, viewers. I am Miles and I'm in Alexandra where on Sunday hundreds of people protested that Runyon Casinos want to demolish this old building behind me and build a casino resort. However, a local group wants to preserve it and develop a MC. Tonight I am going to ask the projects' spokespersons what benefits their projects have to offer. Then you can call us and vote for the one you prefer.'

The camera swung to Jane beside him. She smiled confidently.

Miles said, 'This is city councillor, Jane Kenwood. Jane, would you tell viewers your group's proposal.'

'Thank you for having us on your programme, Miles,' Jane said. She was calm and sharp. 'Our proposal is to restore the old IB and extend it to become an exciting multicultural community centre.'

'What will it have in it?' asked Miles.

'There will be a theatre with a continuous programme of world-class entertainment from many countries and a second theatre putting on ethnic productions with talented local performers. There will be places where people can meet others from their homelands, share languages and customs, commemorate pioneers and eat food from other countries.'

'What is the purpose of your MC?'

'It will celebrate the unique cultures of Robertans, from many places.'

'What difference will it make?'

'A lot. Alexandra will gain racial harmony and it will help Roberta become a strong and confident society.'

'Now let's see the history of this building and what it means today,' said Miles.

We saw a recording of Sunita's presentation from the demonstration, with Jane's voiceover. It was factual and would be respected for its honesty. It ended with an artist's impression of

172

Winkler's design for the restored building and new theatres, merged perfectly and stylish overall.

When it ended, Jane said, 'Our MC will be self-sustaining, with something for everyone.'

Again, we saw Miles with Jane on the steps. 'That was the MC proposal. Thank you, Jane.'

It cut to him standing with Andrea in front of her company's prestigious office building.

'And now to the casino proposal. Runyon's is the company who want to demolish this historic building to make way for a casino resort. Andrea Gough is their project manager.'

'Good evening, Miles,' she said.

'Andrea, will you tell us what your company is proposing.'

'I'll play our video called 'A Better Future for Alexandra City'.

It was the same video we councillors had watched. Runyon's movie was more polished than ours, more Las Vegasy. I hoped viewers would recognise that the gloss concealed an obnoxious development.

Miles' continued, 'That was the casino proposal. What a wonderful resort! Now I am going to ask Andrea how it would benefit the city, apart from providing jobs.'

'Thank you, Miles. It will transform the CBD from a post-colonial city centre into a global tourism precinct. Whole families will come and enjoy the facilities. They will shop in the city and go on excursions. There will be a regular income to the Government from the taxes collected.'

'What do you say to people who are concerned that Alexandra City will be transformed into a place like Las Vegas, where high-rolling foreigners come and squander their money with the possibility of bringing crime?'

'Vegas is magnificent! There is no crime problem.'

'We can see you have a vision, Andrea. Now back to the other alternative, a MC. Councillor Doctor Phillip Keane will tell us its benefits.'

I made the case for valuing cultural diversity, nourishing foreign cultures at a MC and cultivating immigrants' roots. I had statistics about ethnicity and forecasts of audience sizes from my feasibility study.

'Thank you, Doctor,' said Miles. 'There you have it. One site and a choice between two very different projects. On the one hand, the imposing glittering steel and glass mushrooms of a futuristic gambling resort at a hub of tourism. On the other, a restored historic IB, with a parade of theatrical, musical and cultural events, a place where people can reconnect with ancestors' homelands, creating racial harmony.

'Now viewers, we want you to tell us which one of these two proposals you support,' said Miles. 'Would you phone 3403 6666 and vote.

'Thank you, Jane, Phillip and Andrea for your participation. Good evening viewers.'

The programme ended and we clapped.

Miles had been fair. The choice was between an apple and an orange. I felt we were in with a chance. Jane had looked like and sounded like a winner

'That was terrific, you guys,' said Tony.

'A team effort,' said Jane.

'What did you think, Phillip?' Jane asked.

'Andrea was corporate and slick — too slick. The casino's gloss could attract dull people but it will alienate people who want the colonial character of the CBD to be retained.'

'I thought you spoke well, Phillip,' said Jane. 'You looked and sounded like a financial analyst who had done his homework and calculated the economics would be sound.'

'Will we win?' I asked.

'I doubt that many people will be bothered to vote by phone,' said Jane. 'City residents' preferences are not the same as those of a national television audience. The main result could be that local politicians will try to use the poll result to advance their own positions.'

We wouldn't find out until Monday.

Jane had ordered pizzas to be delivered. We ate and chatted for a couple of hours. We phoned ATV to record our votes. Then the others left. It had been a busy weekend. Jane and I watched a movie to unwind.

Although our mood was buoyant, I was apprehensive. I had a premonition of disaster. It was like approaching an iceberg and glimpsing a large and formidable shape beneath the surface. I had no clue of what to expect and no idea what to do.

CHAPTER 43

The next morning the result was on the public broadcast website: casino 41%; MC 59%.

'That's brilliant,' I said to Jane.

'Don't get carried away,' she said. 'It is councillors' voting in the chamber that will decide. The NLP will vote for the casino.'

We spent the day at our ward offices. In the evening I went to her place. We watched the national news. It was followed by a political skit that Cutter and I had recorded a week earlier.

'Good evening, everyone,' I said. 'I'm Simon Spanner. I am going to interview Colin Cog who is a special member of the Cabinet. Thank you for coming in and welcome, Colin.'

Cog was played by Cutter. He sat back in a business suit, white shirt and tie.

'Glad to be with you, Simon,' he said.

'Minister, does the Government debate its policies with the Opposition?'

'We don't need to,' he said glibly.

'Why not?'

'Two reasons. One, we have a majority. Two, they copy our policies.'

'Do you debate policies internally, within your own party?'

'Never.'

'Why not?'

'We always agree.'

He was laconic.

'Who do you agree with?'

'The leader of our Party.'

'How is your leader different from a dictator?'

'We elected him.'

'Does he get cabinet approval for his actions?'

'Always — as soon afterwards as possible.'

'Is the Opposition an alternative government?'

'It is at elections.'

'Once elected, does the Government get it pretty much their own way?' I asked.

'Yes. That's what the Westminster System is all about — autocracy.'

'I thought it was about democracy.'

'You mean with control by the people?' he said. 'We would never allow that. We have bipartisan government.'

'Exactly. The NLP governs and the SLP opposes.'

'You mean they are adversaries? That is the Westminster System.'

'Doesn't bipartisan government require working together?'

'Yes. They do that too.'

'Does each party try to win in the elections?'

'Yes. There has to be balance and we take turns.'

'Thank you, Colin Cog.'

'A pleasure.'

'Thank you, everyone. You have been a great audience. Good evening from me, Simon Spanner.'

The news magazine continued to another story and I switched off.

I asked Jane, 'What do you think?'

'It was fun,' she said. 'You and Cutter did it well. People will admire your wit but it won't make any difference. They will see that the party's game is self-serving, the political system is a duopoly and the Government is a tyranny. But there is nothing they can do about it.'

She was right. Cutter and I had indulged ourselves pointlessly.

'In fact, there's a lot people can do — vote independent for a start,' Jane said.

'She is hopeful,' I thought. *'Bringing the parties down will require a revolution in the public's perception.'*

There could be a confrontation in the Council tomorrow. I was anxious that our MC proposal would be considered fairly. To stop worrying I prepared a pasta dinner. While I cooked, Jane played the piano in the lounge — a Chopin nocturne. She was happy and relaxed, with no sign of any concerns.

177

When we sat down to eat, Jane said, 'We need to meet with Cutter and Barbie first thing tomorrow.'

'What for?' I said.

'Munster and Hubbard are sure to try and get Runyon's PDA approved. It may be our last chance to get councillors to change their minds. We need Cutter on the same page as us. Barbie may have some ideas too.'

'When?'

'How about 9 am in the Members' Lounge?'

'Okay.'

Jane called them and they agreed to go.

We were weary and ate in silence. When we finished she sat watching me, deep in thought, her hands resting on the table. Her presence had an ethereal quality like light rays that came together in a hologram that I could look through without ever seeing the real Jane inside. She was a mystery. Her opponents sometimes found her disconcerting but all I could see was goodness and kindness in her. I was aware of her profound effect on me, causing me to strive to become a better and more worthy person.

After putting the dishes in the washer, we began planning an overseas holiday in Council's next recess.

'Are you thinking of Europe?' I asked.

'We only have two or three weeks,' she said.

'I don't want to go on a tour.'

'Fending for ourselves would test our relationship.'

I didn't like the sound of that.

'Perhaps we should not be too ambitious,' I said.

'How about Vietnam?'

'I was there a couple of years ago.'

'North or South?'

'I wouldn't mind going down the Mekong again.'

'There must be somewhere neither of us have been,' she said.

We decided on a Bali homestay with a Hindu family, well away from tourism. We would go in a month's time.

'I'll see if I can get a booking,' I said.

After dinner, we made love. It got better and better. We lay in bed, talking politics like Eva and Juan Peron. We kept coming back to what was likely to happen in the Council tomorrow. I left around midnight to go home for a good night's sleep to get a smooth start to what could be a difficult day.

At home I tossed and turned, trying to sleep, with the meeting looping in my head, and dreamed of an opera set in the Council chamber.

A brass band was playing 'Entry of the Gladiators' as the Lord Mayor, surrounded by his entourage, swept in, swirled his cloak around him and reclined on his throne. I was a toadying courtier fearful of his wrath. The Chairperson was on her dais and nodded to him to begin. He sang a tedious aria with pomp, in fruity bass tones. It was self-congratulatory and the applause was half-hearted.

I had glimpses of animated action rather than a continuous narrative. It had all the nuances of a real Council meeting. I was watching a game in which I understood how everything worked but was powerless to change anything.

He and the Chairperson sang a duet about the beneficence of their government and how it helped those who helped themselves. Their plump figures indicated that they had helped themselves plentifully. The Mayor's dark bass was mitigated by the Chairperson's sweet alto. The Opposition leader, a dapper tenor, engaged the Mayor in a duet. Their exchange was a parody of political banter.

'We provide the people with what they need,' sang the Mayor.

'We provide them with what they want,' sang the Opposition leader.

There was the sound of a mob chanting outside, *'Save us! We want food! We want shelter!'* The door burst open and a young woman wearing breeches and thigh-length leather boots strode to centre stage. It was Jane. She trilled a soaring soprano aria imploring the Mayor to help her people who were weak from hunger, did not have the strength to help themselves and were throwing themselves on his mercy.

The light faded and in the gloom the Mayor, sotto voce, directed a pair of ruffians who ran across the stage and dragged Jane outside.

Fear gripped my heart as I realised they could take her life. Then I awoke.

PART 3

MISSING

CHAPTER 44

Dread perched on my mind like a vulture, a harbinger of awfulness. There was something ominous beneath my dream that seemed frighteningly real. I had to protect Jane from imminent danger. I was nauseous but I followed my usual breakfast routine and composed myself, in readiness for our meeting.

It was overcast with gusting winds when I drove into the city. I strode across City Square with thunder rumbling overhead. I arrived in the Councillors' Lounge at 8.50 am. Cutter and Barbie arrived together at 8.55 am, holding hands and starry-eyed.

'All right?' I asked with a knowing smile.

Cutter smiled but Barbie scowled. 'I suppose so, Doc,' she said with a shrug. She would be the last to admit she was besotted with Cutter, but I could see she was happy.

We couldn't start without Jane, our leader. We waited.

At 9.05 Cutter asked, 'Where is she?'

'I don't know. She was okay when I left her place at midnight,' I said.

Her house telephone wasn't answering and her mobile was switched off, which was unheard of. She hadn't contacted her ward office. I sent an email to her.

Since I had known her, she had always been reliable. When she was delayed she would phone. I was concerned about what could have happened. I went out to meet her coming in. Lightning slapped down on City Square, with rain lashing and bucketing. She didn't come.

I went back inside. It was 9.15 am.

'The road may be flooded,' I said. 'Let's start without her. She will be able to catch up. Let's anticipate what they will do.'

'They will try and approve the casino,' said Cutter.

'Can you stop them?' asked Barbie.

'We can if the SLP vote with us,' I said. 'We have to persuade them to prefer a MC.'

We went over the arguments.

Jane still hadn't turned up and I was worried.

'She might have had an accident or been injured and not have been found yet.' I said. 'Barbie, would you try the hospital emergency departments and ambulance. Cutter, would you contact the police, water police, state emergency service, fire brigade and coastguard.'

I called her number again as I walked to the garage. Her bay was empty. Her mobile was still switched off.

The storm had ended but on the way to her place there were puddles over the road. Her garage was empty. I let myself in and had a look around but I couldn't see anything unusual.

I drove back to City Hall. I called her family, trying not to sound too concerned. They had not heard from her. I had to admit she was missing without explanation and they became very concerned. Anxiety had been simmering in me for weeks and now it was close to boiling over. I called Cutter.

'Has she turned up yet?' I yelled into my mobile.

'Steady on,' said Cutter. 'There is probably a simple explanation. Where are you?'

'In reception.'

'Hang on. I'll come out.'

He stayed with me and we searched for her.

'Perhaps something happened to her on her walk to City Hall, or inside, or on her way to our meeting, or she could have received a message that turned her around.'

It was 10 am, time for our committee meeting. I called Munster.

'Jane is missing. Cutter and I are looking for her.'

'Get in here as soon as you can,' she said. I knew she wouldn't wait for us and the Government would do what it wanted — but that was the least of my worries just now.

We walked the route she would have taken from the garage, knocking on office doors in City Hall along the way. We inquired if anyone had seen Jane or heard anything unusual around 9 am, but no-one had. She could have been intercepted before getting to City Hall.

'Let's go to the meeting and if she doesn't turn up, take it to the police,' Cutter said.

We went to the committee room and joined the meeting.

'Ah, Phillip, any news of Jane?' asked Munster.

'We were expecting her at 9.00 am but she didn't show.'

'I hope she's alright. Could she have gone to be with family or friends?'

'It's possible,' I said doubtfully. Jane didn't operate that way. She would have let us know.

'Before you two got here we discussed the PDAs for both projects,' Erskine said. 'The committee has accepted both. The recommendation being considered is that the applicants put in closed bids for the site and the winner prepares a DA for the Council to assess.'

'The MC doesn't need to bid for the site,' I said. 'It would operate in buildings owned by the people of Southland.'

'That would never happen,' said Munster. 'The Government won't saddle itself with a new public enterprise. The Government is privatising, not getting into new public investments.'

'You mean you want to sell the site to get money to leverage your re-election,' I said. 'The IB belongs to the people. It should not be used as an election fund.'

Munster shrugged as if it was already decided. Jane's absence would result in the casino winning unless I did something.

I tried not to sound desperate. 'The public prefer a MC on this site. This was shown in both the Council's and ATV's polls. Selling it for a casino would be wrong.'

'That is your opinion, Phillip,' said Munster. 'Had you been here, you would have heard our reasons for moving this motion. But it is now too late. Erskine, please proceed with the vote.'

'The motion is to recommend that applicants bid for the site. Those in favour?'

Munster, Fenwick, Penny and Shelly raised their arms.

The SLP had sold out to them. I wondered what their reward would be — perhaps they had gained an approval or a disapproval for another project they were interested in.

'Those against?'

Cutter and me.

'Motion carried,' said Erskine. '4 to 2.'

It was a catastrophe. The committee had recommended to build the casino on the rubble of the formerly iconic IB. But Jane's disappearance was a greater concern. This could be the danger that my subconscious had forewarned me about: it was real and present.

CHAPTER 45

Cutter walked with me to the police headquarters (HQ). Cutter was Jane's oldest friend and, like me, he was rattled by Jane's disappearance.

I asked for Detective Chief Inspector (DCI) Wall. Peggy had been my favourite detective when I was a forensic investigator. We went up to her floor and she met us at the lift.

She led us, erect and brisk, to her office. She was in a white shirt, with tie and epaulettes, her hair pulled back into a tight bun, blue serge uniform trousers and shiny black Oxfords. Her office window was floor to ceiling and with a panorama of the towers of the CBD and a cathedral spire.

Her desk had an open laptop and a second screen. Her sole concession to humanity was a fireman's calendar on the wall with bulging biceps and washboard abdominals. Peggy liked men. She was an attractive woman. She leaned back in her desk chair with her fingers making a steeple.

I introduced Cutter.

She looked at me and said, 'What's wrong, Phillip?'

'Do you know Councillor Jane Kenwood?'

'I know of her, of course.'

'She's my partner. She drove in to work this morning and drove out again 11 minutes later. We don't know why.'

I recounted our actions in looking for her.

'Was she in any kind of strife?'

'Only the usual conflict between politicians. Nothing personal.'

I gave Peggy Jane's mobile number and she would check her calls since 6 am, when I had left her. A few minutes later Peggy had the phone company's calls on her screen. There had been one from an unregistered 'burn' phone at 7 am and then it was switched off at 8.59 am.

It was now 12 noon.

'Did she normally switch off her phone?'

'Hardly ever,' I said.

'I'll check her credit card.'

I gave her Jane's bank and account details from my payee list when I sent money to her after she had paid for me. Her bank told Peggy there hadn't been any transactions since she went missing but they would block her card.

'She has been expected for three hours with no news, Doctor,' said Peggy. 'We usually wait longer but I will post her missing. We have reasonable and justified fears for her safety and welfare.'

Peggy called uniformed branch and asked them to cordon off her parking bay and adjoining areas, including nearby cars.

'I'm going to put DI Gary Malcolm on to it, Doctor,' she said and called him in.

His attire identified him as a detective with a difference. He wore jeans, T-shirt, shoulder-length brown hair and joggers. His arms were brawny with tats and his handshake was strong. Peggy recounted to him how Jane had disappeared.

'I want to help in the search,' Detective Inspector,' I said.

'We can work together, Doctor,' Malcolm said. 'I need as much assistance as you dudes can give. Let's go and have a look at the CCTV recordings around City Hall.'

I doubted he would get cooperation because he looked so unkempt.

The three of us went to the city centre precinct station. Malcolm requested playback of footpath cameras near City Hall. I gave the officer a description.

'She's 170 cms, medium build, auburn hair in a ponytail.'

'What was she wearing?'

'Probably a smart business suit in a bright pastel colour – yellow, green or blue,' I said. 'Medium heels … and a matching shoulder bag.'

He played the recordings on fast forward as we watched over his shoulder. The pictures were fuzzy. He and Malcolm looked carefully. It took an hour. She could have been there but we didn't see her. We thanked him and left.

'Would you show me where she would have parked her car,' Malcolm said.

Cutter and I walked with him to the parking garage. We searched Jane's bay and vicinity and found only some lolly wrappers. He called a Crime Scene Investigator (CSI) who arrived with her equipment and began dusting for fingerprints, taking photographs, looking for footprints and other traces.

My phone rang. It was my mother.

'How are you?' she said.

'Not so good.'

My anxiety was messing with my head. I was seeing villains wherever I looked.

'What's wrong?' she asked. She had a knack of knowing when I was bothered.

'Jane's missing,' I replied.

'What do you think has happened to her?'

I told her what we knew. Not much.

'There may be a simple explanation,' she said. 'She's probably alright somewhere. Your father and I will come up to the city and help look for her.'

'We are doing everything.'

She had gone.

Helping DI Malcolm investigate allayed my anxiety.

'Do you think she could have disappeared between here and City Hall?' Malcolm asked. 'Would there be anyone around when she came in for your meeting?'

'We arranged for 9.00 am,' I said. 'I arrived at 8.50 am. That is my car over there. The garage was quite empty. I didn't see her or her car. Most councillors come in around 10 am for their meetings.'

'Someone could have seen her. I'll ask the garage attendant.'

He didn't remember seeing her car. He asked us to get her parking permit number from admin. We came back with it and he checked the record.

'She drove in at 8.54 am and drove out at 9.05 am.'

'I must have walked across the garage just before she arrived. Cutter and Barbie arrived a few minutes later. We came close to seeing her — she might have been with someone.'

189

'Why would she leave after 11 minutes?'

'She could have gone to get something.'

'Somebody else could have driven her car out.'

'They used her card.'

'Perhaps she went with them.'

'They could have taken her card and stolen her car. She could still be here somewhere.'

'Let's have a look around,' Cutter said.

Her parking bay was number 14. We peered into all the cars on Level A.

'She could be in a car boot,' I said.

'Maybe she fled. Where would she have gone?'

'She was under pressure in a political fight,' I said. 'We talked about holidays last evening. It is conceivable that she dropped her bundle and took off.'

I found myself saying these words but I didn't believe them for a minute because she would have let me know.

'She could have gone to the airport. I phoned there but they had no record of her checking in or being on a passenger list.'

'Has she ever flipped before?'

'Not that I know of.'

'There are traffic cameras on main roads. Her car should be easy to pick out if we can tell them what time it would have passed by.'

Malcolm called Peggy on speaker phone.

'Would you get Roads to check their traffic cameras for Jane's car, a yellow Porsche, plate number JANE 01, after 9.05 am,' he said.

'Until when?' Peggy asked.

'It takes about half an hour to the city boundary in a straight run from the City Hall,' Malcolm said. 'Allowing for traffic, a stop and a delay, say up to 10 am.'

'It will take them a while to do a check,' Malcolm said, turning to me.

'Shall I check if she's in a hospital or somewhere?' I said.

'We'll do that — but it won't do any harm if you ask too.'

Malcolm left us at the car park.

'I'll call the hospitals,' said Cutter. 'Do you know her GP's name?'

190

I gave him the name of her medical centre.

I called her parents again but they hadn't heard from her. 'Has anyone contacted you about her?' I didn't want to alarm them by using words like 'hostage' or 'ransom' or 'abductor'. The Kenwoods were quite well off but they wouldn't be able to assemble a heap of cash quickly.

'No. Nothing.'

'If anyone does contact you, will you go to the police?' I asked.

He paused. 'Probably.'

They proposed coming into the city but I said they should stay at home in case Jane or the abductors called them. It was bad enough having my parents hanging around. I didn't want more oldies looking over my shoulder.

By this time I was close to a standstill. Cutter and I went for a sandwich and coffee. It was 2.30 pm and time for the Council meeting. We walked back, into City Hall and arrived in the chamber as the Chairperson started the meeting.

After prayers I interrupted.

'Madam Chairperson, can I speak to the meeting briefly?'

'Yes, Councillor Keane.'

'Councillor Kenwood has disappeared under mysterious circumstances,' I said. The room went quiet. 'She drove in from home at 9 am and drove away again a short time later. We have searched for her without success and have reported her missing to the police. They suspect foul play. If anyone has any information, would they contact me or the police. Councillor Kenwood was to be our main speaker this afternoon in a debate of a motion to delay consideration of Runyon Casinos' PDA. Councillor Barber and I were late attending this morning's committee meeting. Because three of us were absent due to circumstances that were unforeseeable, I request that the committee declare invalid the committee's recommendation to auction the IB site. I wish to propose a motion.'

'Very well, Councillor Keane. Move your motion.'

I tried to sound resolute. 'I move that the DA committee's recommendation from this morning's meeting be rescinded and a decision on Runyon's PDA be postponed until Councillor Kenwood is found, or until Council decides to proceed.'

191

'Thank you, Councillor Keane. Does any councillor wish to speak for or against Councillor Keane's motion?'

Jane's disappearance was a sensation and councillors were agog. If the SLP voted for it and with Cutter on our side we might have the numbers to scrape in.

Munster stood up and leaned forward to speak into her mic. 'I am sympathetic about Councillor Kenwood's unexplained absence but concerned that postponement is unnecessary. Runyon's are expecting their large investment in this project to be resolved today and we should honour that. There will be another opportunity for those who oppose the casino to submit an objection after the DA has been submitted and assessed. We should proceed with the important work of the Council and hope that Councillor Kenwood will soon reappear.'

It was a callous call. Perhaps Munster thought Jane was hiding or malingering.

Fenwick said, 'Because Councillor Kenwood wanted transparency, her friends in the Opposition should be happy that the committee has recommended selling the IB site to the highest bidder.'

'Point of order,' I said.

'Councillor Keane.'

'The committee recommended an auction, which has lower transparency than tendering. A property under auction goes to the highest bidder in money alone, whereas a tender would normally be awarded for the most attractive offer, including commitment to a specified development. Because the nature of the development matters very much, you should rescind an auction by voting for this motion.'

'Are there any other speakers?'

No-one said anything.

'The motion is to rescind the committee recommendation. All those in agreement, say 'Aye'.'

There was a chorus of 'Aye'.

'Those against, say 'Naye'.'

A chorus of 'Naye'.

'A division. Ring the bells.'

The SLP were for it. Shelly and Penny had backflipped. Cutter stood with the Opposition, deserting the NLP.

The result was 12 For and 11 Against. We had won a delay. The NLP had not succeeded in taking advantage of Jane's absence to progress the casino. They had counted on Cutter's support, but he had opposed them.

'Motion carried.'

The NLP chagrin was evident in the abuse they levelled at us as we left.

'Scabs! Hoaxers! Faking her absence! Tsk, tsk, tsk!'

'You won't be able to stop the casino.'

'You'll get your come-uppance at the election.'

When the Hubbard Government had swaggered into office, it had had a majority of 13 against the SLPs 10. Since taking office they had alienated Jane, Cutter and me. Now they had their just desserts: a hung Council.

I didn't stay around to talk about it. Jane hadn't phoned and I was desperately concerned for her safety. Something had happened that was preventing her from contacting us.

CHAPTER 46

Jane was missing and my brain was numb with apprehension. After the Council meeting, I went for a drink with Cutter, Barbie and Sunita. Tony joined us after work.

'Where is she?' they asked me.

I shook my head. I told them how Jane's car had exited from the garage minutes after entering.

'Maybe she has gone travelling,' Tony suggested. 'She could be starting a new life somewhere else. People disappear all the time.'

'Jane would have had more consideration,' I said. 'If she had bolted she would have let us know not to worry about her.'

'Maybe she couldn't face telling us she was leaving,' said Tony. 'Tired of the struggle, wanting to pursue a dream, unable to pull the pin openly, she has split. Maybe she went with someone. A person can think they are in a sound relationship and then one day without any warning their partner walks out on them.'

Did Tony think I was gullible? If Jane had taken off with Manfred she would have told me. She wouldn't sneak away.

'Do you know something I don't?' I asked him.

He shook his head sheepishly.

'Maybe she has joined a movement,' said Cutter.

'I would know about it,' I said. 'Her ideals are transparent.'

'Was she down at all? Did she ever mention suicide?' asked Tony.

I looked around at the others and they shook their heads.

'She was sometimes frustrated and negative but that's normal,' I said. 'People who are in good health and spirits don't drive into work then drive away and commit suicide.'

'Could she have staged it for publicity?' Tony said. 'She likes to have her name in the news.'

'That's true but Jane confronts people to get her way: she doesn't deceive them,' I said.

'She's not above a ploy to get attention,' said Tony, persisting. 'The election isn't far away. Could disappearing for a time get her voted in as Lord Mayor?'

'No,' said Cutter. 'A faked kidnapping would have the opposite effect — showing she is a loose cannon. Her opponents would have a field day.'

I left them in the bar and went home, tired and dejected. My aloneness bore down on me like a heavy weight. I grilled sausages and ate them with a can of baked beans. I watched the TV news, hoping for something but there was nothing. I turned in early and was unable to sleep. I felt lost and hopeless without her. My mind churned through the awful possibilities. I must have slept because I awoke early with my adrenalin primed for a fight. I was too anxious to have breakfast. I set off in my car without a destination in mind, driving to anywhere I might come across Jane.

Everything seemed hyper real. Details stood out vividly of people, cars, trees and houses. It was like a buzz from something — a visual distortion. The amygdala in my brain must have been sensing danger. My adrenalin was pumping. I couldn't think clearly. My cerebrum was inoperable like a corked muscle, making me unable to solve problems. I took some wrong turns.

I went to the same places as yesterday. I drove to Jane's house and searched high and low for any clue but without success. Her parents and several friends phoned. No-one had any leads. I read her postal mail and emails but there were no unusual messages. I checked her recent computer activity but I saw nothing suspicious.

I knocked on neighbours' doors. No-one had noticed anything unusual. It didn't seem possible that someone from her past had come and taken her away. Everything seemed so normal. In the park, children were turning cartwheels and trying to do handstands, looking around for approval.

I couldn't think where to search next. I would work in with the police to find her. I went to see Peggy. We hadn't had time to catch up.

'How long have you been together with Jane?' she asked.

'Four months.'

'What happened with Connie, Doctor?'

Peggy had liked Connie.

'We divorced.'

'I'm sorry.'

'Thank you.'

'What are you up to these days, Peggy?' I asked.

'I spend my time behind a desk, Phillip,' she said, 'but I still get my jollies from nailing villains. How about you?'

'Being on the Council is a bit different from the forensic unit. It's the same skulduggery without as much blood.'

We talked about old acquaintances and the police department.

'What do you think has happened to Jane?' I asked presently.

Peggy paused. 'She broke with her routine and left the City Square parking garage 11 minutes after she arrived.'

'She could have been hijacked,' I said.

'Her car could have been photographed by a traffic camera, Doctor. Traffic Branch are doing a search.'

'Where would they take her?'

'Where they could hide her and hold her, Doctor.'

'Why?'

'Not to kill her — they could have done that in the garage. Not for sex — she's attractive but there are other attractive women who would be less trouble. She was targeted for some other reason.'

Later that morning Peggy called me.

'Doctor Keane, we have found a photo of her car crossing the Horton Bridge going north, 10 minutes after leaving the parking garage. When they blew up the picture there were two occupants, a woman driving and a man beside her. They are sending me a copy. Can you come in to my office? You can identify her.'

It was a relief that she was alive — even though she was with an unknown person. We looked at an image of Jane at the wheel taken from ahead and above. Sitting beside her was a broad dark figure. Their faces were in shadow. In the corner of the screen a clock showed 9.20 am. Peggy tried zooming in but couldn't get any more detail.

'Is that her, Doctor?'

'Yes. The car is hers and it looks like Jane.'

'What about him?'

'Never seen him before.'

'Where did he get in?'

'In the garage.'

'Could he have been with her when she arrived?'

'Why would he go in there with her? It is more likely he got into her car there and she left with him.'

'She picked him up?'

'Or a hijack. She could be driving under threat.'

'Could he be holding something in his lap under the newspaper?' Peggy said.

'A gun or a knife? He could have it covered so people can't see.'

'Maybe.'

'She seems okay driving,' said Peggy. 'It's a hard call whether he's benign or threatening.'

'I don't see any benign,' I said. 'What is under the newspaper may not be benign. If he's benign then why was her phone switched off at 8.59 am?'

'He was making her drive to the hiding place where she is now, Doctor.'

'Why didn't he drive?'

'He wouldn't be able to hold her captive. He couldn't stop her attracting other drivers' attention.'

There were no other cameras further along from where the photo was taken. The Northgrove Road went through the northern suburbs and out into rural Southland. It was possible that they had left the city. A search of camera records showed the car had not returned that day.

'What could he want her for?' I asked.

'If it was a ransom or a demand we would know by now. It's been 28 hours.'

'Why her?'

'She's a councillor, an influential one. They may want ... to take her out from doing her job ... for some time.'

'She was trying to stop a multibillion dollar casino project,' I said. 'They could kill her. We have to find her urgently.'

'I have put out an all-stations alert with a description of her car. DI Malcolm is following leads from the photograph — broad, dark villains and any hijacks.'

'I want to help,' I said. 'I'm available full time.'

'What about your Council work, Doctor?'

'I can't work — not knowing is messing up my head.'

'It would mine too,' Peggy said kindly. 'Doctor, you need to do something that takes your mind off it or it will drag you down. Why not keep your job ticking over? You may hear something useful at the Council.'

'Hmm. Good idea. There's a meeting tomorrow. I'll go.'

'Let me know what you're doing,' she said. 'Call me anytime.'

Peggy's support meant a lot to me. My girlfriend had been taken away from me without trace and I was in despair. Although everyone was sympathetic, it was business as usual for them, as if time would heal the wound. In my mind it was festering and I felt poisoned by the vileness of the crime. If Jane was never found my life as I had known it would be ended.

I decided to go to the Council meeting, continue searching and let Vero and Robert look after my ward work.

CHAPTER 47

When my parents arrived, we had lunch at a nearby coffee shop. I had been independent for many years and their involvement now put me on the defensive.

'There was no warning,' I told them. 'He snatched her away.'

'Could he have left her somewhere?'

'If she had been set free, we would probably have heard by now. Movies with amnesiacs wandering around in public are fanciful.'

Nevertheless, we searched her haunts: shopping malls, public parks, meeting places, museums, art galleries, libraries and riverside walkways. By evening I was exhausted. I took them to their hotel, had a meal and got an early night.

I awoke refreshed. The other parents – hers – called me on Facetime for any news. I told them about the photo of her in her car.

'It must be foul play,' her father said. 'We'd better come into the city.'

'There isn't anything you can do here,' I said. I couldn't cope with them too. 'It's best you stay there because Jane or the kidnappers might try to contact you. I'll keep you updated on what's happening.'

They called me every morning and evening.

They were devastated. They had more genes at stake than my parents. As the days passed without finding any clues, their concern became dismay and then anguish. I had nothing good to tell them to ease their pain. They were inconsolable.

Day after day we searched the streets parallel to the highway beyond the Horton Bridge, looking for anywhere she could be hidden. We passed several addresses to the police to investigate.

They broadcast an appeal to business people to look out for signs of new occupation of premises, new comings and goings, increased consumption of takeaway food, changes in lighting, electricity, water, parking, ventilation or disposal of waste and sewage. Some reports of suspicious changes were received and they followed them up but there were no arrests.

Alone in the evenings, I speculated about possible motives of the abductors. They had not identified themselves or their cause. As a scientist I didn't put much credence in abduction by aliens — no evidence had been substantiated. Nor could she have been taken to become someone's wife, or to be made to work in the sex trade. Jane would never cooperate.

If a 'tiger kidnapper' had wanted to force me to do something by threatening her, he would have contacted me by now.

The worst prospect was that she had been taken by a sex monster and murderer. This thought hastened my search.

Jane had been a thorn in the side of the Provincial Government and Council and her abduction could have originated there. The leaders could have had her removed to get their own way but I had no evidence of any wrongdoing. Confronting those who could benefit from her absence would not uncover incriminating evidence. Surveillance could be noticed and punished. They had minders. They had influence with law enforcement agencies. An accusation could bring reprisal.

Peggy and I were Government employees. We could not investigate the possibility of Government wrongdoing without evidence.

'We are not getting any closer to finding her,' I said.

Peggy heard my frustration. 'We are following up every line of enquiry, Doctor. There is nothing more we can do.'

I couldn't just sit back and wait. My head was full of questions. Did Jane have a meeting arranged with the man in her car? Did she set off with him voluntarily? Or did he force her to drive him? Worrying, I slept badly.

Next morning I arrived at my ward office, stressed. It was a relief that Vero and Robert were doing a great job covering for me. Vero forwarded an email from the LM.

Dear Phillip,
Council is shocked by the unexplained absence of
Councillor Jane Kenwood under suspicious
circumstances. Our thoughts are with her family and

friends and our hopes are that she will soon be found
unharmed
Martha Hubbard
Lord Mayor

Andrea Gough had emailed too.

Dear Councillor Keane,
Everyone at our Alexandra office is concerned that
Councillor Jane Kenwood has disappeared. We hope she
will be found unhurt and will be back at work soon.
Andrea Gough
Manager
Runyon Casinos

It was sobering to be acknowledged formally as Jane's partner after only a few months together. The weight of responsibility on me was heavy for making sure she would be found as soon as possible. My role was to find her and in the meantime I had to protect her interests. If Jane was not found soon, Council would approve the casino. Day by day, the casino was becoming a reality and prospects for a MC were receding.

'Could you pair someone with Councillor Kenwood?' I asked Fenwick. He could arrange for a NLP councillor to abstain from voting to balance Jane's absence.

'No. Pairing is only for party members,' he said with a smirk.

The Council was hung and before the Government put up any motion, the NLP checked that Cutter and I would support it. They were annoyed that we would not return to the NLP fold or go into coalition with them.

One day Cutter and I found our car tyres spiked, our wipers, aerials and mirrors snapped off and our filler caps stolen.

'No-one else has reported damage,' Cutter said after checking with the parking attendant.

'We are the only independents,' I said.

'Someone is trying to intimidate us.'

'From what?'

'Going against the Government.'

'Then why not intimidate SLP councillors too?'

'They are dyed-in-the-wool opponents whereas they could expect their bullying to frighten us off.'

'Wouldn't it provoke us?'

'Initially, like now, it would. But if they continue it could eventually wear us down until we come around to voting with them again. At least, that could be their theory.'

'They would have to be stupid to think that would work with us.'

'There could be other shit on the way.'

'It won't work on me.'

'Nor me. I'm with you bro'

We were vulnerable because our votes were decisive in the hung Council. I was paranoid that we too might be abducted. I asked Peggy to get some capsicum spray so Cutter and I could protect ourselves.

CHAPTER 48

Jane had gone missing on Tuesday morning.

On Friday morning I received a call from DCI Wall.

'Doctor Keane? This is Peggy Wall. We have found her car.'

'Where?'

'At Northgrove, near the highway north.'

'Are there any leads?'

'The CSIs are there now.'

'I want to go there,' I said. 'What's the address?'

'Anston Street, Northgrove.'

My GPS took me across the Horton Bridge and along the highway, turning off on to a local road, then along a side street to where Jane's car was fenced off behind crime-scene tape. Two uniformed police stood guard. The doors were open and a forensic officer in white overalls was doing fingerprints and taking photos.

The duty officer was expecting me and waved me past the tape.

'Good morning,' I said to the CSI who was dusting the dashboard. 'Inspector Wall said I could take a look—I was in forensics a couple of years ago. My name is Keane.'

'I know you, Doctor Keane. You are okay to have a look around.'

'Who reported it?'

'A helicopter spotted it and we sent a car. The doors were unlocked with the keys inside on the floor. A neighbour said it was here at 10 am on Tuesday morning. A gold-coloured bag was on the back seat with an iPad, ID, credit cards, coin change and personal items.'

I sat in the driver's seat and inspected the interior of the car.

'There is a syringe wrapper by the passenger's feet,' I told the CSI. 'It may have prints. Would you sample some dust from the floor on both sides — separate bags, please.'

'Yes, sir.'

'Have you talked to the neighbours?'

'We door-knocked first thing this morning. It was there on Tuesday morning but no-one had seen anything else.'

I went back into the city then, but I came back at 5 pm and parked where I could see the Porsche but would not be seen. One of the police officers was standing by the cordoned-off car. I told him who I was and stayed in my car. The light was fading when a tow truck came, winched it on and drove away.

The police officer came over.

'I'll be going now, sir,' he said.

'Don't sir me,' I said. 'I'm off the force now.'

'Will you be staying here, Dr Keane?' he asked.

'For a while.'

'You won't speak to the locals, will you? We will be interviewing them tomorrow.'

'No, I won't,' I said, lying. Talking to the locals was exactly what I had in mind. The police were slack. There is a theory that a person's memory halves daily in the amount of detail retained. Three days had elapsed and only one eighth of the detail could be remembered, soon to become one sixteenth. The police interviews would be too late for anything much to be recalled.'

'Goodnight, sir.' He drove away.

Two small boys began kicking a ball in the street near where her car had been. I went over.

'Excuse me, lads.'

They stopped playing and were sullen.

'Did you see a yellow car parked here?'

'Are you police?' one asked.

'I'm a crime investigator, working with the police.'

'We saw it. Stolen, was it?'

'We don't know yet. Did you see another car parked here earlier in the week?'

'Might have,' he said.

The other boy nodded tentatively.

'What colour was it?'

'Black.'

'What type of car?'

'Dunno.'

'Did you see anyone?'
'No. When we come home, it was gone and the porky was here.'
'Did you see anyone?'
'No.'
'Well, that's all for now. If you can think of anything else, call me at this number.'
'Is there a reward?'
'Yes,' I said, lying.
'How much?'
'Enough to buy a Ferrari, or a plane, or for your whole family to go to Disneyland.'
'Cool.'
It was almost dark when a woman came out from one of the houses. She spied me talking with the boys and marched over.
'What've they been up to now?'
'Helping the police with their inquiries.'
I was not impersonating police.
'They saw two cars here. Did you see them?'
'I saw a yellow one — it was here all week.'
'When did you see it first?'
'Maybe Tuesday. Yes, it was Tuesday. I was late for work that day and I saw it outside when I left the house.'
'What time was that?'
'About 10 o'clock. I told them this morning.'
'On Tuesday, what time did the boys leave?'
'About 8.30.'
'Did you see another car there earlier?'
'No. I stayed in the back except when I went out the front door to work. Is that all? Boys, come in for your dinner now.'
'Could I have your names please?'
'I'm Rachel MacMillan and these are Andrew and Richard.'
'Thank you for your help.'
They went into the house. I went back to my car and read a Kindle book, while keeping an eye open for comings and goings. A bush pheasant scooted across, its guilty head low to the ground as it peered into driveways for an escape route.

Darkness slid over the cul-de-sac. Cars arrived and parked or garaged. Dogs were walked. Lights came on.

I had some food with me — sandwiches and a flask of coffee. It was too dark to read. I dozed fitfully. I got out a couple of times to stretch. At around 5 am, the sky was lightening when a man walked past.

I called out the window, 'Excuse me please.'

He spun around fearfully. He hadn't seen me sitting in the car. He turned and walked away.

I got out and called again, 'Excuse me, sir.'

He stopped and I walked up to him.

'Thank you for your cooperation,' I said. 'I am helping the police investigate a crime. Do you live around here?'

'Yes,' he said.

'Are you going for a walk?'

'I work at the shopping centre. I do security.'

'Was there a car here yesterday?'

'Yes. A yellow Porsche.'

'Was it there previously?'

'Yes, for several days.'

'Did you notice anything?'

'I looked inside. I was going to report it. There was a gold bag on the back seat. Cars have been abandoned here before.'

'When did you first see it?'

'Hmm. About Tuesday evening.'

'Was there another car before that?'

'Yes — about this time on Tuesday morning I think.'

'What sort of car?'

'A Merc I think. Black.'

'Did you see anyone?'

'No.'

'Would you have a look at some pictures of Mercedes to see what model it was?'

I showed him photos on my iPad.

'I think it was that one.'

'That's a C-Class sedan. It would be at least 10 years old.'

'It wasn't new.'

'Thank you for your help, sir. Would you give me your name please?'

'Graeme Newberry.'

'Can I see your ID?'

I took down details from his driving licence.

'If you think of anything else, here's my number,' I said. 'Good morning.'

On my way home I called Peggy Wall.

'I have a description of the getaway car, a Mercedes C-Class, black.'

'There are a few around.'

'It could be sitting outside the hidey hole.'

'I'll tell the search team. How did you find out?'

I explained how I had talked with the boys and the man.

'What do you think happened, Doctor?' Peggy asked.

'He had parked the Merc there earlier. She drove the Porsche up behind it. He jabbed her and she passed out. He lifted her out, carried her and put her in the Merc, probably in the boot.'

'How heavy is she?'

'About 60 kg.'

'A heavy lift for one man. Wouldn't he have made her walk?'

'She could have screamed and got a look at him. I reckon he injected her while she was in the driving seat. There was a wrapper from a syringe on the floor.'

'Of course we will have to check all this, Doctor Keane,' Peggy said. She sounded put out. I gave her Newberry's driving licence number and she typed it into her computer.

'It's kosher,' she said. Her voice changed, becoming hard. 'Doctor, you are not authorised to question witnesses. It won't be admissible in court and you could have put ideas in witnesses' heads.'

'I thought the police had finished.'

'We haven't. You know very well we don't finish at a crime scene until the case is closed,' she said angrily. 'For fuck's sake, when you do your investigating, would you *not* question suspects or witnesses. Leave that to us.'

'Here … I am sending you a copy of my notes.'

She opened it on her PC and began reading. It was a record of my conversations with the MacMillan boys and Newberry.

'That's useful information,' Peggy said when she finished. 'Thank you for that, Phillip. If you come into my office tomorrow, I'll fill you in on progress.'

'Thank you, Peggy.'

I needed to stay onside with Peggy for the police to put their best effort in to finding Jane.

I spent the rest of the weekend and Monday driving around and looking for the hiding place.

*

On Tuesday I went to the DA Committee meeting. It had been a week since I had seen them.

'Are the police making any progress?' Cheryl Munster asked me. They had heard on the news how Jane had exited the parking garage and seen the photo of her crossing the bridge. I told them about finding her car.

'It looks like abduction,' Munster said. 'They could make some demands even now.'

'They wouldn't get much ...' said Fenwick, as if Jane was of low value.

'That is a stupid thing ...' I began but he interrupted me.

' ... I mean, the police wouldn't allow kidnappers to be paid off, would they?' he smirked.

'You are a slimy two-faced worm,' said Shelly. 'She is a friend of ours and we want her back at any cost.'

The atmosphere was tense. No-one mentioned that the reason she was abducted was because of her influence in the Council. It could have been done by someone present — and they might strike again.

There was little talk and the meeting finished early.

CHAPTER 49

By the end of the week, I was in a dark hole. Jane's passion for life had hooked me like a drug and without the fixes of her presence, it was difficult to keep going.

My parents did not like living in a hotel and returned home. They had been a support and I talked with them on Skype daily. Joseph and Jennifer Kenwood came into the city to make sure that everything possible was being done to find their daughter. They tried to tease out the personal antipathies in Jane's Council work before her disappearance, which were mainly with councillors she had clashed with about Runyon's casino.

'I thought you would have seen this coming,' Joseph said to me reproachfully.

'What do you mean?'

He turned to his wife. 'He doesn't realise yet what he's done. You should have made her realise she was playing with fire.'

I had supported Jane in making a stand against the casino but I had not foreseen any real threat to her safety. Violence against city councillors was unheard of in Southland. I realised grief was speaking and I forgave him. Losing a daughter could cause even more mental stress than losing a spouse. Joseph was hurting at least as much as I was.

'I agree,' I said. 'I never imagined anything like this. I'm very sorry.'

I was alone with my thoughts almost continually. There was no escape from my past. What I had done was predetermined in my genes and childhood. Fate had determined this cruel blow. I stood at the edge of an empty existence. It wasn't enough for me and time passed excruciatingly slowly.

I went to her house to check emails. I wandered aimlessly through her home. A tap dripped in the cavernous silence. I turned it off. I felt shafted by anxiety. If I ate something I might feel better. There was a half bar of chocolate in the refrigerator and I ate it all. Since Jane had been gone, months of dieting and exercise work on my abs and pecs had gone by the board. I no longer cared if I got fat.

In the dining room, her silk scarf was draped over a chair. It was orange in a Paisley design with maroon and dark green swirls. I held it to my face, remembering its touch when she had worn it. Her breathing had been uneven, her body quivering like a bird's. The smoothness of the silk reminded me of her face. I sniffed it and her smell, a pure flower note, flooded my senses. I sobbed, grieving for my loss, blinded by tears.

I locked up her place and went home. When I got into bed, she was not there to put her arms around me. She would kiss me and we would chatter about our plans for the weekend. Tired from work she would fall asleep in my arms like a trusting child, warm and heavy. My life was empty. Night after night I curled up in a foetal position and wept, the salty tears running down and soaking the pillow. Mornings were easier and I remembered how she would climb on top and put me inside her, rocking me awake.

I became exhausted and dull from searching for her. Several times I imagined I could hear her calling faintly, 'Help me, Phillip. I can't hang on much longer.' My heart pounded, ready to fight. I couldn't rest.

As the days and weeks passed she was slipping away from me. My memory of her blurred. The hard outline of my pain softened to an ache and I began to forget her. When I took time off from missing her I felt guilty.

In the evenings, I had time to mull over the possibilities: accident; eloped; fled; abducted; suicided; murdered. She was like Schrodinger's cat, shut in a box with poison it might eat, to an outsider both alive and dead at the same time. I learned to keep going with her existence a question mark. As I ran out of places to search for her, hope was replaced by sadness. I dreaded finding her dead. I was near to melting down.

In the weeks after she went missing, Jane's disappearance continued to make news headlines. There was public outrage that a politician had been abducted. The police had appealed for information and were inundated with possible leads. Police officers, emergency

210

squads and armed forces personnel were brought in. But the search eventually petered out.

I tried to keep active by looking for her. At the least, the police would be reminded that someone cared. It was a dastardly crime and someone would have to pay.

No-one had been arrested and no justice had yet been served on anyone for perpetrating this savage blow. It was wrong that the abductor could get away with it so easily. I knew that anger, bitterness and alienation were unhealthy so I assiduously avoided negativity, at least in my talk.

I cut myself off from friends and from social life. I stayed at home and ate tuna and beans from the can. I streamed movies at night from my Apple TV. Darkness was fearful and I would doze off with the light on, listening to her Spotify playlist and the songs she loved.

When I was interviewed by media, interviewers concentrated on finding anything controversial in Jane's work in the Council. I said that her attention was fixed on serving residents. I would not speculate on who might be behind her abduction. I had no evidence. That she had opposed a project that the Government supported was insufficient grounds to accuse anyone.

Fenwick, the NLP whip, enraged me by trying to get me to change my story.

'Telling people that Jane was standing up to NLP bullying is damaging us,' he said. 'You must stop making these derogatory comments.'

'Fuck you,' I said. 'Her family and constituents are the ones suffering, not the NLP.'

'You've got it all wrong, Phillip. It's what the Government wants that matters.'

'No,' I said, shaking my head. 'It's what the people want that matters.'

'Exactly. People want us to decide for them.'

It was like hitting my head against a wall.

'No, the other way around,' I said. 'We have to do what they want.'

'But they don't know what they want,' he said. 'We do what *we* want and tell them that's what *they* want. Then they will re-elect us.'

211

Fenwick made a hyena seem genteel. Unfortunately, he was technically correct. Philosopher Edmund Burke had established over 200 years ago that a political representative was a moral agent rather than a delegate or spokesperson. A politician was not a conduit for local views. It was a precept that Roberta's politicians embraced, an endemic tyranny.

A TV reporter said on air, 'Shocked by Jane's disappearance and the possibility of treachery in their Government, Alexandrans are hard at work. They are determined not to let the possibility of a political crime hold back development of their city.'

I spent most of my time searching for places where Jane could be held. Cutter was a loyal friend and kept me abreast of happenings at the Council. We set up crime information booths with placards requesting information at pedestrian precincts Jane had visited in the weeks before she disappeared. We received a few interesting leads and gave them to the police.

I fell further and further behind with my Council work. I was unable to plan ahead and blackness was closing in. I knew I was becoming depressed but I didn't know how to prevent it.

When I glimpsed someone lurking outside my apartment building I was upset.

'I think I'm being stalked,' I said to Cutter.

'Are you sure?'

'No. It could be paranoia. It doesn't make sense—why would anyone follow me?'

'The people who have Jane could want to find out if you are getting close, so they can stop you.'

'What should I do?'

'Nothing. If you try to grab him, he could get physical. Don't give them any opportunity to hurt you.'

'I want to force him to tell me where she is.'

'He wouldn't know. The mastermind is hardly going to risk him telling us.'

'Maybe I am being stalked means she's still alive?'

It wasn't good logic but it was the straw I grasped to buoy me up.

CHAPTER 50

For three weeks I had gone to Jane's ward office every day. I helped her assistants, Barbie and Simon, to respond to local events and residents' wants. Barbie was good at relating to ordinary folk. She could discuss current issues with a self-educated knowledge of politics, law, history and civic affairs. Her arguments used words such as: 'truth', 'right', 'ought', 'good', 'fairness', 'equality', 'greed', 'honesty' and 'duty', words that I didn't use any more. Legalese had replaced them in 'Politically Correct' circles. Barbie was not PC and people understood her better than me.

Barbie was dynamic and full of ideas. While we were having coffee together, I questioned her about her background.

'How did you get on at school?' I asked.

'I hated it. I left as soon as I could.'

'Why did you hate it?'

'Teachers told me I was lazy and incapable. I was okay with being lazy but I wanted to show them that I was capable when I was interested. Unless the work interested me, I didn't try.'

'Why were you so unwilling?' I asked.

'I needed all my will to be myself.'

'Did it take will to be yourself? Couldn't you just do what you wanted?'

'No. They tried to force me to do what they wanted and to stop me being myself. I wouldn't jump through their hoops. Education destroys your real self. What we had to study was nearly all bullshit.

'Sitting through lessons was an agony of boredom. I wanted to have all my brain going at near the speed of light, staying younger relative to the slow and careful thinkers.'

I was amazed. She wanted to live fast like the space travellers who Einstein had predicted would live slower and longer.

'The teachers told us that people with the best marks would get the best-paid jobs, but I found out that's not true. You get most money

213

from doing work that other people don't want to do. In an uncool job, you can get paid heaps. Everyone wants work that is fun, so those jobs get more than enough workers and they pay them shit. For work that no-one wants, you don't need good marks. I wanted to be a prostitute.'

'Being a prostitute wouldn't be enjoyable.'

'No, but I would earn a lot and would then be able to have fun outside work.'

'You said you are yourself by will power. If you were paid a lot, you could afford to be whoever you want, without doing prostitution.'

She hesitated as if she didn't recognise my chicken and egg contradiction. Preferring prostitution could be for her a renegade's bravado to conceal lack of conventional achievement at school. It seemed she hadn't launched this career yet, fortunately.

She chewed gum and looked at me defensively.

'What did you do?' I asked her eventually.

'In my final year I did work experience in Ms Kenwood's ward office. She lived near me and we used to talk. She was my hero. She used to come to my school to give out awards.'

'Did you get one?'

'Fat chance. Jane told me it didn't matter. As soon as I was 15, I left school. Although my marks were bad, Ms Kenwood gave me a job. That was three years ago. I really like it a lot. It was difficult at first. Sometimes I felt I was falling ... like Alice in Wonderland. I would get smaller and smaller until I was almost disappearing. Then Ms Kenwood would help me up and I would be able to get going and try again. Then I would get larger and larger ... until Ms Kenwood would tell me to pull my head in. Then I would get back to normal again.'

'You gained real self-confidence.'

'I was so grateful to Ms Kenwood. I'd do anything for her.'

'She really values your work. She told me that you have a lot of potential.'

'All I want to do is work for Ms Kenwood.'

Jane had told me about Barbie, 'Whereas life puts most of us on the back foot most of the time, Barbie has had the courage to climb out of her mould and trip blithely around in No Man's Land, looking

214

under stones to see what crawls out. She wants to understand everything. She has no fear of anybody or anything. She hasn't discovered her own limits yet.'

I smiled. I was jealous of Barbie's relationship with Jane. She thought the world of Barbie. Her disappearance was tragic for both of us.

*

On one of my visits to Blake Ward office I asked Barbie how she was getting on in her job.

'Okay, Doc,' she said, 'but it's not the same without Ms Kenwood.'

'Keeping the ward office going is very important,' I said. 'You are doing a great job.'

'There's not enough to do here,' she said. 'It used to be fun.'

I was struggling with my work load and needed help. Barbie had skills I lacked, such as in chatting up people so they would spill the beans.

'Barbie, how would you like to help me search for Jane?' I said.

'Really? When, Doc?'

'Starting tomorrow first thing.'

'What, every day?'

'We'll see how we go.'

'Who will do my work here?'

'If Simon needs help, I'll send Vero or Robert over.'

'Awesome, Doc,' she said, her eyes sparkling.

'You will have to be careful. You could get into some tricky situations.'

'Could I get done in?' she asked as if this would be an advantage. The amygdala part of her brain was too young to be wary of danger.

I laughed. Sleuthing had risks but I didn't want to scare her.

'If they catch you snooping they are not going to be kind to you. I am counting on you not to get caught. Don't tell anybody what we are doing.'

Her loyalty to Jane was fierce and I trusted her.

'I won't. This is what I've always wanted to do — be a detective.'

215

'I have a private detective licence and you can be my assistant. We can't do everything the police can do, such as interviewing suspects. But we can do some things better than them, such as investigating every possible angle before the trail goes cold. Mostly it will be sleuthing.'

'Fantastic,' she said. 'Detecting a crime!'

I looked down on her at her desk, with my chin held in; her eyes were looking up at me. They met my eyes and she knew me. I was mesmerised – I knew she knew me. She looked into my eyes and my being acknowledged hers. She knew me and she was not daunted.

Her eyes dwelled upon me and their sampling seemed to have pierced into my brain. She was measuring me up. I saw her immodest right eye looking into me, calculating. I felt her indomitable will confront mine. She would be in control and I was possessed by her.

As she looked up I knew the way her brow furrowed. I knew her freckled nose and the clear whites of her black eyes. She followed me with her eyes as I walked away across the room, her head tilting towards me, half amused, half intent and cunning. I left her, not sure whether to be pleased that I had a helper who knew my inner self or dismayed that I had recruited a wild animal, a feral cat or a fox, unafraid as she came into my territory. She was beautiful and dangerous.

'Come to my ward office tomorrow at 8.30 am,' I said. 'Let Simon know where you are. I'll square it with the Council's bean counters. I will tell them I am supervising your work in Councillor Kenwood's absence.'

CHAPTER 51

Next morning Barbie was at my ward office at 8.30 am. She draped her long body over Vero's credenza, studied her beigey-gold nails and chewed gum.

'Them who took Jane are going to be sorry,' she said, biting off her words in the Yorkshire way. 'They're not going to get away with it.'

'I'd like you to spend the day in the Council's offices,' I said. 'You can find out the road maintenance programme for Blake. When they know you work for Jane, they will tell you what they think has happened to her — the rumours, the gossip. It won't be reliable but there could be a lead.'

'Okay, boss.'

The next day she came into my office, lolling against the door jamb, mini-skirted, spaghetti legs crossed, hand on hip.

'Hiya, Barbie,' I said. 'How did you go?'

'There are heaps of rumours, Doc. Some of them said the party bosses had her taken out. Ainsley Montague, the CEO, said it was Runyon's that did it.'

'Maybe Montague did it himself,' I said.

'Or had it done for him. No-one likes him.'

'Or he wanted to divert attention away from someone who did it.'

'Or he has it in for Runyon's. Several of them said that.'

'Perhaps Runyon's really did do it,' she said, 'to get their casino through Council.'

'A bit obvious, isn't it? Is there any evidence?'

'Not that I heard.'

'People probably made it up. How did you get them to talk?'

'I told them that there was a reward for new information leading to Jane.'

'What reward is this?'

'I said a large sum had been put up by family, friends and Blake residents. People think I'm too dumb to lie. They think I have nothing in my brain.'

'If only they knew! So no-one had any evidence?'

'Not yet. Someone could still come forward.'

'Good job, Barbie!'

She glowed with pleasure.

'What do you want me to do next, Doc?' she asked.

'Let's go and see Peggy Wall.'

We drove to Police HQ with Barbie at the wheel. Peggy sat with us at a round table in her office. I brought her up to date on what we had been doing.

'We are trying to get a lead, Doctor,' Peggy said. 'We haven't matched the prints they got from her car. He could have been wearing gloves or had superglue on his fingers. All we can do is look for where they are holding her. We have two officers and a squad car on the job.'

'How can we help?'

'DI Malcolm will tell you what we're doing.'

She took us to his office and left us with him.

'Where do you think she is?' I asked him.

'She is out of sight and out of earshot,' Malcolm replied.

'Inside somewhere, gagged, tied up or locked up?' I said.

'Wouldn't she scream when they take the gag off to feed her, Doc?'

'It could be away somewhere or soundproofed.'

We looked at a city map occupying one wall, dotted with pins.

'These are the places our cars are investigating:' Malcolm said, 'unoccupied commercial premises; industrial estates; riverside warehouses; disused factories; new office blocks; residential blocks; and buildings under construction.'

'What about out in the countryside?' Barbie said, pointing off the diagram with her lips.

'A farm shed,' I said, 'or a livestock barn; or an empty house.'

'They notice strangers out in the country,' said Malcolm.

'We could help you look in town,' I said. 'Could we look on the north side of the river, seeing as how he was heading out that way?'

'He could have doubled back,' Malcolm said, shaking his head. 'If you stay west of the Northgrove Road, we'll take the east. If you want somewhere gone into, give me the details.'

I called Cutter and he agreed to drive his car, looking for hideouts. I dropped off Barbie to go with him. They would like to be together. I had given her a map with an area outlined. I went to another area, driving up and down the streets, looking for possible places, getting out, snooping around for signs of human traffic, listing places for the police to follow up.

It would be easier to leave it to the police but we had to find her urgently. They could be mistreating her. If Jane had found out who they were, the danger to her was increasing with every passing day.

We assisted the police with our two cars, driving up and down streets all day, looking.

That evening I went for a brisk walk in the local park by the river. It was almost dark. I heard footsteps behind me and there was a blow on the side of my head. I saw stars and crumpled up. When he tried to boot me in the face, I rolled aside. It was a big man wearing a dark track suit. I kicked his legs from under him and he went down. I tried to pin him down, but he was strong and pushed me off. He got to his feet and ran away. By the time I had recovered and gave chase, he had disappeared.

I was shaken. He hadn't taken anything. It seemed that he had wanted to injure me. Too late I remembered the capsicum spray in my pocket. I hadn't had a good look at his face because it was dark. He was wide enough to be the man in the bridge photo. I went to the local police station and reported the attack. The duty officer took down the details.

'This area is densely populated, Doctor Keane,' he said. 'We wouldn't be able to find him. There are too many people about at this time of day. He will have disappeared. Sorry, Doctor.'

I left the police station angry with myself. I had missed an opportunity to find who was holding Jane and where.

I called Peggy and informed her what had happened.

'He may have wanted to frighten you off, to deter you from investigating, or to stop you opposing the casino in the Council, Doctor.'

'Well, it didn't work. I am going to get that bastard and stop the casino, if I can.'

'Be careful, Phillip,' she warned. 'They are dangerous.'

In the evening at home I wanted to see Jane and opened my photo album. In some of the photos there were the two of us together. She had been cut away from me like an amputation. It ached and I was disabled. I had to try and get along without her. It took all of my strength to hold in the hurt and continue to live. The hope that she would be found and returned to me kept me going. I wouldn't ever give up on getting her back but she had been missing for a month and my memory of her was fuzzy.

CHAPTER 52

The attack in the park worried me and I slept badly.

The next day I drove in for our weekly Committee meeting. I arrived a little late.

'Ah, Phillip,' said Munster. 'You are just in time to vote. The motion is to recommend the casino for the IB site.'

The month's delay time had expired.

'That's not possible,' I said. 'The survey showed the public prefer a MC for that site.'

'There are other considerations,' said Munster, 'such as the high price Runyon's would pay for it.'

'Council rescinded bidding for the site.'

'When?'

'On the same day Jane disappeared, about a month ago,' I said, '12 councillors voted to rescind bidding against your 11.'

'We are not now proposing to hold an auction,' said Munster. 'We will vote whether to recommend acceptance of Runyon's PDA for that site.'

I argued that this was logically excluded by the Council's earlier rejection but Munster was obdurate.

Erskine conducted the vote. Shelly and Penny abstained. They must have been persuaded not to oppose the NLP somehow. Cutter hadn't turned up. There were only Munster and Fenwick in favour. It was 2 against 1.

We had lost.

I stayed in City Hall where there were people around, missing out on lunch because I was isolated and vulnerable and the mugger might try it again at any time.

In the Council meeting that afternoon they took it straight to a division without anyone speaking either for or against the recommendation. Shelly and Penny, who had abstained in the committee, now came out against the casino with the rest of the SLP. They may have felt safer opposing the Government in a group.

'Motion failed, 11:11,' said the Chairperson. 'The PDA for a casino on the IB site is rejected.'

The IB was saved. I breathed a sigh of relief. Our MC would now be in the box seat to get the IB site. Jane would be pleased if she knew. I felt hopeful for the first time in weeks. I wanted to whoop and jump about but dignity demanded that I behave as if I had expected this all along.

'Runyon's will be disappointed,' I said to Shelly.

'Yes,' she said. 'This morning we thought you weren't going to show.'

I wondered why she had thought that we wouldn't come. Had she known I would be mugged? Had she known Cutter wouldn't be there?

I phoned Cutter. 'What happened to you?'

'I was driving in, when a car pulled alongside me and forced me into a parked car. Hell of a smash. The bastard drove off. He didn't have plates.'

'Were you hurt?'

'No. The airbag worked. My car's a mess.'

'Did you get a look at him?'

'No. His car had tinted glass.'

'Who could have done it?'

'I don't know.'

'Maybe Samantha's husband?'

She had been his lover before Barbie.

'Fuck off,' he said.

'You missed an important meeting.'

'What happened?'

'The committee sneaked through a recommendation to accept the casino but we threw it out later in Council. The vote was 11 all. I nearly wasn't there — I was mugged last evening.'

'Shit. What happened?'

'Some thug knocked me down in the park. He got away.'

'Were you hurt?'

'A few bruises — that's all.'

'What the hell's going on?' Cutter asked.

'Someone is trying to take us out. It could be the same people who got Jane.'

'Well they failed. Is the site ours now?'

'Yes. Runyon's will have to find somewhere else to put it or pull out. Now we have to prepare a DA.'

'For fuck's sake. When are we going to have time to do that?' said Cutter.

'We'll have to make time,' I said.

Preparing a DA would take a big effort and I would have to take the lead. My time had been taken up trying to find Jane but I would ease up. I had wanted an intense police search but I reckoned a low-key search would be safer. The villains holding Jane could be holding her like a monkey with a clenched fist of food stuck inside a jar. The more it panics and tugs, the worse it becomes jammed and has to bite of its hand to get free. If we caught them by surprise, they might cut off Jane's life to get away.

CHAPTER 53

I was at my office, planning another sortie into the suburbs, looking for the hideout, when I received an email.

From: DCI P Wall
Subject: Kenwood car dust analysis
Date: 16 July
To: Dr Phillip Keane

Begin forwarded message:
From: parcher741@rob.gov.fsu
Subject: Kenwood Case
To: DCI P Wall

'Lithium in dust collected from the victim's car.
Chemical Analysis: NMR tests were done for 20 metallic ions. Lithium is present in the dust on the passenger side. It could have been deposited there from a passenger's footwear. The concentration is higher than is usual in soils and waste materials.
Lithium carbonate is an anti-manic agent used in preventing and treating symptoms of bipolar disorder. Lithium metal is used in anode material for high-performance batteries for digital devices. Although batteries are sealed, lithium compounds can leak and disperse as a fluid, solid or powder, contaminating ground near a battery dump.
Lithium comes from a mineral, spodumene, produced in only a few countries.
If samples from different locations are compared, relative quantities of different isotopes may establish a common source.

My report is attached.
Dr Peter Archer

Phillip, can we discuss this?
Regards,
DCI Peggy Wall

I talked with Peggy on the phone.

'Is Jane Kenwood bipolar, Doctor?' Peggy asked.

'No, I don't think so,' I said. 'Why? There wasn't any on the driver side.'

'Did she take many passengers?'

'No. She gave me a lift a couple of times.'

'Then it could have come from the man in the photo.'

'Quite likely. About every two months she had her car cleaned, inside and out.'

'Is it possible he dropped a pill?'

'We found only dust. He could have crushed it underfoot,' I said, 'but that is unlikely because the pills are hard.'

I knew about lithium tablets from my ex-wife who took them to prevent bipolar disorder. She said being married to me made her depressed – but she was already taking them when I met her.

'I'll get our people to check for a wide male who is bipolar and on lithium.'

Peggy put me on hold. Ten minutes later she came back.

'We didn't find anyone like that. Profiles are keyed in before mental health is evaluated. Bipolar might not be discovered. Conditions found later may never get recorded.'

'He might not have any police record, Peggy,' I said.

'It's possible,' she said, 'but that toe-rag hijacker is likely to have form.'

'But we can't use the lithium to find him. Shit.'

'Sorry, Councillor,' said Peggy. 'Until we get a sample from him we can't link him to the lithium in her car. I'm going home. Have a good evening.'

Peggy clicked off. It was 6.30 pm.

225

The next day I showed the email to Cutter and Barbie at my office.

'How would he get lithium on his footwear?' asked Barbie.

'He could have brought it from his own car, from his residence, or he may have picked it up from the ground somewhere,' said Cutter.

'What places have lithium lying around?'

'Mental hospitals,' I said. 'Jane could be locked up somewhere.'

'They can lock up anyone if a shrink signs the form,' said Cutter.

'Jane would deny she was mad.'

'Denial is evidence of madness,' said Cutter. 'I heard of a perfectly sane woman who was held in a mental hospital for five years because she was angry that a relative had got her sectioned.'

'Jesus, we'll have to visit every mental hospital in Roberta,' said Barbie.

'Prisons too,' said Cutter.

'Hospitals.'

'Pharmacies.'

'It's a humongous task,' said Barbie.

She yawned and stretched.

'Where else could the passenger get lithium on his shoes?' I asked.

'Battery manufacturers and recyclers.' said Cutter.

'Are lithium batteries made or recycled in Alexandra?'

'No, I don't think so. When they go flat they are dumped or returned to the manufacturer.'

'What about the tablets? Where are they made?'

'The ingredients are imported and made into tablets locally.'

'So lithium is here in Alexandra in bulk?'

'Maybe. I'll check.'

I phoned my local pharmacy. Although it was 8.30 pm, Jessica, the manager, answered.

'Hello, Phillip. What's the problem?'

'Jessica, the police are trying to track down traces of lithium found in a car at a crime scene. Do you know if lithium tablets are manufactured in Alexandra? ... I see. Where did they make them before that?'

I wrote down the address and thanked her.

226

I turned to the others.

'They come from China now but they used to be made in Alexandra,' I said.

'Until the Depression,' guffawed Barbie.

'It would have been crazy to keep making them,' said Cutter, deadpan.

'The old factory is at 205 Commercial Road.'

Barbie used Google Earth and found a two-storey building of about a hectare in an industrial area.

'She could be there now,' said Cutter.

'It looks disused,' I said. 'The car park is empty.'

'Duh. It's an old photo.'

'If we surprise them they could harm her,' Cutter said,

'Can we wait until they come out?' said Barbie.

'She might not be there.'

'Let's do a recce and see if we need police,' I said. 'Softly, softly, catchee monkey.

'It's 10 pm now. If we go blundering around in the middle of the night they'll hear us coming. Let's go at first light.'

Barbie pointed to herself and raised an eyebrow quizzically.

'Yes, you come too, Barbie.'

'I wish I had a gun,' Cutter said.

'These people are dangerous,' Barbie said. 'They mug people and ram cars. We could get hurt.'

'We are going on a recce,' I said, 'not a raid.'

CHAPTER 54

It was 6.30 am and just getting light when Barbie parked on the street a block away.

'How long should I give you, Doc?'

'Half an hour. Then call the police.'

'Okay.'

Cutter and I vaulted over the delivery gate. There was a gravel pathway to the back door. I couldn't see any footprints. Behind a bush was a broom that could have swept away footprints.

The door was locked. I stuck a sink plunger on to the window, put a loop of string over the handle and tied it to a diamond glass cutter. Keeping the string taut, I scored a circle. Tapping with the metal handle of the cutter, I cracked around the score mark. I hoped the villains didn't hear. I lifted out the glass disc. Reaching through the hole, I released the window catch and slid it open.

'Better than a brick,' I said.

Cutter and I climbed inside. There was the smell of acrid chemicals. Machines the size of cars stood in rows like gravestones. Upstairs there were empty offices. A garden hose led into a free-standing cubicle half the size of a shipping container. In one side was an open door. I shone my flashlight in. It was soundproofed with black rippled plastic foam lining the walls, a booth designed for audio recording. The stench of human waste came from a bucket in one corner. The hose came through the wall and was fitted with a handgun. On the floor was a sleeping bag.

'She was here,' I said.

With my flashlight we looked at a blood spot on the floor.

'It's recent,' I said.

'I hope she's alright,' Cutter said.

'She could be dead.'

'There's a vial here labelled Propofol,' said Cutter.

It was a common anaesthetic. It could have been synthesised in a home laboratory from easily obtained chemicals and catalyst.

'They could have used it to control her when they moved her out.'

'How long ago?'

'Under an hour. A blood spot would dry in an hour or two. This one is still sticky.'

'Perhaps they found out we were on our way and took off.'

'Why not leave her here for us to find?'

'Maybe they haven't finished with her yet.'

'Where would they take her?' asked Cutter.

'To another hiding place.'

'If they're in the Merc the police can look for them.'

I called Peggy.

'Phillip here. We have found where they held her. We are there now. They have just now taken her away.'

'Where are you?

'Commercial Road number 205. It's a disused factory.'

'Just a minute.'

Peggy put me on hold.

When she came back she said, 'I've put out an alert. It's gone out to all cars and stations. They could have her in the Mercedes at CS2 but there are a lot of black C-Classes out there. There's not much hope of finding it without a plate number. I've sent a CSI team, Doctor. How did you get in?'

'The back door is open.'

It was now.

'What else is there?'

I had another look at the blood spot on the floor.

'They might have injured her, killed her, or she might have died and they have gone to dump her.'

'Where would they take her?' Cutter said.

'Where she wouldn't be found. Or where they could hide her — in a place where no-one goes.'

'In the bush.'

'There's bushland along Blackland Road.'

'They might still be there. It's worth a try.'

We ran back to the car. I told Barbie the way.

'Fast as you can,' I said.

Cutter called Peggy. 'We are on our way to Blackland Road. We figure they might try to hide her body in the bush there.'

'Stay well back — they are dangerous.'

Barbie was way over the speed limit.

It felt good to be with Cutter and Barbie. We worked well together.

'Shh!'

Barbie turned up the radio news.

' ... A woman has been found on a building site in the Central Business District and taken to the Alexandra South Hospital. She is in Intensive Care.'

'That could be her,' I said. 'Stop.'

Barbie stood on the brakes and we slithered to a halt on the verge.

'Steady, Barbie,' said Cutter. 'It might not be her.'

The radio continued. 'The woman is unconscious and in a very serious condition. Her identity is not yet known. It is possible she is Councillor Jane Kenwood who disappeared five weeks ago.'

Her name burst into my consciousness like a bomb.

'It is her. Quick — to the hospital. She sounds in a bad way.'

With tyres squealing, Barbie did a U-turn.

'She was found at a construction site on Fortescue and Endicot Streets,' the radio continued. 'It has been cordoned off as a crime scene. The police would like to hear from anyone who noticed anything suspicious there this morning before 7 am. Their number is 3386 1190. Now for the weather.'

Barbie wove from lane to lane past slow and turning vehicles.

Jane was alive but she sounded precarious. I would confirm it was her and make sure the medics were doing all they could for her.

The traffic dithered as parents dropped children off at school. Driving on the wrong side of the road, Barbie roared past them.

'Slow down, please,' I said to Barbie, 'or we'll be in hospital too.'

'We were a bit too late getting to the factory,' Cutter said.

'Maybe just as well,' I thought. *'A confrontation could have been disastrous.'*

'Perhaps they knew we were coming and decided to get rid of her before we got there,' said Cutter. 'We left town at around 6.00 am and arrived at the factory at 6.30 am. They must have left the factory before 6.30 am for her to be dumped on a construction site when no-one was around.'

'Did you two mention to anyone that we were following a lead?' I asked.

'I didn't,' said Cutter.

'I told Tony we were on to something, Doc,' said Barbie defensively, 'but I didn't say what.'

'Only four of us – Barbie, Tony, Cutter and Jessica the pharmacist – knew,' I said. 'Could it have been a coincidence that they fled just before we arrived?'

Barbie switched her gaze momentarily from the road and her coal-black eyes looked straight into mine. She bristled as if rebuffing an accusation. Her glance became a stare as she projected her superior right. I was bested in an encounter with her wild-animal mind. I winced, pursed my mouth and turned away. Her presence intimidated me.

I said slowly, 'It was only a few days ago that the casino lost the IB site in the Council. They no longer needed to hold her and that was the cue to get rid of her. It could be a coincidence.'

I wasn't happy with this conclusion. Coincidence was a last resort. It was more likely someone had told them we were coming. I have learned during my time in police work never to completely trust anyone when investigating a crime. Barbie seemed intent on the road ahead.

Why had she lasered me with an ocular burn?

PART 4

FOUND

CHAPTER 55

When we arrived at the hospital, Cutter and I went to the reception desk while Barbie parked. The queue was moving slowly and I pushed to the front.

'Excuse me. Where is Intensive Care?' I asked.

'Are you a doctor?'

'Yes. I am a doctor of philosophy in forensic science.'

The receptionist frowned.

'Are you a proper doctor?'

'Yes,' I said.

'What is the patient's name?'

'Councillor Jane Kenwood. She is critical.'

'Is she a relative?'

'I'm her partner and I'm on the City Council with her.' I indicated Cutter. 'He is a councillor too.'

Her attitude changed to helpful.

'Take the lift to Floor 6.'

We went up. There was a crowd with cameras and notebooks pressed against a glass door with a 'No Entry' sign. The time was 8.34 am.

'Is this Intensive Care?' I asked a reporter.

'Only doctors can go in.'

'I am a doctor,' I said.

'Which patient?'

'Councillor Kenwood.'

They clustered around, jostling for position and taking photos.

'Would you answer a few questions, Doctor Keane?' said a busty brunette with a toothy smile. She could have recognised me from a Council event she had covered.

'Not now. I am in a hurry.'

I pushed towards the door to go in.

'Who is behind this, Dr Keane?' asked someone, following me.

'Go away,' I said.

As Cutter and I pushed through to the 'No Entry' door, Barbie arrived. The media people were in a tight scrum.

'Stand aside,' I ordered.

I had played rugby and was able to force a pathway for Barbie to come through and go in with us.

'Get out of my way,' I said and elbowed through.

'Ouch,' a reporter complained.

We arrived at the nurses' station, where we had to show identification.

'Only next of kin may visit critical patients,' said the nurse.

'I'm her partner.'

'You may visit her, Doctor Keane. Our Registrar, Doctor Kaur, will take you in.'

Cutter and Barbie went to the waiting room.

A pretty coffee-coloured young Indian woman with a swathe of glossy black hair tied loosely down her back came to meet me.

'I am Doctor Kaur.'

She was wearing a pale-blue embroidered kamees, a dress top, over dark blue baggy salvar pants. She pressed her hands together in a humble Sikh greeting.

'Sat Sri Akal,' she said. 'God is the Truth. Call me Jasmine, please.'

I gave her my Council calling card. She looked at it.

'Are you a medical doctor, Doctor Keane?'

'No. I am a doctor of forensic science.'

'I am pleased to meet you, Doctor Keane. You must be worried about her. I will take you to see her. She was rescued from drowning in concrete.'

'Did you say concrete?'

'Yes. She was covered with wet concrete, immersed in it. They dragged her out from under. An ambulance brought her here at 8 am. She was unconscious.'

I was shocked. I had not expected Jane to have been so mistreated.

'There was a gag in her mouth. Concrete is corrosive to soft tissues. Prolonged contact with skin, eyes, mouth and clothing may result in burns. She was immersed for only a few minutes. She is

236

recovering from a large dose of anaesthetic and has bruises possibly from a fight or from being handled roughly.'

'Has she recovered consciousness?' I asked.

'Not yet. When they rescued her she was moving but she lost consciousness and has been out ever since.'

'Could she have appeared to be dead when they covered her?'

'The concrete workers said she was covered by accident.'

'Was it an accident?'

'They didn't see she was there. She had ropes around her wrists and ankles. I'll take you in to see her now. You may visit her for three minutes. You cannot come within one metre of her or touch or try to communicate with her or make any noise. She is weak and we must protect her from infections and stresses. I will be present throughout. Do you agree?'

'Okay,' I said. I was reeling from hearing what had been done to her. Burial alive was heinous, hideously brutal, as compassionate as a charging rhinoceros.

She gave me a face mask.

'Follow me. Tell me when you can confirm who she is.'

We entered the room where she lay.

The room was dim. I was shocked by Jane's appearance. Her poor bruised face was thin, hollow and pale. Her long locks were dirty and tangled. She seemed barely alive and I wanted to weep. A drip was connected to a scrawny arm. Her eyes were hooded and her expression was pained, as if she had been away from sunlight and joy for a long time.

It was no publicity stunt.

I recognised a small pale scar at her right temple from a bike accident as a child.

'Yes, it is Jane Kenwood,' I whispered to Doctor Kaur.

I felt angry and wanted revenge.

She was wired up to sensors that monitored her life functions at regular intervals. I slipped into my familiar former forensic role, analysed the polygraph and my anger cooled.

Her temperature was high and feverish. Her heart rate, breathing and blood pressure were cycling dramatically.

'Can you stabilise her, Doctor?' I whispered to Kaur.

237

'Shh. We shouldn't be talking.' She drew me away from the bed. 'We want her to bring it under control herself. We are trying to boost her immunity. If she gets an infection, it could be fatal. If the cycling continues, we might medicate her.'

'She seems very pale,' I said.

'She could have been in the dark.'

I tried to imagine how she had been treated but could not.

'Her muscles are wasted. Why is that?'

'DCI Wall has a theory — ask her. Time is up now. We will go outside.'

Peggy Wall was there with Malcolm.

'Good morning, Chief Inspector. Good morning, Malcolm. How are you?' I said, shaking hands.

'How is she?'

'She's alive but she's in a bad way. Peggy, I am told you have a theory about her muscles being wasted away?'

'Yes, Doctor Keane,' she said. "What sort of physical shape was she in when she disappeared?'

'Good shape,' I said. 'She played tennis and did gym. She had muscles.'

'She may not have had any food.'

I didn't get it.

'When?'

'Never.'

'What — not for five weeks?'

Peggy let Dr Kaur answer.

'It looks that way,' she said. 'When a person is starved, they metabolise their fat first and when that is all gone, they digest their muscles. When the muscles are all gone, they die. She has no fat left and has used up almost all her muscles. She was near death when they found her.'

I was stunned. Starvation was cruel. Anger surged in me again but I stopped it. If I was going to help Jane, I had to keep a cool head.

'Will she recover, Doctor?' I asked.

'The physical damage may not be permanent.' Dr Kaur said.

'Are you sure?' I asked.

'Fairly certain, Doctor. A young man who was lost in the Himalayas without any food for six weeks consumed 40% of his body mass but had no organ damage. He had minor nerve damage from vitamin deficiency and was left with a small vision disability.'

'Did he suffer trauma?'

'No.'

'Was he in a coma?'

'No.'

'Jane could have permanent effects.'

'We will have to wait and see.'

I understood now why Dr Kaur had not told me Jane had been starved. I was a suspect and my visit to Jane could conceivably be to divert suspicion from me. They were testing to see if I knew she had been starved, as evidence of my involvement in the crime. I could have come to the hospital to finish her off. I was not offended. I supposed hospital doctors used the ploy routinely when a family member could be implicated. I was worried about her condition, which was precarious.

CHAPTER 56

As I left the intensive care ward, the brunette reporter blocked my path.

'Doctor Keane, would you answer a few questions now, please?'

'Will it take long? I have urgent business.'

'Only a few minutes.'

'Okay then.'

'Is she still in a coma?'

'Yes.'

'Does she have an enemy who would do this to her?'

'She has political opponents who have had her excluded from Council meetings. There has never been any physical violence.'

'Does she stop the Government getting its own way?'

'Jane is our best councillor,' I said. 'Week after week, often alone, she has stood up for her residents and run the gauntlet of the party bullies. She prevents greed from holding sway and demands that developers contribute to the public good.'

'Could her abduction have been motivated by business or political interest?' said a reporter.

'Yes,' I thought but antagonising people would accomplish nothing.

I said, 'She has always followed the rules, played the ball, not the opponent, worked tirelessly for the interests of her constituents and all the people of Alexandra.'

'Do you live with her?'

'Yes, sometimes.'

'Dr Keane, what is your relationship with Ms Kenwood?'

I didn't have words for it. We had had a delightful relationship for several months but it could be ended forever. I realised how much I had lost and it was like a punch in the guts.

'We are good friends,' I answered sadly.

'Is your friendship with her sexual?' she asked.

'That is none of your business,' I said.

'Is your relationship with her err ... physical?'

They pushed in around me, cameras gaping, wanting a story of foul play and romance.

I spoke testily.

'You seem to be more interested in whether we do or do not copulate than in the political significance of this abduction. You should tell readers how the democratic rights of city people have been breached. Now stand aside, my good woman.'

She let me pass.

Another reporter, a man, pushed in. 'When will she be able to tell us who did it?'

I saw red. For him, it was simply a story to be hyped up for the news. Jane might not live. I wanted to trash him.

'Get out of my way.' I shouldered him aside and went to find the Medical Director. His luxurious suite was in the newest building on the top floor.

'I want to make a complaint,' I told his secretary.

'Can you give me some idea of what it's about?'

'It's about safeguarding Councillor Jane Kenwood.'

'One moment please.'

A few minutes later she showed me into his office. A middle-aged man in shirtsleeves was concentrating at a computer screen. He got up, came around the desk and shook my hand.

'Good morning, Doctor Keane. My name is Henry Carter. I understand that you are concerned about Jane Kenwood. Her situation is very serious.'

'Thank you for seeing me, Mr Carter.' I was deferent to bureaucrats when I wanted something from them. 'I am concerned to stop the criminals who might try to finish her off while she is here in hospital.'

'I have discussed it with Chief Inspector Wall, Doctor,' he said. 'An assailant would have to get to Floor 6, go past the nurses' station, find the room she is in and get away afterwards without being seen. It would be quite difficult and it is unlikely.'

'In my opinion too easy and very likely. He could come in as a reporter and hide among the mob up there.'

The Medical Director swallowed and looked out of the window.

'Do you think it is likely they will try again?' he said

I raised my voice a notch. 'Very likely. They have already tried to bury her in concrete. Two councillors have been attacked. Now we need a very determined defence to stop them finishing her off. Councillor Kenwood is an important public figure and must be protected. Anyone could slip in and hide among the crowd of reporters up there.'

'We can stop the media people from going up,' Carter said. 'We can have daily conferences with them, at 10 am, on the ground floor. A doctor and a member of our public relations team can update them on her condition.'

'She also needs to be guarded 24/7. As soon as she starts to talk they could try to silence her permanently.'

'We will review the situation after we see how she's progressing.'

'But ...'

'Sorry. That's all I can do for you now.'

'Thank you, Mr Carter.'

He showed me out.

*

I slept badly. In the morning I heard the crane driver interviewed on the radio. He told how he had swung the spout along to where Jane was found and spewed concrete in.

I imagined her captor watching with psychopathic interest from a nearby pedestrian bridge. It was a miracle Jane was still alive.

The next day, I returned to the hospital at 10 am for a media conference. The room was full of reporters. Henry Carter stood at the lectern.

'I am the Medical Director and this is our Medical Registrar, Dr Jasmine Kaur, who will give us an update.'

'Ms Kenwood slept most of the night,' said Jasmine. 'She was sedated for several hours by the anaesthetic the abductors had injected but its effects have now worn off. She is still unconscious. She is stabilising but she is still critical. It has not been possible to diagnose her mental condition but post-traumatic stress disorder is a possibility. She has been given a medication to quell anxiety.'

'Detective Chief Inspector Wall will now summarise the police investigation.'

'We are investigating five crime scenes,' Peggy said. 'They are the place where she was taken; where her car was found; where she was held; another location; and where she was found.'

'Is there a suspect?' a reporter asked.

'We are pursuing several leads but so far there is not enough evidence to bring anyone in.'

'And now Councillor Dr Phillip Keane will speak. He is Ms Kenwood's partner and colleague.'

I stepped up to the lectern. My voice was loud because of my outrage.

'Those who have done this to Jane have attacked the people of our city, the ordinary folk who want freedom, equality and justice. The abductors have taken her away from them.

'I appeal to you to ask members of the public to contact the police if they have any information that could help identify those who did this to her. Hers is such a brilliant star; perhaps she has attracted the attention of unscrupulous people. If they have information would they call 3386 1190. Thank you for your support,' I said and stepped back.

'Thank you, Doctor Keane,' said Peggy. 'We want to hear of anything suspicious.'

Henry Carter said, 'When Ms Kenwood's condition changes, we will hold another media conference. Give us your contacts and we will keep you informed.'

CHAPTER 57

The next day, Jane's parents, Joseph and Jennifer Kenwood, were in the waiting room after a visit at her bedside. Joseph stared at the wall without speaking. I sat down beside him.

'How are you?' I asked.

'I'm very worried about Jane,' he said.

'Me too. She is very special to many people. Blake people regard her as one of their own.'

He turned and looked at me.

'I have always been close to Jane,' he said. 'She accomplished what I couldn't. I ran for Council, but lost.'

'She had you to help her.'

'She got there pretty much by herself. Did you know that before she ran for Council she was doing well as a barrister?'

'Why did she change to politics?'

'She's idealistic and wanted to make a difference. We should have talked her out of it.'

'Could she be finishing what you started?'

'Her getting on the Council wasn't my doing,' he said. 'I coached her in the principles of democracy, politics and debating. She got there by herself.'

'Do you have an enemy who could have done this to her?'

'No.'

'What did you think about her going independent?'

'Hmmph. She shouldn't have quit the NLP. Once she gets an idea into her head, nothing will stop her. She won't be able to get far on her own. Have you crossed?'

'Yes. Richard Barber has too. The three of us help each other.'

'Three heads are better than one.'

'Jane said you taught her to play chess.'

'I did,' he said. 'Her opening game is brilliant; her middle game is very good; but her end game is pretty ordinary. She doesn't have a lot of patience. She is impetuous.'

'That's Jane. Has she always been like that?'

'She gets bored easily and believes in change for change's sake,' her father said. 'Basically, she's an inventor.'

'It's hard to keep up with her sometimes.'

'You could be good for each other.'

'I hope so. Thanks, Joe.'

*

Later that day, Richard Barber aka Cutter came to the hospital. He was quite drunk. He was sucking on a Coca Cola can and stank of rum. He went with Barbie and me in to see the recumbent Jane. When we came out he seemed upset.

'Will she be alright, Phillip?' he asked. His words were slurred.

'No-one knows,' I replied. 'We're waiting for her to come round.'

'How long will that be?'

'They don't know.'

'Shit.'

He sat down heavily next to Barbie in the visitor's room.

'Cheer up, Cutter,' she said. 'She is getting better. We just have to wait.'

'I can stay for an hour, I suppose,' said Cutter. 'Hospitals make me sick.'

After a while he said to us, 'Who did this to her?'

'Political or business people, probably,' I said.

'Council people?'

I looked at him and shrugged. 'I don't know.'

'It sucks,' said Cutter. 'Disappearing a representative of the people is bad.'

'I agree,' I said. 'The bastards who did this are going to suffer.'

'Count me in on that,' said Cutter, with a hiccup.

*

Sunita and Tony met with us for a drink at a city bar after work.

245

I told them about the cell where she had been held. They were horrified.

'They treated her like shit,' said Sunita.

'Because she went out on a limb.'

The mood was sombre and I became reproachful.

'We should have taken better care of her,' I said.

'No, Phillip. The fault lies with whoever did this to her,' said Sunita. 'If you think any of us could have foreseen this, you're wrong. In Southland, politicians are never abducted.'

'We let her become a target,' I said.

Cutter shook his head. 'That's not fair. We couldn't have expected this.'

Sunita burst into tears. 'Phillip, you are being a prick. This kind of violence is associated with drug barons, dictators and espionage, not with the ACC.'

'Why are you crying?' I asked. Her histrionics annoyed me.

'We need to be sensitive to each other's feelings,' said Sunita. 'Friends are supposed to support each other — that's what friendship is all about. It's not like any of us have been up this particular shit creek before, have we?'

There was a lot of guilt going on besides mine.

'I should have looked after her better,' I said. 'I should have reined her in.'

'She wouldn't have let you.'

My eyes were watering and I wiped away a tear that slid down my cheek.

'I don't know how to share in your feelings,' I said, 'but I have a big share in the blame. I let her go out in front for all of us. Now she is taking the rap and it makes me feel like a piece of shit.'

'No-one is to blame except the motherfuckers who did this,' said Tony.

'We shouldn't have let her be singled out,' I said.

'It's too late to do anything about that now, Doc,' Barbie said. Her eyes had an animal look, on alert as she stared me down. She watched me tremulously and I imagined tiny twitches as she waited. I realised that Barbie was keyed up, watching us as if to discover which one of us was implicated.

'We can help her recover,' I said.

'And find out who did it,' said Tony.

We were a sombre group without Jane. We got drunk and the hurt eased a little.

CHAPTER 58

'How is Jane?' the LM asked when our paths crossed.

'No change.'

Hubbard's interest in Jane's welfare could be concocted to allay any suspicion of her involvement in the abduction. The LM was the person benefitting most from her absence. I didn't want her to know about Jane's gradual improvement because she might try to prevent her recovery.

'I'm going to visit her,' she said, 'tomorrow at 2 pm.'

She would assess how soon Jane would be back voting in opposition against her again. Her hung Council was barely surviving. Before her Government tabled bills in the legislature, Cutter and I had insisted she run them past us so we could veto any we disagreed with.

'The way you pick and choose is disgraceful,' the LM complained. 'We'll get all those bills through in our next term, you'll see — if you're returned, which isn't likely.'

I was there at the hospital to meet the LM when she came out of Jane's room.

'She's getting over something awful. Do you know who did it?'

I shook my head.

'She must have pressed someone's buttons once too often,' she said.

I nodded. 'Maybe.'

'She was a bit impulsive and wild sometimes, don't you think?' she said, as if Jane had got her comeuppance.

I leapt to her defence.

'She is neither impulsive nor wild; she is passionate about good government.'

We didn't talk any more after that and the LM left.

Seeing Jane in a coma was unpleasant and I kept my visits brief. I was uncomfortable with sickness. When I could, I avoided sick people. Going to a hospital invited infection and I didn't stay for longer than I had to.

*

I was sitting with Cutter in the Council's tearoom.

'We two can cause an election,' I said.

'I'm waiting for an offer I can't refuse,' he said.

'After Jane crossed she turned them all down.'

'That's why she was taken out — because they couldn't control her.'

'It wasn't necessarily Government people. Did anyone from outside ever threaten her?'

'She didn't mention it to me,' he said.

'Nor to me.'

'We may not know what happened until she comes around.'

*

In our Committee meeting Munster tried bullying us.

'The Premier wants to get the casino approved,' she said.

'It's pretty low to approve it while Councillor Kenwood is in hospital.'

'I object. The councillor is inferring motive,' said Fenwick.

'I am not,' I said. 'The committee will miss her. If the Government goes ahead without her, it would be despicable behaviour because it was decided two weeks ago not to approve the casino for the IB site.'

'Your MC is not home and hosed yet,' said Munster. 'Until a DA is approved the casino could still get the IB site.'

The meeting went on to other business.

'Our DA is needed urgently,' I said to Cutter afterwards. 'Preparing it is a huge task.'

'Now that we have Jane back with us, we can take up where we left off.'

'I'm giving it everything I've got.'

'She would want that.'

249

CHAPTER 59

On the day after they pulled Jane out from under the concrete, Peggy, Barbie and I visited her in hospital.

She lay unconscious, with continuous monitoring of her cardiac and respiratory systems.

'How could anyone have wanted to do this to her?' I thought.

For 10 minutes we stood at her bedside. She lay still, with her vital signs pulsing weakly on the polygraph. It seemed as though she would never recover.

We met with Doctor Kaur afterwards for an update.

'Is she getting better, Doctor?'

'She is no longer critical,' said Kaur. 'She is being fed through a nasogastric tube, with intravenous hydration and morphine to calm her. She is not yet stable and cycling randomly. She could relapse at any time. The psychologist is coming at 11 am.'

'Why is she so pale?'

'Light triggers the skin to grow pigmentation cells called melanocytes. When she was admitted she had none. She could have been in complete darkness for all five weeks she was missing. Sensory deprivation can cause mental issues too.'

Her experience had been horrific.

'What mental issues?' I asked.

'We won't know until she comes out of it.'

'Could she have been unconscious before she was dropped into the hole?' asked Peggy.

'She could have been under from the anaesthetic. Or she might have feigned death, remaining conscious until her rescuers hosed her down and put her in shock.'

'What would be happening to her in a coma?' I asked Dr Kaur.

'Suppose she was a computer. Her systems have overloaded and she has shut down voluntary behaviour. She is slowly rebooting.'

'Could her brain be hung indefinitely?'

'The polygraph shows she is not in a loop and could be improving.'

Psychologist, Terry Cline, arrived and we went with Jasmine into a conference room.

'What is happening in her mind, Terry?' I said.

'We don't know much yet,' he said. 'Her abduction, imprisonment and handling were traumatic enough to cause post-traumatic stress disorder (PTSD), even before she was covered with concrete.'

'What was the effect of the concrete?' I asked.

Kaur answered, 'She would be chilled, crushed and asphyxiated. The pressure on her abdomen would increase as the concrete got deeper, preventing her drawing breath even if there was air available, which there wasn't. Being unable to move while being smothered by heavy concrete would have terrified her,' the psychologist said. 'There could be damage to her mind that may never be undone, or will repair only slowly. There is little we can do other than wait for her recovery.'

'I have to go,' said Peggy. 'Doctor Kaur, will you let me know of any change in her condition, please?'

*

I visited Jane for an hour every morning with Barbie. Her other visitors came in the afternoons and evenings.

Several times, Jane stirred slightly, with a tremor in her abdomen or a limb. It was movement and it was increasing.

I spoke to her softly. 'Jane, it's me, Phillip.'

A few days later I noticed she was responding.

'Nurse,' I said, 'she startles whenever anyone talks to her.'

'Startles?'

'Destabilises on the polygraph. It happens when we get close to her. Look, I'll show you.'

With my mouth close to her ear, I said quietly, 'Hello, Jane, this is Phillip.'

We watched as her heart rate that had been flatlining spiked and she gasped. Her muscles tensed up.

251

'Is it fight, flight or freeze?' I asked the nurse.

'One of those, I should think,' she said. 'You shouldn't be experimenting. I'll ask the psychologist to talk with you.'

Terry Cline arrived a few minutes later. He said that Jane wasn't strong enough yet to be stimulated. My take on the psychology was that stimulating her had an observer effect, like a physicist trying to look at an atom by firing electrons at it, which would inadvertently change it. Jane's responses to stimuli could be negative and would alter her, giving a distorted image. The medics wanted Jane revealed unaltered, au naturel.

'She seems to panic with human contact, whoever it is,' said Cline. 'It is expected because her most recent human contact has hurt her. We can try to soothe her panic cycles — get her used to being touched and spoken to.'

Kaur said her main therapy was food. The hospital was feeding her starved organs, like the gaping maws of nestlings, so they would recover and fly in a wheeling flock of wellbeing.

We left Doctor Kaur and Barbie drove us to my ward office where we looked for leads by piecing together the information from the crime sites.

'We don't have much to go on,' I said.

'The police want her to tell them who did it,' Barbie said.

'She might not be able to talk about it for months,' I said. 'By then traces could have been cleaned away. Witnesses could forget. Suspects could disappear. We must investigate now before the trail goes cold.'

PART 5

RECONSTRUCTION

CHAPTER 60

On the fifth day, I was caressing Jane's hand when a cycle that was building up dwindled away. I was excited because it could mean she was on her way back to the real world.

I ran into Peggy at the hospital.

'Is Jane talking yet?' she asked.

I was impatient. 'No. She seems to be improving. We should interview the main political and business players before they can say they don't remember what they were doing.'

'Doctor Keane, I am under orders to wait for Councillor Kenwood's testimony,' Peggy said. 'Until we have evidence we can't go looking under stones to see what crawls out.'

'Whose orders?'

'Government — at the political level.'

Peggy must have received a ministerial edict.

'We could be waiting for months,' I said to Peggy. 'Essential evidence could be lost. We need this as soon as possible.'

'I understand how you feel. If you need help, Doctor, let me know,' said Peggy. 'I may be able to do something.'

It had been two years since I had investigated a crime but you don't lose the skills. As long as I didn't break the law, they couldn't stop me.

I felt for Peggy. Having the Government on her back was like carrying a heavy weight. If she slipped it could crush her.

'I am doing a reconstruction,' I said to Peggy. 'I am starting with the features of the crime scenes that caused Jane's condition when they found her.'

'Okay, we have information from her car and from the construction site,' said Peggy. 'As for her condition, DI Malcolm is arranging to meet with the hospital's pathologist, Doctor Semple. Doctor Keane, you are welcome to go along with him but I am warning you, it won't be easy for you to hear about the damage that's been done to her.'

'I'll be okay. I am used to shutting out my feelings.'

'We don't want you to make any emotional calls.'

'They call me Spock.'

'Even Spock has a heart. You could bias the evidence.'

'Being dispassionate is deeply ingrained in me,' I said. 'You don't have to worry about me being biased.'

'I look forward to hearing how you're getting on, Doctor,' said Peggy.

DCI Peggy Wall and DI Malcolm allowed me access to the evidence the police had collected. I suggested leads and forensic tests. It was not unlike my old job, when I had advised the detectives, lawyers and law courts. The main difference was that then I had a team who conducted forensic work. Now Peggy's people gathered the evidence and did the tests. It was careful and slow. I found it difficult to contain my impatience but when I proposed doing a reconstruction of the crime, Peggy let me get on with it.

My reconstruction had to be the best possible explanation of the evidence. I would have a 'think tank' that would do lateral thinking because many heads were better than one for solving puzzles. I knew how to set one up from a friend who had researched how to organise for creativity. My think tank would be unlike police case conferences and briefings. Authoritarian instruction would be replaced with a discussion culture I would nurture by feedback of outcomes. I would ask our group of friends to meet on one evening each week.

I needed a place where we would be comfortable and undisturbed. My ward office had three rooms and a small kitchen on either side of a passage behind a reception desk. One room was my office, another for my assistants. In the reception area there was a cork wallboard with a schedule of local events and posters advertising them.

I leased an additional room next door, accessible from the office. It was windowless but had air conditioning. I put in a table and six chairs, a settee, armchairs and a coffee table. We already had a capsule coffee machine.

I fixed a map of the city to the wall and attached a whiteboard with my plan for reconstructing the abduction. It was a diagram with arrows numbered 1 to 8, making a continuous route connecting the four intersection points in a kite shape, entering at Step 1 at the bottom and going through a network with several reversals of direction, without retracing, finishing at Step 8.

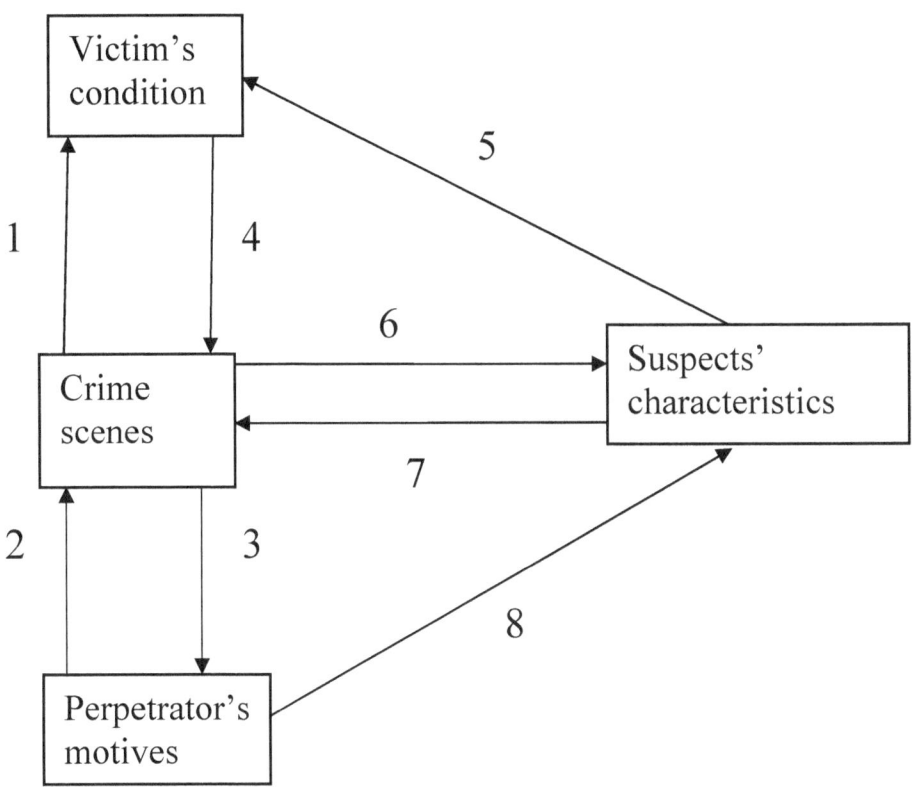

THE RECONSRUCTION LINKS

Cutter and Barbie looked at the diagram sceptically.

'Geez, do you have to get so technical, Phillip?' asked Cutter.

'It's similar to solving a maze. It's an Euler walk,' I said, pronouncing it oi-ler. 'He was a Polish mathematician who defined the rules for finding a pathway through a network.'

'If we are going on a walking tour of the crime, Doc,' said Barbie, 'how should I dress in case I meet the criminal?'

'Nothing too revealing,' said Cutter.

They laughed together, deeply affectionate. He was twice her age, old enough to be her father, but their affair was none of my business.

'What network is this?' asked Cutter.

'The four types of information about the crime are the victim's condition, crime scenes, suspects' characteristics and perpetrator's motives. We will proceed from effects at each of these to their causes that connect in a logical chain of hypotheses, which is the reconstruction. There are 12 possible pairings, of which we will do eight, one at a time.'

'What about the other four?'

'They are not necessary. If they were included, there would be no way out of the maze.'

'Beginning at the end with the victim's condition after the crime, we will take the only route possible through the maze to where the crime began, at the motives. The rest of the data is at two other intersections, having several paths in and out: crime scenes and suspects. Euler's discovery was that every intersection has to have the same number of exits as entrances or you will get stuck there.'

'Duh!' said Barbie. 'If you go in more often than you come out, of course you will be stuck inside. How smart is that?'

'The same if you come out more often than you go in.'

'Then you would be totally fucked,' said Barbie.

'It seems obvious,' I said, 'but Euler was the first to apply that rule in solving network problems.'

'Holy cow! Why don't we do what they usually do, make up theories until one fits the data?' Cutter's tone was scathing.

'That's haphazard,' I said, 'and inefficient. There are too many combinations to consider. We could go around in circles without getting anywhere. My approach will use our time better.'

'Have you tried it?'

'Yes. I tested it during my PhD research on three crimes that had been investigated by the police. My reworks of the cases showed definite benefits — more effective solving of crimes.'

'Why not start with the motives?' Cutter said.

'It is more logical to enter with the victim's condition because it is more objective. We will end up with motives, because in this crime those are more conjectural.'

Cutter and Barbie looked at each other.

'Do you understand?' Barbie asked Cutter.

'No,' he said. 'I trust he knows what he's doing. He usually does.'

'I don't normally like logic,' said Barbie. 'But it makes sense and I'll give it a go for Jane's sake.'

'That's the spirit,' he said. 'You can't go wrong with logic.'

Cutter seemed besotted with Barbie. They had been together on a date or two and had some sort of private communication going. He hung on her every word.

'Holy reconstruction, Batman,' Barbie said, chewing gum. 'You are invincible.'

I laughed. 'More like industrious. We're up for a lot of work.'

'It's a piece of cake,' said Barbie.

'It's worth a try,' said Cutter. 'It makes more sense than blundering around, hoping to stumble on clues, going over and over the same ground, like they do in whodunits on TV.'

It was good to have their support. I looked forward to convincing them by solving the abduction puzzle.

CHAPTER 61

Cutter, Sunita, Barbie and Tony came to the first meeting of our think tank. They brought in cups of coffee from my office next door. There were sandwiches from a delicatessen.

'Thanks for coming,' I said.

'Smoked salmon, yummy,' said Sunita. 'What do we have to do?'

'I want you to have ideas about what happened to Jane so we can catch whoever did it.'

I pointed to my diagram on the whiteboard. I had checked the logic many times. I was confident of a good outcome. It was a strategy for forensic reconstruction I had developed with much commitment and it was part of my karma.

'I want this to be our plan,' I said. 'I've already talked with Cutter and Barbie about it.'

I explained it to Tony and Sunita.

'It seems very thorough,' Tony said.

He was being polite.

They will understand when we get underway,' I thought.

'Shall I tell you who I think abducted Jane?' said Sunita.

'Who?'

'Montague.'

'Why him?'

'He was in the military. They kill people.'

'Then Jane would be dead.'

'He's ex-military.'

'Exactly.'

We laughed.

'It was just an idea,' said Sunita.

'Nice one,' I said. 'Thinking outside the box is what we want.'

'Don't expect me to be creative,' said Tony. 'I have enough on my plate trying to be normal. Odd ideas mean trouble.'

'Not here they don't,' I said.

'Give it a try, Tony,' said Cutter. 'You can be as odd as you like with us.'

Tony glared at him.

'It seems like a good plan,' Barbie said loyally. 'Thinking up weird stuff will be fun.'

'Thank you, Barbie,' I said. 'Ideas don't have to be weird — just good and useful. We will make a start today with Link number 1, which is how the various crime scenes could have caused Jane's condition.'

I switched on my iPad voice recorder.

'During the five weeks she was missing, Jane changed from a healthy, thoughtful, vibrant person to the barely conscious emaciated woman I visited in hospital earlier today. Let's have some ideas, please, about how she got into that condition.'

'She was already in a bad way before the concrete,' said Sunita.

'It was supposed to finish her off,' said Tony.

'It doesn't make sense he kept her alive all that time, then tried to bury her,' Cutter said.

'Perhaps he panicked.'

'Alive, she would set off a manhunt and he might be caught,' said Tony. 'Perhaps after he finished with her he wanted to kill her and get rid of the evidence.'

'Then she would be dead.'

'He didn't expect them to rescue her.'

'Perhaps he wanted her dead but couldn't bring himself to kill her.'

'Perhaps he was taking her somewhere when he thought she had died,' said Cutter.

'While he was driving?'

'Perhaps he stopped and she seemed dead. After that he tried to hide her body.'

Tony said, 'How did he know where the concrete would go? It couldn't have been just his good luck. He didn't spy them concreting and carry her across. He must have known when they would be pouring beforehand. He arranged to arrive before 7 am when they started work and he knew which formwork they would be filling.'

'That makes good sense, Tony,' I said.

261

We discussed what would be in someone's mind when they buried a person alive.

'Perhaps to kill her humanely such as by strangulation would be accepting too much responsibility.'

'He could have had a fantasy of entombment.'

'Barbie,' I said, 'would you find out who knew the when and where of the concreting that day?'

'Okay, boss,' she said.

'We will suspend Link 1 until we get more details of Jane's condition and figure out what happened to cause it. We have made good progress.'

We agreed to meet again in a week and finished our meeting.

*

Barbie and I went with DI Malcolm to see pathologist, Dr Semple, at the hospital. He met us at reception and we went down in the lift to the basement where his office was near the mortuary.

'I usually investigate cadavers,' said the pathologist. 'I look inside victims, which isn't possible in this case. So I might not be of much help to you.

'I have had a look at her from the outside and I have done some tests,' he said. 'The starvation she suffered would have killed many people. She has lost 20 kilograms from 60; that's about 30%. She wasn't packing much spare tissue. She metabolised her body fat and most of her muscle tissue.'

'How much longer would she have lasted?' Malcolm asked.

'A week or two.'

'What would cause her to die?' asked Barbie.

'Hunger strikers have contracted respiratory tract infections, such as bronchitis or pneumonia, and become too weak to cough or to swallow and drowned in their own mucous secretions,' said Semple.

'Yuck.'

'Could she have been on hunger strike?' asked Sunita.

'Hunger striking is to leverage release supposing the captors do not want voluntary death on their hands. There were no signs of forced feeding.'

262

'Maybe when she wouldn't eat they were going to release her.'

'We will have to wait until she recovers to find that out,' I said.

'Could she have lost condition by illness?'

'There is no evidence of blood poisoning or food poisoning, dysentery, cholera, or another infection caught from food, from water, from the air, or from surfaces or vectors such as rats or mosquitoes,' Semple said. 'After a bacterial infection, her white cell count would be high but it isn't. Nor was she affected by poisonous foods, seeds, plants or insects. We did not find any toxic substances in significant amounts.

'We looked for evidence of other illnesses. There was no evidence of hypothermia or heat exhaustion. We found no organ failure or tumours.'

'Was anything else done to her, Doctor Semple?' asked Barbie.

'She was injected only an hour or two before she was rescued. There was Propofol residue in her blood,' Dr Semple said. 'It knocks out people within minutes and keeps them under for a period of several hours, depending on their body mass and the size of the dose.

'It could have prevented her escaping, or calling out, or seeing her captors, or being able to identify them.'

'Could it have been to kill her?'

'If they were going to kill her they wouldn't have blindfolded her,' said Malcolm.

'Might they have tried to put her down the way a vet finishes off an old dog?' Barbie asked.

'They didn't succeed,' said Semple.

'Why didn't they keep on until they did? They had time,' I said.

'Because they were not trying to kill her,' Semple said. 'Her condition when rescued was the cumulative effect of non-lethal harm done at all the crime scenes.'

'How could it be otherwise?' I said.

'She could have been incapacitated by only one of the events. Or her condition could be of indeterminate causation. But my conclusion is that it resulted from the shock of burial at CS6 when she was emaciated from CS3. Together they put her in hospital. We don't yet know all the effects. Her brain may be partly shut down. There could be permanent brain damage.'

Dismay bounced around in my head. I couldn't deal with her mind being impaired. Of all her lovely features, it was her mind that I most adored.

'It doesn't look like attempted murder,' Malcolm said as we rode back up to Jane's ward.

'We know more or less what was done, but we don't know who did it,' Barbie said disconsolately. 'We don't even have a suspect.'

'Cheer up, Barbie,' said Malcolm. 'Phillip's method is working. We have created hypotheses for how her condition was caused. From what we know of the crime scenes, they caused the effects on her. We will get to finding out suspects soon enough.'

'The test will be when Jane tells us what really happened,' I said.

'I think it will be soon, Doc.'

We had established Link 1 in the reconstruction, that Jane's near-comatose state when she was rescued could be explained by conditions at the crime scenes.

I asked myself, *'Why did they impose these harsh conditions on her?'*

CHAPTER 62

It had been a month since Jane was found. I was shaving at 7 am to go to the hospital when my phone rang.

'This is Alexandra South Hospital, Jasmine Kaur here. Jane has opened her eyes.'

'Fantastic,' I said. 'Thank you for calling, Doctor. I'll be there shortly.'

A weight had been lifted off me. I dressed in a rush, putting on the clothes I wore yesterday, not bothering with socks. I would feed my goldfish later. I went without breakfast, my favourite meal. I galloped around checking the three outside doors were locked. I went out the front door and set the deadlock.

In the garage I realised I had left my car keys behind and went back for them. Before re-exiting, I rechecked the outside doors. I reset the deadlock. Then I checked my shoulder bag for my wallet. After trying the various pockets several times, I had not found it and went back in again. It was not in the likely places. Flustered and cursing, I rechecked the shoulder bag and there it was, after all. In my haste, I shut the front door on my hand and it hurt for the rest of the day. It was then I noticed my mobile phone was missing from its pocket. Hot and bothered, I started to go back but fumbled with my keys and decided to go without my phone.

I drove straight to the hospital. Feeling incomplete in my car without my phone, I reflected on my inefficient getaway and my autism. My flexibility under pressure was woeful. My life was a series of routines. My subconscious could be trying to delay me from finding out the likely bad news of Jane's psychological injuries.

I arrived at the hospital at 8 am. Miraculously she was conscious with Terry at her bedside. Her eyes were closed, her jaw was clenched and her mouth was pursed, as if from an unpleasant taste.

Her eyes fluttered open but she did not see me. Her gaze was over my head but she was aware we were there.

'Welcome back, Jane,' I said with tears streaming down my face and my voice choking up. 'Thank you for coming back to us.'

'Speak softly,' Terry said. 'Her hearing is very sensitive.'

It had been nine weeks since she had heard a friendly voice. Although her eyes were open, there was no communication with me. Her right eye was half-closed, dull and unfocused, as if the left side of her brain had lost interest in reality because it was too awful. Her left eye was round, clear and bright, indicating her inner-self was well.

Although she did not engage, it was enough for now. I left it to her other visitors to hug and kiss her. My role was as a scientist to ensure her recovery, protection and achievement of justice. I would be unemotional. Defence counsel could reject my investigation as compromised by my relationship with the victim. They could say that because I was emotionally involved, my reconstruction would be biased. In any case, she was in no fit state for cuddling. The damage done to her stood in the way of restoring our relationship.

Jane's improving condition had been closely followed in the news. A media conference was held at the hospital to announce her return to consciousness.

I went to see Medical Director, Henry Carter, in his office.

'I hear she's come round, Doctor Keane,' he said. 'Fantastic!'

'She must have an armed guard 24/7,' I said. 'When the abductors hear she's talking they could try and silence her permanently.'

'Hmm,' Carter said. 'We have guards for public figures in top jobs, Doctor. But for a city councillor ... I'm not sure. We don't have funds for a 24-hour guard.'

'But you do have security guards.'

'We can't pull them off their regular work.'

'Guarding needs to start immediately. Can you request extra funding when your regulars complain?'

He glared at me. He wasn't used to being told what to do by a patient's lover, even if I was a city councillor.

'I'll see what I can do. I'm not making any promises.'

I went back to intensive care and asked Dr Kaur if I could stay in Jane's room until a guard arrived. I fetched a chair and started my bedside vigil with a book.

I had to be ready to tackle an assailant but I struggled to stay awake. I tried standing up but when I dozed off my legs buckled. I found the best way to stay awake was to work. I got out my iPad and used the hospital's Wi-Fi connection.

At midnight a nurse whispered that the security guard had arrived. I went outside and met Owen, a strapping 30-year old. His shift was until 8 am when another guard would take over. A baton hung from his belt but no gun. I had asked for an armed guard but a hospital would not endorse violence. It would be like celebrating Ramadan with a smorgasbord.

'Doctor Keane, you can go home and get some sleep,' said Owen.

*

I spent a part of each morning at Jane's bedside. I tried talking to her.

'How are you, Jane?'

I felt a little foolish speaking to someone so inert. She slept most of the day. At first, I got little or no response. She looked at me but did not see me, focusing on me briefly then looking away, as if searching for words.

'Jane, hello! This is your partner, Phillip. Do you remember me?'

There was no sign that she had heard.

'Today is Wednesday, July 16th. Your birthday is next month. How old will you be?'

Her eyes looked past me.

'Let's see, you are two years younger than me, so you'll be 36. If you can hear me, blink or move a little? No — well, never mind, there's plenty of time.'

Day by day, her interaction with me improved in small steps. In-between she had several panics. She would be lying in bed, staring at nothing one moment, the next her heart rate would soar and the alarm ping. Her head would jerk from side to side on the pillow, with her eyes rolled back, screaming, convulsing, threshing and pulling out her drips and tubes.

'What is setting her off?' I asked Terry.

267

'It's difficult to say. Perhaps a bad memory.'

'Will the memories fade?'

'Hopefully yes,' he said. 'Her panics should become further apart. Don't expect her to pick up where you left off. It's normal for trauma victims to forget people and relationships. It's called emotional numbing.'

I was talking to her when her eyes blinked open and she looked at me as if I was a stranger. I could hardly believe it – it was months ago we last had eye contact. My heart surged.

'Hello, Jane,' I said. 'It's me, Phillip.'

She stared at me blankly, swallowed and turned away.

'Are you hungry?' I said.

She looked at me, licked her lips and nodded slightly.

I asked a nurse to bring some food.

'I'll help you sit up,' said the nurse. She tilted her up to sitting position and fitted a table across the bed, with a bowl of clear soup.

I offered her a spoonful. She opened her mouth and took it. She finished the bowlful. Afterwards she slept.

It was a good feeling that she had accepted my help.

CHAPTER 63

At a Council meeting, during Any Business, I stood up.
'Yes Councillor Keane?'
'Madam Chairperson, I would like to announce an event.'
'Go ahead, Councillor.'
'LM, Madam Chairperson, Councillors,' I said, 'next Saturday, in the afternoon and evening, I invite you to a multicultural festival where you can sit in a grandstand in front of the IB to watch the parade with your families and friends. The proceeds will go to applying to develop a multicultural centre there. Your attendance would show your support for Alexandra becoming a multicultural city.'
I sat down.
'Thank you, Dr Keane.'
The meeting continued.

*

Sunita and IBAG arranged the greatest multicultural celebration ever held in the CBD. It attracted tens of thousands, including many councillors and other civic leaders. Brightly lit floats with throbbing ethnic music and scantily clad dancers cruised slowly along streets crowded with onlookers. Between the floats were performers from many countries: troupes of dancers, clowns, jugglers, fire twirlers, stilt-walkers and a marching band.

In front of the IB there was a large screen with a CCTV image of Jane sitting up in her hospital bed. She wasn't up to waving or even smiling yet. People knew the MC idea was hers and she would soon be back in charge.

Wallets opened to support the project. A 'Jane's MC' website received donations. A steady stream of money flowed in and spurred on our preparation of a DA.

269

Visiting Jane could be fraught. I had never been in a bedside caring role before or had to deal with anyone having acute PTSD before. She could be friendly, indifferent, in hiding, aloof, cold or rude. Always she was preoccupied as if the hurt of her experience was in the forefront of her mind.

'Do you remember me?' I said. 'I am Phillip. We are friends. We see each other every day. Do you remember me at all?'

She looked past me, thinking.

'Do you know who I am?' I prompted

She nodded slowly and her lips shaped. 'Yes.'

'What is my name?'

She looked at me blankly. I was someone she used to know. I figured she was incapable of a close relationship at present.

She bottled up her feelings, or bagged them until they burst out dramatically. You never could tell when something would set her off.

I was leaving and turned off the light when she was lying with her eyes almost closed.

'No, no, no,' she said, her voice anguished. She whimpered, her legs and arms working, trying to flee. Terror roller-coasted on her polygraph.

She ripped out her needles and tubes, her arms flailing, the cot sides of her bed preventing her from falling out. She threw down onto the floor everything around her, including an intravenous drip stand and a bowlful of fruit. I turned on the light again and she curled into a foetal ball and sobbed, her thin body shuddering. A nurse loaded a syringe with Propofol, but she couldn't find enough muscle in her arm. She settled for Jane's skinny buttock. Immediately Jane calmed down and slept. The nurse reinserted the drip in her arm.

Psychologist Terry Cline arrived.

'How is she?'

'Alive and kicking.'

I told him about her panic.

'We can stop her tearing herself apart but we need to find the cause and deal with it,' he said.

When she awoke, he questioned her softly.

'What upset you, Jane? Tell me what you were thinking.'

Jane looked at him and mouthed quietly, unaccustomed to speaking.

'He ... it was dark.' Jane's voice was faint, unsure of pitch and volume. 'I couldn't hear anything ... no-one came.'

'How did you feel?'

'I was scared. I was hungry. I screamed.'

'Did anyone come?'

She shook her head.

'You're wrong, Jane. A nurse, Phillip and I came. There will always be someone to come to you here. You are safe. There is nothing to be afraid of.'

Jane spoke a little more each day. They put a small light in her room, gradually reducing its brightness. Soon she no longer feared darkness.

*

As Cutter and I waited to visit her one day he said, 'Are you hooked on Jane?'

'It wouldn't be right to walk out on her when she is in hospital,' I said.

'You are being honourable,' said Cutter.

'What should I be?'

'It's her birthday today — I thought you would want to be alone with her.'

'We're not in a relationship.'

It had taken effort to stop myself from touching, holding and caressing Jane. I might have seemed unfeeling, but the best I could do would be to concentrate on finding the abductors, so she could move on towards resuming a proper relationship with me.

'Have you tried?'

'She's not up to it. It is better that I stand back and stay objective.'

Cutter scratched his head.

'Events have split you two apart. It could be months. In the meantime you can enjoy other women.'

'I don't want other women,' I said. 'Have you never wanted one woman?'

'Not for long. The more you get to know a woman, the more her differences become intractable.'

'Intractable?'

'Women have compulsions: health, food, fitness, hygiene, clothes, decor, communication, travel, relatives, children, men, manners and sex. You cannot dismiss or change their preoccupations and you may not be able to live with them. It is best to know what you are getting into before trying to settle down with them, or you are going to be uncomfortable.'

'Do you want to have children?'

'Yes, theoretically. A notional child is appealing. But a real child would be an encumbrance. I can't be bothered with children.'

'I suppose you expect to have a better time by keeping relationships casual?'

'Absolutely. Every time I fall in lust I believe it will be forever. You can't beat the emotional experience of a new conquest and you can have it time and again.'

'You are afloat on a sea of lustful sex.'

'I am. Like Bonobos I subscribe to polygamous fornication as the definitive action in social and communal bonding.'

'You randy sod.'

'It's a compulsion. I spend most of my waking hours teeing up my next fuck. It's like an all-consuming itch that can only be scratched by orgasm.'

'Don't you grow bored with sex?'

'Never. I have an infinite appetite for different women.'

'Because you want diversity?'

'It's more than that. Monogamy is dependence, like having a dog. I do not want to be anyone's master or anyone's dog. I want to be a free individual.'

'Is Jane my dependent?'

'If the two of you so choose.'

'I want to care for her. I would like to have other women too but it wouldn't work.'

'Why not?'

'I would feel guilty dividing my affection between them.'

'I know what you mean. I find having more than one woman at a time very demanding. In polygamous marriages the women usually work out a roster.'

'I could muster women to stand in for Jane but I don't want that. I'll stay celibate.'

'An open relationship is the ideal but the women have to be compliant. Barbie is sexually demanding and she is cramping my style. I couldn't cope with two females like her.'

'Don't worry. Intractables will kick in soon and you'll be free again.'

'Monogamy with Barbie is like polygamy with other women. She has many sides.'

'Do you feel too dependent?'

'No. I love it.'

'Treat that girl kindly, won't you? Or you'll have me to deal with.'

'What do you think I am?'

'I know you and I hope for her sake you will change.'

Barbie and Cutter's relationship piqued my appetite for sex. But I knew Jane wasn't up to a sexual relationship yet and I had to bide my time.

*

One night Jane saw the door of her room open. A dark head looked in, saw her and quickly withdrew. Owen, the guard, had gone out and she was alone. She pressed the emergency buzzer. A nurse ran in.

'He was here,' Jane said shrilly, pointing at the door and bursting into tears. 'I saw him.'

'Who?'

'The one who took me. Cobra.'

Jane told me this was the name her hijacker had used.

Owen returned. He had been to the toilet. He and the nurses searched for the intruder but they didn't find him. I lodged a complaint with the Medical Director and it was arranged that when a security guard needed to be relieved, Jane would be guarded by a nurse.

Jane was badly upset and it was a week until her mind got back to where it had been.

'Have you been trying to find him?' she asked me.

'Yes.'

'Why haven't you found him? You have to catch him and lock him up.'

This threat had to be removed to allow Jane to relax and recover.

'He might not have expected me to see him and thought I might scream. He could come back later.'

She was preoccupied and distant with everyone.

'She is so uncommunicative,' said Barbie. 'It's as if she doesn't want to know me.'

'That's what PTSD does to victims – it dries up their emotions,' I said, quoting from my reading. 'Victims withdraw, remain hyper-vigilant, won't connect and avoid intimacy.'

'She has these high walls around her,' Barbie said sadly, 'but I know that she's still the same as she was inside.'

'Barbie, you are getting through to her,' I said. 'You brighten up her day.'

'I wish it was true, Doc,' Barbie said tearfully, 'but I'm only a wallflower.'

On Barbie's moral compass Jane was north. With Jane incapacitated, she was lost.

'It's enough,' I consoled her. 'You are making her happy. She'll knock down the walls when she's ready.'

My earlier suspicion of Barbie being an informant was unfounded. My questioning of her loyalty to Jane had put her in feline attack mode. What I had perceived as fear was hubris. She disdained me for suspecting her. Untamed, splendid, wilful and proud, Barbie was a true ally.

CHAPTER 64

Jane's speech was becoming more fluent. Every day Peggy Wall asked me for her testimony but she was not able to recount what had happened without going to pieces. Her panics were becoming less frequent and less debilitating. She had gone from intensive care to a shared room in a general ward. So she would have plenty of opportunities to talk, I had organised a roster of friends and relatives.

A week later she seemed quite normal when I arrived.
'Hello ... Phillip,' she said in a small voice.
'Hello, Jane. How do you feel today?'
'Okay,' she said. 'How long have I been here?'
'Let's see. Today is August 23rd. They rescued you on July 22nd – a month ago.'
'Why do I have to stay in hospital?' she said. 'I'm not sick.'
'Yes you are. Yesterday you panicked. You have to rest and get over what happened to you. We want you to tell us all about it.'
'I hate to think about it. I get scared.'
'It is getting easier, isn't it?'
'Maybe.'
The close relationship I had once had with her was over the horizon. We never discussed it. It was as though I had never been more than a platonic friend. She was in denial.
'I am not ill. Go away! I don't want you!' she said when I reminded her she was ill.
It was as if I didn't measure up. I had never seen her like this before. The rejection hurt. I continued to visit her and after a couple of days she took my hand again.

A few days later, Barbie was with Jane when I arrived.
'Hiya, Phil!'
'Hi, Barbie,' I said. 'How is she?'

'Talking a little, on and off ... more relaxed than yesterday. She's coming good. I think I'll go now,' she said. 'I expect you want to be alone with her.'

'No, stay,' I said. 'We can talk with her together.'

Barbie told her about what was happening in the Council. Barbie was always a full bottle on unofficial Council happenings. I talked about my design work for the MC PDA. These topics were okay for Jane. We never mentioned the think tank or our reconstruction because the speculation could confuse her testimony.

Later at the office, Barbie confronted me.

'Why don't you want to be alone with Jane? What's wrong with you?'

'We're not in a relationship.'

'Have you tried?' Barbie said.

'An investigator has to stand back.'

'Oh phooey! She needs you to help her get better.'

'Yes — by finding the abductors.'

Barbie pulled a face. 'A bit of loving would do her good.'

Her romantic notions were well meant but she didn't understand that neither Jane nor I wanted a romantic relationship just then.

Later that week Barbie was propping up the doorway of the visitors' waiting room when I came out from Jane's room. She had the intensity and poise of a hunting cheetah. She gave me one of her 100% smiles. I wondered why she hadn't come in to be with us.

'I wanted to talk with you alone,' she said. 'I heard something.'

She followed me into the waiting room and sat down beside me. I tried to ignore her smooth bare thighs.

'What's happening?' I asked.

'Fenwick is an evil bastard,' Barbie said. 'No-one has a good word to say about him. His ward assistant told me that when they rescued Jane he gave a big sigh and said, 'Pity. They should have left her there. That woman's a menace.''

Barbie's recall of people's behaviour was extraordinary. It was nothing for her to mimic, word for word, something said months previously, including facial expressions.

I wanted to go and confront Fenwick but I knew he would conceal any involvement. I would find it out in due course.

'Is that all?' I said.

'Yes. When I heard that I wanted to hurt him.'

'It's good that you didn't. I feel sorry for him — he's unbalanced.'

'It could have been him that took Jane.'

'I don't think so, or he would have been more guarded in what he said. He's annoying, I know. But try and forget about him.'

'Okay. I'll try.'

*

Cutter and Barbie were often together when they visited Jane. Their liking for each other was real. Cutter was courteous and concerned when he was with her, unlike his usual supercilious self. They still romped around and partied together. But they were making time to find out about each other and Barbie began to rely on him. Cutter had been treating her well so far.

CHAPTER 65

In the fifth week after she was found, Jane started telling us her version of events. The police wanted a testimony that would stand up in court, free of prompting and hysteria. Peggy and Terry left it to me to question her. I would make a voice recording and Barbie would transcribe it.

I wanted Jane to recall her experiences in the order: last in, first out. There would be three interviews so as not to tire her, commencing with events leading up to the rescue, rather than proceeding forwards from her disappearance. By telling it backwards it would be better corroborated by the rescue evidence and more credible.

Jane was sitting up in bed ready for her first recount.

'Tell me everything that happened after he came and injected you to take you away,' I said.

She spoke quietly, pausing after each sentence.

'I came around in the boot of a moving car. I could hear traffic noises. I was blindfolded, with a gag in my mouth and my wrists and ankles tied together. I was uncomfortable and I felt faint. Then the car stopped and I heard the boot open. I held my breath and didn't move.

''If I seem dead,' I thought, *'he might leave me alone.'*

'Fingers held my wrist and then pressed against my neck and tummy.

'He said, 'Fuck.' He felt my wrist, neck and tummy again and again. 'Fuck, fuck, fuck.' He sounded angry, as if his plans had gone wrong.'

'Did you recognise his voice?' I asked.

'It was Cobra.'

'What happened?'

'He slammed the boot shut and drove on. I heard other cars. When he stopped he pulled me out of the boot, put me over his shoulder and carried me like a sack of potatoes. He carried me and dropped me

278

down hard. I hit my head and I must have passed out. I woke up with concrete thumping down on to me. I struggled but it covered over my head and I couldn't move or breathe. I thought I would die.'

Jane was distressed and her pulse raced. I held her hand. She was trembling.

'It was ...' she began, then her eyes rolled up, she gagged and closed her eyes.

'Jane, it's over,' I said. 'You are safe in hospital with friends.'

After a minute she opened her eyes. She looked sheepish.

'I've wet myself.'

'Never mind. They'll change you in a minute. You were saying that you were under concrete and couldn't move. Do you remember anything after that?'

'It got into my eyes, nose and mouth. Then someone started pulling at my arms and dragged me out on to the ground. Someone put their finger in my mouth to get the concrete out. They washed me with cold water. I must have passed out. When I came round, I was here in hospital.'

'Okay, Jane, that's enough for today,' I said. 'Thank you. You don't have to think about it anymore. You have given us some leads to follow up. We are going to find who did this to you.'

Jane's information confirmed our view of the perp's motives. He had been going to release her, stopped the car somewhere and was volubly dismayed by something, which could have been that she seemed dead. He drove to the construction site and dumped her where her body would be hidden under concrete. He may have tried to murder her.

Barbie transcribed the recording and I sent a copy to Peggy.

I showed a copy to Dr Kaur.

'Is it possible that the perp thought Jane was dead in the boot of his car?' I asked.

'Yes,' she said. 'It would be hard to feel her pulse in the cramped space of a car boot, or to feel her tummy moving with breathing. She was in poor shape and her signs would have been weak. He might have concluded she was dead.'

Jasmine's Kaur's information made it a real possibility that he had been going to release her.

279

'Can you explain why he injected her with Propofol?'

'Criminal psychology is not my expertise, Doctor,' she said. 'He might have wanted to subdue her to take her in his car.'

'We need to continue our reconstruction to deduce what his motives had been earlier on.'

CHAPTER 66

Two days later, I was in my office, writing. Barbie was at the computer, making up questions to ask the concrete workers, ready-mix drivers, dispatchers and office personnel at the Bridge Works construction site.

'I'll ask two questions,' said Barbie. 'One: What persons knew that concrete would be poured there and when?'

'Not many would know. Your question could winkle out the perp, unless he is in hiding.'

About half an hour later I asked aloud, 'What are all the possible crime scenes?'

'Do you want me to tell you, Doc?' said Barbie.

I handed her a list. 'Check these, please.'

CRIME SCENE	DESCRIPTION
CS1	City Square car parking garage
CS2	Roadway, Anston Street, Northgrove
CS3	Factory, Commercial Road
CS4	Vehicle to transport victim from CS3
CS5	Hypothetical release site between CS4 and CS6
CS6	Construction site where victim was rescued
CS7	Hypothetical place where the mastermind paid the abductor(s).
CS8	Hypothetical place where mastermind acquired funds to pay.

Barbie studied the list in silence.

'I am okay with CS1, the City Square parking garage,' she said. 'What happened in the roadway at CS2?'

'That's where they found Jane's car.'

'Okay. CS3 — that's the factory we went to?'

281

'That's right.'

'I don't get CS4?'

'The car that took her away.'

'Okay. Where was CS5?'

'We don't know. Cutter suggested that the *perp* was taking her somewhere when he stopped and she seemed dead.'

'Who is the *perp*?'

'The *perpetrator* is the one who did the hands-on stuff.'

'So the *mastermind* did the scheming?'

'Yes.'

'How can a crime scene be *hypothetical*?'

'We guess that there was a place somewhere where he was going to release her.'

'Okay, I get it. CS6 is okay too,' Barbie told me. 'Now for CS7. How do you know the perp was paid?'

'My hunch is that it was done by a professional for money.'

'By a kidnapper, Doc,' Barbie said. 'Perhaps it was an amateur.'

'It wasn't done amateurishly,' I said.

'Where would they get a professional from?'

'He could be in a job with the mastermind.'

'I don't think so,' said Barbie. 'If the mastermind is a political or corporate leader, he would have security people and bodyguards but not a professional hit man.'

'What about hijacking, mugging and car-ramming?' I said. 'Who would they get to do that?'

'Runyon's might have a pro.'

'Do Runyon's operate in Alexandra?'

'Only a project office,' she said.

'Could they bring in someone from out of town to do the job?'

'Yeah,' said Barbie, 'or hire a freelancer.'

'He could be difficult to trace.'

Barbie pouted thoughtfully as she read down the list.

'Why these scenes? The action was continuous.'

'We will look at the puzzle piece by piece, then fit the pieces together.'

Barbie thought for a moment.

'These eight crime scenes are the places where her suffering was caused.'

'People will want to refer to them at tomorrow's think tank. Would you please write them on the whiteboard.'

'My writing is crap.'

'No, it's okay,' I said. 'Just do your best.'

'Righto.'

'I'll send you a MP3 recording of the discussion at the previous think tank. There is a part where Sunita said that Jane was already in a bad way when the concrete was poured over her. Would you cue it ready to play at the meeting.'

'Okay.'

I never had to tell Barbie anything twice.

CHAPTER 67

On Saturday, five of us gathered at the think tank.

Barbie had made a plate of nachos in the microwave. I took a bunch, rounded up the strings of cheese with my finger and ate them. Then I started the meeting.

'I'll play back to you the first part of Jane's testimony.'

We listened in silence to Jane telling how she was transported, dumped and buried.

When it finished Sunita said, 'How terrible for her, poor girl.'

I had heard it several times but I still felt claustrophobic imagining it. I hid my feelings by getting technical.

'Jane's story confirms our Link 1: that the effects on Jane had accumulated. Now I will play back the voice recording of the insight we had last time because it will reinforce the type of talk that can lead us to somewhere useful.'

We listened. When it finished I said, 'The idea built up like a snowball. Sunita started it rolling with an observation that the victim was in a bad way before being buried; then Tony gave it a push by suggesting that the perp would kill her and hide her body; but Cutter said it seemed he was taking her somewhere when he thought she had died.'

'You kicked the ideas around. It was pretty loose and imaginative,' said Barbie.

'It was positive,' Cutter said. 'No put-downs or sarcasm or posing.'

'Have we shown which crime scenes caused her condition?' asked Tony.

'Yes. The evidence is that she was starved probably at CS3 and buried as a corpse at CS6,' said Cutter.

'It was a good team effort,' I said. 'Let's do it again now. Our task is to uncover what motivated them to cause these crime scenes. I have coded them to make discussion easier.'

We looked at the list of crime scenes on the whiteboard.

'Good idea, Spock,' said Cutter. 'It seems like a good way to put events on a timeline.'

'Perhaps their motive was to change her health, her location, her career, her attitude or her behaviour,' said Sunita. 'There are heaps of angles.'

'Not all of those could be changed overnight.'

'Her behaviour could be changed right away.'

'What behaviour would they have wanted to change most?' asked Barbie, waving a clump of nachos around.

'They would want to stop her opposing the Government in Council meetings.'

'Also she was doing hostile interviews with the media.'

'She was a threat to the Government's majority.'

'She was campaigning against the parties,' I said.

'She was also campaigning against the casino.'

'She was campaigning for a MC,' said Sunita.

'Perhaps they wanted to stop her campaigning by removing her.'

'Why would they want to stop her campaigning?'

'She was stopping them getting money, votes and control,' I said.

'Would her absence have benefited particular people enough to have her abducted?' said Cutter.

Barbie took a wedge of nachos and nibbled delicately.

'She was stopping some greedy ones sticking their snouts in the trough, hey, Doc!' she said.

'Who do you have in mind?' asked Tony.

'Let's not go there yet,' I said. 'We'll look for suspects later. We have to figure out why they did what they did.'

'Jane's an attractive woman and a public figure,' said Cutter. 'Her abductor may have been a psychopathic misogynist, or conversely a sex maniac.'

'Tell us about those, Cutter,' Sunita said.

Cutter ignored the jibe.

'We don't have any evidence of sexual attack,' I said.

'Was her campaigning a threat to the national political parties?' Tony asked. 'She wanted to persuade councillors not to follow party

285

lines and desert their parties. Do you remember how when we were at Singh's, she said she was declaring war on the parties?'

'I remember she was worried they might be listening to us,' said Cutter. 'She made us change tables. Maybe they did hear us and abducted her to stop us.'

'Was she a figurehead of dissent?' Tony asked.

Cutter nodded. 'Yes. She was always in fights with the NLP. Before that it was the SLP. She crossed swords regularly with most of Alexandra's political leaders. I suppose that made her vulnerable.'

'She was a scapegoat,' I said. 'She was feared by City Hall and provincial executives because she criticised them publicly. She thwarted the plans of corporation leaders such as Sindona of Runyon Casinos. They probably hated her when she revealed their misdoings, stymied their projects, lost them lucrative bonuses and ruined their reputations. There would be plenty of people glad to put her out of action.'

'It is a long step from benefiting from her absence to taking her out,' Tony said. 'Abducting someone because they are campaigning for democracy in Alexandra is far-fetched, isn't it?'

'It happens in other places,' said Barbie, 'so why not here?'

'I used to work for Amnesty International,' said Sunita. 'In other countries people who have opposed the government have been imprisoned or simply disappeared. In Myanmar, Aung San Suu Kyi was detained for 15 years. Less commonly, the Opposition may abduct Government leaders. Ingrid Betancourt was campaigning for the Colombian presidency when she was held captive for six years. Political leaders of countries with internal conflict are sometimes abducted to influence the course of the hostilities. Lord Bandon was held hostage by the IRA for six weeks to dissuade the British from executing prisoners. Others have been abducted for ransom money, to generate publicity and to foment racial hatred. So I agree with Barbie, why not here? Our leaders are ruthless too.'

Sunita stopped and took some nachos.

'Could a leader really have wanted to have Jane abducted?' Tony asked.

'Yes, because the Council is hung,' I said. 'Jane was holding Council in the palm of her hand. Her opposition to Runyon's casino could have been the last straw.'

'There were plenty of people with plenty of reasons to want her out of the way,' Cutter said. 'She had a casting vote that could trounce the casino, cause an election and unseat the Government.'

'Perhaps a nutcase did it,' Barbie said. 'Someone with a set against Jane.'

'It's possible,' I said. 'There were city residents who believed that Jane's disruptions were reducing the City Government to chaos, because they thought she was overreaching, going too far and further than she was allowed to go.'

'What could they do about her?'

'Because she was law abiding, nothing legally.'

'Could there be a 'Get Jane' organisation?'

'The big players would have their own 'Get Jane' organisation. They had most motive,' Cutter said. 'The casino's large potential profit was a sufficient motive for her abduction. The cost of hiring a professional abductor would be peanuts compared with the billions at stake.'

'Once they had decided to take her out, how long would it take to grab Jane and hold her somewhere?' asked Barbie.

'Jane was a spanner in the mastermind's works for months,' I said. 'He didn't think up a scheme to abduct her overnight.'

'Perhaps she did something that pulled his pin,' said Barbie.

'When Cutter and I crossed and the Council became hung, it could have been the final straw,' I said. 'With her out of the way, he might have thought Cutter and I would go back to the NLP.'

'He thought wrong,' said Cutter. 'Dirty play like that caused me to quit the NLP.'

'The mastermind might have given it to a junior as initiation, or assigned it to a henchman, or employed a mercenary,' I said. 'The perp would have to risk Jane identifying him when he released her, unless he hid from her or left town. He could want to preserve his anonymity in all his interactions with her. If he was taking care of her, the difficulty of keeping his identity from her would increase with the duration.'

'It would be difficult to feed her anonymously, Doc,' said Barbie. 'So he never tried.'

'He was probably hired to hold Jane for a few days,' Sunita said. 'He might have expected a short stay. Perhaps he had never held anyone for so long and when they wanted to hold her longer he had no plans for feeding her.'

'He would want ...' Tony began.

Sunita interrupted, excited. '... extra money to care for her because of extra duties, extra time and extra risk. If he wasn't paid, he might have refused to feed her. Sorry, now your go, Tony.'

'He would want to receive his fee even if the victim died or was in poor condition when found,' Tony said. 'The burial at CS6 was the best way to cover up his lack of care. He could concoct a story about her dying due to ill health to tell the mastermind, so he would still get paid his fee.'

'Do you think it was a coincidence that he left CS3 shortly before they poured concrete at the Endicot Street construction site?' I said.

'No. He could have timed it to be able to dispose of her body if he needed to,' said Barbie.

'How precise was that?'

'She wasn't in the hole for long before the concrete went in.'

'If she had been, she would have been found.'

'How did he know when?'

'No-one at Bridge Works offered to explain how he would have known where and when the concrete would be poured.'

'If he worked on site he could have found out,' said Tony.

'So concrete burial was intended all along?' I asked.

'More likely it was a contingency plan,' Cutter replied. 'If she had died, he would be able to hide her body.'

'Could she be a victim of indifference and neglect? They might not have intended to harm her.'

'Is neglect a crime?' asked Barbie.

'Yes,' I said. 'The legal position would probably be to do with whether there was a responsibility of reasonable care that had not been fulfilled.'

'Setting it up so he could hide her body if she died was tantamount to murder,' said Tony.

288

'Attempted murder,' said Cutter.

The think tank was working well. People had tuned into each other and were able to follow their ideas into new territory.

'We have Link 2,' I said. 'Jane did not get under the concrete by accident nor did the perp intend to kill her. Burying her was a premeditated contingency. He tried to escape justice by hiding her body when he thought she was dead.'

'Well done, everyone.'

We ended our meeting.

To confirm these motives, we needed Jane's account of the second part of her ordeal: her imprisonment.

CHAPTER 68

Barbie and I met with Peggy and Malcolm to update them on our think tank's reconstruction of the crime. I told them ideas we had about motives.

'We don't believe they would have planned to bury her alive,' I said.

'Why not?'

'It is just too cruel.'

'Her long solitary imprisonment was cruel too, Doctor,' said Peggy.

'I agree but they may not have wanted to kill her. If they were going to kill her, why tie her up and drug her?'

'Perhaps they changed their mind. She left CS3 alive and Jane heard his swearing at CS5. He expected her to be alive He was thwarted. He didn't set out to murder her. If he had, he would have done it at CS3 or CS4. He must have imagined that she had died after he loaded her into the car at CS4.'

'He thought that he could be up for murder and hid the evidence by concealing her body, to prevent it triggering a manhunt,' Malcolm said. 'He didn't bother to remove the ropes from her wrists and ankles, as these would assist in carrying her. He dropped her into the foundation hole as if she was already dead.'

'Finding she was dead when she was really alive could have been in error.'

'An honest mistake or wishful thinking?' Peggy asked.

'We can do a test. Barbie, if you will lie in the boot of a Merc, I will try to feel your pulse and detect your breathing.'

'Will I have to starve first?'

'No. The reconstruction hypothesis is that in the car boot it was not possible to detect her pulse and breathing. Hers would be easier to feel than yours, buried under tissue. If I observe a pulse or breathing, we can throw out the error theory and conclude he tried to murder her.'

'You'd better hope no-one sees you, Doc,' said Barbie, 'or you might get arrested.'

'We can tell people that we are making a movie about people smuggling,' I said. 'I can be checking your vital signs in case you have died in transit.'

'You will need someone with a camera,' Malcolm said.

'I'll ask Cutter,' said Barbie.

'We need a Mercedes C-Class,' I said.

'Ask a dealer if you can borrow one, Doctor,' said Peggy. 'Tell them you want to check if someone in the boot is alive or dead. You can reassure them there won't be any blood.'

'Too easy.'

The meeting ended.

The next day we tested Barbie in a car boot. I didn't detect either a pulse or breathing. The perp had thought she was dead and tried to conceal her body.

We had reconstructed Link 2. Six to go.

*

When I visited Jane she made eye contact for the first time. She had the most amazing azure eyes. They bored into me for a moment then looked away to some inner horizon. I was haunted by her haggard right eye, which revealed she was having difficulty coping with reality. Her left brain must be a mess. The stress of abandonment may have caused her to escape into paranoid delusions. Her dendrite pathways could be tangled with unreal associations. Unravelling them would take time and skilled counselling. As if, Jane's mind could be turning alternative memories to a combination that matched reality, like solving a Rubik's Cube. She was giving it her best shot but she was distracted by the constant unease from perceiving herself in danger.

'You are safe here,' I said to her for the nth time.

Her look at me was sceptical.

To regrow her wasted muscles, a physiotherapist did exercises with her. Jane began raising her limbs and lifting her body. She was weak at first but made rapid progress.

She was in the 'denial' phase and did not acknowledge what had happened. She wanted to be treated as if she had recovered. Her mind would get up, then something would set her off and it would be knocked down again. She would mentally flee without confronting and dealing with it.

'Her abductors are still at large,' Terry said. 'She has grounds for having fears and has to learn to talk about them and seek support.'

The danger to Jane was real. When I visited her, Owen told me how the previous night security had been breached at the ward.

'Owen!' Jane had called out.

He stood up and went across to her. She was taking large breaths, panicking, her eyes rolled back in fear.

'He ... coming,' she gasped, pointing at the half-open door. It was kept closed but now it was open.

'Who was it?' asked Owen.

'Him. Cobra,' she replied.

Owen and the nurses searched the ward but the intruder had disappeared. They concluded that either a lost stranger or a villain had opened the door to Jane's room, seen Owen reading and left. They couldn't figure out how he had entered the ward unseen.

I phoned the Medical Director and asked that the perimeter doors be kept locked when not in use.

'It will mean staff have to let themselves in and out with keys, Doctor,' Carter grumbled. 'It will hinder their work.'

'It is worth it,' I said.

'Do you think he'll be back?'

'Yes. Jane has started recalling incriminating evidence. It's in the news. They know she can identify him and they'll want to silence her.'

'Okay, we'll keep the doors locked.'

CHAPTER 69

Jane was rested and relaxed in bed when I turned on my voice recorder.

'Jane, tell me everything that happened, after you were in your car and he injected you.'

'I came round lying on a floor in complete blackness. I tried to find a light switch but there wasn't one. I was inside a small room. The door was locked. I banged on it and yelled but no-one came. My voice seemed muffled. The walls were soft, made of wavy plastic foam. I dug my fingers in to break out but there was metal behind. The blackness and silence were scary and I panicked, screaming until my throat hurt. I was terrified. I thought I was dead. When I calmed down I was crying for a long time. It could have been hours or days. I only knew time had passed because I had to pee. All I could do was fight the panic and wait.'

'Were there any sounds outside?'

'No.'

'What did you do?'

'I lay on a sleeping bag on the floor. There was no furniture. I stood up sometimes and I nearly fell over in the dark. There was a water hose with a handgun and a cup. I drank and washed my face and hands. I stayed motionless to conserve energy. I didn't exercise or take showers. I stayed in the sleeping bag, getting out to pee in the bucket. Sometimes I moved about to keep my body functioning.'

An auxiliary nurse brought Jane's lunch, steamed fish and stewed apple.

She wept as she ate.

'What is it, Jane?' I asked.

'I stopped waiting for food. I could have given in and died. But I wanted to survive to put the criminals behind bars.'

'Did you receive any food at all?'

'No,' she said, tears streaming down her face. 'No-one came for the whole time I was there. The hunger hurt. I sucked on a corner of my sleeping bag.'

'Was your hunger painful?'

'There was a hollowness always inside me. I felt tired and seemed to sleep a lot. I didn't move often.'

'How did you fill in the time?'

'I thought up stories and sang songs or played mental chess.'

'Did you remember the positions of the pieces?'

'Yes. I played white. My other self played black.'

'Who won?'

'Sometimes white, sometimes black, sometimes stalemate.'

'Did you lay traps or do feints to catch yourself out?'

'Yes. We kept our moves to ourselves.'

'How long did the games last?'

'I don't know. I concentrated and time flowed. I would forget about being hungry.'

'Jane, that's amazing. Could you tell the time?'

'No. Nothing was happening. I only had distant memories. I would imagine I was eating, chatting or listening to music. When I rocked from side to side, time seemed to pass more quickly.'

'Were you ill at all?'

'No.'

'Diarrhoea?'

'Are you kidding? I shat once at the beginning and never again.'

She had been lithe and strong but when they rescued her she had looked like a holocaust victim.

'What else did you do?'

'Sometimes I posed questions like 'Why am I here?''

'Did you think of an answer?'

'Everyone has to be somewhere.' She gave a weak laugh. 'Spike Milligan said that.'

I laughed.

'Why did you think you were there?'

'I wasn't sure. It could be because I had tried to stop the casino.'

'What did you think about that?'

'That there were evil people.'

'What did you imagine would happen?'

'Sometimes I thought about Jesus' suffering.'

'Are you a Christian?'

'No. But Jesus' life gave my suffering meaning.'

'What meaning?'

'That I was a scapegoat, taking the blame for others.'

'Who?'

'People who were opposing the Government.'

'Was it a group, like a political party?'

'No. I was independent. They were friends. We talked about stopping the Government.'

'Did God inspire or strengthen you?'

'No. What was happening to me could be explained without God's agency. Even when I was mentally ill and hallucinated, I never totally lost the plot like that. But I came close.'

'What happened?'

'I thought I was a messiah like Jesus. I was being persecuted.'

It could have been a schizophrenic delusion. Her shrunken right eye indicated she had withdrawn from reality, whereas her left eye was enlarged by imaginative self-talk.

'What did you do?'

'I stayed true to my cause.'

'And what was that?'

'I was an elected representative of the people. I willed myself to survive until I was rescued and could get back to my job as councillor.'

'How did you 'will yourself'?'

'I would not give up. I would do the best I could under these circumstances.'

'What happened next?'

'I lay in the dark, drinking and peeing, getting lost in my thoughts. Dreams and reality were mixed up and went on and on.

'After a very, very, long time someone unlocked the door. It was a huge noise. I thought he might have come to harm me. I was lying on the floor. He shone a light in my face. My eyes hurt.

'He said, 'Get up.' It was Cobra's voice.'

'Did you see him?'

295

'No. It was dark, except for the flashlight. I couldn't stand. I couldn't even kneel — I was too weak. He kicked me in the side.

"Get up,' he said again.

"I can't.'

'He left the flashlight on the floor and I could see a little. He went outside and came back with a syringe. He filled it and put the bottle down. He squeezed the air out and grabbed my arm. When he felt how bony my arm was, he rolled me over on my face, pulled up my dress and went to inject me in the bum. I rolled away and kicked him hard in the crotch. He sprawled forwards. I grabbed the flashlight and shone it on his face. He swiped it aside but I had seen him.'

'Good for you. What did he look like?'

'Youngish, small mean eyes, a long, thin, oval face, long narrow nose, coffee-coloured skin, short brown beard, brown hair. His left ear had a small gold ring.'

'What did he do?'

'He grabbed the light and punched me in the face.

"Bitch,' he said. 'Do what you're told or I'll kill you. Don't move.'

'I lay quietly. He stuck the needle in my bum. It hurt. Then I must have passed out.'

I stopped her recounting there. She had already told the next part, about being in the car boot and under the concrete.

'Thank you, Jane,' I said. 'You went through hell.'

'Sometimes I think it is still happening.'

'It is over, Jane. Try to forget.'

I requested Peggy send an Identikit artist to get Jane's impression of Cobra. We could look for him.

CHAPTER 70

When Barbie had transcribed Jane's testimony, I sent it to Peggy.

I discussed her story with Terry Cline.

'The treatment Jane suffered was even worse than I had feared,' he said. 'It is surprising that she survived. Prisoners have often given up and died in solitary confinement. Without the will to live, a person may sink into a torpor and expire within a few days. Survivors mention the debilitating effect of being unable to monitor the passage of time, of being unable to assess the prospects of rescuers coming and consequently being without hope.'

'What was the main trauma?' I asked.

'The deficit of attention. Jane was discarded as if her life was of no more significance than a cockroach's. A human needs frequent attention, preferably affectionate. Even harassment is better than no attention at all. Lacking attention, people become morose and sink into debilitating depression or become paranoid, continuing into hallucinations and eventually madness. They go into a catatonic state from which they may never fully recover. Only a few mentally strong prisoners have withstood prolonged solitude. By comparison, her long starvation and total darkness were less severe.

'I have not heard of anyone, until Jane, who survived for five weeks without human contact, companionship, food, warmth, exercise, recreation, fresh air, comfortable sleep, light and indication of time. She suffered extreme privation and can be expected to be very disturbed. Her recovery will be slow and possibly incomplete.'

A week later, Peggy emailed me a copy of her CSI officer's report.

CRIME SCENE INVESTIGATION AT 205 WELLINGTON ROAD
Our purpose was to verify the victim's testimony and gather any evidence missed earlier.

Ms Kenwood was held on the upper floor of a disused pharmaceutical factory.

The perp had used a key for access to the building. We confirm Ms Kenwood's observations that she was held in a cell of size about 4.2 m x 4.8 m x 2.2 m high. The door could be locked with a padlock. There was no window and the walls were sound absorbent. The power was off. There was no light. A bucket had been used for ablutions and there was a drinking mug. A garden hose entered through a hole in the wall, recently made, supplying water to a handgun and connected to a janitor's tap. The perp may have found the water on or turned it on at a mains valve.

There was no evidence of any food in the cell, consistent with the victim's testimony that she did not receive any.

The fingerprints we found in the cell were Ms Kenwood's. Surfaces inside and in adjacent areas had been wiped clean. It is probable that the perp(s) stayed away and when they were present, they wore gloves. We found skin, garment fibres and hairs in adjacent areas but these could have been left earlier by factory people.

DNA analysis of a blood drop found in the cell showed it was Ms Kenwood's.

We found a jacket and shoes that belonged to Ms Kenwood and a sleeping bag. An empty vial of the sedative Propofol was found in the cell. There was a gum wrapper.

Before it was shut down, the factory had manufactured medications, including lithium carbonate pills, from ingredients brought in drums from overseas. Samples of dust from the floor contained lithium as did dust found in Ms Kenwood's car. NMR imaging showed that dust samples from these two crime scenes contained isotopes of lithium in similar proportions, indicating the samples probably originated from the same mineral source and possibly had later provenance in common. Lithium could have been taken on the perp's footwear from the factory to Ms Kenwood's car.

Our investigation verifies Ms Kenwood's testimony.

Signed,

(CSI)

'The absence of DNA-containing material and fingerprints is unusual,' I said to Peggy 'The perps were ultra-cautious in avoiding leaving traces.'

Our best lead was to match lithium at CS3 with a suspect's shoes, his car or his house.

Now that the police had obtained most of Jane's story, they started their investigation in earnest. Peggy and Malcolm familiarised themselves with her testimony and our reconstruction so far.

Peggy came to our next think tank.

We sat around the table eating pizza and listening to Jane's CS3 testimony.

'Wow!' said Cutter. 'It couldn't have been much worse for her.'

'How are you going with your oily walk, Doctor Keane?' Peggy asked condescendingly. 'Time is slipping by.'

She pretended to look at her watch. Peggy was driven by immediacy of results. She didn't trust my theory.

'We have done the first two links,' I said. 'Let's replay the recording of our talk just before we figured out Link 2, that he left her at CS6 to conceal the crime.'

I played back the voice recording. When it ended I said, 'We all contributed positively, without anyone being a prima donna. Next we will find out how events at the crime scenes affected the perp's motives.'

'Don't you mean the other way around, Doctor, how the perp's motives affected the crime scenes?' Peggy asked.

'No — we have done that,' I said.' Now we're wondering how the perp may have modified his motives in response to events. For example, during the crime, when Jane got a glimpse of his face, he could have changed from wanting to keep her alive to wanting her dead.'

'Oh I see,' she said, chastened.

I wanted Peggy to appreciate the painstaking nature of our reconstruction, so she would realise why progress seemed slow. Unfortunately, she might have taken my correction as a putdown. It was clumsy of me. If she jumped the gun and went rushing off after suspects, our sync with the police would be lost.

'The abductor may not be a casino interest,' I said. 'They have not demanded that the Council approve it.'

'Approval under duress could be revoked,' said Peggy.

'They could have wanted to warn Jane off from meddling in their dirty game,' Barbie said.

'Some warning. They almost killed her.'

'Would they have wanted her to suffer as much as she did?' asked Cutter. 'Would they be that heartless?'

'Yes, for revenge,' said Sunita.

'Revenge for what?' said Cutter.

'For hanging up the Council. As if it was all her doing rather than party nonsense.'

'Did she actually stop the Government ...?' asked Peggy.

'Yes. The casino was her Waterloo.'

'Others were opposed too,' I said. 'She was the scapegoat.'

'Some people liked her fireworks,' said Cutter. 'Me for one.'

'Could anyone have abducted her because she was so glamorous?' Cutter asked.

'Jane hasn't mentioned there was any sexual interest in her.'

'Their interest was to remove her from political action.'

'We've narrowed it down,' I said. 'Let's have coffee.'

It had been an intense session. The test of a coherent reconstruction was to imagine you stood in the perpetrator's shoes. I wasn't there yet. A person who was so indifferent to alleviating Jane's suffering could have a psychological disability or illness.

CHAPTER 71

'We have to ask ourselves why the perp treated Jane the way he did,' I said when we resumed.

'What did he gain from abandoning her?' said Tony.

'Not being traced,' said Barbie.

'Would that have concerned him so very much?' Cutter said.

'He may not have been hired to care for her.'

'Or he refused to do it for some other reason,' Barbie said.

'The abduction contract might have been only for a day or two,' I said.

'Would they really have had a contract?' asked Sunita.

'A verbal one.'

'Without a victim care clause,' said Tony.

'The perp could have thought feeding her was too risky,' said Cutter. 'Carrying food into a disused factory, he would stick out like dogs' balls.'

'We know he was paranoid.'

'Did he lock her in and leave her simply because he was paranoid?' Barbie said. 'Come on! There has to be more to it than that.'

'Did he want her to suffer?' said Sunita. 'Perhaps she hurt him when she fought him?'

'Yeah,' said Tony. 'She kicked him in the nuts.'

'That was at the end,' said Sunita. 'I mean at the start, when he got into her car. Maybe she did something to him.'

'It's hard to imagine that she had hurt him that much or that he was scared of her,' Cutter said.

'I will ask her,' I said. 'What about later when he thought he had killed her and went to bury her? What did he want?'

'Perhaps he was angry that she had got a look at his face and he over-injected her,' said Barbie.

'It is easy to over-inject when you are inexperienced,' I said.

301

'Maybe. Because she had eyed him, perhaps he wanted to murder her to protect his identity,' said Cutter.

'He could tell the mastermind she had died from an illness.'

'If he wanted her dead, why go to the trouble of injecting her?' asked Cutter. 'Why didn't he strangle her or smash her head in?'

'The mastermind might not pay him.'

'How would he find out?'

'From the autopsy.'

'If her body was found. He had a good way of making her body disappear.'

'Did she live because he failed in his attempt to kill her?'

'There wasn't deliberation to kill her,' said Peggy. 'We have evidence that he changed his intention from releasing her, to concealing her corpse.'

'If he had released her alive, she could see him and identify him,' said Barbie, 'unless she was sedated.'

The perp's motives seemed ambivalent and we were stuck. The silence was awkward.

'I think it was attempted murder, Chief Inspector,' said Barbie. 'He had tried very hard to stop her seeing him. He wore a mask, knocked her out with anaesthetic and kept her in the dark. When she fought with him and saw his face, he thought he wouldn't be safe as long as she lived. He wanted to kill her, against the mastermind's orders that he release her. He may have over-injected her with anaesthetic.'

'This is another situation for Schrodinger and his cat in a closed-up box, Doctor,' said Malcolm. 'The perp had locked her in and she was both alive and dead at the same time.'

'Such equivocation does not fit the statutes,' said Peggy to Malcolm severely. 'He either attempted to murder her or he did not.'

'People's behaviour is not always convenient for dispensing justice,' I said, trying to help Malcolm's argument along. 'People do try to have their cake and eat it too. When he took her to release her, he might have preferred her to be alive but was frustrated and angry because she had seen him. He therefore treated her roughly, unconcerned that she might die. The injection he gave her could have been excessive, through antipathy and hurrying, rather than being

302

coolly calculated. He left fate to decide whether she arrived at CS5 dead or alive, like Schrodinger did with his cat.'

'Doctor, tell us, in your opinion was it attempted murder or not?' Peggy was impatient.

'If she dies, it will be murder.'

'It does not seem much like premeditated murder to me, Doctor,' said Peggy. 'How sure are you?'

'It fits the evidence,' I said. 'Firstly, he didn't try to keep her alive, He left CS3 angry with her just before the pouring of concrete started at CS6. He went through the motions of the release planned. When he opened the boot at CS5, he was ready to believe she was dead.

'Meaning he was aware he could have killed her. If she died, that would be murder.'

Peggy showed the fingers of her left hand one at a time: 'Neglect, anger, scheduling, expectation of death and victim identification. Five reasons for attempted murder.' She lowered her hand. She held up her other hand in a fist.

'The reasons to think he did not attempt murder her are: 1. Burying her could have been a spontaneous act.' She uncurled the forefinger. 'Perhaps he dumped her there on the spur of the moment.'

'Not likely,' said Barbie who had spent the day before asking questions at the site for anything that could relate to the crime. 'The chance of concrete being poured in within an hour after dumping someone into a random hole on a construction site is very low.'

'You're right.' I said. 'Someone must have noticed something. We'll continue tomorrow. We can ask other questions.'

'Anyway, why keep her alive for five weeks to delay killing her?' said Peggy. 'It doesn't make sense. He must have intended to release her. She put up another finger. That's two reasons against a murder attempt. He took precautions against her seeing him, as if she might live. That's three.'

'He was taking her to release her,' said Barbie. 'That's four.'

'Releasing her would avoid a dead body and have a lower penalty,' I said. "That's five.'

'That makes five reasons it was not murder. We also had five reasons it was murder,' said Peggy, displaying the fingers of both hands. 'It's as clear as mud: it could be either.'

'She didn't die, so what does it matter?' asked Barbie.

Everyone looked at her.

'Motives do matter,' said Peggy. 'Attempted murder is more serious than grievous bodily harm, or wounding, or concealment of a corpse, or deprivation of liberty, or interfering with political liberty. It gets a higher penalty.'

'Don't we have to catch them first, Chief Inspector?' said Barbie, with naiveté belying sarcasm.

Peggy glared at her.

I interrupted on a positive note. 'Now we have found Link 3: the material circumstances of the crime modified the abductor's preconceived purposes. Leaving her body at CS5 could be traced so he took it to hide it. After that, Link 2 was that he concealed it at CS6. Then Link 1 was that her condition when she was found was the cumulative effect of a series of mistreatments.'

'Are you sure your reconstruction is correct?' asked Peggy.

'They are hypotheses,' I said. 'The evidence does not refute them. They are the best we can do. We have inferred what happened up to this point from our understanding of how the perpetrator and mastermind most likely behaved.'

'Can we really predict the villains' behaviour with confidence?' said Peggy. 'They would not behave like you and me.'

'Are you sure of that, Chief Inspector?' I said. 'Their genes are almost identical to ours. During 99.9% of their lives they have done the sorts of things we have done. We have considered possible variations in their behaviour at the crime scenes and selected those that seem most likely. The links are hypotheses and they are as confident as reconstruction can be.'

'It makes sense, Doctor,' said Peggy. 'Let's run with it and see where it takes us.'

We ate the remainder of the pizza and chatted. Barbie went back to Blake and I went through into my office to catch up on my ward work.

CHAPTER 72

Jane was standing up and walking around the ward now. She would not accept that she was ill. She had always been headstrong. Her lapses in behaviour followed a pattern of improvement but she expected each setback to be the last. She would gain mental wellness for a few days, then stall and go backwards.

One day when I visited her I found her bed empty. When I rushed out to the nurses' station, she was there with a taxi driver. She had gone down in the lift and outside. The taxi driver had realised she was ill and brought her back.

'I am fine,' she said.

'That's not what the taxi driver told me,' a nurse said. 'You couldn't tell him where you wanted to go.'

'I did tell him.'

The nurse called Terry Cline and he came up to the ward.

'Jane, you are in the denial phase,' he said. 'You are still ill. You have been going great guns but you have a serious illness and need time to get over it.'

But Jane persisted.

'I want to go home now,' she said to Doctor Kaur.

'You are at risk and need supervision. You must stay here until we discharge you.'

'When will that be?'

'At least a couple of weeks.'

'Rubbish. There's nothing wrong with me now.'

'Besides the PTSD, you are still underweight and need a special vitamin diet.'

'Give me a list for the chemist,' Jane demanded.

'It's not that simple,' Dr Kaur said. 'We have to monitor you closely. Sorry, Jane, please be patient.'

'What are you monitoring?'

'You are safer staying in hospital where you are guarded,' I said.

Cutter brought a bottle of vodka in secretly and he and Jane got drunk together. I was glad when they had finished the bottle because she needed to deal with the causes of her anxieties, rather than alcoholising them.

Jane was beginning to show her old colours. Perhaps it was her idealism that had put her in hospital.

'Jane,' I thought, 'is there a place for brinkmanship like yours? You made your mark as a rebellious schoolgirl who refused to wear the uniform. You took on the establishment. As a barrister you wanted truth and justice until you found these could belong to whoever undertook the most costly preparation of the case. So you switched to politics and adopted holus bolus the democratic ideals that your experienced colleagues had learned to decline. Now you have been silenced. Will you ever regain your focus? Will you have the strength to impress your will on others? Only time can answer what will become of your idealism. I will do everything I can to make sure it survives, so that it can inspire others the way it does me.'

We hoped that resuming work would help Jane recover. I went with her from the hospital to Council meetings at City Hall. On the day she returned, the public gallery of the debating chamber was filled with her supporters. There was a standing ovation when she walked in. The applause went on and on.

'Thank you,' she said in a small voice unlike her usual strident tone. 'Thank you very much for your support while I have been away. It is good to be back.'

Some councillors dabbed at their eyes.

It was courageous of her to be there because her abductors could be there too.

'It might take some time for me to participate fully, but that is my intention.'

There was more applause as she sat down. When Jane left the building her supporters surrounded her in City Square.

'Who did it, Jane?' someone asked.

'The police are investigating,' she said. 'When they know they will be arrested.'

At a meeting of the Council, Jane panicked and began sobbing hysterically during an O'Connell rant. I helped her outside to a cab and then to the hospital.

'What were you thinking?' I asked her.

'O'Connell was staring at me. I thought he was the hijacker.'

'It couldn't have been him,' I said. 'He isn't wide enough to be Cobra.'

She looked at me intently, deep in thought. 'I suppose not,' she said, as if I had dispelled only one of many fears she had.

'He could be the mastermind,' I said, 'but so could several others.'

Jane was continually anxious and watchful around other people. She had difficulty concentrating and was unable to contribute to discussions. Improvement was slow and I would have despaired without the support of Terry, Cutter and Barbie.

'Don't fret, Phil,' said Cutter. 'It took them many weeks to mess her up and it will take as long again to unravel her. Don't expect too much. There is no hurry. Stay loose – you are her best therapist. You are working wonders.'

*

Jane sometimes went out to city shops, or to meet friends for coffee or lunch, accompanied by a security guard. Her visitors came to the hospital in the evening.

'What did you talk about today?' I asked Barbie after she had visited Jane.

'I asked her what I should do about Cutter, Doc.'

'What about him?'

'He's got another woman.'

'What did Jane say?'

'She said that Cutter was too old for me and too selfish. I don't know what to do. What do you think?'

'Keep on doing what you have been doing. Trust in your feelings. Presently the way forward will become clear.'

'Good idea. Thank you, Phillip.'

It was not often that anyone asked me for relationship advice. I was getting better at dealing with people.

I received a call from Peggy Wall.

'Have you reconstructed who did it yet, Doctor?'

'No,' I said, 'but we are making progress.'

'Get your skates on. We want a suspect pronto.'

'Deducing suspects is the step after next. We will have someone for you soon, I promise. Ice hockey players sprint to where the puck will go next, not to where it is now. Today we are getting the final part of Jane's testimony.'

'Awesome, Doctor,' Peggy said. 'When you have it we will be able to start interviewing suspects.'

The last part of Jane's testimony would be the hijack 11 weeks previously. Since then she had suffered five weeks of hell followed by six weeks recovering in hospital.

She was sitting up in bed, ready to begin. I started my voice recorder and set it in front of her.

'Jane, would you tell me what happened when they seized you,' I said. 'What were you doing?'

Her eyes were on her fingernails.

'I drove in for our meeting ... at 9 am, I think.'

'Who knew that you were going in at that time?'

'You, Cutter and Barbie.'

'Anyone else?'

'No ... Oh, yes! I nearly forgot. That morning, before I left home, I got a phone call from a Blake Ward resident who wanted to meet with me urgently about something to do with planning — rezoning, I think.'

'Did you know who it was?'

'No. He said he was new in the area. I told him I had a meeting at 9.00 am and another at 10.30 am. I could only do it at 10.00 am. We would have half an hour.'

'Then what happened?'

'I drove my car in and went to my bay as usual. Someone wrenched opened the passenger door and jumped in beside me. I was too scared to scream. He was wearing a mask.'

'What kind of mask?'

'Captain Kirk of Star Wars. I started screaming and he punched me hard in the face. I stopped screaming.'

308

'He said, 'Don't do anything stupid and you won't get hurt. No-one can see or hear.'

'It was true. The glass in my car was the darkest you can get. My nose hurt and bled. I was crying and I couldn't see.'

'Tell me about his voice.'

'A Southlander.'

'Did he say anything else?'

'He pulled a knife out of a newspaper he was carrying and jabbed me in the side. I squealed. He said, 'Drive.' When I reached the exit he said, 'Go to the Horton Bridge.' Then he used his mobile and said, 'Cobra here. Got her.''

'What happened next?'

'After we went over the bridge he said, 'Stay on this road.''

'What else could you see of him?'

'Black hair, coffee-coloured skin. Black vinyl jacket. Blue jeans.'

'Rings, jewellery?'

'He looked at his watch several times, as if he was on a schedule.'

'Footwear?'

'Joggers, grey and white.'

''Gum?' he asked me. I said no. He chewed.'

'Then what did he do?'

'We drove for about 20 minutes along the highway north. He didn't know the way. He used a GPS on his iPhone. When we got to Northgrove, he counted down the distances to the turning. We went through some back streets and he told me to stop.'

'Behind a black car?'

She looked at me, surprised. She may have thought hers was the only evidence we had.

'Yes.'

'What type of car?'

'Mercedes.'

'Did you get out of your car?'

'No. He said, 'If you try anything, I'll kill you.''

She began to weep.

'Take 10 deep breaths,' I said. 'One, two, three, come on, you can do it, four, five, six, that's great, seven, eight, nine, ten ... There ... feel better now?'

309

She nodded, wiping her eyes. I waited for her to stop sobbing.

'He filled a hypodermic,' she continued. 'His hands were so ... deliberate ... and cruel. I was too frightened to resist. He stuck the syringe into my thigh and I screamed.'

'Did anyone hear?'

'There was no-one about.'

'Then I must have blacked out. I woke up in the dark, lying on a floor. I was locked in.'

'We'll stop there. You have already told us about that.'

'I hope you have enough to catch him.'

'I would like you to tell the Identikit artist anything else you can add.'

'Okay.'

'Thank you, Jane. You have done well to remember it without panicking. That's it, the last piece of your story. Now put it all out of your mind.'

CHAPTER 73

I was in a meeting with Peggy and Malcolm at Police HQ to update them on our progress.

'This week we met at an apartment overlooking a beach. We listened to a recording of Jane's hijack testimony. Then we brainstormed Link 4, which was how Jane herself affected the crime scenes.

We had looked out over an endless ocean swept by a strong onshore wind bringing a steady procession of gigantic rollers that crashed on to the beach below us.

I recounted to them the highlights of our meeting, reading from my notes.

'What Jane was doing influenced the date they snatched her. The timing of the hijack was precisely before a debate to approve the casino. Without Jane being there, the Government almost got its own way.

'When they grabbed her they might have expected to hold her only a few days but they kept her until Council finally rejected the casino for the IB site, when further opposition was unnecessary.

'They had a window of opportunity to take out Jane that spanned the weeks until the casino site was decided. By then she was in no fit state to oppose anyone. If they had known her condition at CS3, they might have changed what they were doing to her — but they didn't know.

'Link 4 is that they took her to release her when she could not affect the casino outcome. They had prevented her voting against it. It was only when they took her away and thought she had died that her condition caused them to adapt the crime scenes to burying her.'

Peggy interrupted me. 'It explains the evidence, Doctor, but we haven't come very far. We have all of Jane's story now but we still don't have a single fucking suspect. Tell me there are some persons

311

of interest we can interview for Chrissake. I am getting stick from upstairs.'

'We have started trying to identify suspects,' I said.

More accurately, I was starting at that very moment.

'What the fuck have you been doing all this time?'

'We have been reconstructing what happened.'

'If we tell that to the media, it will make the front page: Kenwood Case: Month 3 — Police Start Looking for Suspects. There will be outrage — the city's favourite lady desecrated and not one suspect after all this time!

'I will be a laughing stock,' she said, trying not to shout. 'How has your 'reconstructing' helped us exactly?'

I wanted to remind her that while the police had sat back and waited for Jane to tell her story, we had investigated steadily. The police had stood aside until three weeks ago when Jane finished her testimony. Now they were blaming us for a lack of results. They had done some searching for hiding places but they had left it to our think tank to work out what had happened. It had suited Peggy well because she had been warned off investigating Government people. If there was going to be any heat from politicians, it would be my head on the block, not hers.

But I thought I would not criticise Peggy — I needed her to deal with the abductors.

'We have backed out what happened and we will soon know who could have done it,' I said.

'I have let you run with it so far, Phillip,' she rabbited. 'Now it's time to deliver. You had better find me a suspect double fucking quick. Jane is a heroine, remember that. When a heroine has been savaged in Alexandra, if the police drag their feet there will be hell to pay.'

DCI Wall put on her braided hat and stomped out. Innocent bystanders were not safe.

When she had gone Malcolm asked me sympathetically, 'How are you going to get a suspect, Doctor?'

'Barbie has been looking for people who could have motives. Heaps of people would have benefitted from Jane's absence. She has crossed swords with politicians, government ministers, town hall

312

bureaucrats, CEOs, union officials and others with a financial connection or directorship. We have to find out who wanted her gone so badly that they masterminded it.'

'The identity of the mastermind is wide open then?' Malcolm asked, with only a hint of derision in his narrowed eyes.

'Yes,' I said. I reflected, 'But not totally wide.'

'What about the perp?' he asked. 'Do you have any leads?'

'We have Jane's Identikit description of Cobra. We're going to ask at the construction site if anyone saw him there.'

'Did you trace who called Jane just before she disappeared?'

'It was an unregistered phone.'

'Bummer. They were super careful.'

Later I was working in my office when Barbie came in. She had been searching online for people connected with the Endicot Street site.

'Guess who is managing the construction work for Roads, Doc?'

'Bridge Works?' I said.

'No. They're the contractor. The manager is the Council.'

'Really? Now that is interesting,' I said. 'The burial of Councillor Jane was managed by her employer: the Council.'

'A bit too convenient if you ask me, Doctor,' said Barbie.

'Maybe the mastermind is on the Council. It is a good lead. Well done, Barbie,' I said with a smile. 'Now we can look for the Council person who arranged for Bridge Works to bury her.'

CHAPTER 74

Malcolm came to our next think tank to help us draw up profiles of the perp and mastermind.

Barbie passed around mint chewies.

'No thank you,' I said. 'My fillings aren't up to it.'

'Next time I'll get suckers.'

'We're here already,' said Sunita.

'I don't suck,' said Cutter, taking one.

'Nor me,' said Tony. 'Sucking chews me up.'

I started the meeting.

'Our think tank today will infer Link 5: who do we suspect of causing the condition Jane was in when we found her? We have to infer from the victim's condition the suspects' physiques, personalities, foibles and anything else — except traces and motives.'

'Did the perp really abandon her?' asked Cutter. 'He seemed never to look in on her. She could have died without him knowing.'

'Was he unable, paranoid, negligent, indifferent, vindictive, or just unpaid?' Tony asked.

'Brutal,' said Sunita. 'He hit her in the face.'

'He may have been greedy and holding out for more money to feed her. If it wasn't in his contract, he might think it wasn't his responsibility,' said Cutter.

'It's a moral responsibility,' said Sunita indignantly. 'It was indefensible not to feed her!'

Sunita was prickly but she engaged with the task and made a valuable contribution always.

'Like feeding a prisoner of war?' said Cutter.

'The Geneva Convention is a mutual agreement to treat prisoners of war humanely. It wouldn't apply to Jane. Starving a captive would be punished under criminal law.'

'Abduction would be punishable. Would feeding her make much difference?' asked Tony.

'It would allay recrimination for neglect of responsibility,' I said. 'If they were going to release her, they would want her in good health. If she returned in good health, the police might be less vindictive and would treat them more leniently.'

'So why didn't they feed her?' asked Tony.

'He wouldn't be seen bringing food; and she wouldn't get to see him.'

'Perhaps the perp stayed away and just came back to release her.'

'It fits a paranoid psychopath,' said Malcolm. 'The absence of remorse is tell-tale. He abandoned Jane without fear of consequences.'

'Somehow he knew what the concrete pouring schedule was,' Cutter said.

'No-one at Bridge Works would admit to telling it to an outsider,' Barbie said.

She took another chewie.

'The perp could have been an insider.'

'Would you chew with your mouth closed, please,' said Sunita to Barbie. 'I don't want to see.'

'Air brings out the flavour. Try it.'

'No thank you,' said Sunita. 'I don't want air in my head.'

Barbie glared at her.

'Ronald Yelling seemed to have something to hide. Tell them, Barbie.'

'When I asked an engineer for names of those who knew where the concrete was going, he told Yelling and he came to reception,' said Barbie. 'He was suspicious and rude. When I said I was with the Council's safety unit he told me to request the information from Ainsley Montague. Then he saw me out.'

'Was he trying to hide something?'

'Yes, I think so.'

'I'll see if he has form, Doctor,' Malcolm said.

'Would you check up on Montague too, Inspector,' I said. 'He has been slippery.'

We stopped for coffee.

When we resumed, I said, 'What sort of a person is this Cobra?'

'Cobra is physically strong,' Malcolm said. 'He was alone when he did the hijack and transferred her to CS3. He is a competent professional thug. He was violent, strong, adopted disguises and did an injection.'

'He showed no sexual interest in her,' I said. 'He was a misogynist.'

'It is possible for a man to be indifferent to Jane without being deviant, Phillip, even if you have difficulty imagining that,' said Cutter.

His humour could be supercilious but Cutter's laconic presence had a practical bent and kept the group grounded.

'He could have been a homosexual,' Barbie said.

'There are some about,' said Tony.

'Or he could have been a faithful husband,' said Malcolm.

'What about the mask, the injections, the darkness, not letting himself be seen and the abandonment?' I asked.

'It is quite normal for an abductor to try and conceal his appearance from his victim, Doctor,' Malcolm said.

'Keeping her locked up in the dark and neglecting to feed her were a bit extreme.'

'He must be paranoid,' Barbie said. 'He could be crazy — trying to become the invisible man.'

Barbie had been rather self-conscious but she had gained in confidence and was contributing well.

'It didn't work. She did get a look at him,' Tony said.

'Not a good look. He was wearing a mask or he was in the dark,' Sunita said.

'We have an Identikit image,' I said.

'A likeness isn't enough to identify him the way DNA or fingerprints would,' Malcolm said.

'But we don't have his DNA or prints,' I said.

'He was careful ... meticulously paranoid ... obsessive,' Malcolm said.

'Was he stupid or just deluded in thinking he could abandon Jane for so long without endangering her life?'

316

'He didn't care — as if her life was someone else's concern. Either that or he was deliberately cruel. Perhaps he has an agenda with harming women.'

'We don't know how much of the planning was left to Cobra to do,' said Barbie.

'Not much. He was told where to go — he was from out of town,' Malcolm said.

'I wonder where he hung out every day,' I said.

'He wasn't taking care of Jane,' said Barbie.

'Maybe he came back to check on her, without her knowing,' I added.

'Check on what? She was not okay, was she?' said Malcolm. 'He didn't check.'

'What if when he unlocked CS3 to release her he had found her dead?'

'He would take her to CS6. He knew of an open grave.'

'It was a carefully planned contingency.'

'Like he has carefully disappeared.'

'We are looking for him,' said Malcolm.

We had our Link 5; that Jane's condition had declined because the perpetrator and one or more masterminds had neglected to care for her while she was captive. The link resonated with her cries for help.

Barbie fetched the jug. 'More coffee anyone?'

We refilled our cups.

'What about the mastermind? What sort of person would he or she be?' I asked.

'Motivated by personal ambition or by financial gain,' replied Malcolm.

'Would he know Jane from her work with the Council?'

'Yes. Or know someone who did,' Malcolm said.

'Would it be a powerful person?'

'Yes, Doctor,' said Malcolm. 'Someone who could pay to have a person removed and who would take the rap if they were caught.'

'Would he meet with the perp?'

'No. Both would want to avoid the other being able to incriminate him,' he said. 'They would use the telephone, post, email or social media.

317

'What would a mastermind do?'

'Get a pile of money, hire a villain, supply a car, provide keys to CS3, give instructions for setting up, then order when and how to capture her.'

Barbie stretched long and luxuriously like a cat.

'So who fits the bill, Doc?' she said.

'How about Sindona, Doctor?' asked Malcolm.

'He had the motive but we don't have any evidence of his involvement, yet,' I said. 'We are still looking.'

'I can't see Sindona masterminding everything. He could have hired Cobra but someone else would have set up the heist and hideout.'

'It could have been one of the NLP bosses,' Barbie said.

'Bentley Leach had most to gain from Jane's absence,' I said. 'Or it could be Martha. Someone lower down in the Council could have been a go-between,' I added.

'Like who?'

'Montague, O'Connell, Munster or Fenwick, or Yelling.'

'Yelling wasn't Council.'

'No, but he practically worked for them. They could lean on him.'

'We can look for evidence of any skulduggery by these officials. That has narrowed it down. Well done, everyone.'

I ended the meeting.

*

It was difficult for us to investigate a suspect. The police could interview unwilling people, take materials in evidence, bring suspects in and hold them for questioning. My role was limited to advising them who to investigate, when and how.

Malcolm stayed and called Yelling's office, pretending to be from a business wanting a timeline on the Endicot Street construction. He got Ronnie's mobile and landline numbers from his secretary. He had Peggy obtain a magistrate's order for the phone companies to record and divulge any mobile and landline conversations around the time of the abduction.

CHAPTER 75

I worked with Barbie to find who had scheduled the concreting job that buried Jane.

'We need to know who decided to pour in that place on that particular day,' I said.

'If I ask about that, they'll want to know if I'm police,' Barbie said.

'Last time you told them you were with Council's safety unit. You can say you are running a safe sites competition and ask if they have a procedure to check for any pets in the formwork. That should prompt them to tell you about Jane and who would have decided when to do that pour.'

'Awesome, Doc. I can say there is a prize for the safest site.'

'I like it. Let's go with that.'

*

Now that Jane's panics were less frequent it was tempting to think that she had fully recovered. However, I could see by her right eye that fear still stalked her. There was no hope of rekindling our relationship until I had allayed her concerns.

'You'll be well again soon,' I said. 'Be patient with yourself. After such a terrifying experience, you are bound to feel fearful and panicky.'

After another panic, I asked Terry, 'Does she feel she is in imminent danger?'

'She may still be experiencing delusions,' he said. 'While she was imprisoned, she may have clung to a buoyant inner reality, a madness to stop from going under. She mentioned a hallucination in which she was persecuted as a Messiah. The schizoid thought patterns that sustained her while she starved in the dark could be like wheel ruts taking her back and forth, keeping her stuck in the past.'

Before she was abducted, Jane had a bright and bubbly personality. Now she seemed preoccupied and hopeless. She did not value herself highly. She had been an elegant dresser, who set the style for the women councillors. For Council meetings, she now dressed inconspicuously.

'My clothes are all too large for me and hang off me like a scarecrow,' she said.

'The way you are eating, it won't be for long.'

Jane had never been precious but the abductors had pricked the bubble of her vanity. Her allure had been taken away. She was a victim of a crime of contempt — her femininity had been spat upon.

Jane gained enough strength to resume her Council duties. While staying at the hospital, she returned to working at Blake Ward office in a blaze of publicity. They held a parade for her down the high street. I rode with her in the tray of a chromed-up ute with huge wheels, its muffler burbling, the crowds pressing forward and calling out in their excitement.

'We love you, Jane!'

'I have waited a long time for this,' she told the crowd when we halted at the civic centre. 'I am happiest here, working for you, the residents of Blake.'

There was rapturous applause.

'When I was locked up in the dark, I remembered your loyalty and it kept me going. Now I am going back to work for you and for all the people of Alexandra City. Together we can do great things.'

Her road back to normalcy was rocky. Something sudden could cause adrenalin to set her heart pounding, ready for fight or flight and tentativeness we had not seen before. At the hospital after work she was sometimes wound up like a spring.

'What is worrying you?' I asked.

'They might have another go at me at any time.'

She was able to relax sharing a bottle of wine with me, but it was only temporary. Beneath her surface she was stressed. For her to recover, her abductors had to be brought to justice.

When Jane returned to the hung parliament, both Government and Opposition solicited her support but they could not buy her vote with favours.

When they asked her which party she would side with she said, 'I will vote on my conscience, as you should do too.'

There would be an election in six months. Jane needed to re-establish herself in her constituency. As an independent, it was gruelling for her to campaign against parties who could dispense largesse and had a pool of money to advertise their brands. She could offer only herself and her band of hard-working volunteers.

Preparation of our DA was proceeding. I managed to borrow a suite of offices in a building next to Council's executive building. Our team set up drafting computers and got down to work. The solicitor, architect and engineers were working partly pro bono and others were involved in design, preparing an impact statement and drawing artists' impressions of the development. We had funds for them from the concert and from donations.

In the DA Committee, Munster said, 'Phillip, are the MC group preparing a DA?'

'Yes.'

'They need to submit it as soon as possible.'

'Can we wait until Jane is back at work?'

'Why?'

'The MC is her idea. Council should wait for her to speak to it. Her absence is not her fault.'

Munster pouted as if she thought it might be.

'How long will we have to wait for her?' she asked.

'At least two months more,' I said.

'That's too long,' she said. 'It's been two months since we approved the PDA. Another month is the most I can give her, then we'll approve Runyon's for the site. Make sure you have evidence of funding.'

Funding was a problem. Profits generated by a MC would not be high and financiers would look for other merits of the project, such as support from Government. That was obviously a problem.

'Can you be finished in a month's time?' I asked Sunita.

'Why?'

'The committee want our DA.'

'We'll do what we can, Doctor,' she said.

'Thank you,' I said.

Sunita and her colleagues needed to put in some long hours. Sunita could be a pain sometimes but I had come to rely on her.

*

I went around town with Jane, meeting corporate leaders, seeking funding.

'Until our DA is approved they won't commit,' Jane said, 'but we can get them to promise an amount they will hand over later.'

'What is in it for them?'

'Corporate image, sales and kudos. Quite a few heads of corporations are immigrants and would like to foster in customers' and suppliers' memories of the homeland. They can attract compatriots to their products by hitching to our wagon. The CEO of Eurobuild has promised $5 million. Others will follow.'

'We have been promised $20 million so far,' I said.

'It's not nearly enough to construct a MC,' she said.

'When we show the promises to the banks, they will lend us the rest.'

'Will Council accept that?'

'Yes. When the banks are onside, governments will get behind us.'

'Can we ask the Federal Government?' I asked. 'They want to be seen to be encouraging a MC but they will only come to the party when they are obliged to. They won't knock us back if we ask now and they could feel obligated later.'

'If we can get a celebrity on board to open doors for us, we can get patronage from the big end of town,' said Jane. 'They could get sponsors to join in a consortium or combine in a syndicate. I'll contact Femma Fleet. Everyone knows her — she's an Alexandran girl and her family were migrants.'

Femma Fleet was a celebrity vocalist who dabbled in public causes. She would entice sponsors.

The slow progress of the Jane investigation created uncertainty that was holding up Council's approval of development of our MC.

CHAPTER 76

I met with Peggy at her office to update her on our progress.

'How are you getting on, Doctor?' Peggy asked. 'Do you have a suspect for me yet?'

'Not yet.'

We had been trying to link someone to the crime scenes for three weeks.

'Any progress?' she asked impatiently.

'We haven't identified Cobra, the man in the car, yet,' I said. 'We need to match traces or show he was at one or more of the crime scenes. Until you bring him in or get a search warrant, Chief Inspector, we are stuck.'

'Do you know where he is?'

'No. We could do a manhunt if there were grounds to bring him in. Are there?'

'No. The lithium in Jane's car matches dirt on the floor at CS3 but it could have been left by an earlier passenger.'

Peggy was curt. 'We have all Jane's testimony now but we haven't got very far. Do you want me to takeover, Doctor Keane?'

'No. It's under control, Chief Inspector. The lithium is our best lead. We're looking to see if Cobra was involved earlier at the construction site in some other role. Have your people found any matches for Jane's description of him?'

'No,' she said. 'It's like looking for a needle in a haystack. Was anyone else at the crime scenes?'

'Barbie has been investigating who went to the factory,' I said. 'It was owned by Roberta Government who have sold it to Runyon Casinos!'

'You're kidding! When?'

'Three months ago — the purchase contract was signed just before Jane went missing on June 17th. Settlement was a month ago.'

'What do Runyon's want it for?' Peggy asked.

'They said it is an alternative site for a casino.'

'Do you believe it?'

'It's possible.'

'The mastermind could be Runyon's CEO,' she said, 'or an underling.'

'We have no evidence of that.'

'A Runyon's mastermind wouldn't have had to look far to get a perpetrator, Doctor,' Peggy said. 'Casinos have strong-arm men on their payroll.'

'Lawbreakers too.'

'It's a bit too obvious,' Peggy said.

'Would another mob take Jane and frame Runyon's? I don't think so. No-one would dare to stitch them up. They're too powerful.'

'The villains could have used the factory to hold Jane without an inkling that Runyon's are buying it, Doc,' Barbie said

'Too much of a coincidence,' I said. 'Someone from Runyon's probably proposed it for the abduction.'

'Would you find out from the Provincial Government when Runyon's first got interested in the place? Then ask Runyon's the same question. It is more than a coincidence.'

Peggy had to go and I went to see Jane.

Peggy called me the next day. She had had a chat with Andrea Gough.

'When their PDA was opposed in Council, Runyon's began looking for another site for their casino,' Peggy said. 'Three weeks before Jane went missing, Andrea got a list of Government properties for sale from Montague and he loaned her a set of keys.'

'At that time, Runyon's were set to get the IB site,' I said. 'It doesn't make sense.'

'Gough said it was a contingency plan.'

'Was buying the building where Jane would be locked up bad luck? Or was it a way to internalise risk?'

'Would they shit in their own backyard?'

'Perhaps they thought the CS3 location and its ownership would never be discovered. Jane wouldn't know where she had been because she would be unconscious coming and going.'

324

'The abductors must have had Runyon's permission, assistance or connivance,' Peggy said.

'We don't have evidence of other Runyon's people at any of the crime scenes,' I said. 'Cobra did the job alone.'

'There would be a mastermind behind the scenes. He could have worked with Cobra previously.'

'At Runyon's?'

'Again, it's too obvious,' Peggy said. 'Perhaps they were both involved with the Endicot Street construction?'

'Employer and contractor?'

'Could be. Payments for the abduction could look like legitimate remuneration.'

'I'll get Barbie to check who was there.'

*

On the way to my office I stopped at a shopping centre and bought a chess set.

'What's this for?' Barbie asked when I gave it to her.

'It's a token of my appreciation for all your hard work,' I said. 'Do you play?'

'No. But I can learn.'

'Cutter plays. Get him to teach you. I know you'll be good.'

'Thanks, Doc.'

'Would you make up a survey form to collect employee names, fasten it to a clipboard and give it to the receptionist in Bridge Works' office to fill out.'

'After last time when they saw me off, she won't give me the time of day.'

'I'll ask DI Malcolm to go with you and show his ID. He can say the Kenwood Inquiry wants to know names of everyone who was on the site in the past six months.'

The great thing about Barbie was you never had to tell her twice.

At the end of the week, she sent me a table of information. The receptionist had listed 15 companies or subcontractors who had brought 136 employees onto the site.

'Cobra was from out of town. If you leave out all the locals, how many are left?'

While Barbie searched the data, I made us both a cup of coffee.

'Fourteen.'

We sent the names and information to Malcolm. He found two with previous convictions: Claus Panovic and Arnold Steele.

'Our man may never have been convicted,' I said. 'Any of the 14 could have done it. He could still be working on site. Could you wait outside and spot him from Jane's Identikit picture?'

'I'll have a go,' she said, sipping her coffee. 'If I do spot him, should I follow him?'

'Make sure he doesn't see you. Don't scare him away. Call me and I'll get Peggy to bring him in.'

Two days later Barbie breezed into my office.

'I sat in my car outside the site entrance, Doc,' she said. 'Two hours later the security guard came over. 'What are you doing here?' he asked.'

'"What's it to you?' I said.'

'"You are on private property."

'"I'm looking for someone,' I said. 'One of the workers here raped me and I am pregnant.' I was weeping. 'I want to find him to get maintenance.' I showed him the Identikit picture. 'The police are too busy to look for him. I am trying to find him myself but he's from out of town. He's medium height, wide and strong. This is a picture. The police gave me this list of people who worked here. If I can get his name, I may be able to find him."

'"I see,' said the guard. 'I'm sorry. Look, leave that picture and those names with me. Someone may know or remember the bastard. Come back in a few days."

'On Friday he gave me three names and some details. 'We reckon it's one of these three,' he said. 'They're not working here now. We know where two came from. They fit the description, young single men and forceful."

Barbie showed me names and details of three men.

Alwyn Caddie's job had been drawing construction plans. He had finished several weeks ago and had not left an address. He may have returned to his home town of Wharton.

Arnold Steele had worked for a subcontractor – CTS. He was a body builder. There was no address. They thought he was from out of town. He hadn't been seen for months. Malcolm had supplied that he had been convicted of aggravated assault, getting six years but paroled after two and released a year ago. He had been off the police's radar until we matched him with Cobra.

Guy Fall was a carpenter who had built forms for concreting. He had previously been a professional football player. He had done several stints at the site. He was from Denwich, a country town.

'This narrows it down. Thank you, Barbie. Were you really weeping?'

'Yes. I believed my own story.'

'The guard believed it too. It worked. One of these three could be our villain doubling as a construction worker,' I said.

'Arnold Steele fits the bill. He's done time.'

'What about a construction worker doubling as our villain?'

'Could we check for lithium on footwear?' said Barbie.

'The police must find him first.'

'Is there any other way we can connect him to the crime?'

'Can we check if any of them received a large sum of money about the time Jane went missing?'

'I'll get local police to find out their bank accounts. I'll ask Peggy.'

The police found bank account numbers for the draftsman and ex-footballer from the Council's property rating database. Neither's bank had received a large cash payment recently. For the third, Arnold Steele, we only knew his employer – CTS.

'What does CTS stand for?'

'Concrete Testing Services.'

'So Arnold Steele was into concrete?' I said. 'How much of a coincidence is it that when he wanted to dispose of her body he buried her in concrete?'

'He seems more like a murderer by the minute,' said Barbie. 'He did more premeditation than the Maharishi Yogi.'

'Would the mastermind hire an abductor because of his concreting experience? I think not. The concreting job was only a cover.'

'He snuck into the hospital to get Jane, tried to mug me and rammed Cutter's car.'

'His pay could equally well have been laundered if he was a ranger who did a flora and fauna survey for the Parks Department.'

'Then he would have buried her in a forest,' Barbie said, 'under the floor. It would be a good way for a ranger to hide her body.'

'Exactly,' I said. 'The concrete was a means, not an end. The CTS job was a way for the mastermind to pay him, not an alibi.'

'Having a job that enabled him to hide her body was a bonus.'

'He looks like Cobra. It must be Steele.'

'Perhaps CTS paid him for snatching Jane,' I said.

'And the mastermind paid CTS,' said Barbie.

'Would Ronnie Yelling have the motive and the money to be the mastermind?'

'I can't see him driving this thing,' I said. 'He is basically a manager. He could have been a middleman. He might have supervised the bogus concrete work as well as the abduction.'

'Why?' asked Barbie.

'Good question. Would you look into Ronnie's possible motives, please.'

CHAPTER 77

Cutter dropped by after lunch. I told him about Cobra being Arnold Steele.

'To find the mastermind we can look for who paid CTS,' said Cutter.

'If Council paid them it would be on record,' Barbie said. 'Can we get access to Council's accounts?'

When I had investigated the Council's accounts for corruption two years ago, I had tangled with CEO Montague.

'Ainsley won't let me poke around in the accounts unless the LM authorises it.'

'Would Martha okay you?'

'No way. She and Montague are in cahoots. They will keep me out until they have covered up anything fishy.'

'How about we watch to see if they do a runner when we start looking under stones.'

'What do you mean?' Cutter asked.

'If they fudge the accounts to look kosher, we can find it out and use it as evidence.'

'Getting a look at the accounts could be tricky,' he said. 'The only access we have is by logging into the account from the computers at our desks in the Council chamber. The files are read-only.'

'We need to download copies.'

'Could you use a screenshot app?' Barbie asked.

'No. I have tried and they are blocked,' I said.

'Could we use a camera?' Cutter asked. 'When no-one is around.'

'How about after a Council meeting?'

'What account do you suspect?' he asked.

'Works,' I said. 'That is the account they use to pay Bridge Works and they could pay CTS.'

'You have to get logins from the Works' Committee chairman,' Cutter said. 'That's Jock O'Connell. He won't give you access — you're Opposition.'

'I'll ask Shelly to take the photos — she's on Works' Committee.'

'She's Opposition too.'

'The SLP and NLP work together, remember? O'Connell won't say no if she has a good reason.'

'Are you sure Shelly will do it?' Cutter asked.

'Yes. She would do anything to nail the abductors who took her friend, Jane.'

'What reason can she give O'Connell?' Cutter asked.

'That she wants to compare spending in her ward with the other wards,' I said.

'Jock would tell her to have Montague's people dig out the numbers.'

'She can say she needs to see the whole account to make a fair comparison.'

'It could work.'

Shelly was a brick and agreed. She persuaded O'Connell to give her the logins. I lent her a document camera. After the next Council meeting she photographed the account. She gave me 20 photos on a flash drive. I checked they would open and phoned CEO Montague.

'Ainsley, have there been any large payments from the Works account in the last few months?'

'What for?' he said.

'Non-budgeted one-off items,' I said.

It was a question that would shake the apple tree. He knew I was investigating the abduction and would cover up anything fishy.

'I'll look into it and get back to you,' he said.

It took two weeks and three reminder phone calls before he responded.

'No, Phillip. Works hasn't paid any large unexpected items. Who said we had?'

'I predicted it from looking into Jane Kenwood's abduction.'

'Well, you gave yourself a bum steer,' Montague said 'There's nothing like that in the accounts. You should leave it to the police.'

He hung up.

A week later I asked Shelly to photograph the accounts again. When I compared them with those she had taken earlier, I found $500,000 had been recorded as paid out to CTS shortly before Jane's abduction on June 17th. A further $500,000 was paid out on July 23rd, the day after she was found. In the later version, the payments to CTS had disappeared from the account. The same amount had been inserted as paid to University Material Testing Services (UMTS). The payments to CTS had been concealed.

'I've found something,' I said to Cutter. 'I need to find out if UMTS really did get paid and what for.'

'Someone must have approved the payments,' Cutter said. 'They should know.'

'I'll ask Ainsley Montague,' I said. 'Face to face could be interesting. I may be able to see how bent he is.'

CHAPTER 78

It would not be a friendly meeting. Ainsley made no secret of his contempt for councillors who were not under Government control. I went alone because if I took Barbie with me she would be a witness and he would be more guarded. I didn't want his cover-up story. I wanted to find out what he was covering up. It would be my word against his but it could lead to evidence.

I could see he didn't have anyone with him but he kept me sitting outside his office for 20 minutes

'It's good of you to see me,' I said, hoping my sarcasm was evident.

'What can I do for you?' Montague said, lying back in his chair and turning a pencil end to end. He was ambitious and highly organised. His financial domain exceeded many national economies.

'Where did that $1 million go from the Works Account?' I asked. 'It couldn't disappear.'

Montague went crimson. He sat forward. His shirt collar seemed to be throttling him.

'Who says anything went anywhere?'

'It was recorded as paid out to CTS from the Works Account two weeks ago but a few days ago the account had been altered and it was gone.'

'What do you mean it was altered?'

'The copy of the Works Account we made two weeks ago is different to the one we made a few days ago.'

'You made copies?' Montague spluttered. 'You are not authorised to copy that account. You have stolen information from us.'

'Yes, Ainsley,' I said agreeably. I knew that the Government would not take action against me because the LM had claimed publicly that Council's operations were more transparent than ever. 'This could mean that the money that appeared to go to CTS wasn't

332

actually sent to them and someone else has it. Did Council pay $500,000 to CTS on July 8th and another $500,000 on July 23rd?'

'Let's see,' he said, looking at his screen. 'We paid it to UMTS. They did the work.'

Our later account photos showed $1 million sent in four payments to UMTS.

'Why was the destination account changed?' I asked.

'My expenditure authority is limited to $350,000. For more than that I require the LM's approval. My people corrected it to four smaller amounts.'

The four payments were for $250,000 each, which was within Ainsley's authority. It was a cover-up of a minor misdemeanour. I was disappointed. We were no closer to finding the mastermind.

'Who checked the tests were done?' I said.

'They sent us a report,' said Montague.

'May I see it?'

He picked up his phone and punched an extension. 'Isembard, would you bring in the CTS report.'

A nerdy looking guy entered, carrying a thin, bound document.

'This is Isembard Harditch, our Principal Civil Engineer,' the CEO told me. 'He designed the concrete testing programme.'

'Who wanted the tests done?' I asked.

'Roads,' Montague said.

'What was their purpose?'

Harditch held his chin in defensively and mumbled. 'It was to be a quality check on the concrete being used at 10 of their projects in the CBD. I worked out a sampling and testing programme.'

'Was one of the sites where Councillor Kenwood was found?'

'Yes, the Endicot Street overpass,' said Montague. 'It was horrific. Do the police have a suspect yet?'

'Not yet,' I said. 'How was CTS to obtain the samples?'

'By swiping across the stream from the trucks with three-litre buckets,' Harditch said. 'It's the standard method.'

'Where did the samples go?'

'To UMTS to set and cure for strength testing.'

'Was the work finished?'

Harditch looked at Montague.

'Yes,' Montague said. 'It is in this report.'

'Did you okay it?' I asked Harditch.

'We sent it to the LM ...' he said uncertainly.

'Yes, Isembard did okay it,' said Montague brusquely.

'Who did you send the money to?'

He fidgeted. 'CTS would forward the money to UMTS.'

'When you arranged the contract, who was the person you dealt with?' I asked Harditch.

'CTS's manager ...' Isembard began.

Montague frowned and shook his head but Harditch blurted out, '... Arnold Steele.'

'What does he look like?' I asked.

Harditch shrugged. 'We used phone and email.'

'Had you employed CTS before?' I said.

'No.'

I said quietly to Montague, 'So you paid out $1 million of Council money for work you did not see to someone you had never met?'

'There isn't a problem,' said Montague. 'Trust us, Phillip. This is how we work.'

I pointed to the report. 'Can I have a copy to take away?'

'What for?' Montague asked.

'I want to check that all the tests were done,' I said. '$1 million is a lot of money.'

Montague reflected for a moment, as if weighing up whether to refuse.

'UMTS are reliable,' he said.

'Is there a UMTS person I can talk to?'

'Helen ...' began Isembard.

'Bill Prescott,' interrupted Montague. 'He's the manager.'

'I would like a copy of that report,' I said firmly.

'Isembard, make him a copy,' said Montague, with exaggerated patience.

Harditch went out.

Montague and I eyed each other. Neither of us mentioned returning the photos to Council. I hoped he had forgotten them.

'Where did the money come from that you paid to CTS?' I asked. 'Or was it UMTS?'

Montague did not clarify the confusion. 'From Works Department.'

'Where did Works get it?'

Montague shrugged. 'It arrived in our account with the money to pay Bridge Works for the Endicot Street construction.'

'From Roads?'

Montague shrugged.

I waited.

'Yes,' he admitted.

One million had been laundered whiter than white. It might not be missed immediately.

'How's Jane Kenwood?' asked Montague, changing the subject, pretending he cared about her health.

There was no love lost between the two. At the end of the previous year Jane had said in a Council meeting, 'Ainsley, your lack of cooperation throughout the year leads me to wish you a Very Unhappy Christmas.'

We talked briefly about Jane's condition.

Isembard came back and handed me a copy of the report.

'Thank you.'

'Is that everything?' said Montague, as if it ought to be.

'Can you give me a contact number for Concrete Testing Services?'

Ainsley reflected for a moment, then wrote on his business card from a phone book on his desk.

'Here's their office number.'

I thanked them and took the lift down. On the ground floor, I was going out through the foyer when Isembard Harditch caught up with me.

He spoke furtively, as if he didn't want to be seen talking to me. 'About me approving that report, Montague bullied me into it,' he said. 'The data was made up.'

Before I could say anything, he ducked away and walked back to the lifts.

*

Peggy called me later that day.

335

'I am shutting you down, Doctor Keane,' she said. 'I have been instructed by the Police Commissioner (PC) to inform you to return to CEO Montague all the information you copied from Council's accounts. If you use it to question the Government or pass it on to others, you will be arrested and charged with theft.'

Someone was trying to cover up something big. Whose side was Peggy on? She had always been a straight shooter with me but we were into something so threatening that to survive she had to follow orders that conflicted with her ethics.

I tried to appeal to her decency.

'Chief Inspector, we have found a transaction in the Council's Works account that is a concealed payment to the abductors.'

'You obtained that evidence illegally and it will not hold up in court,' she said.

I told her we had uncovered account tampering and explained what we had found.

'It might simply be that Montague exceeded his authority,' she said.

'That's what he wants us to believe, Chief Inspector, but I am trying to find out what the money was used for,' I said. 'It may have gone to something they want to hide. The phone number Montague gave me is disconnected.'

'Maybe they have moved.'

'CTS was registered as a vendor to Works, with Arnold Steele as owner operator. His appearance matches Jane's glimpsed description of Cobra. His home address was a motel. He's no longer there,' I said. 'We are going there to see if we can get a lead to find him.'

*

Barbie and I went to the motel.

I showed the Identikit pictures of Cobra to the receptionist.

'No, I don't remember him,' she said. 'It is too long ago. We get a lot of people through here. You could try room service. One of the girls might remember him.'

336

We hit pay dirt with Annie who was cleaning rooms. 'Yes, I remember him. One gold earring, left ear. He was here for more than a month.'

I thought, *'So Cobra is Arnold Steele.'*

'Did he say where he was from?' I asked.

'No,' said the chambermaid. 'He never talked.'

'It's a way of hiding,' I thought.

I called Peggy. 'I have a suspect for you, Arnold Steele. He looks like Jane's picture of Cobra. He has done two years for grievous bodily harm. He worked at the Endicot Street site. He may have received $1 million for the abduction from CTS.'

'Good work — although it's circumstantial. We still need to link him with one or more of the crime scenes.'

I wondered why Peggy was reluctant to arrest the suspect.

337

CHAPTER 79

I called Jane at the hospital.

'I need your help for a couple of hours. Can I pick you up in 15?'

'What for?'

'I need you to meet with some people who can help our investigation. It won't take long.'

'What should I wear?'

'It's outdoors but smartish would be good.'

'Okay.'

Jane wore a crisp white shirt, blue jeans and ankle boots with low heels.

I drove with her to Endicot Street. We started to walk across the site but when Jane realised where she was, she wanted to flee. I held her hand. The concreting crew and crane were putting formwork around a column. Bob and Brian were uncoupling wire ropes. Norman switched off and climbed down from his cab. They stood around us and Jane managed a smile.

'Morning, Ms Kenwood,' Norman said.

'These are the guys who rescued you, Jane.'

'You look a bit better than last time we saw you, Miss.'

It had been 10 weeks.

'Thank you for saving me,' she said and gave each of them a hug.

In overalls covered with dust, they were awkward and blushing. Jane was pristine and glamorous, although gaunt.

'Have you caught up with them what done it yet, Doctor Keane?' Bob asked me. 'It ain't been on the news.'

'Not yet,' I said. 'The police are working on it. I want to ask you something. Did you see anyone getting buckets of concrete about a month before you rescued her?'

'I might have seen a guy over there at the trucks a couple of times,' Norman said.

'What did he look like?'

He scratched his head.

'I can't remember.'

'Did he look like this?' I showed him the Identikit picture.

'Oh him,' Norman said. 'He came over and had a look at what we were doing. Big bloke. He says to me, 'I have to tell them where the concrete is going.' 'Columns for a road overpass,' I said and he wrote it down.'

'His name was Arnold Steele. Did he say anything else?'

'His mobile rang. 'I'm finished,' he answered it. It sounded like he was talking to the boss, Ronnie Yelling who I could see standing at his office window. 'Leaving in about five minutes.' Then he got into an argument on the phone.'

'Why didn't he go inside and talk to him?'

'I dunno.'

'Could Ronnie have come down?'

'He never does,' Norman said. 'Ronnie always stays in his office and talks on the phone with me and the lads.'

'What did he and Steele talk about?'

'They argued.'

'How do you know they were arguing?'

'Steele was shouting. He was pretty upset.'

'What about?'

'Money it was. He wanted to get paid more.'

I thought. *'Steele must have worked for Yelling.'*

'Could they have been talking about the next pour?'

'I didn't hear because I got back into my cab.'

'Thank you. I hope we haven't delayed you too much,' I said.

'No worries, Doc,' Norman said. 'Glad to see you looking so much better, Ms Kenwood. Keep up the good work on the Council.'

'Give those fat bastards a hard time for me,' said Brian.

'I saw in the paper what you said in the Council, Ms Kenwood,' said Norman. 'You put them lot to rights properly.'

'Why, thank you, Norman,' said Jane graciously.

'See ya,' said Bob and Brian as they went back to work.

As we walked back to my car, Jane said 'Now you have a lead.'

'You opened up their memories. We are lucky to find Yelling — he stayed at a distance where he thought he wouldn't be discovered.'

339

Peggy rang with bad news. The phone company had not found any conversations between Yelling's mobile and either Steele or Cobra. Triangulation from microwave towers was unavailable because the phones were no longer transmitting, possibly destroyed. They could have used prepaid unregistered 'burn' phones. We would have to find another way to incriminate them.

CHAPTER 80

The UMTS's building was situated behind Civil Engineering.

Barbie parked in one of the visitors' spaces.

'We are from the City Council,' I told the receptionist. 'Could we speak with Helen?'

It was the name Montague had wanted to prevent Harditch from telling us.

'What is it about?'

'Some tests done for us recently.'

'Who is us?'

'City Council. My name is Dr Phillip Keane.'

'I'll call her.'

A young woman in a white coat came to reception.

'I'm pleased to meet you, Dr Keane,' she said, offering her hand. 'I've seen you in the news. I'm Helen Gabriel, research assistant.'

'Pleased to meet you,' I said and introduced Barbie.

'Are you investigating Jane Kenwood's disappearance, Doctor?'

'Yes.'

She paused. 'I hope you catch whoever did it. What they did was terribly cruel.'

'I apologise for just turning up like this. We were passing. I hope we are not interrupting your work?'

'Not at all. How can I help?'

'We are trying to find out about some work done here in June by a company called Concrete Testing Services.'

'I remember. What do you want to know?'

'Council received a copy of a report from CTS with results of some tests done here. We want to know what the tests were. Isembard Harditch mentioned your name.'

'I was away on holiday at the time. The testing was done by CTS people. Have you talked to them?'

'We haven't been able to contact them. Did you meet any of their people?'

'Yes. Arnold Steele was here for a couple of weeks, I think.'

I showed her the Identikit picture. 'Is this him?'

'Yes,' Helen said. 'Is he suspected of something?'

'He is helping us with our inquiries. Do you have an address or number for him?'

She looked at her mobile. She had the same number Montague had given us that was disconnected.

'Could you give us CTS' bank details,' I said. 'They may have a contact address.'

'I'll see if it's on file.'

We followed her into the office.

'Here is the report with the test results,' she said, 'and here's our invoice.'

She showed us a copy of an invoice for $500,000 for 'testing'. It was stamped: 'Paid June 12th', a few days before Jane was abducted.

I thought, *'If the tests had been faked, payment for them could be faked too.'*

'Who deals with accounts receivable?' I asked her.

'The manager, Bill Prescott.'

'Is he around?'

'He's away today.'

'What work did CTS have done here?'

'I'll show you our set-up,' Helen said. 'They stored their samples in that building over there.'

We went to a large shed. On the floor were hundreds of identical plastic cylinders, like small buckets, filled with concrete.

'Customers leave their samples here for a couple of weeks to dry and cure.'

'Did you see anyone bringing CTS's samples in here?' I asked.

'Yes, Arnold Steele.'

'How many did he bring?'

'Five thousand — it's on the invoice.'

'How many of them did you actually see?'

'Oh ... only a few, at the start. I don't come in here normally. I left him to get on with it. When I came back from holiday, he had finished and gone.'

'What tests were done?'

'Compression strength. The equipment they use is through here.'

We went into an equipment bay, a high building filled with hydraulic presses, some the size of a bus.

'He used that one over there,' she said, pointing to a large hydraulic press.

'How is a test done?'

'I'll show you.'

She fetched one of the buckets filled with concrete and hefted it onto the press. She lowered the ram to rest on it, dialled a loading rate and touched a button. A warning klaxon sounded. We stood behind a screen.

An electric motor murmured. We waited. Nothing seemed to be happening, until there was a bang and the cylinder bulged outwards. The concrete had fractured apart.

'Pieces fly off sometimes,' she said.

'I'd like one of these for macadamias,' said Barbie.

Helen read a digital pressure gauge.

'Hmm — 700 kilograms per square centimetre.'

'Is that okay?'

'Seven hundred is okay for a small building with a broad foundation. But for a heavy building with narrow foundations, steel reinforcement would be needed.'

'Were any of the CTS samples not okay?' I asked.

'I don't evaluate the results. Clients interpret them for their own situation.'

'Is it usual for clients to use your equipment unsupervised?'

'Yes. We train them to use the presses,' said Helen

'How long were you away?'

'Two weeks.'

'That's 500 per day,' I said. 'Wow. Did Arnold Steele have anyone working with him?'

'I didn't see anyone.'

'They must have worked around the clock,' I said.

343

'It happens.'

'How much does the university charge?'

'It works out at around $100 per sample.'

' ... times 5000 ... that makes half a million dollars.'

'That's what was on the invoice.'

'Are the crushed samples here somewhere?'

'No. We truck them to a landfill. Why?'

It was time to stop beating about the bush.

'Helen, our hypothesis is that the tests never took place. CTS only pretended to do them.'

'What?' she sounded surprised. 'Why would they do that?'

'So Arnold Steele could have an alibi and get paid for doing a crime somewhere else.'

She looked at the ground.

'Well, they fooled me. I feel really stupid. What about the results in the report?'

'The numbers could be made up. Is there any other evidence that the tests were actually done?'

'Concrete evidence,' Barbie prompted. I frowned at her and gave a small shake of my head. Helen was upset and it was not a good time for her irreverent humour.

'I wasn't here. He started off as though he meant business,' said Helen.

'What dates were you away?'

'From June 14th to 29th.'

'Who approved your holiday?'

'The manager, Bill Prescott.'

'Was it his idea you took a holiday at that time?'

She seemed surprised. 'Yes, as a matter of fact, it was.'

'Could the test results have been made up?'

'I don't know,' she said, shrugging.

She didn't reject it.

'Helen, do you have any doubts that the tests were actually done?'

She hesitated. 'You should talk with Prescott—he's the manager. I just do what I'm told.'

She gave me his card.

'Now, if you will excuse me, I need to get on with my work.'

Tight-lipped, she turned away. We thanked her and left.

'It seems like a scam,' I said as we drove back to the city. 'CTS have no premises and only one employee, Arnold Steele. Very few tests were done.'

Steele had pretended to be taking samples to UMTS for a couple of weeks before the hijack. Helen was away for the first two weeks after Jane went missing and Steele supposedly did the testing while she was away.

'So what do we do next, Doc?' Barbie asked.

'Ask Prescott for evidence that CTS passed on to him the Council's half a million dollars.'

'His invoice is stamped 'Paid'.'

'It may be faked. We need evidence. I'll ask Peggy to interview him.'

I called Peggy and told her about the UMTS scam.

'It looks as though the Council sent $500,000 to CTS to cover Bill Prescott's invoice, Chief Inspector. Then they sent a further $500,000 just after Jane Kenwood was rescued.'

'Was there a second invoice?'

'Helen Gabriel didn't mention it. Montague only mentioned one invoice. If he paid the second $500,000 without an invoice, it is damning.'

'It stinks,' Peggy said. 'I'll bet CTS never paid UMTS anything at all.'

'Do you think Prescott was duped?'

'No,' said Peggy. 'He abetted a fraud by writing an invoice and pretending to receive the money. He enabled CTS to obtain money under false pretences.'

'Could he be in on the abduction?'

'I doubt it. He may for some time have been money laundering to pay for Government dirty business, Doctor. He could have been sending bent invoices and pretending to receive payment for years without ever knowing what felonies he was funding.'

'Why pretend to be doing the tests?' I asked. 'Why not send an invoice for them without having Steele go there?'

'For the money to be legit, the tests had to be more than fiction.'

'Why not do all of the tests?'

'Steele was too busy grabbing Jane and locking her up,' Peggy said.

'He might have stayed at the factory to keep an eye on the place.'

'UMTS provided him with an alibi for the hijack and for two weeks after. If Harditch hadn't talked, the tests could have put us off his scent.'

'Would you find out how they faked those 5000 tests?'

I gave Peggy Prescott's number.

CHAPTER 81

Two days later, Peggy emailed me a copy of Malcolm's report of their interview.

October 13ᵗʰ, Kenwood Investigation
Interview by DCI Wall and DI Malcolm with Materials Testing Laboratory manager, Bill Prescott, of the Civil Engineering Department, Alexandra University.

1. *Prescott said he had provided Isembard Harditch, a Council engineer, with a quote for 5000 client-operated compression strength tests by a company: CTS. The cost would be $100 per sample.*
2. *Helen Gabriel was on leave from June 14th to 27th. These dates had been suggested by Prescott.*
3. *The meter on the hydraulic press counted the number of tests conducted. It could be run forward by manually depressing a switch once to simulate tests being done.*
4. *After her return, Helen Gabriel submitted activity reports for two weeks with a metered total of 5000 tests done for CTS. She estimated weekly quantities of 2345 and 2655 respectively.*
5. *CTS called Prescott on June 30th to say they had finished.*
6. *Prescott sent an invoice to CTS for $500,000 on July 1st.*
7. *Prescott receipted $500,000 from CTS on July 24th to cover their invoice but provided no evidence that the money went into the UMTS account. He said the money had gone into a UMTS general account to defray costs but when details were requested did not comply.*
8. *No evidence was obtained to refute that very little testing had been done. There were no witnesses who had observed CTS doing the tests.*
Signed
(DI Malcolm)

In the report we had obtained from Montague were several pages of data. To determine the authenticity of the measurements, I used Benford's statistical technique and found abnormally few low-strength samples as if the measurements had been made by a false process that omitted problem values. This supported that the tests did not take place.

'We have enough to indict CTS for fraud,' I said to Peggy in her office. 'Unfortunately, CTS have disappeared.'

'Have you tried twisting Montague's arm for an address, Doctor?' said Peggy. 'He must have a record of where the money was sent.'

I called Montague.

'Would you give me the number of the CTS bank account into which you paid $1 million.'

'We have no record of any transaction with CTS,' said Montague.

'There was a transaction with CTS that was altered to UMTS,' I said. 'Where is your back-up file with the payee's account number.'

'They don't keep the back-ups forever,' he said. 'I'll find out if we still have it. I'll call you.'

But he didn't call.

After two days, I phoned Montague.

'We didn't find account details for CTS,' he said.

'You will have to tell that to the police,' I said.

'It will be the same,' he said. 'We don't have their details.'

I called Peggy.

'I have asked Montague but he claims the bank account number they had for CTS has been erased.'

'They must have it. They are required to retain it. Tell him if he won't give it to us, I'll come with a court order and search for it.

'This is financial negligence,' she said. 'I'll get it on record and lay charges.'

Later that day Peggy phoned to tell me she and Malcolm had gone to Montague's office. She had cautioned him and requested evidence that statutory payment procedures were being adhered to. He came up with a bank account number.

'CTS were with Roberta Bank and their signatory was a Peter Pradel,' said Peggy. 'The bank had their postal address as the Bridge Works office building. On the day after Jane was found they received a second payment of $500,000 from the Council. They closed the account and sent the balance of $1 million to the joint account of Peter and Megan Pradel at the National Bank in Chesterfield. The bank has supplied the home address and telephone number of the Pradels.'

'So our suspect is Peter Pradel aka Arnold Steele aka Cobra,' I said.

'If we had Harditch's testimony we could contact Chesterfield police and bring him in on suspicion of defrauding Council,' said Peggy.

'Do we have other evidence of a fraud?'

'Not enough,' she said. 'It is impossible to show that the tests did not take place. There cannot be evidence of a non-event. Even if the hydraulic press was broken at the time, the tests might conceivably have been done another way.'

'My statistical analysis shows that the results were fabricated. Isn't that enough?'

'It is circumstantial. We need to sheet home the fraud by interviewing Isembard Harditch.'

'Can we keep Harditch out of the limelight?' I asked. 'He has already been bullied to take part in the cover-up. If he looks like being a whistleblower, they might give him a hard time.'

'Once you start pussyfooting around, Phillip, the villains are winning,' said Peggy. 'I'm going to call him.'

Harditch's phone did not answer. She asked to be put through to Ainsley Montague. Peggy was on speakerphone.

'I would like to talk to Harditch,' she said. 'Would you ask him to call me.'

'What about?' Montague asked.

Peggy couldn't reveal that she wanted Harditch to testify to their money-laundering scam.

'I want to know the purpose of the tests and the conclusions,' she said.

349

'The purpose was to check the quality of concrete at 10 sites,' Montague said.

'We want to know how you analysed the results.'

'You are implying that something is amiss,' Montague said with indignation. 'What is your evidence? You are insulting me and my staff. It was a routine testing programme carried out correctly. Get off our back or I will request the Police Minister to stop you harassing us.'

He hung up.

Would Harditch have the courage to blow the whistle?

CHAPTER 82

I was in Peggy's office to update her.

'We are up to looking for anything the suspect could have taken away that could be traced back to the crime scenes.

'Until we know what traces the suspect could leave at the crime scene we won't know what to look for there. It is a 'Catch 22' that a person must be connected to a crime scene before they can be investigated to find a connecting substance, such as this lithium.

'Link 6 assumes Cobra carried lithium from CS3 to CS2 but it remains to be confirmed by finding traces on him. We don't know of anyone else who could have carried it. The connection is weak but we have to accept it for now.'

'What about the money — isn't that a trace?' asked Peggy.

'CTS took away $1 million from CS7 that came from CS8, which was the Works account.'

'How did it get in there?'

'I'll ask the Premier.'

I listened to Peggy on speaker phone as she called the Premier and was put through to one of his aides.

'I would like to see the Government accounts to find out how testing was done for Council by a company called CTS.'

'What do you want to know?'

'Who authorised payment of $1 million to Works for it and from what account?'

'I'll get back to you.'

*

Peggy and Malcolm came to our next think tank meeting. I introduced Sunita and Tony to them.

'Barbie has brought some cherries. Help yourselves.'

I said, 'We have reached the penultimate Link 7, evident by traces the suspect left at the crime scenes, such as voice messages on phones that show involvement with the crime.'

'When the phone company searched calls from Ronnie's registered mobile to persons of interest, they found only one conversation between him and Hubbard,' Malcolm said.

'She made one call to Yelling on her registered mobile,' Peggy said. 'Every other time she may have called him from a burn phone.'

'What did they talk about?' I asked.

'It was a cryptic conversation and difficult to understand,' said Peggy. 'It seemed to be about the abduction. There is not enough evidence to bring in either of them.'

'Is there evidence that Hubbard is the mastermind?' I asked.

'No,' she said. 'There are other possibilities.'

'Would it be enough of a link if the mastermind had purchased the place where they took Jane?' said Tony.

His impish ideas enlivened the group.

'Gee, that's a tough one, Tony,' said Sunita. 'The mastermind would have to be brazen, stupid or unlucky.'

'He could have been framed.'

'It is circumstantial,' I said. 'Runyon's could have made a genuine purchase for the reasons they have given us.'

'Fat chance,' said Barbie. 'It stinks.'

'Perhaps they were looking for an alternative site for the casino and stumbled on a good place to hold Jane.'

'It fits. Sindona could be the mastermind,' said Sunita.

'We need evidence of Sindona's intent and whether his money went right through Government to CTS and to Arnold Steele,' Peggy said.

'It won't be easy, ' I said. 'They will try to stop us investigating — the Government employs us and can force us to comply.'

'Malcolm and I have been warned from a high level not to follow the money trail into the Government,' said Peggy.

'Who warned you?' I said.

'My super. He told me any investigation had to be cleared with him and done by the police, not by you.'

'What did you say?'

'I said that I couldn't stop you if what you were doing was legal.

'He said, 'Stop them. That is an order— from the top.'

'I told him it is illegal for a public official to break the law and his order was illegally given.

'His reply was, in this instance, the Premier's authority was superior by emergency powers and must be obeyed.

'I told him I wanted it in writing.

'If I refused, he'd transfer me, he told me.'

Peggy seemed to be complying with a tyrant but I forgave her. I knew that she was trying to passively resist this shit. Politicians had no constitutional right to decide how laws would be policed.

'It is a cover-up,' I said.

'I would watch my back if I were you, Doctor,' said Peggy. 'They are ruthless.'

'We need to interview Sindona about the money they paid for the factory, Chief Inspector,' I said. 'Maybe some of it had strings.'

'You will be lucky to get to talk with him,' Peggy said. 'He skedaddled overseas at about the time Jane disappeared and hasn't been back since.'

I telephoned Andrea Gough.

'How's Jane?' she asked.

'She's back at work, phasing in,' I said. 'She's getting stronger all the time.'

'I hope she recovers soon.'

'Can I speak with Sindona?'

'He's overseas and hard to catch,' she said. 'He'll be here in three weeks.'

'Perhaps he imagines the heat is off and it is safe for him to return now,' I thought. *'Because he went overseas before Jane disappeared, he probably isn't the mastermind.'*

'Is there any possibility he could come back sooner?'

'I'll ask him.'

'Thank you, Andrea.'

'Good afternoon, Phillip.'

She ended the call.

*

'Will you interview the Premier?' I asked Peggy at our next meeting.

'Hmm,' said Peggy, 'if I question whether there has been misappropriation of funds, he will throw me out. I could take it to Wallace Templeton, the Crime and Corruption Commissioner (CCC). It's his job to deal with complaints about the Government.'

'It was the Premier who appointed him,' I said. 'Do you think he would play it straight?'

'He's our only hope.'

Risking the ire of her boss, the Police Commissioner, Peggy contacted the CCC. He seconded Peggy Wall and Gary Malcolm to move the police's investigation to his offices.

'I have initiated a Jane Kenwood Abduction Inquiry,' the CCC told Peggy. 'You can summons witnesses and requisition documents.'

'Terrific,' Peggy said. 'It will be so much better than pussyfooting around, having to get evidence before I can ask questions. We already have samples of lithium, hair, dust and dirt from the crime scenes. If we can get samples from suspects we might get a match.'

CHAPTER 83

Two days later, Peggy called me.

'Have you heard from Harditch yet?' she asked.

'No. Have you?'

'He's disappeared,' Peggy said. 'His wife said he seemed preoccupied on Monday evening and when he left the house on Tuesday morning he was agitated. He never arrived at work. I've checked the hospitals. He hasn't been reported in any accident. His wife is in quite a state.'

'He was scared when he told me Montague had bullied him,' I said.

'They could have threatened him.'

'Could he have done a runner and be hiding out somewhere?'

'His wife said he didn't take any clothes.'

'Suicide?'

'Possible, although he has children.'

'Perhaps he has been taken out?'

'Taken out or not, the CCC wants him found.'

Peggy issued a general alert, giving a description of Harditch and his car.

I went with Peggy and Malcolm to a meeting with the CCC in his office.

'Can we place Steele at any of your eight crime scenes?' the CCC asked.

'Yes, possibly all of them. Link 7 is that the person who grabbed Jane, locked her up, unlocked her and dumped her was the same person: the suspect Cobra.'

'What's this link business?' The CCC was puzzled.

'Councillor Keane is doing a ... reconstruction,' Peggy explained. 'He has a chain of hypotheses that describes how Cobra, step by step, put Jane in hospital.'

'Have you put out a warrant for his arrest?'

'Not yet. We aren't certain it was him. Jane's glimpses of Cobra were only partial sightings. The defence could argue that because Jane was kept in the dark, her eyes were dazzled, unable to focus and her recall of Cobra's face could not be reliable.'

'The lithium in Jane's car probably came from the factory and there was $1 million found in Cobra's account,' I said. 'He could also be involved in Harditch's disappearance. Isn't that enough to bring him in, Commissioner?'

'Shit yes,' said the CCC. 'The burial in concrete when he is a concrete worker is too much of a coincidence. It's got to be him. Bring him in.'

The PC had been under political orders and had held Peggy back until now. The CCC's authority could kickstart the stalled investigation. Peggy could go after Steele.

'We have to find him first, sir,' Peggy said.

'Surely you have enough to ferret him out?'

'Yes, sir,' said Peggy. 'I'll get the local police on to it.'

The meeting ended.

*

Peggy wrote a warrant for the arrest of Arnold Steele aka Peter Pradel at the address obtained from his bank and emailed it to Chesterfield Police.

'He is big, strong, intelligent and a psychopath,' Peggy told their Sergeant Norris on the phone. 'We suspect him of attempted murder — he is dangerous. Go in strength, surround the house and if necessary force your way in. His woman lives there with three children, so be careful. Let me know how you get on.'

Norris called from the Pradel home two hours later. Megan Pradel and the children were there but Arnold was out of town on a job. She didn't know where he was and hadn't heard from him for several months. She didn't have an address or phone number and didn't know when he would be back.

'A likely story,' said Peggy. 'Get a couple of recent photos of him, if possible with and without a beard. Get some of his worn clothes, dirty work boots and dirty shoes. Collect dust from door mats. Get a description of his car and registration. Also phone numbers, phone companies, email addresses and internet providers. Bring in any computers and search them. Check them for any communication in or out and any sus docos. We can send someone to help you to do that.

'Steele is a body builder. Ask for him at local gyms. Get photos from the woman and show them around.'

*

The following day as I was having breakfast I heard on the radio a police report that a family man, Isembard Harditch, was missing under suspicious circumstances. He had last been seen in Alexandra leaving home to go to work. A picture of him was posted on the Missing Person's website. Anyone with information was requested to contact the police urgently.

I went to see Peggy. She was on the phone in her office, listening intently.

'Yes, I agree,' she said. 'Ocean currents and tides would not carry him further than about five kilometres along the shore.' She hung up and looked at me.

'They have found Harditch's car at Pelican Bay, parked near a boat ramp. Forensics are going over it,' she said. 'Light planes are searching for a body, from the waterline to a kilometre offshore. Volunteers are searching the flotsam along beaches for clothing and shoes.'

The phone rang.

'That's terrific,' Peggy answered. 'Label the items with where they were found, take them to lifesaving stations and lay them out on tables in groups of similar items. I'll bring his wife there this afternoon to look through them. We'll be there around three. Thank you.' Peggy hung up.

She said to me, 'They have collected half a truckload of clothing and shoes. I'll be leaving in an hour.'

'I won't come,' I said. 'I have to catch up with some Council work.'

*

We had been working on the DA for months.

'I think that's everything,' I said.

We lodged it with Council for assessment and sank back, exhausted.

357

CHAPTER 84

The following morning, I called Peggy at her office.

'Did Mrs Harditch recognise any of her husband's clothes or footwear?'

'Nothing definite. There's more coming in.'

We ended the call.

'Can I go to Pelican Bay?' asked Barbie. 'There could be evidence that Arnold Steele was there.'

It was about half an hour's drive northeast.

'Okay, see you later,' I said.

Later that morning, Barbie called me, distraught.

'Harditch is dead, Doc,' she cried. 'A fisher found him by the boat ramp under two metres of water. It looks like suicide. It's terrible — he was a good man, a father,' she choked.

'Why do you think it was suicide?'

'He had on a backpack full of rocks.'

'I see what you mean. Stay there. Try to work out what happened. I'll be there in an hour.'

When I arrived, Barbie was on hands and knees searching the ground beside the car. Nearby was a clothed body on the sand in a taped-off area, face down, wearing a backpack. Peggy, Malcolm and several police were standing around, talking.

'He could have walked into the sea and fallen over, Doctor. The backpack has about 30 kilograms of rocks. He was unable to regain his feet and drowned.'

'He would have to be very determined to do that,' I said. 'Rocks underwater lose about 40% of their weight due to buoyancy. He could have stood up, breathed and walked up the beach.'

'I think we need to check that,' said Peggy. 'Suicide is possible. Virginia Woolf in 1941 filled her overcoat pockets with stones and walked into the River Ouse behind her house and drowned.'

'Harditch wasn't depressed, Chief Inspector,' I said.

'It has been staged to look like suicide. He may have been forced into the sea somehow and the rocks held him under.'

'How could they have got him to walk in deep enough?' Barbie said.

'He was found at 11 am at mid-tide. When we know what time he died, we can use tide tables to find out how deep the water was.'

'Would the murderer be able to make him walk in?' Malcolm said.

'There are no signs of struggle or physical violence.'

'If there are no marks on him, then it was suicide,' Peggy said.

'He could have threatened him with a gun or a knife.'

'Steele doesn't carry a gun. A knife would leave marks on him. He would have to drag him in.'

'We haven't found any bruises.'

'Perhaps we can find out who supplied the backpack and where the rocks came from?' I said. 'If he brought them himself, it would be suicide.'

'I'll have someone look into that.'

*

I contacted Henry Carter to alert Jane's guards to beware of an assailant. Because Harditch's killer was at large, she was safest in hospital.

Peggy okayed an ambulance to take Harditch's body to the mortuary.

'We need an autopsy to tell us exactly how he died,' she said.

'I want to be there,' I said. 'Would you let me know when?'

'Okay. Will you tell his wife?'

'Yes, right away.'

I went from Pelican Bay to the Harditch home. It was a painful duty. Angela Harditch had phoned me every day since her husband went missing. Her hope had descended to despair.

When I told her, she retreated within herself and was very quiet. The savagery of murder had been replaced with the possibility that she had a personal role in her husband's suicide. I felt sorry for her.

'Will you tell the children later?' I suggested.

She nodded.

'You don't have to identify him,' I said. 'Someone else can do it.'

'I want to.'

I picked her up the next morning and left Barbie to look after her children. We went to the hospital. My investigation had been a cause of his death and I felt very small.

Angela identified him and afterwards I took her home. Her sister was there to help her with the children.

Barbie returned to work and I went back to the hospital where I met Peggy and the forensic pathologist, Dr Evans, who would perform the autopsy. I knew him from when I was with the police. He was a tall man, with a slight stoop and a hooked nose.

'How do you like being on the Council, Phillip?'

'It's different,' I said. 'It's not like solving forensic cases one at a time. You have to be a juggler.'

'Keeping people up in the air?'

'Avoiding collisions. There are many fingers in the pie.'

'Many pies too.'

We took the lift down to the basement and entered a bare room where a sheet covered a corpse on a trolley wheeled out from a cold room. Under it was a naked rather thin and unfit body, lying on its back. The face was unmistakeably Isembard Harditch's with his eyes and mouth open. He had the beginnings of a dark beard growing from his grey face. Evans pored over the corpse, peering intently, his long nose seeming to be sampling odours. I smelled salt and seaweed, with a hint of putrefaction. He peered short-sightedly at all of the outside of the body and inside the mouth. He pulled on plastic gloves and scraped some skin from the neck into a sample bottle and handed it to an assistant, who labelled it.

After finishing with the front, they rolled over the rigid corpse with a slam and examined the other side minutely.

Evans removed the kidneys and examined them in a kidney-shaped dish. They turned him onto his back again. With a scalpel Evans slit open the belly and pulled out the intestines into a container. He sliced into them and took samples. The assistant photographed the condition of each organ and labelled each sample.

The acrid stench caused me to retch.

'Sorry about the smell,' said Evans. 'It helps if you pinch your nose.'

Peggy was looking rather pale.

Evans pulled down a circular saw suspended from a gantry and cut the chest open along the sternum. The sweet 'burnt hair' smell of the hot bone was not unpleasant. With hydraulic callipers he prised the ribs apart, with bones breaking and tendons snapping noisily. He lifted out the liver, inspected it and removed the lungs, stomach and heart. He sliced into the lungs, sampled the liquid that flowed out and measured its salinity with a probe and meter.

'Lungs filled with water, Sample 12, conductivity 4.8 Siemens per metre, probably sea water, consistent with drowning.'

Evans opened the stomach and took a sample, then inspected the heart. He sliced through it and sampled the blood from within. Lowering the saw again, at right angles, he cut across the top of the head, exposing the brain, which he removed and examined.

Finally he returned all the organs to their cavities and sewed up the openings with thread.

He pulled off his gloves and spoke into a recorder while his assistant took photographs.

'Harditch autopsy, August 28th, 10.15 am. Subject is a male, age 40-ish. He was submerged in sea water fully clothed for about 12 hours, judging by skin, wrinkled and separating from fingers. Death at about 11 pm; found at about 11 am.

'Lesions on face and hands from small fish feeding. Wrists chaffed where bound. Slight bruising and abrasion on shoulders from struggling to remove a heavy backpack. Six pairs of small red spots on neck and two on palm of right hand. Sample 1 - skin scraped at two small lesions, 25 mm apart, left side, 60 mm below left ear.'

Peggy and I looked at the spots closely.

Evans concluded his examination, 'The deceased's death was probably due to drowning while unconscious due to an electrical discharge from a stun gun.'

'Is that why his face is contorted, Doctor?' I asked.

'Yes. He could have convulsed while trying to breathe underwater.'

361

'Shocks could have got him into the backpack and into the water,' Peggy said. 'They would have to be painful without felling him.'

'The effect of an electric shock from a stun gun depends on voltage and duration,' said the pathologist. 'A brief discharge of 10,000 Volts would lock his muscles and hurt a lot. Partial immersion in sea water would increase current flow and cause a greater shock. A half-second zap of 50,000 Volts would cause a huge immediate pain, muscle contractions, spasms and paralysis of the muscles, enough to knock a person down. A long zap could submerge him with involuntary inhalation of water.

'Threatened by the gun, he possibly walked into the sea as far as he could, toting the rocks. Then the perpetrator stunned him and he went under. Unable to get to his feet, he would drown.'

'Where would he get a stun gun?' I asked. 'Would he need a licence?'

'Not for one from overseas, by the Internet,' said Peggy.

'Do you think he was held under?' I said.

'I don't know,' said the pathologist. 'The bruises were caused by the backpack. It would have pulled him under if he lost his footing or went out of his depth.' Evans washed his hands and dried them. 'Do you have any other questions?'

'Could anything else have caused the red spots, Doctor?' Peggy asked.

'Hmm. I don't know of anything else that would cause such regular spacing,' said Evans.

'How can we be sure it was a stun gun?'

'Electrical discharges would leave metal residues on the skin from the electrodes but they may be washed away by now. Also there could be slight charring of the epidermis. I've taken samples.'

'We may need to do a forensic simulation,' I said to Peggy.

'That's a good idea,' she said. 'Let's wait for the samples to be analysed first.'

'Would he have struggled much, Doctor?' I asked.

'The bruises are small and could have come from the backpack,' Evans said.

'The stun gun would have knocked the fight out of him,' said Peggy. 'The perp may have thrown it into the bushes near the boat ramp or out of his car window as he left. I'll get them to look for it.'

Peggy received a call. A geologist had found quartzite rocks like those in Harditch's backpack at a road cutting on the city ring road.

'The murderer could have parked, filled the backpack and used the stun gun to get Harditch to strap it on,' she said. 'No-one would have heard his screams.'

'Alternatively, Harditch could have gone there by himself and filled his pack with rocks,' I said.'

'The red spots indicate foul play,' said Peggy.

'Could the perpetrator really force him into the sea?'

'They might not be seen,' Peggy said. 'Few people walk past the boat ramp at night.'

'The poor man got out of his depth,' I said.

As Evans covered the corpse and pushed it back into the refrigerator, we stood to attention. Respect was the most we could give him. I wanted to salute him for trying to tell the truth despite ruthless bullying.

I hoped that the inquest would be over soon so they could tell Angela Harditch that it wasn't suicide and she would be able to move on with caring for her children. She needed justice to be done as soon as possible. I hoped the abduction I was reconstructing would provide a lead to the killer.

CHAPTER 85

I provided a slab of lager and a six-pack of vodka juice for our next think tank. Peggy and Malcolm were on duty but they drank with us anyway.

'What are we celebrating?' asked Cutter.

No-one said anything.

'Something good must have happened to someone, somewhere,' said Barbie.

Cutter looked pleased with himself. 'I didn't get a speeding ticket.'

'There is no justice,' said Sunita with a grimace.

'I wasn't speeding,' he said, teasing Sunita as usual.

'We didn't need to know that,' she said with exasperation.

'It's better than having nothing to celebrate.'

He gave me a small wink.

I drew their attention to Link 8 on the whiteboard: how their motives affected what the suspects did.

'This is the last link,' I said, pointing to it on the whiteboard.

'Can we be sure it was Steele who got rid of Harditch?' asked Cutter.

'It's a no-brainer,' I said. 'He had the motive. His hands were dirty already. He would kill Harditch to stop being put in the frame for the abduction. He may already have had a stun gun. He had the opportunity. He snatched him on his way to work, like he did Jane.'

'Harditch went missing on Monday but he wasn't found until Saturday morning, four days later. He was in the sea for 12 hours — so where was he for four and a half days?'

'Steele was holding him captive somewhere,' said Tony.

'We can guess where, Doc,' Barbie said. 'Steele would have locked him away in a soundproof box, like he did Jane.'

'Steele could have done both crimes,' I said. 'He had motives for disposing of both bodies.'

'Having motives is not enough,' said Peggy. 'We need evidence.'

364

'What evidence is there that Steele murdered Harditch?' asked Sunita.

'We need to find the stun gun or traces on him from contact with Harditch,' I said.

'The murder of Harditch was probably to cover up the abduction.'

'Ainsley Montague had bullied Harditch to approve a faked report.'

'Do you think Montague was the mastermind?' asked Cutter.

'No,' I said. 'He didn't have enough motive. He could be a middleman.'

'How about Martha Hubbard?' Cutter said. 'She could have had Steele do the dirty work and used Montague to pay him.'

'Who would she get to bully Harditch into approving the faked test results?'

'Montague?' Cutter said.

'Yes; and when Harditch looked like spilling the beans,' I said, 'who would she get to silence him?'

'Not Montague — he wouldn't get his hands dirty.'

'Montague must have put two and two together and told the mastermind that Harditch was about to squeal. He sicced Steele on to him.'

Peggy had failed to protect a witness.

'My mistake,' said Peggy. 'I didn't realise how ruthless they were. Catching Steele is our top priority. A confession from him would uncover the mastermind.'

'Hmm. How can we catch him?' asked Tony.

'I have an idea,' I said. 'Chief Inspector, can we get together afterwards?'

We had another round of lagers and juices.

'Masterminds who could be implicated are Sindona, Leach and Hubbard, with Yelling and Montague as middlemen.

'Link 8 must be Sindona, the empire-building sycophant whose money the Government hierarchy laundered and paid to Steele. *The others lacked a motive sufficient to abduct Jane.* We have completed the reconstruction. Here is our reconstruction.

'Leach took Sindona's money and used it to hire Steele,' I said. 'Steele hijacked Jane, took her to CS3 and kept her locked up.

Lithium from CS3 was carried away by Steele. Steele neglected her, causing her condition to decline. The mastermind delayed releasing her until it would not affect the casino outcome. Leaving her body at CS5 would reveal the crime and Steele wanted to hide her body. He left her at CS6 to conceal the crime. Already weak, the rough treatment when she was rescued put her into a coma.

'That, fellow thinkers, is our chain of linked causes and their effects.'

Malcolm was frowning. 'It's not the type of reconstruction we are familiar with, Doctor. It has to convince a jury beyond reasonable doubt. Other explanations are possible aren't they?'

'It can be used to confront the suspects, interrogate them, extract confessions and bargain pleas.'

'Could I call it a preconstruction?'

'Nice word. It gives the police leverage on the suspects but it is not necessarily the last word on what happened. I will work with Peggy to strengthen it.

'That brings us to the end of our last think tank session,' I said. 'What's next, Chief Inspector?'

'Thank you all,' said Peggy. 'We are now in a good position to interview the suspects. I think the outcome might have been quite different under political control. Your think tank created a more logical, considered and just approach than the Government would have allowed. Your investigation has been very thorough.'

'Thank you, Chief Inspector,' I said. 'I like to think we have left no stone unturned. Thank you, everybody, for a job well done. Keep in touch with any further ideas, or contact Peggy and Malcolm.'

I could not rest yet. I hoped the police would resolve the case speedily, for Jane's sake. We closed up the think tank and the others left. Peggy and I made a cup of coffee.

'Now, what's this idea of yours, Phillip?' Peggy said.

I took my coffee to an armchair.

'How can we set a trap and catch Steele?' I asked.

CHAPTER 86

'The way to catch a villain,' said Peggy, 'is to find his weakness, put out a bait, hook him and play him in.'

'Our villain is a fucking shark,' I said. 'Are you sure he has a weakness?'

'I have asked our people in Chesterfield to find out about him. I'll ask them.'

She called on Skype and spoke with DI Webber.

'Inspector, I have Dr Phillip Keane here, a private investigator who is working on the Kenwood case,' said Peggy. 'What can you tell us about Cobra, aka Arnold Steele, aka Peter Pradel?'

'We showed photographs of him around town,' Webber said. 'A gym manager said he was Brian Payne, a body builder. We talked with his schools, teachers, welfare, employers and neighbours. We found his sister. He stays with her when he is around, which isn't often.'

'He grew up on a smallholding near Antrim, a country town 30 kilometres from Chesterfield. His parents were alternative lifestylers. Their oldest child was a girl, Joni, and then there were identical twin boys, Arnold and Graham. The Payne property was poor land and Brian's father did odd jobs for neighbours. Payne was known to police as drunken and violent.

An Education Department psychologist had investigated Arnold's school records when he was prosecuted for grievous bodily harm. Webber read to us the psychologist's assessment presented to Antrim Court when they were considering taking the children into care at the instigation of the school.

Arnold is a good-looking and pleasant child. The twins play together and depend on each other, excluding others. They have developed their own language and games and language. They choose not to mix with other children, not even with their sister. Each is 'a twin' rather than an individual. Individual identities are declined by teachers reluctant to give

367

them different marks in case it would be unfair or could be construed as favouritism.

The following statement by Arnold's father had been recorded.

'Arnold's mother was a shambles. She left me when the twins were five and went off with another man. She would not take her children with her because she didn't think she could cope in her mental state. She said she was depressed. I did my best to look after the kids but we didn't have much. I usually didn't know where the next meal was coming from. I depended on the child allowance. I sent the children to school every day. I was strict but fair.

'Joni helped me with her brothers. The school gave used uniforms, writing things and books. The twins kept to themselves at school. When Joni was 11 she passed the entrance test to the local girls' grammar school. Two years later, the twins took the test to the boys' grammar. Arnold passed but Graham failed. They would go to different schools. They had always been in the same class but I reckoned it was high time they learned to stand alone. Arnold went to the posh grammar school, learning to go to university, while Graham had to go to the comprehensive and learn a trade.

'Arnold resented that the exam wasn't fair to his brother. They travelled into the town to their schools on the bus together and then went to their different schools. But it didn't work. Neither of them made friends. They kept to themselves. Arnold was down on himself. He wouldn't try the work, misbehaved and was put into a slow class. He got attention by getting into trouble, by bullying other students. He was always in trouble up at the office. He was a show-off but the other kids, because they were scared of him, left him alone. The one thing he did well at was javelin throwing and he won competitions. He was irresponsible, wild and dangerous.

'At the school athletics carnival, he came close to spearing one of the judges. They said it was deliberate and suspended him for a week.

'He was large and strong and when he was 15, he broke a teacher's jaw and was expelled. He lived at home and took labouring jobs locally until he went to live with his sister. His brother helped me on the farm.'

DI Webber read the psychologist's assessment when Arnold had been suspended.

The result of the entrance exam result was unexpected and catastrophic. Arnold passed and was promoted to privilege. Graham was labelled dumb. Their commonality was destroyed. Although they were together much of the day, the difference between them in their schooling was pervasive. They both experienced a deeply disturbing loneliness never experienced by singletons, possibly like the pain from amputation of a limb. Graham was disabled, emotional and subservient, while Arnold became dominant, unemotional and cruel.

Webber said, 'I went to the Payne farm. Graham was feeding the livestock. He said he hadn't seen his brother for months. I tracked down the sister, Joni, to the house she rents in Chesterfield. She had a toddler on her hip and was smoking a cigarette. 'He stayed with me when he moved out from home,' she said. 'I was working as an aide at a crèche.''

''Where is he now?' I asked her. She said, 'I don't know.''

'When did you last hear from him?' ''About six months ago,' she said. 'He phoned but he didn't say where he was.''

'What was he doing?'

'He didn't say.'

'Do you believe her?' Tom asked Webber.

'I don't know. She knows he's into crime. He was surly, reckless and wild. He joined a bikie gang and got into drugs.'

'We knew him only too well,' said Webber. 'He was an imposing figure, wide and strong, with coffee-coloured skin and tattoos covering powerful arms. His hobby was body building.'

369

"Then he met Megan,' Joni continued. 'She became pregnant and he moved in with her but after a couple of months she threw him out because he was running around with someone else. She had the baby alone. He came to the hospital but she wouldn't see him after that.

"Arnold wanted Megan but she didn't want him. He became depressed and was always drunk or stoned.

"On the night of his 25th birthday he got drunk and drove his car into a tree. It killed his passenger and he was in hospital for months, with his legs and face smashed up. He had permanent injuries: autism, emotional numbing and speech impairment. His style was severely cramped and depressed. He had no friends.

"When he got out of hospital he had nowhere to go,' Joni said. 'He stayed in our yard in a caravan we bought for him for nearly two years. He gradually recovered but was withdrawn and isolated.''

Webber told us he had inspected the caravan. It was dusty and without any evidence of recent occupation. He surveyed and listed Arnold Payne's belongings. There were a few expensive garments, work boots, joggers, fancy suede, Italian leather, gold buckled. Swim togs, grip developers, chest expanders. Personal deodorant, a dozen toothbrushes. Car tools, accessories. TV, CDs, videos, magazines, martial arts, violence, SM, porn.

Joni told Webber that Arnold had hung around there until he'd got work. He collected debts, ran errands and delivered packages for a racketeer in Chesterfield.

'Our records show that he became a nightclub bouncer, then a bodyguard. His work was making threats, beating people up, minding bosses, collecting debts, pimping prostitutes, selling drugs and protecting gambling rackets. He didn't care about anyone and hurt people without remorse. His specialty was extortion with menaces. His bosses relied on him but he ratted on everyone else.

'He was arrested for his part in a turf war and convicted for grievous bodily harm. He was sentenced to four years.

'He didn't make friends in prison and survived by being big, tough and watchful. He was a model prisoner and concealed his psychopathic nature. He stayed under the radar, did rehabilitation and was paroled after two years.

370

'Out of prison, he was a loner with an aggrieved sense of social justice — that he had not had a fair chance and that his crimes were a just retribution against society.

'He had a paranoid fear of going back to prison. He believed people were trying to find him and kill him — which was probably true. He seldom went home to Joni's place. He established the legitimacy of Megan's child using the Peter Pradel identity to forge a birth certificate. But Megan would have nothing more to do with him. He changed his appearance several times, grew a beard, shaved his head and had his arms tattooed. After a couple of months, he went away without saying where to.

'His bank account received $1 million recently from a company called CTS. He took out a few thousands by online transfer to a bank in Alexandra. We have frozen both accounts by court order. He has never stayed anywhere for long and we have not been able to find him to serve the warrant.

'Jon would contact me if she heard from him or he came back. She never asked me what he had done.'

*

Peggy passed Webber's report to a police criminal psychologist. A week later she received the following profile.

Arnold Steele is certainly a sociopath and psychopath. He is nervous, has rages and does not form attachment to others. He lacks empathy and manipulates people. He is without conscience, remorseless, disturbed and dangerous.

He developed this character from a series of bad experiences: desertion by his mother, from being raised by a brutal father, from the trauma of separation from his twin brother at school, from alienation at school, from taking drugs, from wild living in a gang, from petty crime, from being rejected by the mother of his child, from his failed suicide attempt, disability from the car crash, from imprisonment and finally from employment in illegal activities. It is a record of deviation that could lead him to act criminally.

The arbitrary separation from his twin brother was pivotal in causing his psychopathy. His imprisonment developed in him an abrasive personality and his countenance became menacing. He had a thing about attractive women, probably because they wouldn't allow him near them. There was self-harm in his past, violence in his present and incrimination in his future. Women gave him a wide berth and he hated them for it. He may have wanted Jane to suffer.

We ended our Skype session with DI Webber.

'Are you inside his skin enough to know what is making him tick?' Peggy asked.

'We have stopped him getting money and he will be aware we are closing in. Cobra's attention to anonymity is obsessive and paranoid. He is desperate to cover his tracks and wants to stop Jane from identifying him. If we presented him with an opportunity to kill her without being caught, we could trap him.'

'Are you sure we can keep her absolutely safe?'

'We can cover foreseeable risks. Even crossing the road has risks.'

'We will have to ask Jane if she is willing to be the bait,' I said.

Peggy said she would ask her.

CHAPTER 87

'Steele could be having delusions of being pursued and finding himself lining up in an identity parade with Jane Kenwood recognising him,' I said. 'He could be sleeping badly or having anxiety attacks. He could fear Jane.'

'Do you think it is enough for him to try and kill her, Chief Inspector?' asked the CCC. 'Wouldn't he prefer to change his appearance or leave Roberta?'

'He has already had two goes at her in the hospital. We think he's still around.'

'So you propose to tether out Councillor Kenwood like a goat for a tiger shoot,' said the CCC. 'It seems risky.'

'We could advertise a democracy rally with Jane as the main speaker,' I said. 'The botanic gardens bowl would be a good place.'

'How do you expect it to play out, Doctor?'

'It will be noisy with the crowd pushing in around the stage. He will get close then sidle up. He could appear to be giving her first aid as he stabs her. He could hope to slink away afterwards concealed in the melee. Once he has revealed himself we would grab him.'

'What if he uses a gun?'

'He never uses firearms. He used a stun gun on Harditch.'

'Would Jane do it?' said the Commissioner.

'I asked her and she is okay with it,' Peggy said. 'Jane is more concerned that he could attack her when she is unprotected.'

'Will it work, Chief Inspector?' asked Templeton.

'It has a good chance,' replied Peggy.

'I like it,' said the Commissioner. 'In a game of chess, exposing your queen is a last resort. But she can't stay in that hospital forever. She would become vulnerable to him sooner or later. This gives her a better chance. Let's do it.'

*

Jane announced the rally, speaking on TV.

'Three months ago I was abducted and locked up in the dark, alone without food for five weeks. I suffered agony and almost died but I am nearly recovered now thanks to the care given me by the wonderful people of Alexandra South Hospital. The police have been investigating and are following leads but the abductors are still at large. This crime has threatened our democracy. Come and show support for democracy at my rally at the Auditorium on Saturday week at 4 pm. Now I want to say this to the suspect who calls himself Cobra: I know you are out there and I will never forget or forgive what you did to me. The police and the public will work together to find you, however long it takes. I know what you look like and you will be brought to justice. If anyone has information that could help to find my abductors, would you call this number: 3386 1190'

Her message was broadcast on the television news.
'That should tweak his paranoia nicely,' said Peggy.

*

We organised the rally to take place in two weeks' time. Sunita and her group made banners demanding democratic rights. A civil rights activist would speak first, then a libertarian next, finally Jane. Peggy supplied a squad of police to protect her. A counter-terrorism trainer developed with them roles of intercepting and holding an attacker. In the rehearsal, Barbie played Jane and I was an assailant who crept up on to the stage. They seized me before I could get near her.

On the day of the rally, a large and festive audience gathered in the open-air auditorium at the botanic gardens. It was a balmy afternoon and people came in droves. A brass band played 'To Every Thing There Is A Season', 'Down By The River Side' and other songs of protest. The atmosphere was happy and hopeful. People filled the auditorium bowl, sitting shoulder to shoulder on the bench seats.

The first two speakers got the crowd wanting their democratic rights. Then Jane walked on to the stage. There was a loud ovation. Everyone who knew of her ordeal listened to her.

'Thank you. I almost wasn't here today because a person who calls himself Cobra kept me locked up in the dark without food for five weeks. Then he dropped me into a hole where concrete was poured over me. But we're on to him and it won't be long before I will be picking him out in an identity parade.'

There was loud applause and a standing ovation. At the side of the stage a hunched figure pushed his way through the onlookers. He lunged forward and wrapped his arms around her like a bear with a doll. The face was obscured by a full beard and a baseball cap. Jane's screams were drowned out by the applause. Just then, a policeman ran in and launched a spear tackle. The bear handed him off and stood his ground but let go of Jane, who crawled away as other policemen surrounded him. Brandishing a knife, he backed away towards an exit.

In yellow luminescent jackets, a string of police, who had been watching from a distance, forced their way through the crowd and onto the stage. A shot rang out and then another. A police officer fell away, injured. They swarmed over the attacker and he went under, weaving from side to side as he went down. Presently the police stood up, leaving him motionless, face down on the stage.

Jane clung to me.

'Are you hurt?' I asked as I held her.

She shook her head. I undid her jacket, unbuckled and removed the armoured vest, leaving her in a T-shirt. I could see a spot of blood where the point of the knife had penetrated the wire matting.

'You have a small cut. Nothing to worry about. You were terrific. Was it him?'

'I think so. I have never seen his face clearly before.'

The audience remained standing in their seats, looking down on the stage where we stood around the body. Daylight faded and the lights came on.

I held Jane close. She was shaking.

A police officer with a loudhailer spoke calmly.

'Ladies and gentleman, a man has been shot but there is no cause for alarm. The police have the situation under control. This event has ended. Would you move calmly and slowly to the nearest exit and go home. Thank you for your cooperation.'

An ambulance officer dressed Jane's wound. My hatred burst into my emotions like a whale breaching. I was elated that he was dead. The outcome was fair. He had caused much pain and unhappiness to Jane, her family, to the Harditches and to me.

The ambulance took Jane away to hospital for checking. I went with her.

I spoke on my mobile to Cutter.

'I didn't know the police were empowered to execute suspects,' I said. 'Who gave them orders to shoot? It wasn't the CCC. He had them standing by for an arrest.'

'They had been told he had a gun on him,' said Cutter. 'They shot him in the arm and when he reached his other arm across to the wound, they shot him in the back of the head.'

'If he really did have a gun, he could have shot Jane.'

'They found one in his pocket but they probably planted it,' Cutter said.

'Someone in the hierarchy must have ordered it,' I said.

'What about his right to a fair trial?'

'He got off lightly,' I said. 'A trial wasn't necessary. Who else would have tried to knife her?'

'I agree that it was him but we needed him alive to tell us who was the mastermind,' said Cutter.

'Someone was counting on that.'

CHAPTER 88

Jane and I went to the mortuary to identify her attacker.
'Are you sure you want to do this?' I asked her outside.
She nodded and we went in.
The corpse was on a trolley. Jane's hand was rigid in mine. A bullet had emerged from his right eye. She held on to the bench.
'It is probably Cobra — I can't tell,' Jane said. She was trembling. She looked at his arm. 'Those are his tatts. It is him. I'm sure.'
We stayed a few minutes and then left. His death should alleviate fears of him that had followed her since the hijack. She had gained closure, but she would not be safe until the mastermind was identified and caught.

*

My mobile rang.
'Phillip, we have Steele's car. It was parked near the botanical gardens. The number plate is the one they obtained from Megan Pradel,' said Peggy. 'There was a stun gun inside. Also a mask – Captain Kirk.'
'What type of car?'
'Mercedes C-Class, black.'
'It could be the one at CS2.'
'He could have used it at CS4 and CS5 too.'
'There was lithium dust on the floor,' Peggy said. 'The same type as on the factory floor and in Jane's car. Steele could have been carrying it around on his footwear.
'We can place Steele at two abduction scenes and the Harditch murder scene,' I said.
'We will have to check that the stun gun was the one used on Harditch,' said Peggy. 'Steele is likely to be the perp for both crimes.'
'It could point to the same mastermind for both too.'

377

Peggy and I met with the CCC in his office to review the inquiry.

'Shooting him has fucked us,' said the CCC. 'We needed him alive, to find and convict the people who hired him.'

'It was a cover-up,' said Peggy. 'Who would have ordered that, do you think?'

'Bentley Leach could have told the PC he had a gun and to shoot him.'

'He could claim Leach misled him about a gun,' said Peggy.

'How badly would Leach want Steele dead?' I asked.

'Very badly, Doctor,' the CCC said. 'Steele could inform on Yelling, who could pass the buck to Leach. What do we have on Leach?'

'No previous, only the usual complaints of corruption and abuse of power,' said Peggy. 'He could have supplied $1 million to Roads that they sent to Works. We need to see the accounts.'

'Have you asked?'

'Yes, sir,' said Peggy. 'I requested an aide of the Premier's. He has not replied.'

'I'll see about that.' The CCC picked up his phone and dialled.

'Premier? Good morning. This is Wallace Templeton, CCC. Yes, well thank you. Our investigation of the Kenwood case is continuing. That's why I'm calling, to inform you that I have sent two officers from this office to the Treasury to get a copy of the Government's accounts.'

We could hear shouting down the phone.

'No, Premier, I believe it is within my powers.'

Templeton held the phone away from his ear.

'Premier,' said the CCC, 'Government funds appear to have been misappropriated. It is my job to investigate whether there has been any malpractice and exonerate people who have behaved appropriately. Having access to the accounts is normal for an investigation of this kind and I have instructed my officers to obtain an electronic copy.'

'We did ask properly. DCI Wall requested to see the accounts from one of your aides several days ago but he has not replied. My people will make a copy this morning. This will not stop your people from doing their jobs.'

378

I heard more shouting from the telephone.

Templeton waited until it stopped. 'Premier, with respect, I agree you do have authority to override my actions, but not if by doing so you are in breach of provincial law. You would be acting unlawfully in denying me reasonable access to the Government accounts, at the time I ask for them, which is now.'

The Premier must have hung up, because Templeton put down the phone gingerly. His hand was shaking.

'If Leach orders his people to refuse me the accounts, there is nothing I can do,' the CCC said. 'He cannot order me to do anything illegal but it is not illegal for him to stop my investigation.'

'If he does we can make his action public,' I said. 'Bentley Leach refusing to cooperate with the CCC would not look good.'

The CCC's officers returned later that morning with E-copies of the Government's accounts. We could now look for a mastermind who had sent $1 million to Works to pay to CTS. It would be the final link.

CHAPTER 89

A week after the Steele shooting, Andrea Gough phoned me.
'Don Sindona is back in town.'
'I'll ask the DI to act for an appointment with him.'
I told Cutter that Sindona was back in town.
'Perhaps he thinks it is safe for him to return now,' he said. 'He might have made himself scarce until he was confident that we hadn't found anything that could incriminate him.'
'Harditch's and Steele's deaths could have let him off the hook,' I said. 'He would be relieved.'
Peggy arranged an interview. We needed a testimony that would stand up in court.
Peggy sent me a copy of the transcription.

Record of interview by DCI Wall and DI Malcolm with Don Sindona, Chief Executive Officer, Runyon Casinos and Andrea Gough, Project Manager, at Runyon Casinos' office, Alexandra City, 26th November.
Detective Chief Inspector Wall cautioned Sindona and Gough.
Wall: 'Mr Sindona, were you involved in any way with abducting Councillor Kenwood?'
Sindona: 'No, I was not.'
Wall: 'Do you know Councillor Kenwood?'
Sindona: 'Yes, I met her on my last visit.'
Wall: 'Is she opposed to your casino project?'
Sindona: 'I don't know. You would have to ask her.'
Wall: 'She has said in the Council that the casino would be harmful. How do you feel about that?'
Sindona: 'You are verballing me. I won't answer a question that is like: Have I stopped beating my wife? Rubbish. Your premise is false.'
DI Malcolm left the room.

Wall: 'Mr Sindona, how much will your casino resort cost?'
Sindona: 'About three billion dollars.'
Wall: 'How much have you spent already?'
Sindona: 'About $10 million.'
Wall: 'If your project is not approved, would you be able to recoup this money?'
Sindona: 'We would try somewhere else.'
Wall: 'On June 5th this year, did you borrow from Bentley Leach keys to the doors of a disused factory at Commercial Road?'
Gough: 'Yes. We looked at several alternative sites for a casino.'
Wall: 'Was it owned by the Government?'
Sindona: 'Yes. The Government had leased it to a factory but now they wanted to sell it for demolition and redevelopment.'
Wall: 'Did you inspect the old factory?'
Sindona: 'Yes but not closely.'
Wall: 'Did you go upstairs?'
Sindona: 'Yes.'
Wall: 'Did you see a recording booth?'
Sindona: 'No. I was only looking at the place to demolish it.'
DI Malcolm re-entered the room and spoke to DCI Wall.
DCI Wall left the room.
Malcolm: Bentley Leach gave the keys to you, Andrea. Did you lend them to anyone?'
Gough: 'No.'
Malcolm: 'Could anyone have taken them and later returned them without your knowledge?'
Gough: 'No.'
Malcolm: 'Where did you keep them?'
Gough: 'In my bag attached to my house keys.'
Malcolm: 'Did you have any copies made from them?'
Gough: 'No.'
Malcolm: 'The circumstances of the abduction suggest that Runyon Casinos were involved in it.'
Sindona: 'Doctor, I absolutely reject that allegation. What circumstances?'
Malcolm: 'Councillor Kenwood was held at the property Runyon's had recently bought.'

381

Gough: 'Runyon's had nothing at all to do with Councillor Kenwood being there.'

Malcolm: 'Did any Runyon's people go there?'

Gough: 'No, not after the purchase went through.'

Malcolm: 'Have Runyon's ever employed a person called Arnold Steele?'

Gough: 'I've never heard that but I'll check.'

DCI Wall re-entered the room and spoke to DI Malcolm.

Malcolm: 'I repeat, did Runyon's give keys to the factory to anyone?'

Gough: 'No.'

Wall: 'How much did Runyon's pay for the factory site?'

Sindona: '$3 million.'

Wall: 'On the property title deed, the amount is recorded as $2 million on the title.'

Gough: 'Really? It is the seller who prepares the transfer documents and records the consideration price — you can ask the Provincial Government about it.'

Wall: 'Did the $3 million you paid include $1 million for something else, or was there to be a donation, or was it for a purpose additional to purchase of the property?'

Sindona: 'No. The price we paid was $3 million for the site only.'

Wall: 'Was some of the money to be used to hire someone to abduct Councillor Kenwood?'

Sindona: 'I have told you: No.'

Wall: 'Did you hire Arnold Steele to abduct Councillor Kenwood?'

Sindona: 'No. I had no contact with anyone of that name. It offends me that you are asking whether I or Runyon's were involved in this crime. Certainly not. I hope you will soon bring the abductors to justice.'

Wall: 'On what date did you leave Alexandra to go overseas?'

Sindona: 'June 2nd.'

Wall: 'You returned a few days ago. Is it correct that you left the day before Councillor Kenwood disappeared and you stayed away during her rescue and while the police were investigating the abduction?'

382

Sindona: 'I left for unrelated business overseas and have returned now for unrelated business here. You are suggesting I was involved in the abduction. How could I be if I wasn't here?'
End of interview.

When I finished reading, I didn't know what to believe. There was no evidence that either Sindona or Gough had masterminded the abduction but they could be lying. Andrea seemed honest but I couldn't be sure of her. She called to say they had no record of ever having employed an Arnold Steele.

I called Peggy.

'Why did you and Malcolm leave the room?' I asked Peggy.

'To rattle the bars of their cage, Doctor. To look as if we were checking facts.'

'Any effect?'

'No. They were very sure of themselves.'

'Thank you, Peggy.'

My intuition was that Sindona was hiding something.

I gave the transcript to Cutter to read.

When he had finished I asked him, 'Do you think Sindona was the mastermind?'

'He could have been,' said Cutter. 'There is no evidence that any of the money he paid for the site was earmarked to pay Steele. Sindona could have concocted the abduction with Leach. We don't have any evidence, but it would fit Sindona's profile. A person I know who used to work for Runyon's told me, 'Don was an inveigler. He began at the bottom as a security guard and worked his way up until he was the one chosen to deal with the police and government officials. He kept Runyon's name out of court and he got government favour while his less meticulous competitors had to shut down.

'Some leaders get to the top by designing products, or by managing people, or by building facilities, or by collecting debts. But Don Sindona got there by getting public officials on his side. He obtains government favour. He is fond of saying: 'Government relations are our greatest asset.' He gets privileges, such as Leach inviting them to build a casino on the IB site.'

'Do you think he bribes people?' I asked Cutter.

383

'He conditions the government donkey with juicy carrots of favours and gifts. As well, he hits it with sticks of blackmail, extortion, menaces and violence.'

'Do you think the $3 million included money for an abduction?' I asked.

'Like it was Sindona's idea?'

'He was hungrier than Leach.'

'I agree,' I said. 'Sindona had egg on his face when Jane identified his company was involved in criminal activities overseas. He could have wanted revenge on Jane — to silence her.'

'For payback?'

'No. To save face.'

'With whom?'

'With his own people,' I said. 'The Don likes to be seen as a hard man. Anyone who trifles with him does so at their peril — especially a woman.'

'So Leach and the others didn't go along with abducting Jane?'

'They wanted it too. They wanted to quash Jane's opposition. The casino could get them re-elected. Their involvement would never be known — they thought.'

CHAPTER 90

We needed Leach to testify where $3 million paid by Runyon Casinos had gone and how payment for the concrete testing had been made. Peggy interviewed a reluctant Premier in his office.

'I have no information that will help you with your inquiry,' he said.

'Mr Premier, it is a formality. Our questions are routine.'

'Alright then, but make it quick. I am busy.'

Malcolm sent me a copy of the transcript from the voice recorder.

Record of Interview by DCI Wall and DI Malcolm with Premier Bentley Leach in his office at 10.00 am on November 27th.

DCI Wall for the CCC informed Premier Leach of the Kenwood Inquiry and cautioned him.

DCI Wall: 'How much did Runyon's pay for the site?'

Transcript of voice recording.

Leach: '$3 million including tax.'

Wall: 'Into what account did the money go?'

Leach: 'General Purposes.'

Wall: 'How was it used?'

Leach: '$2 million was credited to asset sales.'

Wall: 'What about the other $1 million?'

Leach: 'It remained in the account.'

Wall: 'Did the LM send you an invoice for $500,000 for concrete testing?'

Leach: 'Yes. I asked the supplier UMTS to raise it with Roads.'

Wall: 'What was the invoice for?'

Leach: 'I recall it was for 'Roads construction safety testing' or something like that.'

Wall: 'Did you transfer funds from General Purposes to Roads to pay them?'

Leach: 'Yes.'

385

Wall: 'How much?'

Leach: '$1 million, I think. The money would go via Works.'

Wall: 'It is $500,000 more than the invoice.'

Leach: 'The additional amount was for Works to conduct the programme. It paid for Montague's engineer and for collecting samples.'

Wall: 'Were you authorised to pay it from General Purposes?'

Leach: 'Yes.'

Wall: 'How were you authorised?'

Leach: 'By Cabinet retrospectively.'

Wall: 'So you had no authority at the time. You misappropriated the money.'

Leach: 'I did not misappropriate anything. That's how we work. People expect their Government to deal with problems quickly. It is not always possible to get authority in advance We make payments to meet emerging needs and tidy up the loose ends later.'

Wall: 'When did you obtain Cabinet approval?'

Leach: 'A couple of months after. I'll send you a copy of the minutes.'

Wall showed the CTS report Montague had supplied.

Wall: 'Did you receive this report?'

Leach: 'Yes, but we didn't look at it. It had been approved by Martha's people and that was good enough for us. Every Premier has approved expenditures under circumstances such as these.'

Wall: 'Did you contact UMTS about these tests?'

Leach: 'No. Should I have?'

Wall: 'They did not do the work.'

Leach: 'Didn't do it? Who says?'

Wall: 'There is evidence that the measurements were faked.'

Leach: 'Are you sure? That's bad. The Council should have managed it properly. You will have to take it up with Martha. You can't blame me for setting the ball rolling and paying the bill at the end.'

Wall: 'You transacted the sale to an owner of a property where a councillor opposed to their interests would be held captive.'

Leach: 'That is a retrospective view. When Runyon's bought it they were not being opposed.'

386

Wall: 'Did you give instructions for the abduction of Councillor Kenwood?'

Leach: 'No. Certainly not.'

Wall: 'Did you give instructions for the killing of Isembard Harditch?'

Leach: 'No. I object to being questioned like this, accusing me without evidence. I want you to leave.'

End of interview.

I finished reading. Leach's glib responses did not conceal that he had laundered the money from Sindona to pay for the abduction. I passed the transcript to Cutter.

'Leach misappropriated $1 million,' I said.

Cutter read it.

'Not more than usual,' he said. 'Leach was probably untidy about getting Cabinet approval, like all Premiers are.'

I used my mobile to call Peggy.

'Peggy, we're looking at your interview with Leach. Was he lying, do you think?'

'It's hard to tell with politicians, Phillip.'

'Did he show any nerves?'

'He was ill at ease throughout,' Peggy said.

'We need evidence that Sindona's money paid for the abduction,' I said.

'Bentley Leach has admitted he transferred it to Roads to cover the UMTS invoice plus an additional $500,000.'

'Is there any evidence Leach knew it was a scam?'

'If the tests were kosher, why fund them with profit from a land deal?' said Peggy.

'Why not? He would have needed Cabinet approval and some of them wouldn't think it was necessary and would try to stop it. So he took it without authority and squared it away later when it was too late for them to disapprove.'

'Sindona and Leach are safe – for the moment,' said Peggy. 'Maybe Hubbard will inform on them. I'm interviewing her tomorrow.'

I thanked Peggy and ended the call. We could try to find out what had happened to the $1 million by eliminating other possibilities.

CHAPTER 91

Peggy and I went to the CCC's office.

'We need to get answers from Hubbard,' Peggy told us. 'Malcolm and I waited outside her office for two hours. She was there but she wouldn't see us.'

The CCC called her and we listened.

'LM, my officers have been trying to obtain an appointment with you but you have not cooperated.'

'I have been busy,' Hubbard replied.

'My investigation is urgent, Lord Mayor. We need your testimony in order to proceed. Must I subpoena you to provide it?'

Hubbard reluctantly agreed to an interview the next day, with her lawyer present. Malcolm sent me a copy of the notes he had taken.

Record of interview on behalf of the CCC by DCI Wall and DI Malcolm with LM, Martha Hubbard, in her City Hall office at 2.30 pm on November 29th.

Also present: Andrew Bartlett, LLB (for Hubbard).

Permission to make a voice recording was refused.

Notes taken by DI Malcolm.

DCI Wall informed LM Hubbard about her work for the Kenwood Inquiry and cautioned her.

DCI Wall: 'Were you responsible for the concrete testing?'

Bartlett, for LM Hubbard: 'No. The report was okayed by Montague's engineer.'

DCI Wall: 'Did you approve payment of $500,000 to CTS?'

LM Hubbard: 'No. I sent an invoice received from UMTS to Premier Bentley Leach.'

DCI Wall: 'Could the Premier have inferred that by sending the invoice to him you approved of payment?'

LM Hubbard: 'I suppose so.'

DCI Wall: 'Why did you send the invoice to Premier Leach?'

389

LM Hubbard: 'He had requested the tests be done.'
DCI Wall: 'And you told him that they had been done.'
LM Hubbard: 'Yes.'
DCI Wall: 'Who did you expect to pay?'
LM Hubbard: 'The Premier sent money to Roads, who sent it to Works, for Montague to pay UMTS.'
DCI Wall: 'Are you aware that the concrete testing programme was not completed?'
LM Hubbard: 'Really? We understood a report had been received and it was approved by our engineer.'
DCI Wall: 'He was murdered.'
LM Hubbard: 'It was a tragedy. The killer must be brought to justice.'
DCI Wall: 'Did you have any part in causing his death?'
LM Hubbard: 'I did not. Do you have evidence that I did?'
DCI Wall: 'Did you approve payment of an additional $500,000?'
LM Hubbard: 'I did not. The Premier could have added it to reimburse Council's costs for the testing programme. Ask Montague about it.'
DCI Wall: 'Did you instruct Bridge Works' CEO, Ronald Yelling, to hire a person to abduct Councillor Kenwood?'
LM Hubbard: 'I did not.'
Bartlett said LM Hubbard would not respond to allegations made without evidence. The LM would not answer any further questions.
The interview ended.

When I finished reading I showed it to Cutter.

'She didn't tell us anything we didn't already know,' he said.

'Peggy couldn't get much traction but she may have been able to figure out the ruse.'

I phoned Peggy.

'I have read Malcolm's notes of your interview with Hubbard,' I asked. 'Do you think she was lying?'

'Yes, but it is only an impression, for she has covered her tracks carefully,' Peggy said. 'Hubbard was calculating, watching me to know the best way to respond. She consulted her lawyer several times. Her posture was never that of a leader trying to facilitate justice for murder of an employee. She was defensive. She could have been covering for Leach and Sindona. They were trying to shift the responsibility on to her and she was trying to wriggle free without owning up to anything. It's not clear whether Yelling got his orders from her or from Leach.'

'All we have is one recording of a cryptic conversation between Yelling and Leach,' I said. 'We don't have enough to bring them in for questioning.'

Later Cutter and I were sitting in my office, trying to join the dots. We talked through what was most likely to have happened, from Yelling getting Steele to set up the prison cell, through to the hijack.

While we were talking, Barbie arrived and she listened as we constructed a narrative of the mastermind's involvement.

'Are you sure that's how it happened, Doc?'

'No, it's guesswork, but it's the best we can do,' I said. 'Sometimes guesses are all we have to go on in a reconstruction. It's like making a full-size model of a dinosaur from a few bones. You have to make up the missing details.'

'It makes sense,' said Barbie.

'I don't get why Yelling did it,' said Cutter. 'He is a business leader not a gangster. Why did he put up his hand to run Cobra?'

'So he would be paid?'

'I don't think so,' I said. 'He's a CEO not a professional kidnapper. Maybe he had an interest in the casino project.'

'What sort of interest?'

'He's a constructor. Could he want Sindona to hire him to construct the casino?'

'I'll see what I can find out,' said Barbie.

She went off with Cutter. I closed up the office and went home. Discovery was 1% inspiration and 99% perspiration. Today it had been mostly perspiration.

*

Jane phoned to tell us Council had approved our DA for a MC.

'Congratulations,' she said enthusiastically. 'Your hard work has paid off.'

391

'It was a team effort.'

'We've done it!' I said on the phone to Sunita. 'The approval means they will lease us the IB site and we can start restoring it and constructing the MC. Lenders will beat a path to our door.'

'Construction and high finance don't turn me on,' said Sunita. 'It will be good when we start putting on shows. I'll get turned on then.'

*

Barbie got back to me later that morning with some inspiration.

'Yelling has hit the casino jackpot,' she said. 'Sindona has given the contract to construct his casino to Bridge Works.'

'You're kidding! The mushrooms too?'

'Yup. The whole resort.'

'It fits. Bridge Works will go from building road overpasses to constructing the province's most prestigious building complex.'

'Did Runyon's put it out to tender?'

'No, they negotiated it privately.'

'Yelling could have agreed to supervise Steele as a sweetener.'

'With Yelling telling Steele what to do?'

'Yes. Yelling would be the middleman.'

'Was it Sindona, Leach or Hubbard who was the mastermind?'

'Sindona could have provided the money, recommended Steele, found the place to hold her and provided door keys. Then he buggered off overseas.'

'Leach would have decided when to grab her and when to release her and when to have Hubbard and Montague pay for the job.'

'Hubbard could have run Yelling for the others.'

'It's conjecture. A conspiracy could have several masterminds sharing leadership.'

'Perhaps we can get someone to confess?'

'What we need is a confrontation that exposes their cosy cabal. For that we need suspects, an audience and allegations that provoke revelations.'

CHAPTER 92

At a public hearing at City Hall on a Tuesday morning at 9.00 am, the Crime and Corruption Commissioner presented his findings in the Jane Kenwood Abduction Inquiry. He summonsed to attend people who had been interviewed during the inquiry to attend. He told them if they did not attend he would subpoena them to attend a supplementary hearing. The public he invited included all of the city's 24 councillors and the 150 members of the Provincial Parliament. The sitting of Parliament at that time was postponed.

The auditorium was a large and prestigious venue. Its high ceiling boasted a regency chandelier resplendent in gold, with cut crystal which flashed sunlight entering from a glass dome. Gryphons and cherubs peered down from cornice mouldings in gold leaf.

There was a row of 10 chairs across the stage, with a name card on each. The CCC sat second from the audience's left. As people arrived, Peggy escorted those selected to their seats on the stage, while the rest sat in the audience.

Peggy took Premier Bentley Leach to sit on the CCC's left, leaving one chair between them. Glamorous in a peach suit, Martha Hubbard arrived and sat on Leach's left with CEO Montague next after that. They greeted each other perfunctorily and waited with affected nonchalance. Bill Prescott was in the next chair. Ronald Yelling arrived at the back with his concreting crew: Norman, Bob and Brian. Peggy walked Yelling up and onto the stage to sit beside Prescott. He crossed his legs, put his hands behind his head with his elbows wide apart, and leaned back, bemused. When Don Sindona arrived with Andrea Gough, Peggy escorted him up to sit self-consciously between the CCC and Leach. Andrea sat back in the audience. There remained three empty chairs, on the audience's right. The room filled up and buzzed with conversation as those on the stage sat in their chairs, assuming kudos, but chatting, fidgeting and looking around nervously.

When the Police Commissioner came in, Peggy sat him on the stage at the audience's left, first in line, where he sat, perplexed.

In front of the stage reporters and camera persons were seated together on the left-hand side. Members of Parliament and councillors sat in the centre and on the right. Cutter, Sunita, Tony and Barbie were sitting halfway back. Behind them were bureaucrats from the executive and members of the public.

Uniformed police stood in pairs at the three exits. At 9.00 am the doors were closed and the CCC went to the lectern and spoke into a mic.

'Premier, LM, Police Commissioner, Members of Parliament, Councillors, Chief Executives, Ladies and Gentlemen, welcome and thank you for coming. My name is Wallace Templeton. I am Commissioner for Crime and Corruption. This hearing will present to the Government and public my commission's findings in our inquiry into the abduction of Jane Kenwood. The three empty chairs remind us that three individuals are, regrettably, unable to attend. They are Councillor Jane Kenwood who is recuperating in hospital and sends her apologies; Isembard Harditch who is deceased; also deceased is Brian Payne aka Peter Pradel aka Arnold Steele aka Cobra.

'Detective Chief Inspector Wall will summarise events on a construction site at Endicot Street in the CBD, on July 22nd at 7 am.'

Peggy took the mic.

'Construction workers rescued a woman they found under wet concrete. She was unconscious and taken to hospital. She was Councillor Jane Kenwood. Her condition was emaciated due to being without food throughout the five weeks she was missing. Now 16 weeks later she is still recovering. She has resumed some of her duties with the Council, but she may always be incapacitated by the psychological injuries inflicted on her. When police were investigating a possible lead to the abductors, a Council engineer was found murdered. A man who was wanted by police attacked Councillor Kenwood and was shot dead while resisting arrest.

'Thank you, DCI Wall,' said the Commissioner. 'Now I will ask Councillor Dr Phillip Keane, who is a forensic scientist, to summarise his reconstruction of events.'

I stood up in the front row and walked up on to the stage. Peggy handed me the mic.

'Thank you, DCI Wall. Four friends of Jane Kenwood are sitting back there: Councillor Richard Barber, Sunita Lovelock, Tony Hart and Barbie Doyle. We have brainstormed in a think tank to explain the evidence and link back from effects to their causes with a chain of hypotheses that reveal the perpetrators. With the collaboration of DCI Wall and DI Malcolm we have been able to reconstruct the abduction. I will walk you through what we think happened.'

Premier Bentley Leach stared across at me from his seat in the line of accused. He was leaning back in his chair, a tall man, his legs spread wide with clenched fists resting on them. The disdain in his pose was not borne out by face, which was twisted by fear.

'Runyon's applied to build a casino on the site of the old IB. When they couldn't get it past the hung Council, they paid to Premier Leach $3 million for an alternative site, which was $1 million more than its value on the balance sheet. The additional money went down the line, through CEO Ainsley Montague, past engineer Isembard Harditch, to the perpetrator Arnold Steele, code name Cobra, who was hired by Ronald Yelling, CEO of Bridge Works, to abduct Councillor Kenwood, giving the Government a majority vote supporting the casino. Steele was supposed to be conducting tests of concrete requested by Premier Leach and implemented by LM Hubbard, but they never took place and he pocketed the money for abducting Jane Kenwood.

'Rubbish,' Yelling said.

'What is the evidence?' said Hubbard.

'This is nonsense,' said Leach.

Peggy said, 'We have a record of phone calls between Ronald Yelling, Bentley Leach and Martha Hubbard, starting two weeks before Jane went missing, until after she was released.'

We had only one full conversation plus a list of phone numbers that Yelling had called.

'They show that Ronald Yelling was the middleman,' Peggy said. The recording was cryptic and Peggy was being imaginative.

'I deny that,' said Yelling.

'We have a recording in which Leach ordered that Steele should continue to hold Councillor Kenwood captive,' Peggy said.

We had made an imaginative inference.

'I did no such thing,' said Leach.

I leaned on the podium and looked at Leach.

His right eye was large and veined redly. It darted about watchfully as if his left-hand brain was hyper-vigilant to a world that was against him. His head was partly turned, concealing his left eye, which was shrunken and cloudy, as if his right brain was unwell and had ceased to look for moral outcomes.

'The abduction proceeded as follows,' I said. 'When Jane arrived at work six months ago, Arnold Steele opened her car door, sat in beside her, broke her nose with a punch and pressed a knife into her side. He made her drive through the city to where his car was parked. He jabbed her with anaesthetic and knocked her out. He took her to a disused factory, carried her unconscious upstairs, locked her in a soundproof cell and abandoned her totally alone for five weeks in complete darkness, with only water supplied. By then she was almost dead. He unlocked the door, anaesthetised her as she struggled and carried her frail, unconscious, body out to his vehicle and drove away. He stopped to release her but when she seemed to be dead, he drove on and dropped her into the foundations of an overpass because he knew from his pretended employment that concrete was to be poured in there shortly. She would have died but by good fortune she was found and rescued. When she reached hospital she was in a coma. She regained consciousness after a few weeks. Since then her physical and mental health have steadily recovered. She still suffers from PTSD and perhaps always will. That ends our reconstruction.'

I stood back. The next part was unpredictable. We didn't know who the mastermind was. I needed a confession.

PART 6

RESOLUTION

CHAPTER 93

'Thank you, Dr Keane,' said the CCC.

'Commissioner,' I said, 'to conclude our reconstruction, I have some questions.'

I sipped water from a glass on the lectern as I perused the seven sitting across the stage to my left. The postures varied between positive interest and offended disaffection.

'There was a previous abduction,' I said. 'Martha Hubbard, did you study law at Alexandra University at the same time as Bentley Leach?'

The question surprised her and she hesitated before answering.

'Yes.'

'During election of a student council, did you with Bentley Leach and several other students grab the SLP candidate, force him into a car and drive him to a deserted farmhouse, where you kept him locked up for several days until after the election?'

'We didn't set out to harm him,' said Hubbard, red-faced. 'It was high jinks; students having fun, adversarial politics.'

'It might have been fun for you but it was not fun for your victim. His ordeal might have affected his physical and mental health. If he had taken it to the police, you could have been charged with depriving a person of liberty and other offences. He lost an election he might have won. You got away with it. You tried it again with Jane Kenwood, didn't you?'

Hubbard hesitated. A lot depended on her response.

'It was supposed to be a bit of a lark. It was good-natured fun but it went wrong. I thought of her as I would a daughter and tried to protect her. I tried to stop her being harmed.'

'What did you do?'

'I told Yelling to have them take good care of her. I had no idea she was suffering. I was appalled to learn she had starved in the dark.

They were supposed to release her in good health. Leach kept putting back her release.'

'A confession at last!' I thought.

'She is lying. I was not involved,' said Leach.

'They could all be in it together,' I thought. *'We need evidence of a conspiracy or a confession. A confession won't hold up if it is extracted under any sort of duress, or direct or indirect reward. We want to know who the prime mover was. If I hang it all on Leach, maybe he'll unload on to Sindona.'*

Enunciating formally and boldly, I said, 'Bentley Leach, you are the mastermind. You received money for illicit purposes, misappropriated public monies, conspired to commit fraud, deprived a person of liberty, abducted a people's representative, conspired to commit a murder and conspired to cause the death of a person resisting arrest.'

'That is all untrue. What is the evidence?' Leach asked.

His face was twisted by inner turmoil. His nose was turned up in distaste, his cheeks puckered into a grimace, his chin drawn in defensively and his mouth a snarl.

The audience was silent as they waited for me to support my allegations. I paused and sipped water at the lectern.

'You took Sindona's money, laundered some of it through Government and had it paid to the perpetrator. You had Yelling order Arnold Steele to abduct Councillor Kenwood and to murder Isembard Harditch.'

'He's lying,' said Yelling.

'You misled the Police Commissioner that Steele would have a gun, demanded he be shot and ordered that a gun be planted on him.'

Leach stood up. 'I've heard enough of this bullshit.' His right eye was bloodshot and staring as he spat out the words disdainfully. 'It was Sindona's idea and his money. Steele was his man.'

His left eye was veiled with inner sorrows, his mouth pursed so small it could barely suck in air.

'It is not true,' Sindona said. 'Tell us your evidence.'

Their denials could never remove the stains of Leach's confession.

I turned towards Runyon's boss. 'Don Sindona, you funded the abduction and that makes you as much of a conspirator as Bentley

400

Leach. Co-conspirators usually get equal punishment. Subverting a parliamentary process by abducting a people's representative is a repugnant crime. The prosecution does not have to show that every conspirator has been physically involved and who did what; it is enough that they have participated. The conspirators could all face these very serious charges and receive equal punishments.'

'I did nothing illegal,' said Leach, who had been sitting with his head in his hands. 'It was my job to approve the casino.'

'You took Runyon's money and laundered it to pay the perpetrator.'

Leach looked around wildly for a way to escape. Seeing him in torment gave me a warm glow of satisfaction. For months I had striven to obtain evidence of his guilt. There was a giddy pleasure in having an irrefutable case against a person in high office.

He crumpled up and with a groan slid off his chair onto the floor. The audience craned to see. A doctor came from the audience, felt his pulse and rolled him into the recovery position. He was unconscious and breathing. Ambulance workers brought a stretcher, lifted him on to a trolley and wheeled him away.

While this was happening, Yelling stood up, edged across the stage and ducked away into the wings. Peggy sent guards after him. They brought him back and stood on either side of his chair.

I was about to resume when Sindona stood up. He spoke calmly and forcefully. 'You can't hold me here without evidence.'

'Leach has just told us that you provided the idea, the money and the abductor.'

'He is lying, trying to get himself off the hook,' Sindona said calmly.

'The victim was held in a building you owned,' I said.

Sindona shook his head. 'It was a stitch-up.'

'By whom?'

'I don't know.'

It was lame. He sat down heavily.

'Mr Sindona, did you know the deceased perpetrator, Arnold Steele? Andrea Gough told us Runyon's had no previous involvement with him but we have evidence that he worked for your Perth casino eight months ago, until he left town after a gangland killing. Why did Andrea hide this?'

'Andrea didn't know,' he said. 'It has nothing to do with what happened to Councillor Kenwood.'

'Leach's testimony implicates you. You were linked by owning the crime site and now by previous dealings with Steele. There is enough evidence for you to be charged. A court can decide whether it is sufficient to find you guilty beyond reasonable doubt. Thank you, DCI Wall, I have finished my questions.'

'Thank you, Doctor Keane,' Peggy said.

CHAPTER 94

Peggy came up to the lectern.

She turned to the six men and one woman on the stage.

'I am arresting you for conspiracy to abduct and murder. You will be taken from here to the city watch house. You do not have to say anything but it may harm your defence if you do not mention, when questioned, something you later rely on in court. Anything you do say may be given in evidence.'

They looked at her, askance.

'I didn't do anything wrong, Chief Inspector,' said Yelling.

'You conspired to perpetrate an abduction, also a mugging, driving of a motor vehicle with intent to cause harm and a murder.'

'You can't pin those on me,' said Yelling. 'I didn't do anything. What evidence do you have?'

'Your phone conversations with Leach show that you ordered the perpetrator to do those things.'

Yelling was silent. It was a relief that he did not contest my allegations because we had little evidence and much supposition.

'I didn't do anything,' said Prescott cockily.

'You will be charged with aiding and abetting a fraud.'

He did not reply. His pretended innocence belied deep government corruption in his organisation's pretended material testing.

'I did what I was told by my employer,' said Montague.

'Your crime was to abet fraud and improperly pay an account with intent to deceive.'

He said nothing, relieved not to be named as an accessory in the murder of Harditch.

'Police Commissioner, you caused Steele to be shot and a gun to be planted on him to pervert the course of justice.'

The PC said nothing, too fearful to speak. He faced a steep penalty for betraying the public's trust.

I was enjoying these proceedings. I had become a forensic scientist because I wanted to catch villains. Outsmarting trusted leaders who had deceived the public was fulfilling.

DCI Wall beckoned police officers onto the stage. They took the seven accused to a van waiting outside. I was suffused with relief as if from an internal sunrise that warmed the depths of my being. Joy kindled as I stood there on the stage before the assembly. Without thinking, I took out my mobile and called on Facetime to Jane at the hospital.

'Jane, it's me, Phillip. What are you doing?'

'Talking to myself,' she said.

The buzz of conversation in the audience died away as they listened to my phone call on speaker phone.

'How come?'

'There's no-one here,' said Jane. 'Everyone must be with you or watching on TV but I can't bear to see it. What's happening?'

'They are all listening to us. Seven people have been arrested.'

'Who?'

I told her the names.

'Great! So it was a conspiracy?'

'Hubbard and Leach have admitted it but Sindona has said our evidence is circumstantial. I think a court would find them guilty.'

'Brilliant. I want to thank everyone who helped and you especially.'

'Do you think we can take up where we left off?'

'Absolutely. Wild horses couldn't keep me away.'

'We have some catching up to do. I had better go now. See you tonight. I love you. Bye.'

Halfway back in the audience, Barbie stood up, raised her arms in jubilation and yelled, 'Go for it, Phil!' The audience rose to its feet as one and the auditorium erupted with yells, whoops and applause. They had been sitting tensely for two hours. The arrests had delighted them and tension was relieved uproariously.

When things quietened down, the CCC took the mic.

'For the past five years city councillors have followed their party leaders in trying to silence Councillor Kenwood in the Council chamber, dismissing her objections and having her excluded. When other councillors began to join her on the crossbench, they conspired to abduct her.

'These events show how civic leaders were drawn into a foolish crime and then into a cover-up worse than the crime they were concealing. Although conspirators normally bear equal penalty, the accused persons may not all be equal before the law and they could face different charges and different penalties. It is for a court to decide.

'That is the end of today's hearing. I will send a written report of the Commission's findings to Parliament. It will contain recommendations for changes to the legislation and government procedures to prevent a similar situation ever arising again. Thank you for coming. Good afternoon.'

*

Jane watched the news in hospital. That evening, with the abductors locked away, she relaxed. She gave me a soft, wet, tongue kiss.

'I'm sorry I have been horrible to you,' she said. 'I'm better now.'

Before my eyes, as if in time lapse, her body seemed to regain confidence and strengthen. Like a butterfly emerging from its chrysalis, her beauty unfolded and took wing again. Safe at last, her customary curiosity took over and she moved around freely, occupying spaces fully, exploring without fear, pushing the boundaries as she always had.

When we went for a walk in a local park, she said, 'I like it here now that I know nothing bad is going to happen to me.'

The difference in her was amazing. The bright, vibrant Jane I had known before she was taken was restored. Her inventive mind had been sledge-hammered but had recovered. She might have died, or been permanently disabled. We were all fortunate.

Her restored vivacity renewed the attention, love and belonging others gave her, which she returned with smiles, compliments, hugs and kisses.

After her next ward meeting she told me, 'I like these people — I feel like I belong with them.'

405

Although she was staying at the hospital, her work outcomes in the Council confirmed that Jane-the-high-achiever was back. People were esteeming her now for what she was, rather than for what she had been. She resumed her pursuit of excellence with composure and elegance.

'To solve our problems there is no lack of solutions,' she said. 'What we need is the will to implement them. We must dare to succeed. I think I know myself better now. I know what I value and must have, as well as what I can do without.'

She had been starved of the majesty of nature and the euphoria of the arts. Now she became rapt in forests, gardens, zoos, theatres, auditoriums, galleries and books.

'I lose myself in others' creations,' she said. 'Human diversity is amazing.'

Without accomplishment for so long, it took some time for her to recover her legendary tenacity, with courage to seek choices and dare to be herself.

'I am back in control of my life,' she said. 'I can do what I like.'

Terry was optimistic that she would make a full recovery. Jane still needed care and I helped organise her friends into a support network. Jane went home from hospital. She renewed her political ambitions and launched her campaign to be elected Lord Mayor.

I was happy for the first time in months but there was uncertainty.

'Will Jane ever be the same with me again?' I pondered. *'Will our relationship resume?'*

406

CHAPTER 95

Jane's lawn had a marquee for a homecoming party for family, friends, neighbours, constituents and work colleagues. There was a band, balloons, a huge cake, champagne, speeches, exultant clapping and whooping from a crowd that squashed into every space, spilling over into the street.

Jane spoke into the mic, brushed tears away and sniffed.

'Thank you all for coming. I never expected to get well enough to return here.'

Cutter let go with 'Three cheers for Jane! Hip, hip.' His hooray put to flight pigeons from their roost in the eaves of the community hall at the end of the street.

After her speech Jane was surrounded by gawkers who were trying to latch on to her glamour. She moved slowly through the crowd, speaking a few words to rapt well-wishers here, pressing hands there, bending down to children and admiring babies. She was big news and every aspect of her life was closely scrutinised — except our relationship, which we kept strictly private.

My greatest pleasure was that Jane was her old self again. She had lived for six months with the fear of an attempt on her life. Now it was gone she focused on me as a man instead of as an investigator. Instead of a victim she was a woman again. I could show Jane my feelings without having to hold back.

Our relationship picked up where we had left off and a few days later I moved in with her. We achieved a new unity that made us a single organism, a mutualism. She was like a sea anemone, with me a clownfish living amongst her tentacles, in a safe haven, immune to her stings. I ate small invertebrates, dealt with media and saw off her enemies: the butterfly fish and other predators of the political kind.

When Jane said my snoring kept her awake, I went to a sleep consultant.

'You snore when you lie on your back, Doctor,' the consultant said. 'Try to sleep on your side. Sew a dozen practice tennis balls into the back of a T-shirt. Lying on your back will be too painful.'

Lying on my side was so uncomfortable I preferred to sleep on top of the back-gouging balls. My snoring was only reduced when I was kept awake by the pain. Meanwhile, Jane was experimenting with ear plugs. My snores were low in frequency and the vibrations went through the bone of her skull, bypassing her ear plugs.

Despite my snoring and Jane's occasional nightmares, we resisted sleeping apart.

We were past the flexibility that comes more easily to younger couples. Adjusting to each other had its challenges. One night I expounded to Jane at length my theory of inertial balance between individuals in a couple.

A person's inertia was their tendency to want to go on with particular activities or inactivity. One of us had more inertia and was less able to change. The other had to sacrifice more in compromises that balanced momentums of the inertias. It was a matter of physics, I explained.

'What do you think?' I asked when I finished.

'Pardon?' she said. 'I didn't hear. I had my earplugs in.'

This outcome was apocryphal and I didn't try to repeat my recipe. Jane balanced her momentum with mine naturally. When she looked over a brink and didn't like what she saw, she modified her perceptions. She chose to stop hearing my snores. She was that sensible. Our idiosyncrasies were part of who we were. Our sacrifices would balance each other because they had to.

When I had stayed at her place for a month she asked, 'Why do you keep your place?'

'So I can reside in my ward.'

'I don't think anyone cares much about that nowadays,' she said.

The real reason was that it was my bolthole, a place to retreat to if we fell out. My reflex was of pessimism in relationships with females.

'It's insurance,' I said, 'in case something goes wrong.'

'What could go wrong?' she said.

408

'Something ... you never know.'

'O ye of little faith!' Jane said, scoffing. 'Nothing is going to go wrong.'

I put caution aside, moved out the rest of my belongings and put my place up for sale. I felt like I was starting an exciting adventure.

My life with Jane had been a journey into the unknown. Her mission had slowly been revealed to me. I have never had her total attention, for she has always had one eye on the way ahead, like an albatross about to fly away across the ocean. It was that restless quality in her that I revered, for I too craved reform of government.

The abduction of Jane Kenwood was a major crime. It occurred because assessment of the public interest in developments was biased by endemic corruption of democratic processes.

I encouraged and gave support for her idea to run for LM at the City Council election. She could offer genuine participative democracy to our city's people.

CHAPTER 96

When Council had approved the DA, the banks and donors came good with the funds they had promised. We invited people to be board members and they appointed Jane as President and me as CEO. We received loans to start constructing a MC. I engaged contractors to restore the old IB, construct an auditorium and a theatre.

'We must create a centre that people will love to visit and keep coming back to,' I said.

Our concert had kickstarted interest in multiculture and it gathered pace. We hired an impresario who developed full seasons of performances at both venues. Alexandra's burgeoning population, with immigrants from many cultures, ensured a steady demand for tickets. Ethnic groups developed shows. Jane was already inviting people to the opening.

With Don Sindona in prison, Runyon's took their project away to another province.

The Council general election would be soon and Jane campaigned to be Alexandra's next LM. Her platform was humanity, transparency, devolution, consultation, public debate and most importantly non-partisan government. Her name was a household word. She was a people's heroine opposing exploitation and political corruption. She would be the people's champion in the struggle for better government.

Jane toured the streets of each of the 23 wards in an open vehicle, announcing pro-democracy rallies at their local sports grounds. Crowds gathered in festive mood, come to see the legendary councillor who had survived horrendous cruelty.

She stood beside each independent candidate and said, 'I congratulate you for standing on your own merit rather than hiding in a political party. May the best independent win.'

To the people gathered she said, 'My commitment is to true democracy by empowering the people. If you elect me Lord Mayor, I will represent you. You won't need a party.'

*

On the day after city residents voted, an Electoral Commission official led out on to a balcony over City Square the 23 newly elected councillors. The large crowd applauded as he introduced them one by one. The political parties had been routed. Independents had been elected in almost every ward. In Jane's Blake Ward, Barbie was elected. Cutter was returned for Wordsworth Ward with an increased majority.

The final announcement was the result of the mayoral ballot.

'Elected Lord Mayor of Alexandra is Jane Kenwood — 75%.'

It was a huge majority. She stepped forward, elegant in an off-the-shoulder gown and her hair up in a bun, her arms raised in victory. The crowd clapped, whooped and yelled.

'Thank you for voting for me. I will do my best for you. I want to thank especially my loyal team.'

She brought us forward one at a time for applause.

Afterwards, I was there when she descended the stairway from the balcony. She threw her arms around me and we hugged.

'Congratulations,' I said. 'What a fantastic result!'

She hugged the others who clustered around: Barbie, Cutter, Sunita and Tony.

As LM she was now leader of the people of Alexandra City. They idolised her and looked to her to improve government.

'I ran for LM to devolve power to constituents,' she said. 'Electing me has empowered you.'

Jane Kenwood began a new era of freedom from party politics.

'Wards can create and implement their own plans,' Jane said in a media conference. 'Our city government is devolved. Each ward has its own budget and their own sub-council to plan and run it, coordinated by their councillor. There is no need for organised

411

opposition because councillors can unite at any time to oppose what others are doing.

'All 24 councillors will vote on their consciences. Our policies will be decided by the informed voting of councillors. A consensus can develop or a new synthesis can emerge without politicians forming permanent party gangs. Councillors are on their guard against relinquishing their discretion. They don't want interference by political parties.'

Jane was a legend, interested in what people thought and what they wanted. No development would be approved if anyone would be disadvantaged. People felt their lifestyles were protected. She ignited the goodwill of the city's inhabitants.

She had an aura of purity and goodness. Her stately bearing brought crowds to see her wherever she went. People spoke of her with awe in their voices, repeating her sayings as if they were sacred words.

'I'm like you,' she had said. 'I have a right to be treated kindly and with respect. I want to help disadvantaged people. I was treated cruelly by greedy people but they have been stopped and their kind will never again rule here.'

They trusted Jane. There was no limit to what their hard work could accomplish under this woman's leadership. Her new regime invoked a new age of considerate behaviour. People opposed greed and tried to help others. Living conditions improved. A civil society was founded that included isolated individuals. Under Jane's leadership, the obstacles raised by the traditional establishment crumbled and fell. Instead of Alexandra being governed for businesses to make profit, it became ruled by the people for the people.

A person's contribution to local taxes was calculated from the difference between what they took from the community and what they gave back. There began an exodus to other cities of wealthy people who wanted to take much more than wanted to give.

Jane's devolved non-partisan government was copied by other provinces and by the Federal Government. ACC became a beacon of participative democracy, guiding governance everywhere. Jane was nominated to run in Provincial and Federal elections but declined.

'Alexandra City has had a people's revolution,' she said. 'My way won't always be best. I will serve as LM until I have dislodged the parasitical political interests that have been a chancre in the Westminster system. Developments have to be approved with free voting by councillors. Other matters could require different processes and someone else can bring them in — but political parties have to go. When that has happened, the city, province and nation will be governed by the people and my work will be done.'

She told me that she did not expect to run for a second term. I didn't know what she was planning.

CHAPTER 97

Arnold Steele was dead and could not be charged with any crime. The other conspirators: Sindona, Leach, Hubbard and Yelling were brought to trial, convicted and imprisoned for life. The Police Commissioner was jailed for 10 years. Prescott and Montague got five years each. Charges against Andrea Gough were dismissed because she had followed Sindona's instructions without realising the consequences.

The new Council strove for transparency.

'It is difficult to be transparent and look competent all of the time,' said Jane. 'Do you think the parties will try to get rid of me?'

'No,' I answered. 'The parties are not allowed to participate in elections or gang up against individuals. People wouldn't let them get away with it.'

'Without you they might have got away with abduction,' she said, with a kiss. 'Will you explain to me what is so special about an Euler walk?'

I detected a note of sarcasm. It had been my PhD thesis and because it was mathematical I was used to scepticism. I would not be able to change her mind with a few words.

'The rules of our Euler walk were quite simple: we reconstructed from effect to cause. This approach could help solve other crimes.'

'It seems rather inflexible. Why not cut across corners?'

'The police chase obvious suspects instead of investigating the crime scene and motives logically. A rigorous reconstruction is more reliable.'

'I think people prefer vigorous chasing like in the Keystone Cops,' she said. 'It may not catch anyone but when villains see it going on they go to ground and are deterred from further mischief.'

'I disagree,' I said. 'Chasing can do more harm than good. The police shouldn't bounce around like a pinball, hoping a solution will drop into their pocket. The traditional authoritarian mode is less

414

effective at solving problems than brainstorming with feedback to nurture creativity. Our think tank method is being trialled by Peggy's people.'

'Euler walking would bring a revolution to detective work,' Jane said. 'There will be more linking than in a sausage factory.'

My skills in analysis and organisation were now needed as CEO of the new MC, rather than as a councillor moonlighting as a crime investigator. I had not contested my seat in the election. 'Kissing hands and shaking babies' wasn't my style.

*

Barbie had become a successful and ambitious councillor, whereas Cutter wanted to settle down and raise a family.

'Barbie and I are getting hitched,' he said.

I was delighted. 'Congratulations.'

I had changed. I was no longer the unfeeling forensic scientist who had been elected for the NLP. These days my heart often guided me. Jane had inspired me to cross the floor and oppose the Government. I had become passionate about participative democracy.

The shocking corruption I had encountered had shaken my faith in our Westminster system. Jane had not been able to move a motion or ask a question or speak in a debate except by permission of the Government. The only way she could express her constituents' needs was to object to, disrupt, or delay the Council's proceedings. She had done this with such aplomb that the leaders had abducted her. It was fortunate that we had been able to track down her abductors in time to save her.

Jane's journey in local government had taken her from renegade councillor to the city's highest office as Lord Mayor. Her non-partisan Council was revolutionary in Southland, with online voting and frequent plebiscites instead of partisan elections.

Jane still had her eye on the horizon. She confided to me one evening, 'I loathe reviewing plans, preparing budgets and reading dull reports.'

'That's part of the job,' I said.

She was silhouetted against an extravagant sunset with her hair tied up.

'How beautiful she is,' I thought.

'City central planning is too authoritarian,' she said. 'Planning should be done by local people with ownership and passion for their own plans. I want to give councillors even more control, local planning roles and proper debates. Perhaps I can devolve my job completely? Computers have made autocracy obsolete.'

'People want central leadership, a Big Brother who is benign,' I said.

'Paternalism is for children.'

I leaned over the back of her chair with my arms around her shoulders and my face pressed into her neck, savouring her caramel odour.

'Will I be letting people down if I quit?' she said.

'Will you serve out your term?'

'Yes,' said Jane. 'I can put up with it for that long.'

'What will you do then?' I said, kissing the softness of her neck.

'I have other plans.'

'Am I in them?' I said.

'You are essential.'

'What for?'

'Guess.'

I could recall a time when I had indulged her.

'To wait for you in my car?'

'No. More active than that.'

I remembered once when she had expected me to pay our solicitor.

'To pay your bills?'

'No. Something we enjoy.'

'Oh, I get it. You want a baby?'

She nodded and looked at me.

'What do you think?'

'It's a terrific idea. How soon?'

'I don't want to wait four years until the election.'

'You can take maternity leave and go back after, say, six months. You won't have to leave the Council. Your deputy can stand in for you. I can stay home and look after the baby.'

416

'What about your job?'

'I have sorted the big picture for the MC. They will want a person with different skills to finish the interior design and do the start-up. There will be too much bottom-up planning and politics for me.'

'I would like to be the CEO who starts it up,' Jane said. 'It would be fun.'

'We should swap jobs,' I said. 'I could run as Lord Mayor.'

'That requires political skills.'

'I could disrupt Council meetings.'

'You might get abducted.'

'No, never again. Without parties, the Council can't be hung. I think I would prefer to be a househusband.'

'I would like that.'

'A baby is a challenge,' I said. 'I'm ready when you are.'

END

ACKNOWLEDGEMENTS

Thank you to my Alpha readers: Ross Allen, Dianne Bishop, Colin Devine and Phil Heywood for their insights and encouragement.

I am indebted to Vesna McMaster and Patricia Fitzgerald for Beta reading that brought many improvements to my story.

Special thanks to Craig Munro, of Queensland Writers Centre, for his editing advice at an early stage.

Thanks to friends Helga Parl, Trina Allen, Jessica White, Brad Ahern, Jenny Perkins and Ken Kolb for their helpful comments on the work in progress.

Thanks to Marilyn Higgins and editor Zoe Lockley for their consideration and contributions.

Thanks to Brisbane City Councillors Nicole Johnston, Helen Abrahams, Jonathan Sri and candidate Karel Boele for information about political processes.

Cornelie van Arkel, Ville du Grande Saconnex, who explained the Swiss way of democracy to me.

Dr Francoise Pintat-Ferrer supplied information about treatment of Post Traumatic Stress Disorder.

I was fortunate to be involved with Kurilpa Futures Group who enabled me to participate in non-partisan community planning.

I participated in campaigns for more democratic government led by Councillor Jonathan Sri and Calam Hendry of Right To The City.

At Avid Reader Bookshop in West End, Fiona Stager led discussions of general and crime fiction with Book Club members. I was fortunate to be able to discuss writing ideas with Roger and Jan Wooller.

I tested political ideas in critical discussion with the Mind Stirrers group at University of the Third Age (U3A). Convenor Ray Rose was a source of information and inspiration on matters of public policy.

I tested ideas too in the Philosophy and Current Affairs classes at U3A tutored by Lindsay Shepherd. The discussions provided insights into the historical, religious, economic and political contexts of my story.

I discussed writing processes with Holland Park Writers, led by Nancy Cox-Millner. Members provided valuable feedback on my writing and encouragement.

My choir, the Queensland University Musical Society, provided diverse characters who strove for perfection.

My family: Zoe, Tessa and Jason provided helpful feedback and encouragement.

AUTHOR BIO

I was awarded 1st Class Honours in Chemical Engineering from Birmingham University and worked in the petroleum industry in Canada. I researched alternative systems of government at Imperial College, London. I emigrated to Australia and was employed in mining development. At age 40 I became a high school science teacher and wrote a textbook that was published.

I am divorced from two marriages, with children and grandchildren.

Since 2013, my main occupation has been writing fiction novels. My speculative fiction novel *The Grass Is Always Browner* was published in 2011 and my general fiction novel *Love Straddle* in 2014.

I write letters, sing in a choir, draw figure art, discuss books, movies, philosophical ideas, government planning and current events.

Since August 2016, I have been writing *A Girl Short*, an abridged version of *Love Straddle*.

Other books by this author

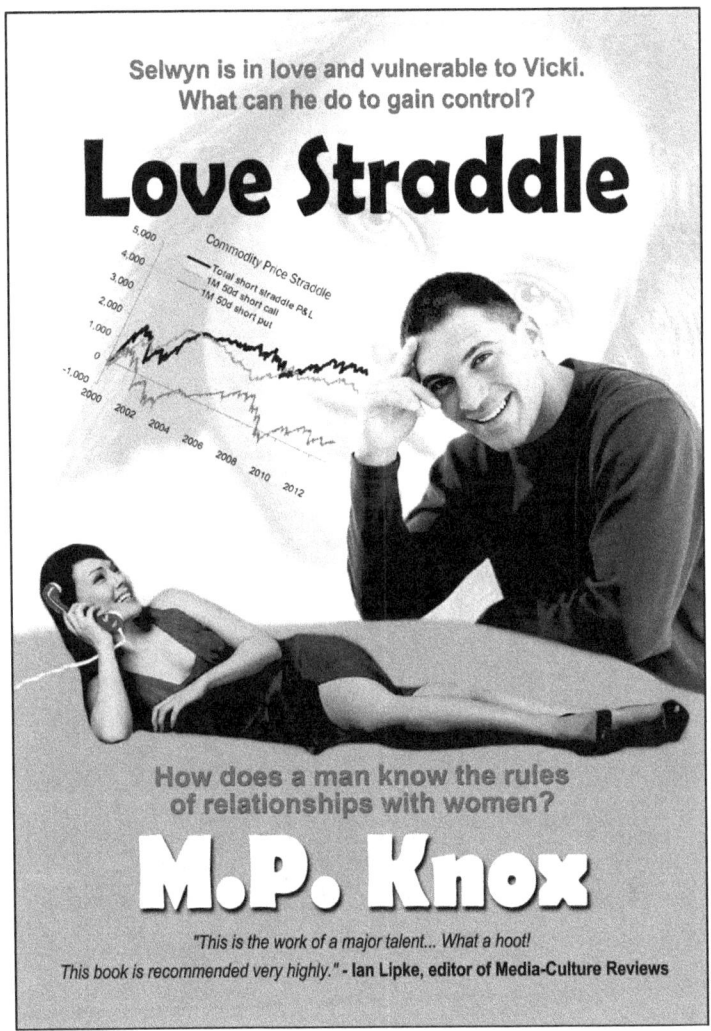

Available at www.amazon.com

421

Available at www.amazon.com

www.ingramcontent.com/pod-product-compliance
Lightning Source LLC
Chambersburg PA
CBHW071932130726
47908CB00015B/187